# Highlanders' Revenge

## PAUL TORS

Matador
9 Priory Business Park,
Wistow Road, Kibworth Beauchamp,
Leicestershire. LE8 0RX
Tel: 0116 279 2299
Email: books@troubador.co.uk
Web: www.troubador.co.uk/matador
Twitter: @matadorbooks

ISBN 978 1785892 691

British Library Cataloguing in Publication Data.
A catalogue record for this book is available from the British Library.

Printed and bound in the UK by TJ International, Padstow, Cornwall
Typeset in 12pt Bembo by Troubador Publishing Ltd, Leicester, UK

Matador is an imprint of Troubador Publishing Ltd

*For The Richmans, past, present and future*

# CONTENTS PAGE

# CHAPTER ONE

# THE MAGINOT LINE

The rain was no more than a mist but it blanketed and drenched the forest as well as the surrounding countryside. Somewhere in the tree canopy an owl hooted forlornly. Mash could feel a drip running down his neck and between his shoulder blades; he shuddered. It was dark in the wood; he could only just make out the members of his patrol as they probed their way forward, merging with the looming trunks of the trees. It did not help that their faces were blackened and many had tucked vegetation into their helmets and kit to try and break up their form.

A twig snapped beneath his boot. Involuntarily Mash flinched. No matter how hard he tried every sound felt as though it must bring a hail of fire down on them. But against the natural movement of the trees and undergrowth along with the rain, Mash knew that the noise they made was minimal. He gripped his rifle and moved on; telling himself it was just as bad for the Germans.

It was the first week of May 1940 and Mash was part of a patrol from the 4th Cameron Highlanders. They were a few miles in front of the Maginot Line, the impregnable defensive system the French had built along the German border, on what the French called the Line of Contact. Mash and the rest of his section were pushing through the Spitzwald wood, just to the south of Flastroff. In better times the countryside would have been described as beautiful; green fields mixed with many dense woodlands set on rolling hills, interspersed with streams and quaint villages. But these were not good times.

Slowly they made their way forward, seeking out the enemy. The men were tired but the knowledge that the Germans were close made every sense strain and the adrenaline pump. For many the last few days had been their first taste of action. They had learnt quickly; they had to as they found that the Germans knew their stuff. Many of the Germans had grown up on the border so they were fighting in their own backyards. The Highlanders had a hint at how close they were to Germany by the place names – villages such as Waldweistroff and Flastroff gave a clue, even Spitzwald wood was part of Foret D'Bouzonville.

Initially the Camerons had a reasonably tough time with a number of their outposts taken and some fierce fights in the Spitzwald. But they were now pushing and probing forward to regain their positions, coming up against an ever more active enemy.

There was a loud rustle to the right. Everyone immediately went to ground, weapons at the ready and eyes staring into the darkness. Seconds passed with no sound. McIntyre, the corporal leading the patrol, signalled Mash and another to move forward to investigate. Tentatively Mash rose to the crouch position and started to creep forward with the other man. Still there was no noise or sign of the enemy. Mash took another step, trying to move as quietly as he could through the undergrowth. He was barely breathing but his heart was beating out of his chest as he swung the rifle from side to side, searching for any clue. Suddenly, inches in front of his foot, it felt like something emerged out of the ground with an enormous racket. Mash nearly jumped out of his skin as he tried to aim his rifle as the blur of motion and sound overwhelmed him. It was a second or two before he could regain his senses. Now ten yards away, a startled young deer was charging its way through the undergrowth, barking its alarm as it sought the safety of the night.

No one had fired. Mash and his companion glanced at each other, the shock and fright written all over their faces. Slowly they returned to the rest of the patrol. Mash could see just enough to reveal a scowl on the face of McIntyre as he contemplated if their presence had been betrayed and Rod's white teeth grinning at him with obvious delight at his friend's discomfort. They stayed still for several minutes after the deer had gone, listening for any sign that they had been discovered. Slowly Mash's heart returned to a more normal rate.

The patrol pushed on. Everyone was on full alert as though it was not just Mash who had been spooked. Mash suspected McIntyre's frustration with him over the deer was the reason he now found himself at point, the first man in the patrol and so the most likely to encounter the enemy.

*I suppose that's fair; the lads back at the estate would be wetting themselves with laughter if they saw that little episode. Now switch on and concentrate.*

After another mile or so, the rain had stopped but Mash could hear the boots swishing through the long grass as they crossed some open ground between clutches of trees. Then Mash thought he heard the faintest sound ahead. He could not say what it was; it was just out of place. He immediately knelt down and signalled for the others to halt. He strained to hear the noise again, but nothing.

*For Christ's sake, the others are going to think you've really got the wind up if this is another waste of time. No, there it is again, a sort of rhythmic tap. Wait! Is that a shadow or something moving?*

A faint rustle announced the arrival of McIntyre. Part of Mash wanted to wait to make sure he was not making a fool of himself, but the more time went on the more he was sure he could hear something or someone moving deliberately towards him. The noise could be a piece of equipment not properly secured; it was not a metallic sound, that would be too obvious, it was more like a half-empty water bottle rhythmically bouncing on a hip. He took the plunge, hand signalled enemy ahead and pointed in the direction of the noise. Quickly and quietly the section deployed, the long grass effectively hiding them. The seconds dragged on. Had he made a mistake? Then finally the first very faint outline of a man was distinguishable. With the rain gone the clouds were starting to break, making visibility a little easier. Soon the dull shape of a second man loomed out of the murk.

*It has to be a patrol, but which side? Should we challenge them?*

He could sense the tension growing in the corporal next to him as the same thoughts rushed through his head. And then, just for a second, a weak and watery moon broke through the clouds for the first time. It gave a fleeting glimpse, no more, but it was enough. The unmistakable shape of a German helmet answered all their questions.

On they came, oblivious of the Highlanders' presence, their numbers growing as it became clear it was another patrol of about the same size. Just when Mash thought the point man was so close he could not fail to spot them, McIntyre opened up next to him and the rest followed an instant later. They had caught the Germans cold and several men fell before they knew what hit them. Mash aimed at a man who seemed to be frozen with the shock and ferocity of the attack. He fired. It was the easiest of shots at this range, despite the light, and the man dropped like a deadweight.

A fierce fight broke out as the rest of the Germans returned fire. Two grenades added further to the enemy's casualties and the remainder realised this was not a fight they were going to win. It was over in seconds. Mash could make out at least three survivors running for their lives and quickly being swallowed up by the gloom. The firing died down and cautiously they moved forward, checking for those who were still alive. They found two seriously wounded Germans in their last moments and three already dead. For most it was the first time they had seen the enemy, let alone a dead body. Pushing back their thoughts and squeamishness, they rifled through the men's pockets, taking badges and anything that might help the intelligence boys in HQ work out what was happening.

Mash searched the man he had shot. He was lying on his back with his legs folded up underneath him, a look of shock on his face. Quickly Mash rifled through his pockets, only pausing when his hand emerged drenched in still-warm blood when he checked the man's breast pocket. And then, without a sound, they rose and resumed the patrol, very aware that the enemy would be in no doubt about where they were.

★ ★ ★

"Last night was a bit up and down for you wasn't it?" smiled Rod as he wolfed down his rations. "The look on your face when that deer shot out."

"I'm glad I was able to amuse you," grinned Mash in reply. "It bloody frightened me to death I can tell you."

They had returned from the patrol without further incident and spent the rest of the following day improving their dug-in positions and barbed wire screens on the outpost line and noting every movement they could see on the German side of the lines. The weather had brightened and the warmth of a spring day had lifted the mood after such a long and hard winter. Now, stood down for the night and in the relative comfort of their dugout, they were coming to terms with what had happened on the patrol.

Mash shifted himself. He was tall at six foot two and broad in the shoulder, so he always found it difficult to get comfortable in the small confines of a trench or dugout. Rod, who was only shorter than him by a couple of inches, seemed to be able to get comfortable anywhere.

"You did bloody well to hear those Jerries mind you," continued Rod. "Whoever sees the opposition first usually wins and I'm glad it was us. It must be down to your game-keeping background."

"You wouldn't have believed I'd ever been a keeper after that deer. It doesn't half make a difference when you think it's a man you're up against. I was sure I was about to get shot when the bloody thing jumped up!"

With a warm meal inside him he was able to see the funny side.

"A lot's happened since we first arrived in France hasn't it, here we are three months later killing Germans," reflected Mash.

"Aye, but the start wasn't bad, bloody cold but what a welcome from the French," replied Rod. "Don't think they could've done any more."

"You'd have thought we'd won the war, not been on our way to it," said Mash. After a pause he continued. "I wonder if the rest of them up north are still having fun."

"All I know is that this winter's been a bugger so it'll have been cold in a trench no matter where you are. I don't suppose they've had to do any fighting though."

Rod and Mash, along with the rest of the Highland Division, had been detached from the British Expeditionary Force and sent south to the Saar front where they relieved the French on a six-mile stretch of the Maginot Line. This was partly in an attempt to get the troops battle-ready and partly as a political gesture to the French. Critically, it was decided to place the division under French overall command, which meant that not only were they separated from the rest of the British forces but also outside their direct control.

"Was that the first time you've killed anyone?" asked Mash.

"Aye, it was," replied Rod. "Not pleasant but that's what we're here to do."

Mash knew that Rod's matter-of-fact attitude was a cover, but it still comforted him a little.

"It makes you think though, seeing them up close like that," continued Mash, trying to verbalise a tangle of thoughts. "Lord knows I've shot enough things on the estate, but the one I shot today, well, he was just a lad like me."

"Given that the Jerries have been stepping up their activity a lot over the past few days, I think we'll both get used to it," answered Rod.

This rather blunt answer was not exactly what he wanted to hear but it was at least truthful. He appreciated it when a minute later Rod tried to lighten the mood.

"Did you hear about the phone tapping?" he asked.

"No," said Mash.

"You know the Jerries pushed some of the lads out of a couple of forward positions, it seems that they tapped the forward telephone cables so that they could listen in to what was going on. The boys clocked what was happening and switched to Gaelic, apparently it flustered them completely."

Mash laughed.

"I can sympathise," he said. "I haven't a clue what you lot are on about half the time and I have to live with you."

"Aye, you're still a Mash Man," teased Rod.

"I remember you explaining the facts of life to me when we first joined up," said Mash, smiling at the memory.

"Well I had to, you were going to get pummelled if I didn't," laughed Rod.

Mash's real name was Edward James. But he was an oddity; an Englishman in a Highland regiment. Rod had been with Mash since they had both enlisted and had watched on as Mash struggled to come to terms with the ribbing he got from the others, particularly why all the other Scottish soldiers kept calling him Mash. What he did not know was that it was the nickname that the Highlanders gave an Englishman in their ranks and they delighted in winding up the new English recruit. It was Rod who had taken pity on him when he could see Mash was ready to explode.

"It's like the Australians calling you English pohms," he had said. "As in Prisoner of His Majesty. You're a potato, a Mash Man."

Mash had bristled at the implied insult, but Rod had just grinned at him.

"They're going to call you it whatever you do," he had said. "So you can either laugh along or keep that face on you. But you won't make any friends that way."

On reflection Mash had decided to take Rod's advice and the nickname stuck, but it became a joke as opposed to an insult. Now, he barely noticed it anymore, in fact he got a shock if anyone called him Ed.

Rod had been a friend from that point onward. He was in his late twenties, only a bit older than Mash and the rest of the section but enough to give him a fatherly feel, something that Rod played up to a little and even encouraged. A number, including Mash, came to him if they needed any advice and he always seemed to have a considered answer.

Rod had been an insurance clerk before the war, something that he reminisced on with little enthusiasm. Instead he quizzed Mash about his position as a gamekeeper, often declaring he should have done something "exciting in the great outdoors." He had always dreamt of adventure he said and now he had plenty of it.

They both sat quietly, remembering the days when they had joined up.

"How's Fiona?" asked Mash as he finished the last mouthful of his meal.

"She's fine," said Rod, smiling slightly as he always did at the mention of Fiona. "She worries about me being out here.

It was easy earlier on as I could honestly say I was in no danger at all, it's getting a bit trickier now."

"I know, it's the same with my mum. She went through it with my dad before he bought it in 1918 so she doesn't believe a word when I say everything's fine." Mash paused for a moment and thought about Fiona. He had only met her once very briefly when they returned from leave just before shipping out to France. His memory was of a very pretty girl who clearly loved Rod. It did not surprise him that Rod had managed to bag such a girl, he seemed to effortlessly glide his way through life. It was that same assured composure that had seen Rod quickly promoted to lance corporal, something Mash wholeheartedly supported.

"How long have you two been together, it must be a while now?"

"Just over two years," said Rod.

"You'd better hurry up and put a ring on her finger, you don't want a cracker like that to get away."

"I know. We talked about it before I left. We both want to tie the knot but I think it's best left until this war's over. You never know what might happen and it'd be easier for her if we kept things simple."

*How typical of him, always thinking of others.*

They were both quiet, digesting their rations. Mash knew that Rod was thinking about Fiona. Mash did not have a girl at home; he wondered what it would be like to have someone waiting for him.

They were shaken out of their reverie by a rattle of machine gun fire close by.

"What the fuck was that?" shouted Rod as they grabbed their weapons and dashed out.

Gunfire streaked the night as the fire fight intensified. It was clear that they were under attack from a well-sized and determined force. Just as they had managed to surprise the

German patrol the night before, the raiding party had been able to get right up to the protecting wire before they were seen.

Mash and Rod fired at every movement and shadow that danced in front of them. More Highlanders were returning fire but the Germans still outnumbered them. The crump of explosions rang out as the Germans, close enough to throw grenades over the wire and into the trenches, peppered the lines. There were screams and shouts from those hit.

"There're loads of the bastards. Are we being overrun?" yelled Mash as he fired round after round at the fleeting targets.

"Don't think so," shouted back Rod. "It's just infantry, no tanks or support. They've got to be probing, testing our strength."

"It's not as strong as it should be!" replied Mash after pausing to fire an aimed shot.

An explosion tore through the trench just to the right of Rod. A grenade had landed on the other side of the man next to him. When Mash looked round he saw the man lying dead and, to his horror, Rod slumped down in the trench. He bent down. Rod was clutching his leg.

"I'm fine, I'm fine!" yelled Rod, although it was obvious he was in pain. "Keep bloody shooting will you."

Hesitantly Mash stood up and resumed firing. Soon after, Rod struggled to his feet and also blazed away. Rounds zipped past, sometimes hitting the parapet and showering them with sand and dirt. Grenades continued to explode but none as close as the one that had hit Rod. A sort of stalemate had been reached, with the Germans either unable or unwilling to breach the wire.

"You OK?" shouted Mash, glancing across at his friend.

"Yes, just keep firing," grimaced Rod.

The fire fight carried on for several more minutes until the arrival of artillery shells. The Highlanders, their position well mapped, called down artillery support just in front of them and the brief salvo decided the matter. The Germans melted away into the darkness, their objective to disrupt and test the defences achieved.

In the trench Rod had doubled over and was holding his leg, blood oozing through his fingers. His right trouser leg looked as though it had been dragged repeatedly through a barbed wire fence.

"It burns like buggery," said Rod, his face pale and shining with sweat. "I don't think anything serious is wrong though as I can still use it."

Mash gently cut away the trouser leg and revealed the wound. He controlled his expression and not a flicker betrayed the concern he felt at the initial sight of it. Fortunately the concern was short lived.

"There are a few puncture marks but the majority of the blood seems to be coming from your calf," said Mash, almost to himself. "There're two flaps of skin hanging down but it doesn't look as though it's done much damage other than the cut."

"So when did you become a bloody doctor then?" replied Rod through gritted teeth.

Mash smiled as he set about applying dressings to the wounds.

"Speaking of deer, I've seen worse injuries on one of the young stags when they're rutting. Mind you I think you'll be in the hospital for a day or two."

Fortunately for Mash he did not understand a word of the wave of Gaelic that then assailed him.

CHAPTER TWO

# COLETTE

Mash's diagnosis proved correct. Though not life threatening, Rod's wound was bad enough to take him to hospital for a couple of days. While he would normally be glad of the rest he was irritated that it coincided with the Camerons being withdrawn from the front line and being relieved by the Seaforth Highlanders. So instead of missing being in a cramped and cold trench he was missing out on being billeted in a warm, albeit tiny, room in a local farm house.

Mash, who was billeted in the same house as Rod was meant to have been, felt sorry for him. Even though the farm house he was staying in was tiny and the family not well off it was a blessing to sleep on an actual bed and be able to wash in water heated by a kettle. The family, the Massons, consisted of a married couple, a mother – though Mash could not figure out which one she belonged to – and two small boys of unknown age who peered and spied on Mash but were too scared to talk to him. On the first night Mash felt awkward invading their home, especially as his French was limited and their English little better, but they got by with a lot of sign language and they were perfectly friendly. They were incredibly busy with the hard work of farming so they left him mostly to his own devices, just serving him three meals a day which, though simple, to Mash were fit for a king.

The morning after Rod was injured, and after a particularly good breakfast of freshly baked bread and eggs, Mash headed to the hospital to see Rod. He took a little of the bread with him, thinking that the food at the hospital would certainly be lacking. His farm was on the outskirts of the village, but it only took him fifteen minutes to walk to where he had been told the hospital was.

What he found shocked him. Carved into the side of a hill was a concrete and steel entrance to a bunker, well guarded but with a stream of people going in and out. Quickly he realised that the hospital was inside the Maginot Line fortifications. With some trepidation he walked up to the sentry post and presented himself. After the language difficulties had been overcome he was ushered inside. Mash had never seen anything like it before and he wandered around like a kid in a sweet shop, trying to take it all in. It was like he had entered an underground city. There were barracks, offices, tunnels that ran forward to the gun emplacements and store rooms of all kinds. It took his breath away when he saw a small railway transporting troops. All the time there was the whir of the electric and ventilation systems, along with the constant bustle of people moving about; it was just like being inside an ant hill.

By this time he had completely forgotten the instructions he had been given on how to get to the hospital. He found an office with an orderly clerk in it and, for no other reason than the word for hospital sounded the same in French, managed to head in the right direction.

The hospital, too, shocked him; there were numerous wards with beds stretching into the distance as well as an operating theatre with all the associated treatment rooms and equipment.

Finally he managed to find Rod's ward with the help of harassed-looking nurses pointing. He wandered through the beds where the bandaged and broken lay alongside those with everyday ailments and was shocked to hear the incredible sound of someone giggling. He followed the noise to a bed where he found Rod propped up on his pillows and talking to a nurse. Rod was grinning and the nurse had stuffed her hands into her mouth to try and stifle her laughter. Mash stared at her; he could see a coil of dark hair escaping from underneath the starched cap. Mash's eyes flicked automatically to take in her figure; he could see it was shapely beneath the unflattering uniform. He quickly brought his gaze back to her face, hoping she had not noticed. When she saw him she dropped her hands and tried to compose her face into a serious expression. He saw her lip twitch as she attempted to hold it together.

"Don't worry lass," said Rod, putting his hand on her arm. "Mash's OK."

The nurse looked at Mash quizzically, seemingly amused by his silence. Mash just stood there holding his bread in front of him like an offering. He did not know what was wrong with him; he was usually alright with women, he could not smooth-talk them like some of the lads but he did OK. But, looking at the giggling nurse, he could not think of a single thing to say.

"Is that for me," said Rod, looking at the bread.

"Er, yes," said Mash and dropped it unceremoniously on Rod's lap.

"They've been kind enough to get Nurse Martineau here to look after me as she speaks very good English. But as you'll know that's not proper Scots so I've been teaching her some of the choicer Scottish swear words," said Rod, as he peeled the wrappings from the loaf. "Say ya glaikit bastard," he said to the nurse.

She smiled and shook her head.

"Ah, go on," said Rod. "You've got a hell of a pronunciation."

The nurse hesitated then said the phrase, trying her hardest to roughen her smooth French vocals. Rod burst out laughing and Mash smiled. The nurse giggled then stuffed her hands to her mouth again and looked round cautiously. Mash knew somewhere there would be a domineering matron lurking, eagle-eyed for any nurse shirking her duty.

"I can't get it right," the nurse said to Mash, her French accent thick. "Rod says I should spit after I say it, to make it authentic."

"Aye, get a bit of Scottish phlegm," said Rod, through a mouthful of breadcrumbs.

"I think you say it very well," said Mash eventually.

Rod eyed the two of them.

"It was kind of you to come Mash but I feel tired all of a sudden." Rod lay back on his pillows and gave a big yawn that fooled neither of them. "I think Nurse Martineau is going off duty, maybe you can take over teaching her the lovely Scottish language."

Mash cringed inwardly at the obvious set-up but he managed to say the words, "I'd be happy to."

Nurse Martineau looked at him. For a horrible moment he thought she might refuse.

"Give me five minutes," she said. "I'll meet you out the front."

Rod winked at Mash as she walked away.

"You owe me," he said. "I saw her first."

★ ★ ★

Mash waited outside the armoured doors of the entrance. He leant against a wall then quickly stood up, almost to attention. Immediately he moved again and sat down on the wall, casually lounging back on one arm. He sat like that for almost a minute then got up quickly and leaned against the wall again. He had not felt this nervous around a woman for a while. He had not been expecting this, he was just going to see Rod, try to cheer him up then enjoy his day of freedom with a few of the other lads. But now he was waiting for one of the prettiest girls he had seen for a while and he was so nervous he could not stay still. He flexed his hands by his side; he did not know what to do with them and he wished he was still carrying the bread so they were at least occupied.

He tried to plan what he would say. As he had walked through the village earlier he had seen a café; he would suggest that they go for a drink or maybe some lunch so he could "teach her some Scottish." He thought that, if she had not already, she would see through this ruse quite quickly when she realised he was not actually Scottish.

At that moment the nurse walked out of the steel side door and looked round for him. He shot off the wall and stood up ramrod-straight again. She walked over to him. She had taken her cap off and her hair was tied loosely at the nape of her neck. It was almost black and more strands were escaping and whipped round her face. Mash wondered briefly why a strand of hair was so attractive on a woman, maybe they did it deliberately to try and get men to tuck it behind their ears and go in for a kiss.

As he was thinking how ridiculous this was she was suddenly in front of him, looking at him with that slightly quizzical smile that she had worn earlier at his tongue-tied silence. He forced himself to speak.

"Hello," he said.

"Hello."

"I'm Edward," he said. "Most people call me Mash."

"Colette," she replied.

"Would you like to go for a drink, Colette?" he asked, savouring the feel of her name on his tongue.

"Alright," she said simply and smiled at him.

She walked next to him and they made their way in to the village.

They had only gone a few steps, and Mash was wracking

his brain for something to say, when he saw Colette glance to the side, then she did a double take and her smile slipped. Mash followed her eye-line and paused himself when he saw that she was looking at three men who were standing under a tree and watching them walk by. One stood further ahead of the other two, with the air of always being at the head of the group. Mash frowned; he recognised Gavin Mitchell and his flunkies. Mitchell was a Glaswegian lance corporal in the Camerons. Mash could usually get along with most people but he had not taken to the man. He did not like the way the corner of his mouth always turned up in a crooked smile. Mitchell probably thought it made him look like a lovable rogue, which was a persona he tried to exude. It never sat right with Mash; the crinkled eyes were always watching and the crooked smile was the smile of an actor, running over the next line in his head, working out the best way he could use the person in front of him.

No one really knew what Mitchell did before he joined up; his usual reply was "a little bit of this and that." As he was a Glaswegian there were rumours of links with gangland activities, though Mash suspected Mitchell spread them himself.

Mitchell was squinting at them through a haze of smoke from his ever present cigarette. The two men behind him were both large and bulky and were almost comically similar, though Wallace Smith had blond hair and had an IQ that Mash was sure was in the single digits, while Douglas Campbell, widely rumoured to be a nasty piece of work, was dark and a fraction shorter. They both followed Mitchell around and, Mash suspected, acted as his heavies when he needed it. They glowered out from behind their leader, who was not wearing his rogue smile today, his expression was blank, but he stared at them as they walked by. Mash knew Mitchell was not very keen on him either. This did not seem to stem from anything more than the fact that he was English. Mitchell was one of the most vocal about not wanting an Englishman in the Highland Division, making snide comments when Mash was in earshot, but never to his face. When Mitchell called him Mash he always heard the meaning behind it, whereas everyone else just called him it out of habit. Rod calmed Mash down whenever he was close to losing it, telling him that Mitchell was the sort to provoke someone into lashing out then running off and telling. Also, Highlanders thought a Lowlander from Glasgow was only one step from an Englishman. So Mash tried his best to ignore him and keep out of his way.

Mash pulled his gaze away and turned to Colette, who was hurrying up.

"Have you met him?" Mash asked her.

Colette nodded.

"Lucky you," muttered Mash.

"Is he your friend?" asked Colette.

"No," said Mash. "He's not."

Colette smiled again and Mash felt a relief followed by a flash of anger at Mitchell and his flunkies for ever causing her smile to slip.

*Christ, I need to get a hold of myself!*

"How come you know him?" he asked.

"He 'suggested' that I went on a date with him," said Colette.

"Suggested?"

"He basically demanded it," she said, gesticulating abruptly. "He sort of sidled up, got real close and spoke into my ear. I think his exact words were, 'you and me tonight, doll.'"

Mash guffawed.

"Doll!" exclaimed Colette.

"He was trying to be braw," said Mash.

Colette frowned.

"What is 'braw'?" she asked.

"Erm, like suave, debonair."

Collette nodded.

"Maybe it works on other girls but I must admit that I burst out laughing."

"I bet he didn't like that," said Mash.

"No," said Colette. "He was quite rude after that."

"Not so braw after all then?" asked Mash. He was feeling a rather childish glee that Colette had turned down Mitchell but agreed to go out with him.

"No, not braw," said Colette, trying out the new word.

They walked along in silence for a couple more minutes.

"It's much more braw to have your friend ask the girl out on your behalf. From a sick bed no less," said Colette.

Mash slowed and looked at her. She was looking at the floor and smiling. He felt heat rush to his face.

"Well, that's what I was going for," he said. "The schoolboy method never fails."

Colette laughed again.

"It worked though," said Mash. He looked sidelong at her.

Colette looked back at him and they were quiet for a beat.

"I can't resist a tongue-tied man," she said.

Mash laughed.

"You know usually I'm a lot better than this," he said.

"Oh, really?"

"Yes. I can sometimes even ask women out myself," he said.

"Impressive," said Colette.

She was quiet for a second.

"What was different with me?" she asked.

Mash looked at her sideways again and saw that she was looking directly at him.

"I don't know," said Mash. "How come you agreed to come with me?"

She did not say anything for a second.

"I don't know either," she said.

★ ★ ★

At the café talk flowed more freely. The place was small but it was packed with soldiers, nurses and other military staff. However, Mash barely noticed his colleagues; it seemed his earlier nervousness had dried up and he questioned Colette about herself with some zeal. He wanted to know where this laughing nurse with the dark hair came from. She told him about her well-off family who could not understand why she had volunteered as a nurse instead of marrying well and settling down to have babies. He was shocked to find that she owned a small motorbike; she was the only woman he knew who could ride one. Colette explained that she had got it partly because she loved the freedom that it gave her and partly because it drove her parents mad.

In turn, he told her about himself, his upbringing in Hull, his time as a gamekeeper and being one of the few Englishmen in a Scottish regiment.

As they spoke the café slowly emptied and the coffee cups built up on the table. Eventually they realised that they were the only people left and that the owner was giving them somewhat unsubtle hints to leave.

They stepped out of the café and into the gathering dusk.

"I'll walk you home," said Mash.

Colette nodded.

They were silent again, but this was not the quiet of nerves as it was before. They walked side by side, not touching but very close. Mash paid no attention to where they were going but would later learn that Colette lived in a small apartment that was only a five-minute walk from the café. Mash's mind was strangely blank yet he felt he could feel more than usual;

the air, the light, he thought he could even feel the small space between them.

In a short time they reached her apartment. There was an infinitesimal pause before Colette said; "Would you like to come in?"

She spoke in a casual manner but Mash could hear the nerves in her voice.

"Yes, please," he said.

Her flat was very small; there was one main room which constituted living-room and kitchen. A bathroom lay off to the side and two doors led to separate bedrooms. Mash stood and looked around the small room. It was sparsely furnished but Colette had added decorative touches; a scarf draped over the sofa, a cheap but pretty print on the wall. He saw a picture on a small table and glanced at it; it showed a younger-looking Colette with loose hair, her arm was around a fair girl. Both were smiling and squinting slightly into the camera.

"That's Gabrielle," said Colette, seeing Mash looking at the picture. "We came together from Caubert to nurse."

Mash studied the picture, the girls made a total contrast; Colette with her almost black hair and Gabrielle's so light that with the sun shining through it, it looked like gossamer.

"She lives here with me but, she is not here this evening," said Colette.

Mash heard the slight pause and turned to look at her. Her previous nonchalance seemed to have gone and she avoided his eye contact, she looked instead at her fingers which were picking at the skirt of her dress.

"Would you like some coffee," she said suddenly.

Without waiting for his answer she walked quickly to the small section of the room that served as a kitchen and started to fill the kettle. Mash followed her slowly and leant against the wall opposite her as she busied herself with the coffee. She stood with her back to him, scrubbing at mugs, clanking them in the sink and then fumbled over the percolator.

Suddenly she paused and leant her arms against the work surface. Then she turned abruptly, walked straight towards Mash and kissed him on the lips.

Mash was caught off guard only for a second as her lips touched his. But then his arms went around her and he was kissing her back with fervour.

They broke apart, still in each other's arms, and looked at each other. Colette opened her mouth as though she was going to speak but then paused. Mash knew speaking was useless. He kissed her again and there was no need for words as the understanding was between them.

They kissed with an urgency, leaning into each other. Mash pushed her against the wall and she pulled him even closer to him, pressing her body against his, harder than ever. Mash could have taken her right there against the wall but she breathed the word "bedroom," into his ear.

They made their way slowly across the room, still attached at the lips. Colette giggled slightly as they missed the door and crashed into the wall and the sound made Mash bury his head in her neck.

After collapsing on the bed they removed each other's clothes with speed. Colette was tearing at his shirt and he knew she felt the same urgency that he did.

And then he was inside her and Colette's gasp mirrored his own. They moved together, bucking faster and faster. Mash's breathing grew ragged; he clutched at her hips and pushed himself further into her. Colette's moans were building with his own.

He thrust faster and could not hold himself back any more. As he climaxed Colette wrapped her legs tightly around his back and he moaned into her shoulder.

He stayed inside her as their movements slowed and finally stopped. Then he rolled off her and onto his back.

They lay next to each other panting. Mash felt the tingling slowly leave his body and his limbs felt heavy.

He slipped a hand onto Colette's belly and looked at her. She looked back and smiled. They said nothing but lay there quietly. Eventually they both dozed.

Mash woke a little later. He did not know how long he had been asleep but he thought it could not have been more than an hour. He rolled over and slipped his arm around Colette. She, half asleep, moved closer to him and buried her head in his neck. Mash pulled her closer and felt himself grow hard again. Colette felt it too and pressed herself against him. In the darkness he found her lips, kissing her softly at first but then hard.

They made love again, this time slower, less urgent but just as intense.

Afterwards, they lay next to each other in the sheets, their bodies slowly coming back to normal and their breathing growing steadier. Mash stared at the dark ceiling, his mind drifted and he felt a peace that he had not felt for a long time, perhaps ever.

Colette rolled over and laid her hand on his chest and moved her head into him. He placed his hand over hers. They lay like that for a while, Mash could not tell how long, it was that time of night where time ceased having any meaning.

He thought she had drifted off to sleep but he heard her voice and felt her lips move against the skin of her chest.

"I wasn't expecting this to happen today," she said.

Mash smiled up at the ceiling.

"Me neither," he said "You came out of the blue."

She looked up at him.

"I hope you know, I don't do this all the time," she said.

"I know," he said.

They were both quiet for a minute then Mash whispered, "I'm glad you did today."

He felt her smile and then they did not say any more.

Mash left while it was still dark. He had kissed Colette

lingeringly at her door, not wanting to leave, but slowly he trudged back to the farm. There was a chill in the air but he hardly felt it; his body was sated and his mind was at peace, yet he felt a pulse of excitement inside of him. All the way back his thoughts were of Colette, the girl he had not even known for twenty-four hours but who he already felt was an integral part of his life and happiness.

He reached the farm around 04:00 and crept in quietly. He lay in his bed and dozed fitfully, his dreams filled with tangled bodies and dark hair splayed across a pillow.

He only managed to sleep for a couple of hours as he had to be up for roll call along with a few hours of exercise and training at 06:30. He did his duties like an automaton, forcing his body to go through the practised moves but in his head he was desperate to get away. He had planned to spend time with some of the other lads in the unit, but he faked a headache and said he wanted to lie down.

Instead of going back to the farm he found his feet taking him in the direction of the hospital. He tried to chasten himself on the way, telling himself it was too early to go and see her; he did not want to appear too keen.

*But then there's nothing wrong with visiting my injured friend. In fact, I'd be a bad friend if I didn't visit Rod.*

He knew this was just an excuse though, he wanted to see Colette. He had never felt anything like it before. He had never believed in love at first sight, but he knew he had felt something when he first saw Colette and after a night together, where most men would have left sated and unwilling to go any further, he just wanted more.

When he reached the bunker he found that he knew exactly where he was going; somehow, subconsciously, he had taken in the route yesterday.

*Was it only yesterday? It feels like an eternity.*

He hurried into the ward and rushed round to Rod's bed.

He came to a standstill and his face dropped when he saw Rod sitting alone with no dark-haired nurse attending to him.

"You don't have to look so disappointed," said Rod. He was trying to sound annoyed but he was smiling.

"She's been hanging round my bed all morning," he continued. "If I'd known better I'd have thought she was into me, but she keeps asking about a certain someone. I take it yesterday's date was a success?"

"You could say that," said Mash.

He sat down on the edge of the bed and for a moment felt the urge to disclose everything to Rod. But he stopped himself. He wanted to keep last night just between himself and Colette for a while. He plucked at the bedspread instead.

"That good was it?" asked Rod.

Mash was silent for a minute but then he said, "Jesus, it was fucking amazing, but I don't want to talk about it."

"Oh, come on," said Rod, looking genuinely upset. "My girl's at home, I need to live vicariously through you."

Before Mash could reply there was the sound of footsteps and Colette emerged from around the corner. She stopped short when she saw him. Her lips involuntarily lifted up into a smile then she forced them down and retained a sensible air.

"Hello," said Mash.

"Hello," she replied.

They were both quiet but the corners of Colette's mouth crept up again and Mash's mirrored hers.

"Well, this is a fascinating conversation," said Rod, cutting through the silence. "But neither of you are paying much attention to me and I'm the invalid."

"I'm sorry Rod," said Mash. "How are you feeling?"

"Terrible, my leg feels like it's on fire and it's turning green."

"He's lying," said Colette. "He's healing very well and he should be out tomorrow."

Rod glowered at her.

A French voice called Colette's name. Colette turned and spoke briefly to a nurse at another bed.

"I have to go," she said.

"When do you finish your shift?" asked Mash.

"One o'clock," said Colette.

"Would you like to have some lunch afterwards?" asked Mash.

"Yes please," Colette replied.

Mash grinned and so did Colette while Rod rolled his eyes between them.

"Nurse Martineau!" came the voice of a matron that made even Mash and Rod jump.

Colette scrambled away, glancing behind her with a smile.

Mash stared after her then turned to see Rod watching him.

"What?" said Mash.

"You've got it bad, son."

Mash looked back down the row of beds where he could see Colette talking to a bandaged-up soldier.

"I think you're right," he said.

When 13:00 rolled around Mash was standing outside at the same wall by the entrance. He did not feel as nervous as he had yesterday when Colette walked outside. Instead, when he saw her he felt a deep fizz of happiness. And he remembered Rod's words; he definitely did have it bad.

Colette walked up to him and without thinking about it he put his arms around her and kissed her deeply on the lips. He pulled away to find Colette smiling at him and he knew she felt the same way as he did.

★ ★ ★

It was lucky that the Camerons were in reserve and that Mash was stood down as he only returned back to the farm sporadically over the next few days. The unexpected amount of time off was a blessing. He spent most of it in Colette's tiny rented room, catching brief hours of sleep between bouts of talking and making love.

They never spoke about the future, it was a silent agreement between the two of them; instead they discussed their past, their favourite books, foods, films and other things that seemed completely meaningless but had all the meaning in the world to them.

The breaks where Mash had to report and do whatever the division deemed was necessary and Colette had to work were put up with, but they immediately returned together.

After nearly a week of this Rod and some of the others from the unit managed to collar him after training and before he ran off to see Colette again.

Rod, who was now out of the hospital, insisted that they meet her properly, or as Rod put it: "venture out of your den of sin and socialise with civilised people."

"And get her to bring some friends," added Murray, a particularly horny member of the unit.

They all went to the local café the following evening. Mash felt a little as though he was introducing her to his family. She brought a couple of nursing friends with her, including Gabrielle, her roommate. She was a couple of years younger than Colette and at first was rather quiet. Meeting her properly now he felt a little guilty that he had only briefly met her at the flat in the times he had ventured out of Colette's bedroom. He made an effort to speak to her properly now. He found that, once over the initial nervousness, she was sweet and could chatter away happily in heavily accented English.

While he spoke to Gabrielle, Mash was pleased to see that Colette was talking to the other men in his unit, including Rod who laughed with her like they were old friends. Mash felt absurdly pleased and he caught her eye. She gave him the ghost of a wink and returned to chatting.

They stayed long into the evening, getting steadily drunker and louder. The only grievance from that night was the presence of Mitchell and his henchmen. Mash noticed them come in an hour or two after he and Colette arrived. She was talking to Rod and did not see them but Mash saw Douglas pause as he walked from the door to the bar. Mitchell looked to see what had made him stop and noticed Colette and then Mash. His eyes fixed on Mash's for a few seconds, then he flicked them up and down Colette quite obviously before smirking and moving along. Behind him Douglas echoed Mitchell's actions, taking a rather long time looking at Colette, who was still obliviously talking to Rod. Instead of a smirk he glared at Mash that gave Mash some pleasure, as it seemed to confirm that his being with Colette was needling Mitchell. Finally he hulked off, Wallace following behind. They went to the bar and ordered drinks. For a moment Mash felt like walking over there and making something of it, but he knew how that would end and a fight in the pub was not how he wanted to remember this night. He slipped over to Colette and put his arm around her waist. He snuck another glance back at Mitchell, knowing full well that he was marking his territory, but Mitchell was not looking at him.

Mash turned his attention to Colette and the others, determining to ignore the men at the bar. The rest of the evening passed in a haze of drinks. Mash felt absurdly happy and hoped that the Phoney War, as it had become known, would last forever so that he could remain exactly as he was.

But this was not to be.

While Mash and Colette had been getting to know each other and enjoying their unexpected freedom, the Germans had not been so idle. The next morning, Friday the 10th May, they had launched an attack through the Ardennes Forest to the north of the Highlanders, effectively going around the side of the Maginot Line and splitting them from the rest of the B.E.F.

The effect on Mash and Colette was immediate. Their free time was rapidly reduced as the Highlanders were put on alert and the hospital braced itself for casualties. That weekend they could only snatch brief periods of time, helped by Rod and Gabrielle covering for them. But the thought that their world was imploding seemed to make their time together more precious, dragging them even closer to each other. It was as though the uncertainty and potential danger heightened their passion.

Then, on the Tuesday, Colette told Mash that the nurses had been informed that the Germans were rapidly advancing and that, because the Maginot Line had been circumvented, the volunteer nurses were free to return to their homes.

"I should probably go," she had said, listlessly.

"You should definitely go," said Mash. "You won't be safe otherwise." He knew his words were true and sensible but speaking them he felt a deadly emptiness inside. It brought home with a crushing reality just how bad things were and that he was going to be parted from her. Desperate for one more night together they begged Rod and Gabrielle to cover for them.

That night they made love with an intensity and fire that was borne out of desperation. They clung to each other in the passion of the moment, neither wanting it to end, before they finally drifted into a fitful sleep, still holding to each other.

They were snatched back to reality by a pounding on the door early in the morning of the 15th. Colette made an indistinguishable sound in French next to Mash as he opened his bleary eyes. The hammering kept going, then he heard the voice.

"Mash! For Christ sake open the door!"

Recognising Rod's voice, Mash rolled out of the bed and opened the front door before he knew what he was doing. He had a brief second to realise that something bad was happening before Rod was suddenly in front of him.

"We've got to go now," he said. "We're withdrawing."

Mash blinked at him as the words sunk in. Behind him Colette emerged from the bedroom just as Gabrielle stuck her head out of hers.

"Are you listening?" Rod asked, his normal laidback attitude gone.

"Yes," said Mash. "What's happened?"

"I don't know much, just that the Germans seem to have broken through and we're in danger of being surrounded. We're withdrawing to Étain, twenty miles away."

Mash heard Colette swear quietly behind him.

"Get your stuff now," said Rod. "They were going to get you from the farm but I managed to bluff them out saying I'd do it."

"Thanks," Mash said, not really knowing what had hit him. But he went back into Colette's room and threw on his clothes. He quickly came back out to find Rod talking to the women.

"If you two've got any sense then you'll get out of here too, you don't want to be around when the Germans come through."

Colette was not looking at Rod but instead had turned to look at Mash. He stared back at her and saw in her face the realisation that they were now going to be separated, just as it hit him.

"Mash, we've got to go," said Rod.

"Can you just give us a minute?" he said.

"I can't we've got to go now."

"Just one, please," said Mash, raising his voice.

Rod looked at him, then at Colette.

"One minute," he said. "But no more, I'll be outside."

With a nod at the women, he left. Gabrielle went back into her room muttering something about packing.

Mash turned back to Colette and for a moment felt

everything he wanted to say overwhelm and cripple him. Finally he managed to speak.

"You and Gabrielle had better leave, but you've got to be safe," he said.

"We can go on the bike," said Colette. "We can go back home to my parents."

"That's bloody miles away," said Mash.

"Yes, 500 kilometres."

"You can't go all the way on the bike across country."

"How else do you propose we go? Anyway, that was how we got here," said Colette.

Mash said nothing.

"We'll dress as men," she said simply.

Mash was about to argue with this when she suddenly turned away.

"I'll give you my parents' address in Caubert," she said. "You can always get a message to me there."

She scribbled the address down and handed the torn piece of paper to him. He took it, folded it and put it in his pocket.

They looked at each other again. Colette made a useless gesture with her hand.

"There's no time to say everything," she said.

"I love you," said Mash. He had not planned to say it but when it came out he knew that he meant it.

Colette's eyes filled with tears.

"I love you too, Mash Man," she said.

Then they were in each other's arms and Mash was holding her tightly while she sobbed into his shoulder.

"Mash!" Rod's voice echoed from the street.

Mash let her go and ran for the door. Then he turned back.

"I will see you again," he said.

"I know," said Colette.

Then he was out of the door and into the street, and he and Rod were hurrying back to their real lives and to the war.

# CHAPTER THREE

# CAUBERT

Though Colette was always in his thoughts, Mash was kept so busy over the next few days that he barely had time to worry. The Germans had unleashed a new type of war: Blitzkrieg. Characterised by the first co-ordinated use of armour, infantry and close air support, the advance relied heavily on effective communication and an unheard of level of autonomy given to a new breed of professional, capable and motivated local commanders. The effect on the out-dated French and British command structures, where it took up to forty-eight hours for a message to be sent from the commander in chief to officers in the field, was staggering. To Mash and the others the most obvious signs of the chaos that ensued was that, as the Germans advanced, it caused orders to be changed or countermanded on a daily, if not hourly, basis. Plus, there was an ever growing flow of refugees that blocked every road to the west.

"I wish they would just bloody well make up their minds," swore Mash out of pure frustration. "One minute it's move to here, the next it's stay where you are, only to be closely followed by go somewhere else. I don't know if I'm coming or going!"

"I heard from one of the signallers from Battalion HQ that two orders from the same French general arrived at exactly the same time, each saying something completely different. Apparently Fortune is as pissed off as we are," said Rod.

It did not mollify Mash that Major General Fortune, the

51st Division's commanding officer, was also struggling with events.

"Well if he doesn't know what's happening then we're in a right mess," he said.

At that moment he saw a commotion further up the line.

"Look out, something's happening, I hope its not another case of hurry up and wait."

All around there was shouting as the NCOs stirred the men into action. At long last they were off and were soon formed up and marching towards the station. Once there they were embarked into large railway trucks.

"Have you seen this," laughed Mash, looking at a sign on the truck. "It says forty men or ten horses. So Rod, what does it feel like to be worth a quarter of a horse?"

"Not a problem for me, just as long as they've cleaned up after the horses first," replied Rod. "Bloody hell, this is going to be cosy!"

The train was overloaded but slowly order prevailed as the men settled down and made themselves comfortable. Eventually the train pulled out. There were ironic cheers and cat-calling until they all settled into a routine of sleep, cards, letters home and chat.

Rod was staring out of the window, his brow furrowed.

"What's worrying you?" asked Mash.

"I don't understand why we're heading south and not west like I thought we would," said Rod. "Also the train is crawling along. I hope we're not needed in a hurry."

Mash looked down at the ground. Rod was right; the speed was pitiful and not more than a brisk walking pace. A quick glance at the sun confirmed they were heading south.

"If the Jerries are just to the north of us then maybe they're taking us a safe way," he said.

"Don't be daft," jumped in Rod. "We're not civilians, we're meant to be where the fighting is. If they're taking us south then either something's up that we're not aware of or the Jerries are making more progress than we thought."

The idea that the Germans were speeding across France shook Mash.

"Do you think Colette's alright? I knew I shouldn't have let her go on that bloody bike."

Rod realised he had opened a can of worms.

"Now don't be daft. That girl's more than capable of looking after herself; I don't think you give her enough credit for that. In any case she's got Gabrielle with her."

"But what happens if she couldn't get through the roads? You saw how they're filling up with refugees." Mash's mind had gone into overdrive. "And what about the Stukas shooting up the roads? She's probably dead in a ditch or something."

"Calm down," said Rod as he put a hand on Mash's shoulder in a vain attempt to stop the thoughts that were racing through Mash's mind. "She left before the roads got really bad, in any case, if I had to pick a vehicle I'd want to get through congested roads on it'd be a motorbike. As for the Stukas, they're only interested in what's in front of their tanks. Colette was further to the south. So will you stop your flapping?"

Rattled as he was Mash could see the sense in what Rod was saying. Somewhat mollified but still highly concerned, he sat on his kit and brooded. He tried to distract himself but thoughts of Colette consumed him and made it difficult to focus on anything else. He resolved that the first opportunity he had he was going to take her with him. He would not be separated from her again.

Rod looked at him

"Young love," he muttered before rolling over and trying to sleep.

★ ★ ★

The journey took six arduous days to cover just over 500 miles. The train ambled its way south and then west through Troyes and Orléans before swinging north at Tours. The boredom was excruciating as the train continued at its snail's pace. The only brief lightening of the mood happened when they passed through Le Mans, which provoked some interest from motor racing fans, before the grind set in again as they headed further north. Finally they reached their final destination, the outskirts of Rouen in Normandy.

The rain poured down as the men disembarked and trudged their way to a temporary site where they hastily erected old French tents.

"If it rains any harder I'm going to need some water wings," grumbled Mash. "At least we can get some sleep."

"I wouldn't bet your bottom dollar on that," replied Rod. He was looking towards a dispatch rider, caked in mud and dripping water, who had just arrived and was searching for the company commander. "In my experience one of those means the end of any shut eye."

Sure enough the order to immediately parade followed not long after. As they stood in the pouring rain they were told that they would be picked up by French transport in thirty minutes.

Three hours later they were still waiting.

"This lot couldn't organise a piss up in a brewery," said Rod, his normally mild face contorted with anger and dripping with water. "They can make all the mistakes they want, but not when it means I'm left standing in the rain!"

Mash was quite surprised that the normally unflappable Rod was showing signs of the frustration. But he did not have time to dwell as around a corner appeared the first of a large number of civilian buses, all with numerous dents and scrapes and not a few bullet holes.

"Bloody hell, have you ever seen anything like that before?"

murmured Mash as a bus pulled up in front of them. A man with a white Gallic moustache was driving, clearly a civilian.

"Vite, vite s'il vous plaît. Dépêchez-vous, tout le monde à bord," he said, ushering them forward with a frenzied waving of his hand.

Soon they were all aboard. The driver let out the clutch with a jerk and they all launched forward.

"How fast is this nutter driving?" shouted Mash as he and the others held on for dear life. "He's way too fast for the conditions and load."

"Perhaps he knows something we don't," replied Rod. "Mind you, have you seen this daft bugger?"

On the side of the road was an open top and very battered Citroen with a French officer standing up and shouting instructions through a megaphone.

"I'm sure that car's half full of water," laughed Rod.

The officer sat down and the Citroen shot forward, pushing its way past the overloaded buses to the front so it could direct them on the next stage of the journey.

"Still, it's a good job it's raining," said Rod.

"How do you work that one out?" shouted Mash, wedging himself into the side of the bus as it hurtled round a tight corner.

"There can't be any Jerry planes up in this weather and it's a good job, we're way too closely packed."

Soon enough, with a squeal of brakes, they arrived at their destination some sixty miles toward the River Somme.

"Allez, descendez-vous tout de suite," shouted the bus driver, waving frantically.

The Camerons had arrived at the Haute Forêt d'Eu overlooking Blangy-sur-Bresle. There they found 150 or so survivors from a Basque regiment who had retreated from Holland. They were on good form, announcing they had many guns and machine guns, lots of ammunition and an abundance of wine. As a result they would hold the river bank for as long as it took. The Basques and the Highlanders immediately struck it off and a dent was soon made in the reserves of wine. Despite the rain, Mash and Rod spent a very pleasant afternoon in the company of their new friends before getting themselves ready to move forward.

That night they and the rest of the Camerons moved up to a village called Limeux, a couple of miles to the west of the River Somme. There they dug in under the cover of a wood.

"It's hard work digging in all these roots," muttered Mash as his spade hit yet another. "And hearing about Belgium doesn't help."

"Aye," replied Rod. "Jerry seems to be charging along. The boys up north must be pulling back to the coast. I hope they don't forget us."

The news that Belgium had surrendered spread like wildfire and the mood was sombre. It meant that the Germans must have pushed the rest of the B.E.F. back and they now knew they were separated from the rest of the British forces.

"Mind you, I heard the sergeant say we're in the woods so that we're out of sight of the Stukas. If that's the case I'm all for it."

"I wonder what's up?" continued Mash. "I've heard all sorts of movement going on, some of it tanks by the sound of it."

"Apparently there was some sort of attack this morning but it didn't work. No doubt we'll find out what's going on eventually," said Rod

"At least we're not going to starve," chirped Mash. "I've never seen so many rabbits as there are in this wood."

★ ★ ★

The next four days passed without incident for Mash and Rod. They could hear a number of engagements, although none came close to them. All the time the incessant movement of tanks, artillery and troops as the French 31st Division arrived told them that something big was in the offing. What they also did not know was that just seventy miles to the north of them, the battered remnants of the B.E.F. were being evacuated from Dunkirk. Finally, on the night of 3rd June, they were called to a briefing.

"Listen in," started the platoon commander. "As you've probably gathered Jerry has advanced rapidly across France and has made it to the sea."

Mash glanced around and saw the concern he was feeling mirrored on the other men's faces.

"Whilst that's bad news, Jerry has a problem. Between him and us is the River Somme, a natural barrier. There're only a few places he can cross and one of them is at Abbeville, which is a few miles to our north. He's managed to get a foothold on our side of the river and he's driven off a couple of attempts to push him back to the other side, that's all the noise you've been hearing. We need to make sure he's sent packing to the other side once and for all. For that reason we've been getting reinforcements in the form of a French division and some of our artillery. Tomorrow's the big push and our chance to give him a black eye."

"Together with the French, the division is aiming to capture about six miles of water meadows in front of the river. That'll ensure Jerry's pushed back into the town of Abbeville on the other side. We're on the far right of the division and the attack. Our job is to secure the right flank by taking and holding the village of Caubert."

Mash felt as though he had been punched in the stomach. The name Caubert was tattooed on his brain.

"Caubert near Abbeville, that's where Colette is!" he hissed to Rod.

"Don't do anything stupid," whispered Rod. "Just listen to the rest of the briefing."

But Mash did not hear another word.

*I'm not going to let her go this time. I'm going to find her and bring her with me, whatever it takes.*

He did not notice Rod looking at him, concerned, from the corner of his eye. He was also taking in all of the details of the attack as he knew Mash was not listening.

When the briefing finished Rod walked back with Mash.

"Tell me you're not going to go after her," Rod said, but got no reply. "Listen, I know what you're thinking but you can't just go on a personal crusade."

"You've no idea what I'm thinking!" snapped Mash as he stopped walking and turned on Rod with an aggression that he had never showed his friend before.

"Are you really telling me that if Fiona was in Caubert you wouldn't move heaven and earth to get to her?"

"Aye, I would. But I wouldn't just charge in there and get my head blown off before I got within a mile of her," reasoned Rod. "She may not even still be there; she might've got back on her bike and continued to head away from the Germans."

"I know she's there. I can't tell you how I know but I do and I'm going to get her."

"The briefing said we've got a lot of open ground to cover before we even get to Caubert. They say that there're not many Germans but Jerry seems to have done a pretty good job of beating back two attacks and they're being reinforced all the time. This is going to be difficult and you're no good to Colette dead."

Mash glared at him, ignoring the sense that Rod was speaking.

"Understand I'm going to get Colette. I don't care how dangerous it is, I'm going to get her. Now you can help me or not, that's your call. But that's what I'm going to do."

"So what happens if you do get her?" countered Rod. "Do

you think the army's just going to let you bring a French girl along with you? You can't do it."

"What are they going to do, tell me to take her back? Everything's fucked, Jerry's made it to the coast, odds are we're going to be evacuated out and I want Colette to come back with me."

Rod looked like he was going to speak again but Mash silenced him with a wave of his arm.

"Enough, I'm going to get ready," he turned and stormed away, leaving Rod staring after him.

As the next day dawned the men were apprehensive; whilst they had been bloodied on the Maginot Line, this was the first major engagement for most of them.

Overnight things had been polite but strained between Rod and Mash. Rod had made one more attempt to talk Mash out of his intended rescue but it had only served to make the atmosphere frostier.

Part of Mash knew that he was being unreasonable, but the thought that he had already nearly lost Colette made his heart override his head.

The French and Scots had managed to gather a reasonable number of artillery pieces, mostly French 75s, and at 03:00 they opened up a barrage lasting thirty minutes. Under the cover of the artillery fire the men formed up and made their last preparations. Men endlessly checked and rechecked their equipment as the nerves set in. Several ducked out for repeated 'nervous pees' or worse, the NCOs watching to make sure they came back. But, although there was apprehension, the Highlanders were ready for the fight; it was their time to get to grips with the Germans.

The clanking and screeching announced the arrival of the tanks. It was an impressive sight. The machines, mainly the light R35 and H39 tanks but with a few of the heavy Char B1s, formed up with the infantry. There were nervous thumbs up between the tank crews and the infantry as the drivers occasionally gunned their engines in anticipation. They were ready.

And then the order to advance was given. The tank engines roared as they moved off and emerged from the wood. The infantry, in extended order, moved forward with them and onto the open field that led down to the water meadows.

Initially there was no opposition. The first sign that the Germans were aware of their presence was when a couple of enemy mortars opened up on them. They soon found the range and the first men started to fall.

From the start Mash was striding out through the foot-high rye crop and getting in front of the tanks and the others. Sharp words from the NCOs brought him reluctantly back into line with a worried Rod.

Whilst Mash's mind was made up, Rod's words had had an effect on him. In addition to getting himself ready, he had spent the evening starting to work through the points and had to concede that he had not thought through the problems. He had wracked his brain to remember anything Colette had said about Caubert. He had her address on a piece of paper in his pocket. He remembered she had said that Caubert was a small village with one main street, the Grande Rue, running through it. Her parents had a big house just opposite the church on the high street, so that should not be too hard to find. But now the most pressing need was to get to her. As he advanced he was not looking for the enemy, instead he was looking at the rooftops of the village, trying to get his bearings and work out where Colette was.

An enormous explosion shattered his thoughts. The tank to his left erupted in flame. The top turret flew up and the tank commander bailed out, but he was the only one who did.

Mash, now looking towards the enemy, searched for a sign of the anti-tank gun but could not see anything. A few minutes later there was another explosion; this time the tracks blew off, leaving the R35 tank stranded and the crew, both of them, made a hasty retreat.

*Still no sign of a gun flash. Wait a minute, there wasn't any sound, no crack of a round. We must be in a minefield.*

They were in a minefield. It was not marked and no one knew if it was a French or German one. But it was taking its toll and forcing the tanks to follow each other as they looked for a way through. Then, to add to the chaos for the tanks, the first of the German anti-tank guns opened up. Rounds slammed into the tanks with devastating effect. Caught between the need to manoeuvre to avoid the anti-tank guns and the need to form columns to minimise their losses from mines, the French tanks were knocked out one by one.

Mash marvelled at the bravery of the tank drivers; one after another was taken out but they still pushed on.

They were now half way across the open field. There were still a couple of tanks with the Highlanders but most had been knocked out. The infantry had taken casualties but were relatively unscathed. But the mortar fire was intensifying and the Spandau machine guns started to open up. The casualties mounted quickly.

*Got to keep moving, no time to stop, I must push on.*

While the others were starting to falter under the now relentless fire, Mash started to run, instantly putting distance between himself and the others. Rod saw him moving ahead and immediately made after his friend. The effect of the two running towards the enemy galvanised the others. The platoon commander and NCOs roared them on as they too also started to quickly close the gap to the enemy guns.

In front, Mash was detached from reality. Bullets zipped and whined all around him. He could see the muzzle flashes getting closer and closer. Twice he felt a thump as rounds struck his webbing and he felt the shockwave of a number more that only just missed him. But he was totally focused on the bank ahead, like a machine, zigzagging back and forth as the ground churned up all around him. Behind him the others were keeping up, only they were not all so lucky and the fire was taking its toll.

*Just a couple of hundred yards. Keep going. What the hell's that?*

Less than a hundred yards ahead of him, in the rye field, Germans were standing up. They had come forward and were in the field, only now Mash and the others were getting close so they were getting ready to receive the charge. Instead of slowing Mash down, it had the opposite effect on him. He sprinted forward and a guttural scream erupted from him. He ran straight for a group of three directly in front of him, who were already unnerved by this lunatic madman. Two fired, but by now, despite the close range, they were thoroughly spooked and shot without aiming. The rounds cracked past him, high and wide, and still he came on. The third lifted his rifle, but Mash fired from the hip, still screaming at the top of his voice. The bullet hit the German in the left side of his chest and spun him round. The other two were now starting to turn to run. Mash dived at them, rugby tackle style, and all three fell to the ground. In a second Mash was up and bayoneting the petrified Germans.

Then, instead of turning to deal with the others, he continued his mad dash forwards towards the village. The remaining Germans were stunned. This mad Highlander had barrelled his way into them and then carried on as if nothing was in his way. Some turned, either to shoot at him or run and the effect was instant. Fear and panic swept through them like a plague and others, seeing men turn and the remainder of the Highlanders about to engage them, turned and ran for their lives. In a scene that would have looked funny if it was not so deadly, they all ran towards the village.

Now panting heavily, Mash reached the trees at the far

side of the field. Ahead of him was a small lake, beyond which were the first of the houses and then the road. He paused for a few seconds to regain his breath before dashing into the trees. The scene was surreal; all around him men were running, the majority German. It was like Mash was floating above the others, watching with an air of detachment. Men ran in all directions, guns fired, mortars exploded, men screamed and yelled, all as though in another world. It was like Mash was part of something else and, his focus purely on finding Colette, he ignored those around him and they seemed to do the same. Behind him Mash could hear the Highlanders running forward, firing as they came. Germans were falling back, trying to find somewhere to form and make a stand.

Mash sprinted up to the garden of one of the houses and hurdled the fence. The garden was like an oasis of calm, but Mash did not linger; instead he ran down the side alley and out into the main road. A burst of automatic fire brought him up with a jolt and he quickly dived down behind the garden wall.

*That was close. Got to keep switched on. Where's the church? That's got to be the easiest way of finding the house.*

He peered out from behind the wall expecting another burst of fire at any second, but there was nothing. Whoever had fired had moved on. He desperately looked around him. To his right the road was dead straight with no sign of a church. To his left the road swung to the right after about seventy-five yards, blocking out any view further on.

*It has to be that way.*

He ran up the road. It was eerily quiet now; the Germans had melted away and the remainder of the Highlanders were still behind him. Throwing caution to the wind Mash sprinted along the road. In seconds he was at the bend and able to see up the main street. There, no more than one hundred yards away, was the church. Hope leapt through his heart as he raced towards it. Still no one appeared or hindered him. He skidded to a halt. The church was on his right, set up on a rise in the ground. A retaining wall, about ten feet tall, ran the length of the church forming a vertical barrier along the side of the road and forming the base for the church. On the other side of the road all Mash could see was a small, white house with blue shutters and door. For a second panic started to sweep over him as he raced forward. And then, set back from the road and hidden behind the white house, he saw an impressive manor house. It was red brick with a light, almost white mortar that gave it a chocolate-box look. It was the house he was looking for and with a shout of delight he ran up the stairs to the front door. He banged on it as he tried the handle. The door was unlocked and he quickly ran inside. He entered a spacious hallway that looked deserted. Mash felt the panic rise in him again.

"Colette, Colette, where are you?" shouted Mash as he passed through the hall and tried other rooms.

He was just beginning to think that she was not there when the door behind him burst open.

"Mash!"

He turned to see her framed in the doorway. For a second, they just stared at each other in silence. Then Mash rushed forward and gathered her up in his arms. They clung to each other and Mash could hear the sobs and feel the tears of joy as he squeezed her tightly. Passionately they kissed before a stream of questions erupted from both of them, so fast that neither had a chance of comprehending let alone answering the other. Embarrassed, they laughed and caught their breath.

"What are you doing here?" said Colette.

"It's a long story, are you alright?"

"Yes, yes, I'm fine," she replied, gripping his hands tightly. "My parents and I hid in the cellar when the fighting started. I heard an English voice calling my name, I immediately knew it was you."

"I'm leaving and I'm taking you with me, but we've got to get away now," said Mash.

"What?" said Colette. "Mash you can't, what would I…"

Mash grabbed her by the shoulders.

"We don't have time for this, it's not going to be long before the Jerries reform. Please just come with me. I need to know that you're safe."

Colette stared at him, her eyes searching his face.

"Alright," she said. "Alright you mad man. Just give me a few minutes to pack some clothes and say goodbye to my parents."

"We don't have time, we've got to go."

"I have to say goodbye to my parents, I can't just leave them. I'll be two minutes I promise."

"OK, I'll go and see where the others are and keep a lookout. Remember to lock the door behind me; it was open when I came in."

Colette kissed him briefly on the lips then ran upstairs.

Mash went out to the road. It was quiet there but in the distance there was still the sound of gunfire. It seemed that the Germans had pulled back towards Abbeville, while the remaining Highlanders, approaching with more caution than Mash's suicidal sprint, were coming up the street from Mash's right and were almost at the small white house. Making sure he was clearly visible as a friend, he made his way towards them and soon spotted Rod at the front of the advance.

"I've found her, she's in the house opposite the church and she's getting ready to come with me," blurted out Mash.

"Jesus Christ," said Rod. "This is a war zone. The British Army aren't going to let you add your sweetheart to the ranks."

"She's coming with me and that's final," said Mash and before Rod could reply he had turned back to Colette's house.

"Where the hell do you think you're going?" shouted a

sergeant. "Get up to the top of that church tower and tell me what you can see."

"I can't," stammered Mash. "I've got to get someone."

It sounded lame to him let alone the sergeant.

"I don't give a flying fucking if you're going to get the Pope, jump to it now!" barked the sergeant, red-faced.

Mash hovered on the spot. His urge to run back to Colette was dragging at him, but he knew he could not ignore a direct order. With a groan he turned and ran off towards the church before the sergeant or Rod could say a word.

In minutes he was at the top of the tower with a panoramic view of the flat countryside around him. What he saw below was not good news. Looking north towards Abbeville he could see the open fields that the Highlanders and French had crossed in their advance. Burning French tanks littered the fields along with many bodies of the infantry. Instantly it was clear that, other than in the far south where Mash was, none of the attacking forces had managed to get to the road or river. The attack had been a failure and only the Camerons had been able to make their objective. Worse, Mash could see that the Germans, realising that Caubert had been taken, were redirecting forces south to regain the village. Mash could see what looked like hundreds of German soldiers, along with several Panzer II and 38(t) tanks and armoured cars, heading down the main road towards him. The lead elements were almost on them and it was only the bend in the road that stopped each side from seeing the other.

Immediately he shouted down to the other Camerons, telling them what he saw. Then he watched as quickly they formed a defensive position either side of the road about thirty yards further down from the church. What seemed like seconds later the lead elements of infantry appeared around the corner. The Highlanders held fire until as many Germans as possible were in sight but without their presence being discovered. They then poured fire into the enemy, who were brought to a sudden halt. After a brief exchange of fire the Germans retreated around the corner, leaving the dead and dying behind them.

From his vantage point Mash could see the Germans bringing forward two tanks to head the next attack, supported by more infantry. He knew the Camerons did not have any anti-tank weapons and was worried that they would not be able to resist the machines.

He was also getting desperate about Colette. They had ended up in a sort of no man's land between the two forces, but with him on one side of the road and Colette on the other.

He ran down from the tower and shouted to the Camerons that tanks were coming, although the engine noises and squeal of tracks had already alerted them. Instead of going back up the tower he ran along the side of the church. At the far end he was blocked from the Germans' view by the wall of the house next to the church and some ten feet above the road where the Germans were advancing. With his back to the wall he waited while the tanks advanced. He was betting that the Germans would not be expecting an attack from above and behind them.

Slowly the lead tank emerged from around the bend. Cautiously Mash peered over the wall and looked down at the tank. He breathed a sigh of relief. Its commander had not closed the hatch on the turret and was peering over the top of the rim to get a better view of what lay ahead. Mash had been gambling that he would do this rather than close up and suffer the very restricted view in a built-up area. In addition there was a group of German infantry behind the tank, using it for cover, and then two more groups of troops advancing on either side of the street. Finally, the second tank was about twenty yards behind the first.

Mash searched through his uniform and found the three Mills bomb grenades he was looking for. He would have liked four but he would have to make do. By now the tank was about ten yards further down the road, so he ducked down and ran forward until he was just coming level with it. He laid the three grenades in front of him then he grabbed the first one and pulled the pin. Anxiously he glanced over the top of the wall and gently lobbed the grenade towards the hatch. He was slightly out. Instead of going into the tank it hit the rim just behind the tank commander's head, who apparently did not notice in the din, and bounced backwards off the back of the tank. Mash cursed himself and immediately pulled the pin on the second grenade. He paused for a second to compose himself and adjust his aim, before throwing it towards the hatch again. As he did this the first grenade exploded right in the middle of the troops behind the tank. Whilst it was not his intended target, the effect was brutal. Many of the soldiers, crammed together to be in cover behind the tank, were hit. The tank commander had no time to react before the second grenade flashed in front of his eyes as it dropped into the body of the tank. In an instant it burst into flames, rounds stored inside the tank banging and ricocheting as the explosion set them off.

Finally Mash threw the third grenade towards the troops on the far side of the road. They had turned toward Mash to look at the explosions and some noticed him pop up behind the wall above the tank. As he threw the grenade rounds from the Germans zipped past and smashed into the stonework around him.

Mash ducked back down behind the wall and sprinted the length of the church. As he did so he could hear fire from the Camerons pouring into the Germans who, in turn, were returning fire. Mash ran down the church steps and charged back to the Camerons, bullets kicking up dust and chips of stone as they burst around him. But the Germans had had enough. The second tank could not get round his burnt-out leader and the numerous dead and wounded on the street. It and the remaining troops were pulling back around the corner and out of the view of the Highlanders.

"Bloody hell, that was brave," shouted Rod as Mash rushed up. "We thought we were in for a thumping when the tank came into view. You were a bloody miracle!"

Around him other Camerons were cheering their support and patting Mash on the back, but he barely noticed.

"I've got to get to Colette," he said to Rod, almost sobbing with emotion.

"Go on laddie, away with you," said the sergeant, who had overheard him. "You've earned it. Be careful though, they'll try and outflank us next."

Mash did not even pause to wonder at the sergeant's kindness; within seconds he sprinted to the far side of the road, past the house and into the garden at the rear. In minutes he was back at the house. He crept round to the front and rushed through the open door. He expected Colette to be waiting for him in the hall, but she was not there. He went from room to room; the sounds of the battle outside were getting closer as the Germans pressed forwards once more and he was desperate to leave. She was not downstairs; he thought she could not be finished packing so he hurried upstairs in search of her bedroom. He opened a couple of doors but there was no one in them. He was starting to grow worried but the adrenaline carried him on. He came to the third door and opened it. It was a bedroom and he immediately recognised some of Colette's jewellery on the dressing table. He pushed the door open and looked around. There was a suitcase on the floor, half packed. Mash called her name and looked around but he could not see her.

He was about to turn and leave the room when he saw it: a foot protruding from the side of the bed. There was a red shoe dangling pathetically from the toes. Colette had been wearing red shoes earlier. Mash stared at the foot and felt the weight of the reality that he had somehow known since he came through the open door into the silent house. He did not want to cross the floor, to see what lay beside the bed, but he knew he had to. In a few swift steps he was there, looking down at her. She was lying on her back, her dark hair fanned out around her. There was a deep and ugly cut across her throat from which her life's blood had splattered onto her face and upper body before forming into a large circle around her that, even now, was dripping through the cracks in the floorboards. Her mouth was gaping open, as though she was still trying to catch her last breath. Her dress was pulled up above her hips, the buttons torn open and her ripped knickers pulled down around her thighs.

Looking back on this moment Mash barely remembered what he did; the shock of seeing her, when only a few minutes before she had been making plans with him, was too much to take in. He only remembered collapsing next to her and clutching her body, listening for a breath but knowing she was dead. Looking at her torn clothes and the ugly bruise around her eye where she had been hit, he realised what had been done to her in the short time he had been away and he gasped with pain and anger. Her life and his world had been destroyed in that tiny space of time.

He did not think about looking for the person who had done this to her, instead he just sat and held her so tight that it would have hurt her if she could still feel.

Mash stayed there until the crash of a German tank shell snapped him back into reality. It dawned on him that he could not keep clutching the still warm body, he had to get out, there was nothing he could do for Colette. As he stood up and started for the door he sensed rather than saw that he was not alone. He started to turn but as he did something crashed down on his head and his world went dark as he crumpled to the floor.

# CHAPTER FOUR

# St Valéry-en-Caux

Being knocked out, falling across Colette and collapsing into her blood saved Mash's life; the main force of Germans swept through the town and the soldiers who came into the house left him for dead, the blood-soaked Tommie who had been having fun before being killed did not provoke a second glance. He woke up sprawled on the floor, a thudding pain in the back of his head. He tentatively lifted his hand to it and felt dried blood. He glanced up and saw that it was dark outside. Slowly he pulled himself up, took one last look at Colette's body then staggered out.

In the gloom outside he looked around. The sound of firing was more distant than it had been earlier; he realised that he was behind enemy lines, alone. He had no idea what had happened to Rod and the others; his only hope was to make his way south-west and try to get back to British lines. He crept through the gardens to where he had last seen his comrades. It was clear that there had been a ferocious fight and, from how close together the bodies lay, it had been done at close quarters. But there was no sign of Rod or the Camerons.

Despite the intense throbbing in his head Mash kept a keen eye out for any Germans. He realised that his best chance was to retrace the line of the attack and then follow the tracks of the retreating vehicles.

Slowly he made his way back to the lake and the surrounding trees. It was eerily silent. He only saw a couple of Germans, walking to and fro as though they were on their holidays, to remind him that a few hours ago this had been the scene of a battle. The only other reminder was the number of dead from both sides; the bodies seemed to be everywhere.

Mash found a thicket in the trees and crawled into it. For the moment he was safe and could not be seen. He shrunk back further into the bush, the damp branches grabbing at his clothes and skin. Now that he had a moment of relative safety, the events from earlier crushed down on him. He knew that the image of Colette lying there with that terrified, pleading look on her face would remain with him forever. The pain at the realisation curled him into a foetal ball and he felt the desolation like a weight. But he could not cry, not like he had howled earlier; he felt empty. It was shock, a part of him knew, shock that she had been suddenly ripped from life. And the fact that somebody had attacked her, he could barely form the word rape in his mind but images of Colette fighting a faceless man ran through his head. He bit back a groan and pressed his head into his hands. If only he had got there sooner, if only he had taken her away immediately.

He struggled against these thoughts but they overwhelmed him. But so did exhaustion; without realising it, tangled in hideous images, he drifted off to sleep.

Dawn was just starting to shoot colour through the dark sky when Mash came to. His head was in the mud and he was damp and cold. He was not sure if he had been asleep or unconscious; his body had just shut down.

He sat up, silently groaning at the cramp in his body. He tentatively tested his feelings and found an emotional void. He felt like all sensation had been sucked out of him, pain, joy, sadness. He did not care. This was the best way to be.

He looked around him. He knew he had to find the others but was not sure if it was better to travel in the day when he

53

could see but also be seen, or if he should wait for darkness when he could move more easily.

Slowly he crawled out of his hiding place. His muscles screamed out in agony to remind him of what he had been through the previous day. His stomach also added to the pain and he realised that he had not eaten for some time.

He made his way to the edge of the wood and looked out across the field over which the attack had advanced yesterday. It was strewn with burnt-out tanks and dead bodies but Mash did not pay any attention to them. He looked around at the fields; they seemed to go on for miles on either side of him. He could try and work his way round to the edge and use the boundary for cover, but that would take him forever and there was no guarantee that the Germans would not be there in force. He could wait until nightfall and use the darkness to cover the open fields, but it was still dawn so he would need to wait the whole day and he was already conscious that he was falling further and further behind enemy lines.

He stared out across the fields. The rye grass was a foot high and there were many tanks burnt out. The thought crossed his mind that he could crawl out through the grass. He remembered how the Highlanders had not seen the Germans in the same fields until they were almost on them so he knew it would hide him. If he got tired, which was likely given the ground to cover, he could rest up under cover of a burnt-out tank and if he saw any Germans he could play dead. It seemed to be worth the risk and he mapped out in his mind the direction he would take. Cautiously, peering left and right, he crawled out into the rye grass.

Initially progress was not too bad. He crawled for about ten yards and then stopped to listen or peer out to check there was no one around. He had a shock as he pushed his way through the long grass to come literally face to face with a dead Highlander. One second just the endless barrier of the grass and then the next a face no more than a foot away from his. He stifled a scream as he fought to regain his composure. The Highlander had been hit in the chest but his dead eyes seemed to stare directly into Mash's. Quickly he detoured around the body and moved on.

Soon the sheer physical effort of crawling on his elbows for such a long distance took its toll. He wearily made his way to the nearest tank, a Char B1. It stank of petrol, burnt rubber and cordite as he slithered underneath it. After taking a moment to regain his breath he peered round the far side of the tank. One of the crew was hanging upside down, his feet still in the tank but his body dangling down the armoured side with his head a matter of inches above the ground. Only there was no head, just a large hole where the face had been. Everything seemed to be held together by the remnants of the crewman's leather helmet, but, being upside down, his blood had poured out of him, like a butchered pig, to form a congealed, bloody carpet on which flies now happily swarmed. Mash retched, but with nothing in his stomach it was dry. The sight provided all the motivation he needed to resume his journey.

On and on he crawled, bitterly regretting his decision. He was exhausted, burning up energy he did not have. Several times he came across more bodies but now he was beyond caring, he just crawled over them rather than waste energy in going round. It took him until well into the afternoon before he finally reached the wood at the far side. Mash was no more than fifteen yards from the tree line and safety.

"It's a bloody good job you made it so obvious you weren't a Jerry or I'd have popped you off," came a broad Scottish voice.

Mash froze, then slowly looked around. For a moment he could not see anyone, then he saw a face among the trees. The man gave a sarcastic wave.

"I've been watching you for an hour or so and you've

made a right meal of that. It's a bloody good job I'm not trigger happy!" he said.

Mash was too relieved to protest. Exhausted, he made his way towards the voice and relative safety. He found a gathering of Highlanders in the wood. It was the remains of the attacking force and it looked pitifully small. Men were dotted about, trying to sleep or quietly chatting whilst others helped dress comrades' wounds.

Mash scanned the faces of the men, looking for one he recognised. His stomach grew tighter as there was no sign of Rod. But then he recognised the stance of a man standing with his back to Mash at the edge of the group.

Relief flooded through Mash as he made his way towards him.

As though sensing him Rod turned as Mash approached. His face immediately broke into a smile of relief, but then froze as he looked at his friend. Mash did not know but the anguish he felt inside was reflected somewhat on his own face.

Mash tried to speak but then his throat closed up. He coughed and tried again.

"Colette," was all he managed to get out.

Rod strode towards him and clasped his arm around Mash's shoulders before Mash collapsed into him.

"Tell me all about it," he said as he supported Mash forward and away from the group.

Over the next hour or so Mash slowly recounted all he could remember from the beginning of the attack. When he had finished Rod asked the obvious question.

"So who do you think did it?"

The question almost came as a surprise to Mash; in his sorrow the thought had not registered much, just the fact that she was dead.

"I don't know," he stammered. "Some, some bastard, some evil bastard."

His voice raised and some of the other troops turned to look at them.

"OK, calm yourself down," said Rod.

"I just," Mash could barely get his words out, there was no way to verbalise his anger and confusion. "I want to kill them, whoever did it, I'm going to kill them."

"It could be anyone, Mash," said Rod, aiming for logic. "Colette was between us and the Jerries and there were locals all around. It was most likely a Jerry and you'll never find him, he could already be dead."

Silence enveloped them. Mash knew Rod spoke the truth but he did not want to hear it. He suddenly felt exhausted again. He felt Rod looking at him but he could think of no reply, so he said nothing.

Somewhat taken aback by the change in his friend Rod was keen to change the subject.

"The rest of us had a hell of a fight. In the end we had to pull out as we had tanks and armoured cars coming down the street and troops coming round our flanks through the houses and gardens," he said. Mash made no reply but Rod carried on anyway.

"We managed to get back to these woods overnight and the stragglers have been coming in all the time, you're not the only one by any means. 2Lt Ross is in command and we're waiting until dark before moving off."

Mash grunted in acknowledgement. A part of him felt very glad that he was soon to be given orders so that he did not have to think.

"You look as though you've had a rough time of it so try and get some rest before we start again. There's almost no food, only what we were carrying or can scrounge off the dead and the land. Here, this is all I've got but you're welcome to it." He held out a few Army ration biscuits. Mash did not move, he knew he was hungry but he had no interest in food.

"You may not want it but you need it," said Rod, still holding out the biscuit.

Mash took it and chewed it slowly. They both sat quietly, waiting for darkness to come.

Eventually, when the sun had set, Lt Ross called the men together.

"The way I see it the attack failed and the Jerries have pushed our boys back on a broad line. Clearly we need to get back to them. I think the easiest way will be to follow the main road, route 28, back until we find them. I want to be on the north side of the road; I'm sure they'll be more to the north as we were the most southerly unit in the attack. We'll have the road on our left but keep to the fields so we can avoid any Jerries. We have to catch up with the others so I'll make a call on whether we keep going at dawn or not when we get there. OK, that's it, any questions?"

There were none so the men readied themselves before moving out.

They cautiously picked their way forward, crossing the road and then following it south-west. Progress was slow. The Germans tended not to move about by night and so there was a constant danger of coming across a group camped up. When they did encounter Germans they would silently detour around them.

However, on one occasion, when they were not sure if they had caught up with the division or met with another group of Germans, they called out in schoolboy French only to be answered in German and a burst of automatic fire. Again they melted away and gave the Germans a wide berth.

They often stumbled across Highlanders trying to make their way to safety. By the end their numbers had grown to around sixty.

When dawn broke the decision was made to keep pushing on as there was a lot of cover. In daylight they could see plenty of movement on the road as the Germans pushed ever further forward.

They nearly made a fatal mistake in the gloom of dusk when they saw a group of British 3-ton Bedford lorries parked up. On seeing them some of the men threw caution to the wind by running towards the vehicles, eager to be reunited with friendly forces. But their run was brought up short by the crack of a sentry's rifle and the sight of German troops leaping out the back of the lorries. They had not realised that the Germans were using their captured vehicles to maintain the speed of the advance. After a brief and inconclusive fire fight the Highlanders withdrew into the gloom and wearily made yet another detour around the Germans.

Other than the enemy, food and fatigue were the two main problems. All the locals were hiding as the Germans advanced, so the men could only find berries or root crops in the fields to sustain them. Most had slept for no more than an hour or two in the last forty-eight hours and they were all dog-tired. After a brief rest in a wood towards the end of the day they pushed on again into the night. They slowly made their way forward, constantly having to reroute, which added miles to their journey.

Finally, on the 6th June they caught up with the rear-guard of the division just outside Martainneville. They had made it back. But if they thought this meant rest then they were mistaken. The Highlanders they had found looked just as tired as they did. It was clear that the division was making a fighting withdrawal and being constantly harassed by the wave of Germans close behind them.

★ ★ ★

One thing that was available was food and soon the survivors of the attack were tucking into the first hot meal they had had in days.

"This is a bit more like it, eh?" said Rod as he sat down to eat.

Mash nodded but said nothing. He could concentrate on nothing but the food and he liked it that way.

"Did you hear about the Stuka attack?" Rod asked as he tried to keep the conversation going. "Apparently three Stukas caught the lads out in the open crossing a field between two woods. Down they came all screaming sirens intent on bloody murder and the lads had no option but to just lie flat and take whatever was coming. The Stukas drop their bombs but don't hit a single person – they say that they're a lot less effective if you take cover, even if it's as basic as lying down. Off they go and the order's given to advance but half of them are asleep! They slept right the way through being bombed. I know I'm bloody tired but I'm not sure I could sleep through that! It seems it took a few well-aimed kicks from the NCOs to get them to wake up!"

Despite himself Mash smiled slightly and he saw the answering smile of relief on Rod's face. He knew his friend was worried about him but he only cared about it in an offhand way. He was in a strange fog of numbness which very little was penetrating.

That night the Camerons pulled back further to the south-west through Le Transloy and the morning of 7th saw them between Blangy and Monchaux. Here they dug in overlooking the River Bresle and prepared to meet whatever the Germans would throw at them. They did not have to wait long. Soon after sun up two German tanks, some armoured cars and lorries, some British, full of troops appeared. The Highlanders only had the Boys .55 anti-tank rifle and the diminutive two-inch mortars, both of which were totally inadequate against the enemy's armour, along with rifle and Bren gun fire. Against them, in addition to the tanks and armoured cars, the Germans had artillery, air support and were particularly skilled in the use of their 8cm heavy mortars, which were soon reigning down their fire on the Highlanders.

Whilst hopelessly outgunned, the Camerons put up a fierce fight lasting into the afternoon. The Germans pushed forward and came very close to breaking through before being repelled. Then they drifted away, not in retreat but to probe another sector, always looking for the weak spot and ready to pour through any gap they could make. The pattern was such since the Germans advanced from Abbeville; the Highlanders marched all night and dug a defensive position before first light, fought off determined attacks by vastly superior forces during the day and then marched back to another position the next night.

On the 8th the Highlanders were ordered to withdraw to a new defensive line the British and French were trying to form called the Bethune Line. The Camerons swung north and headed for the sea, ready to hold the section of the new line along the River Arques around Dieppe.

On the morning of the 9th Mash and the others were grabbing a quick rest.

"Aye, aye," said Rod, stirring from the utter fatigue that they all felt. "What have we got here then?"

Mash and the others looked up.

Coming down the road were a section of immaculately dressed sailors, all in khaki and sporting rifles and tin helmets, with a number of Royal Navy officers in the middle of them.

"That's an interesting development," continued Rod. "If the Navy's here they've got to be talking about evacuating us. It can't be from Dieppe as we're only just holding onto the town so it must be another port further to the west."

Mash did not say anything but just watched the naval men approach.

Rod continued anyway: "My bet is Le Havre. Mind you, it's worrying if they're looking to evacuate us. Things must be properly going wrong. I think I'm going to see if I can wangle an errand to HQ that needs doing, it'll give me a chance to find out what's going on."

Mash watched him go. He felt a slight wavering of his general numbness at the mention of evacuation. The thought of going home was the only thing in the last few days that had brought him close to anything resembling hope.

Word that Rod had been to HQ had circulated so when he returned later that afternoon he had quite a crowd awaiting him.

"It's pretty drastic boys," started Rod. "It seems that all that was left of the B.E.F. were evacuated a week ago from some place called Dunkirk. They now want to do something similar for us. As I thought, they've picked Le Havre as the place for the evacuation and the Navy's here to sort out the details."

There was a flurry of whispers from the men but Rod carried on.

"They're creating a group from the division called Ark Force who are going to Le Havre today to defend the surrounds and make the preparations for the evacuation."

Rod paused as he saw the look on some of the faces.

"No, we're not part of it so we'll just have to wait our turn. But that's not the interesting bit. I heard that, apparently, we've got enough transport for the whole division to get to Le Havre immediately, assuming some multiple runs, but that Fortune has decided not to do it as it would mean abandoning the French and leaving their flank wide open."

"Does the man not know this is our chance to get away?" complained one man, only to be immediately rebuffed by another.

"Fortune's done the right thing," said Rod somewhat sternly. "There's no way a Highlander is going to cut and run leaving the Frogs on their own."

There was a murmur of agreement and several spoke in support.

"Well that's what I heard," said Rod. "I guess we're going to see things come to a head quite quickly, one way or another. I'll try to keep in touch with my mate in HQ so that we know what's going on."

For that they were all grateful; after days of no more than an hour or two of sleep in the bottom of a trench, in between long marches and hard fighting, they were completely exhausted and the news that the end was in sight was a ray of hope.

Later on they heard the newly formed Ark Force form up and pull out to Le Havre, accompanied by some helpful shouts of encouragement and some words of advice for the local girls.

At first light a large number of tanks were seen approaching Dieppe from the east. It looked like a whole tank division and was certainly sufficient to overwhelm the defences available.

Mash and Rod were watching the tanks when a summons came for Rod to go to Battalion HQ. He was to be given a message to run to Divisional HQ about the tanks closing from the east. This was not a job Rod would normally have done as there were runners tasked with this specific role. He and Mash were musing on why he had been chosen when a sergeant came alongside.

"If you're wondering, it seems your info is better than theirs," he whispered and was off before Rod could say anything.

Rod grinned at Mash and headed off to Divisional HQ as fast as he could.

Mash was curious for him to return but he had no time to wonder about it. They were under attack from the air for most of the day; the shelling barely let up.

Finally, after several hours, the Germans retreated. Exhausted, Mash was having a much deserved rest when he saw that Rod had returned. His grin had disappeared and he went straight to the waiting officers. Mash watched as their faces dropped while Rod spoke.

Rod eventually made his way over to Mash.

"I've brought you a present," he said, producing a number of tins and boxes from various pockets. "I managed to grab some grub when I was at HQ so I thought we should have a picnic now we're at the seaside."

Mash smiled at the lame joke and the thought of a decent meal. He realised that it was the first time he had smiled in a while.

"Tell me, then," he said.

Rod made himself comfortable and began.

"Firstly, the Ark Force had managed to get away and is now in Le Havre. However, rumours were circulating that the Germans had cut the link to Le Havre after the Ark Force got through. Turns out these rumours were true; a lot of Jerry tanks were seen to the west of the River Durdent near a place called St Valéry-en-Caux. By the sounds of it the Germans had gone to the south of the Bethune line before swinging north and driving hard for the coast. There's also news that at least one other tank division is driving up from Rouen and is pushing in from the south. In short, we're surrounded with enemy tank divisions pushing in from the east, west and south with the channel to the north."

"Shit," muttered Mash. He realised that, in making the decision not to pull the division back to Le Havre, their chances of survival were significantly reduced.

"My thoughts exactly," said Rod. "The plan is to pull back to St Valéry immediately and the Navy will try and get us off there. I hear it's going to be tricky because it's a small fishing village in a cove and surrounded by hills. The Jerries are closing in all the time and the Navy has already taken casualties while reconnoitring around St Valéry."

Mash was quiet, he could not think of anything to say, he

was exhausted from fighting all day and the thought of more difficulty made him feel even more dog-tired. However, there was one highlight in what Rod said.

"So we're going home," he said.

"Well, that's the idea. Whether we get there or not is another matter," said Rod. "I hear you've had a hard time of it whilst I've been away?" he continued.

"Aye, we've been hard pushed all day. The Jerry artillery and planes have been busy but we've managed to drive off all the attacks, at quite a cost though." Mash paused for a moment. The food Rod was handing him was the first he had eaten in a while and the promise of the hot meal Rod was preparing was a delight. But his expression darkened as he went on.

"Each bloody attack and all the shelling and bombing is taking its toll. We lost more lads today and the bastards are slowly grinding us down. Sarge says we've got to conserve ammo as stocks are getting really low."

He was quiet again and did not notice Rod looking at him askance. Mash had seen more men struck down that day, young men, the same age as Colette. He closed his eyes and fought against the surge of darkness which threatened to penetrate the thin wall he had put up since Colette died. At that moment it felt membrane-thin.

"When's all this killing going to end?" he said quietly.

"Don't you worry laddie," Rod said. "The Navy's coming to get us and we'll be home soon."

He smiled reassuringly at Mash, but Mash could see the doubt behind it.

They ate together, conversing about gossip from around the camp and other nonsense, both pretending that there was not a well of terror inside them.

★ ★ ★

So began another fighting withdrawal, a manoeuvre they had practised for real so many times over the previous week. As dusk fell, blinding the artillery and dive bombers, the Camerons started pulling back to St Valéry. The division was concentrating around St Valéry and the plan was to get them away later that night. But nothing happened. At first light on the 11th the rain was pouring down, drenching everyone and making life even more miserable than normal. Even the Germans delayed their incessant bombardment and probing attacks. In the deluge orders came through to move again and rumours started to circulate.

"Have you heard, no one got off?" said Mash to Rod.

His tone was almost accusatory; the thought of going home had consumed him and become the only thing he could fixate on.

"I heard it all got cocked up," said Rod. "The Navy had worked bloody wonders to get a blooming armada off the beach, enough to get the whole division off. Only when they got ashore there was no one there; the boats couldn't find anyone to evacuate. They had to leave empty handed, save for taking some of the wounded with them."

"What the hell happened?" asked Mash.

"Apparently the Froggie high command hadn't given permission to evacuate and so Fortune had no other option but to stay out of the village and let the opportunity pass.

"Jesus," said Mash, grinding a cigarette into the soaking ground.

"Don't worry, we're getting another chance soon. I heard we're using the cover of all this fucking rain to set up a defensive square around the town so that we can have another go tonight."

"Tonight?" said Mash.

"Yep," said Rod.

"Thank Christ," said Mash.

"Don't thank him just yet, we've got to make it first," said Rod.

As Rod had said, later that evening they were told to gather their kit and they made their way, soaked to the skin, into St Valéry on their way to their new position.

"Jesus," said Rod as they made their way into the port. "Look at the state of this!"

Around them was a scene of utter devastation. The tiny area surrounding the port was packed with men, many dead or dying, and the living struggling to dig in and organise themselves in the pouring rain. St Valéry was in flames, hissing and spitting in the rain, with buildings destroyed and a growing mass of wounded gathering, with no cover, amongst the rubble in the square. To add to the misery the Germans, as if sensing the Highlanders were on the move, started their pounding of the area with artillery. Slowly the Camerons moved out, their concern at what they witnessed etched on their faces.

The Highlanders formed a three-sided square around St Valéry to allow for the evacuation that night. The Camerons were tasked with holding a small hamlet, called Neville, to the south of St Valéry, with the Gordon Highlanders to their right and the remaining French forces on the left. Between them and the coast was the Divisional HQ.

"This'll do us nicely," said Rod as he and Mash settled into their new position. They had managed to pull some debris from a nearby house over the top of the trench they had just dug to deflect most of the rain. Old rafters from the same building were now in the bottom of the trench keeping them out of the worst of the mud that came courtesy of the deluge.

"Just got to hold off the hoards for another day and, hopefully, we'll be out of here tonight," said Rod.

He smiled at Mash and for the first time since Colette had died Mash really noticed it. It was not Rod's usually sanguine grin. It looked similar but Mash could see the tension behind it. It had almost become a lurid grin. In that moment Mash realised that his friend was struggling too. He realised Rod must be scared and desperate to get home to Fiona.

He opened his mouth to say something, somehow thank Rod for carrying him through the last few days. But before he could speak there was a shout of warning and the unmistakeable screech of a German Stuka as it started its headlong dive towards the troops.

And so began the daily ritual. When they were not being bombed or shelled they were beating back attacks from tanks and infantry, only now they were counting every round.

Finally night fell and thoughts turned to the evacuation. Unbeknownst to Rod and Mash it was not until 17:00 on the 11th that the French High Command finally gave their permission for the Highlanders to be taken off. The first they knew was when orders arrived to destroy all equipment other than the weapons and ammunition they could carry.

Soon after they were gathering ready to pull back to St Valéry.

"Remember, you have to be bloody quiet when going down to the port, single file and not a sound," a sergeant was shouting. "The Krauts are on the heights on both sides of the way down and we don't want to wake them up!"

"That's changed since yesterday," whispered Rod. "It sounds as though this is going to be tough."

They set off, most of the men were like Mash, itching to get home. But after a couple of miles they were ordered to halt. It was the early hours, cold and damp. In the wet they huddled together for warmth and wondered what the holdup was.

"Do you think it's going to happen?" asked Mash.

"Don't know," replied Rod. "There's bound to be delays. Just get your head down and try and get some sleep."

Mash needed no second invite. All the troops were out on their feet and, despite the conditions, simply curled up in the mud and debris and were asleep in seconds. Occasionally they were lit by star shells as the Germans searched for them. The eerie scene was enhanced as fog began to roll in, giving the star shells a weird glow as they floated down. From the port and the surrounding hills came the sounds of sporadic machine gun fire and shelling.

"Wake up Mash!"

Mash groaned and, still half asleep, swatted at the hand that shook him.

"Mash!" said Rod, shaking him harder.

Mash jerked awake and stared blearily at Rod.

"Sorry laddie, we're not getting off tonight, they've just passed the word."

Mash looked at him with uncomprehending eyes.

"After the abortive attempt last night the Navy have been waiting for us offshore. They've been bombed and shelled all morning and lost a load of ships so they moved further out. Tonight they came in to try and get us off as they promised but there's thick fog down by the sea and most of them couldn't get close. Those that did found the town surrounded by the Jerries and got themselves blasted, a lot of them were sunk. We've got to form another defensive circle whilst they work out what to do next."

The realisation that their escape had been pushed back once again sunk into Mash as it did all the other tired and hungry men. But there was nothing to do except pick themselves up and move out. As if to add to their misery it started to rain again.

They dug in once more and waited for the inevitable resumption of fire from the Germans. They did not have to wait long before the incessant artillery started up once more. Soon after, tanks and infantry were spotted and the Camerons were once again called on to beat back the attack with brisk fire on all sides.

Eventually the attack moved onto another sector and they got a breather. Mash was taking a slug from his canteen when his attention was caught by a man in the road.

"What the hell is he all about?" asked Mash. It was a French officer who was walking down the road without an apparent care in the world. "What's he got on his back?"

The two of them stared at the officer.

"Looks like a bit of sheet tucked into his lapels. Makes him look like he's got a cape on," replied Rod, equally as bemused. "Maybe it's some form of recognition the Frogs are using."

After a while the officer disappeared as another salvo came close from the German artillery. But the mystery did not take long to solve.

"Sorry boys," sighed the sergeant as he did the rounds from position to position. "The Frogs have surrendered. Apparently they called it a day at 08:00 this morning."

"That leaves us high and dry," said Rod. "At least we know what that officer was all about."

"Aye, just be careful if you come across any more French as we don't know what they're up to now. We're still in the fight," replied the sergeant.

One thing was for sure, the Highlanders had not given in. Fire continued up and down the line as the Germans pushed forward. The shells and mortar bombs continued to seek the survivors out. Having destroyed all the heavy equipment they could not carry ahead of the abortive evacuation, the Highlanders had only small arms to try and hold back the German wave.

They were getting desperate. But then, as if by magic, everything went quiet.

"What's happening?" asked Mash

Before Rod could answer there was a shout to look to the

front. Directly opposite Rod and Mash a Panzer III tank was making its way forward. The tank commander, looking every bit the German Aryan role model with his blond hair and immaculate black Panzer uniform, was standing up out of his turret and a white flag was fluttering behind him.

Mash and Rod looked at each other.

"Looks as though we're in for a front row seat for whatever's happening, he's headed straight for us," said Rod.

A Highland officer tentatively stood up as the tank approached. It pulled up about twenty yards in front of him. In a loud, clear voice and in perfect English the German spoke.

"I have to tell you that your commander has surrendered. You have fought well and bravely but you must now put down your weapons."

There was an audible shock of disbelief as the words sank in. Mash stared at the Nazi poster boy.

"I'm sorry but I haven't received that order," replied the Highland officer. "May I suggest we stay as we are whilst I get this checked?"

"The port is surrounded and the French have surrendered," continued the German. "Your navy has been beaten back and you have little ammunition left. I would have thought the position was obvious."

"Nevertheless I must insist," replied the officer.

The German gave a curt nod and settled back while a runner was dispatched.

Mash looked at Rod, who for once was speechless, then he looked round at the other men; the shock he felt was clearly etched on their faces, some of them were even in tears. Mash turned back to the German who was staring steadfastly ahead. Mash felt something else, another feeling beside the black mix of depression and numbness he had had since Colette died; it was shame.

After a few minutes the runner reappeared. Breathlessly

he halted behind the officer who looked round. Without a word the runner simply nodded and with a frown the officer turned back to the German.

"It would appear what you say is true. Please tell me, who is your commanding officer?"

"I have the honour of serving Brigadier General Erwin Rommel, commander of the 7th Panzer Division and he has taken the surrender from your General Fortune."

★ ★ ★

"I never thought it would end like this," said Rod.

They had just stacked their weapons in a pile in front of their captors and were now sitting on the wet ground.

Rod's disbelief was shared by the others. They were proud men and it was a humiliation to be herded into captivity. Mash felt it too, but almost as though it was at a distance.

Throughout the retreat from Abbeville to St Valéry Mash had fought with considerable courage but in a detached, quiet way that made him more like an automaton than a man. He had no time to properly grieve for Colette but he had been swamped in a darkness that constantly threatened to overwhelm him. Then the possibility of getting home to England and his mother had offered him a glimmer of light. But it had been taken away. Colette was gone and he was a prisoner. Nothing mattered anymore. He knew Rod was worried about him but he could not find the energy to care; he was emotionally and physically shattered.

In total 6,000 Highlanders were rounded up, disarmed and formed up ready for the march back to captivity. The line of troops was nearly a mile long and, every five yards along its length, a German guard was positioned. The guards were relatively old, being the first to be released by the front line units. Luckily, they behaved professionally and treated the Highlanders fairly.

That first day they were marched east. It was not more than they were used to, and they were not ill-treated, but they were hungry and exhausted so the march was long and wearisome.

In the evening they were gathered in a barbed wire compound, which had clearly been hastily erected for them. Inside the compound the men were left to themselves. The only problem was that they were left without food.

"Christ, I'm hungry," complained Rod. "I think the last meal we had was when I brought that food back from HQ. Still, it's good to see Jerry has as many logistical problems as we do."

There was no response from Mash. Rod shuffled over so that he was almost whispering in Mash's ear.

"Listen, when we form up tomorrow I want us to be in the middle of the column, on one of the outer files with you ahead of me."

"Why?" asked Mash, rousing himself.

"Because I think we can make a break for it. I've spent the whole day watching the guards. They may start ten yards apart but they regularly concertina and if we time it right then I don't think they'll see. Anyway, it's not like they're a bunch of spring chickens." Rod said all this while trying to look as casual as possible.

"Why do you want to be behind me?" asked Mash.

"Because, my old sausage, I want you to leave the timing to me. You're not quite on your game so let me make the decision. Just go with me when I give you a shove."

Mash could not disagree with this logic. Rod was smiling at him with an enthusiasm that he had not seen in a while. Mash tried to feel it too but he had taken too many kicks in the last few days. He did not want to get his hopes up only to have them dashed again.

In the morning, whilst there was still no food, they were

allowed to fill their water bottles before being lined up and marched off. As Rod had suggested, he and Mash were in the middle of the line on the left-hand file, in between two of the oldest guards they could find.

They quickly resumed the routine of the march. Mash watched Rod and Rod watched the guards. But the opportunities were few and far between. Once Rod thought he spotted an opening but hesitated and the chance was gone. For the rest of the morning they trooped through crop fields and meadows that offered no cover.

When the moment did come it was courtesy of another Highlander. They were walking around a right-hand curve on a road. On their left was a drop into a drainage ditch covered with bracken and nettles. On their right was a small wood rising up a gentle slope. Without warning there was a rush of activity. A Highlander on the other side of the column and a little further up had made a break for the woods. There were shouts and the guard on the far side gave chase. On the side near Mash, the guard pushed through the column to help his colleague stop the escaping man, although he was blocked and hampered by other Highlanders as he tried to make his way through. The guard behind Rod was looking over the top of the column to see what was going on and the curve in the road hid the two of them from him.

"Now!" whispered Rod, grabbing Mash by the arm and propelling him down into the ditch. As soon as they hit the bottom they edged to one side to be covered by the nettles and bracken. The thorns tore at their skin and the nettles stung, but they were silent as they peered up through the undergrowth. They were relieved to see the other troops, realising what they had done, shuffle over to cover the gap they had left.

Within seconds the Highlander on the far side had been caught and the guards resumed their positions. They looked up and down the line but could not see any gaps and so the column moved off. Just as they did Mash saw the man now standing in his place carefully take his hand just to the lip of his pocket and give a thumbs up sign before returning it.

The column marched above them and it took many minutes before they were past. All the time Mash and Rod feared a guard would look down and discover them but none did, their attention was on their captives and the road ahead.

Rod waited for a good ten minutes before the last of them disappeared around the bend. He then grabbed Mash's arm and they raced over the road and climbed up the slope into the cover of the wood on the other side.

They stopped when they were undercover, panting as they crouched in the trees.

"I'm glad that's over, I was being stung to death by those damn nettles," said Rod.

Mash nodded, still trying to get his breath back.

"I reckon we should wait up until night and then head north back towards the coast. Maybe we can steal a fishing boat or something," continued Rod, checking the sun to see which way to go. "Let's get some sleep now and move off when it's good and dark."

Despite the light, the gnawing ache of hunger and his many stinging nettle wounds, Mash slept soundly.

Later that night they moved off. Rod let Mash lead; despite the state of his friend he knew that his ability to pick a path through country in the dark was much better than his own. Together they made good progress. The land was mainly flat, arable farmland with gentle folds in the ground. There was little in the way of cover but it was easy to see if any Germans, who were relaxing now the fighting was over, were in the vicinity.

They even managed to forage a few berries to eat. Mash would have loved to have bagged a rabbit or pheasant, but both knew they had to remain undetected and there was no time to stop and set snares.

As the first rays of dawn started to lighten the darkness from the east, they reached the coast. There, in the growing light, they found a hiding place in one of the crags along the cliff top. Tired and hungry they looked out across the sea.

"We've got a major problem," said Rod quietly and Mash nodded in agreement.

Either side of them, as far as they could see, the cliffs stretched out into the distance.

"I can only see a few places where we could even think of risking a descent to the beach, everywhere else is a sheer drop," continued Rod. "And even if we could get down no self-respecting fisherman is going to leave a boat in such an inaccessible place."

"What do you want to do?" asked Mash.

"I think the only thing we can do is hole up here, wait for dark and then try and sneak into one of the fishing villages. I think we're to the east of St Valéry so I reckon we should head away from there as we know there're lots of Jerries and continue east to the next port," said Rod. "The only thing I don't like is that there's little cover here. But we'd have to backtrack a long way if we want to find any cover in these fields."

"I vote we stay here," murmured Mash, too exhausted to think about backtracking.

"Aye, I agree," replied Rod. "But we'll need to keep a look out. I'll take first watch and wake you in a few hours."

Mash nodded as Rod patted him on the back and prepared to keep watch.

Three hours later Rod shook Mash awake.

"Your turn. I'm all in," he said. "Give me a shake if you see anything. Visibility's excellent so if you keep a sharp eye out we can move off before anyone gets close. Are you sure you're OK?"

"Aye, I'm fine. You get your head down," replied Mash and with that Rod rolled over.

It took a few minutes for Mash to orientate himself and fully awaken. For the first hour he looked out, searching for any sign of movement, but could not find any. Then, with the sun out and a gentle breeze, Mash found himself starting to drift as sleep looked to claim him.

*Snap out of it, stay alert.*

For another ten minutes he regained his senses but before long the sun and the breeze dragged him down once more.

They both woke with a start. A dog was barking loudly only feet away from them. In panic they looked around to see two men about twenty yards away.

"How the fuck did you let them get so close?" whispered Rod as they tried to push themselves into the ground.

"I'm sorry, I'm sorry it's all my fault," replied Mash

Rod squinted at the men, they were not in uniform.

"At least they're not Jerries," he whispered. "Let's hope they're friendly."

Slowly the two Frenchmen walked over to where they lay. They got so close that they were directly above them. Mash held his breath, trying to peer up at them. Beside him Rod was completely still.

One of the men hushed his dog whilst the other, pretending to look out to sea, spoke in very broken English.

"I think you Ecossaise, oui?"

"Oui," said Rod cautiously.

The Frenchman nodded, glanced at his colleague before resuming his stare out to sea.

"Attendez ici. Tonight I come. Au revoir." And with that he and his friend resumed their walk along the cliff top.

They lay in silence until the men were out of sight, then Mash turned to Rod.

"I was an idiot, I'm sorry. I just couldn't keep my eyes open."

"Don't worry," replied Rod with a sigh.

"No I mean it, I know I've been useless and if it wasn't for you we wouldn't have got away. I'll try and pull myself together now."

Rod looked at him. "It's alright Mash, I know you've been through, well, hell. Who knows, this might just turn out to be the best thing that could've happened. We'll just have to see if they come back on their own or with a bunch of krauts. Now, I'll stand guard for a while."

But there was no way Mash, exhausted as he was, could sleep after that scare. Rod scanned the approaches whilst Mash looked out across the field.

"When it gets dark we'll move out and hide behind that patch of long grass," said Mash. Rod, who had not heard a proactive word from Mash in days, stared at him.

"We'll be close enough to see them, and if they come with any Jerries then we'll have at least a chance of avoiding them, well, more of a chance than we would staying here," continued Mash.

"OK, that's fine with me," Rod slowly replied.

The rest of the day passed uneventfully. As soon as it was dark they moved out of their hiding place and lay down behind the long grass. Nothing stirred until after midnight when they heard footsteps approaching. Whoever it was made sure to scuff their boots on every stone to ensure they knew he was coming. They strained their ears but could only hear one person. Eventually they saw a man loom out of the darkness above where they had been hiding. Seeing that there was no one there the man looked around.

"Let's do this," said Rod and together they stood up and walked forward.

It was the man from earlier in the day. They stood looking at each other for a moment, then he held out a bundle of something. They stepped forward to see that he had brought them clothes. Quickly they put the trousers and jackets over their uniforms.

"Je suis Jacques. You come my maison," with that he turned and headed along the cliffs to the east.

Quickly Mash and Rod followed. Together they walked in silence to the village. Jacques took them round the backs of the houses until he came to a small cottage which they were ushered inside of. Once the door was closed a lamp was turned up to reveal the other man they had seen earlier and a woman stirring a cauldron of food over a fire. Jacques went to her and said something in French that neither of them understood. She looked at them and smiled before reaching for two old and chipped bowls that she filled with a fish stew from the cauldron. She put the bowls on a rough wooden table and gestured to them to come and eat.

Without any hesitation they threw themselves at the meal.

"This is the best food I've ever tasted," said Rod as he almost launched into the bowl. "Merci beaucoup madam, tres bon," he said to the woman as he stuffed a piece of bread into his mouth.

Mash too was in heaven. He scolded his mouth as he slurped down the soup, but it was the sweetest pain he had ever felt. The woman smiled again, happy at the obvious enjoyment the two strange men got from her meal. After several helpings the two sat back and groaned in pain and pleasure. Seeing they had finished Jacques pulled over a chair.

"Morning you, me and Charles," he began, pointing to the other man. "Go fish. My bateau. We find bateau Anglais, oui?"

"Oui," replied Rod.

"Soldat Allemand we see, no parlez," Jacques continued, pointing at the two of them.

"Oui," said Rod again.

With that Jacques nodded, rose and ushered them to a couple of chairs by the fire.

"Sommeil," he said, putting his head on his hands.

After the meal the two did not need a second invitation.

The warmth of the fire soon dragged them into a deep sleep.

They were awoken when it was still dark. After a quick breakfast of bread and cheese they headed for the door. The woman put down what she was doing and met them at the door. She hugged them both and whispered "Bon chance." Mash squeezed her hands in his. She smiled at him before turning back into the house.

Mash and Rod followed Jacques and Charles down to the beach. On the way they passed a group of Germans huddled round a large fire. A couple of soldiers glanced across but they were only one of a number of other fishermen heading for their boats and the soldiers soon went back to their conversation. When they reached the beach there were a number of small boats pulled up away from the water. The fishermen helped each other push their boats down to the water. Rod and Mash did exactly what Jacques did. They could feel the eyes of the other fishermen looking at them, seeing them as strangers, but no one said a word. Once all the boats were in the water Rod and Mash climbed aboard Jacques' boat and they headed due north. The other boats headed in different directions at the same time, as though they were making sure the Germans would not see one boat leave the group.

It was not long before they started to see activity. About five miles out, beyond the range and accurate sighting of the land based artillery, a couple of vessels could be seen patrolling. Jacques immediately headed to intercept the nearest. As they approached Charles stood in the bows and frantically waved a French flag he had brought with him. The ship, a destroyer, slowed and altered course towards them. Rod and Mash took off their French clothes to reveal their uniforms and joined Charles in the bows. The destroyer came to a stop close to them and a Jacob's ladder appeared over the side.

"As fast as you can please chaps, there're rather a lot of German bombers about!" came a very English voice through a megaphone.

Mash turned quickly to the two Frenchmen, trying to think of a way to express his thanks in a few seconds. But Charles just smiled at him then clapped him on the arm.

"Go," he said.

Mash turned and scaled the ladder. He was unceremoniously hauled over the side to join Rod. They had just enough time to turn and wave to Jacques and Charles, who were already turning about and heading off to their fishing grounds.

"Merci beaucoup!" they shouted at the top of their voices to be rewarded by waves and friendly shouts that they did not understand. As soon as the fishing boat was clear they both felt the destroyer surge forward as she got underway.

CHAPTER FIVE

# GREYSTONE MANOR

They arrived in Portsmouth and were immediately debriefed, quickly and efficiently, by the assembled intelligence officers. The last man had been evacuated from Dunkirk on the 4th June, two weeks before, and so by the time Rod and Mash arrived the process had been perfected. Before long they found themselves on a train heading north. They had been granted a week's leave before having to report to the Inverness barracks that the Camerons called home.

Mash sat in the carriage, his head leant against the window, his eyes looking unseeing onto the passing countryside.

"Are you alright?" Rod asked him in the gentle tone he adopted whenever he tried to broach the subject of Colette.

Since returning it appeared to Mash as though Rod was on a one-man mission to get him to talk about Colette, as if it would heal the wound. But for Mash it was too early, like salt on an open wound and whilst he knew his friend was trying to help he was starting to dread the attempts. He nodded with a grunt but said nothing else, hoping Rod would get the hint.

"You'll let me know if you need anything?" Rod persisted.

Mash nodded again. But Rod would not leave it alone.

"It's OK you know," he said. "You've seen awful things and on top of that there was Colette."

Mash winced at the sound of her name and Rod paused.

"Being around your friends and family, that's what will help," said Rod with a confidence he did not feel.

Mash said nothing again. For another minute or so they were quiet. Rod picked imaginary fluff off his knee as he thought of something else to say.

"It'll be good to see your mother again. How long is it since you last saw her?" he asked eventually.

This question brought a spark to Mash's set face.

"It's been a while. God I can't wait to see her," he mumbled.

The train rumbled on and Rod gently questioned Mash about his plans, slowly teasing him out and getting him talking. The arrangement was that Mash would leave the train on its way north to see his mother in Hull. From there he would go to the Highland estate he called home before re-joining Rod in Inverness at the end of their leave. Mash found that talking about his mother and the estate pierced the gloom somewhat; plus, it put Rod off Colette and France.

By the time it came for Mash to leave the train he was feeling brighter. Although when he said goodbye to Rod he found himself feeling downcast again, even though he knew he would see him in a few days' time. He put a brave face on it and said goodbye breezily before leaving to catch his connecting train.

As the train to Hull approached his stop he started to see familiar surroundings and his heart grew lighter. He willed the train to get to the stop quicker. Finally it arrived and he was one of the first off the train. The day was glorious and he squinted as he exited the carriage. He caught sight of the newspaper stands, which were full of doom about the impending German invasion that everyone was expecting. Mash ignored them, walked right by and out of the station. It was only a ten-minute walk to his mother's home. The sun on his back and the knowledge he was nearly there quickened his step. Before long his boots were clacking down the cobblestones on the street of working men's two up, two downs where his mother lived. As he approached the door he paused, he had been impatient to get home but now that he was there he felt hesitant. He desperately wanted to see his mother but he knew that after the greeting she would question him on all that had happened. He did not even know how to begin talking about it all, or whether he even wanted to.

He stood there for almost a minute feeling the sun beat down on his back. He was exhausted and hot and his whole body ached. He took a deep breath and knocked on the door.

He knew his arrival would be a surprise to his mother but he did not expect the shriek and the bone-crushing hug that his normally poised mother delivered when she opened the door.

Mash put his arms around her and felt his body relax and tears creep into his eyes.

His mother drew back and looked at him, putting her hand on his face. She did not say anything but patted his cheek as tears rolled down her own.

"Come in," she said eventually.

The house had not changed; it was small and cramped but immaculately clean and infused with a cosiness that only his mother could make. As she fussed about him, complaining she had nothing prepared, Mash looked at her. She was a tall woman with long fair hair that she always wore tied up on her head. She had an elegance that underpinned everything, even when she was cleaning and scrubbing for her customers. It was opposite to her working-class roots but also born from it; a pride and forbearance that only a hardworking woman had.

Mash did not realise it but his mother was watching him too and she knew that this was a different son to the one who had gone to war.

That first evening they talked and talked. To begin with it was all one way as Mash's mother poured out all the news and gossip she could think of, sensing that Mash was reluctant to talk himself. Eventually she started to probe him, asking about the friends he had made and the places he had been. At first every innocent question felt like a jab and Mash gave as short answers as possible. But eventually, when his mother asked if he had met any girls, he felt the story of Colette well up inside him. He started slowly but soon momentum gathered and the tears rolled down his cheeks as the story of Colette and her death came out. He told her everything, how they met, their time together and then her death, he only left out the way he had found her, with her clothes torn, he could not bring himself to say it. But he suspected his mother knew. She was holding his hand and trying to keep her expression strong but her eyes were watering and her hands clutched his too tightly. By the end he was sobbing almost uncontrollably, the first time he had properly cried since it happened. He felt lost but the strength of his mother's hands anchored him. Eventually the sobs subsided and he found that he felt as though he had leached some of the poison a little. He found that he wanted to keep talking. He told her about the war, although he still held some back to save his mother from the true picture. When he finally climbed the stairs to go to bed and sank into fresh sheets and pillows for the first time in what seemed like a lifetime, he fell asleep in seconds.

Mash slept the sleep of the dead for a full twenty-four hours, oblivious to the checks his mother made on him and the precious time that was passing by. When he finally did wake and came down to the kitchen he found his mother had prepared a meal fit for a king. Mash was utterly ravenous and eagerly wolfed down the food. It was not until he was finishing the meal that he noticed that his mother was not eating with him. Whilst rationing had not yet tightened its grip to the degree it would later in the war, it had started and it dawned on Mash that his mother must have called in every favour she had and gone without herself to ensure he had all he could want.

"God I'm sorry Mum," he said, ashamed of himself. "I didn't think."

"Don't worry," said his mother before he could finish talking. "You deserve it and it's lovely to be able to cook for you again."

Mash stopped eating and as he did so he plucked up the courage to ask his mother a question. He had actually wanted to ask it for a while, ever since he had joined up and met the other lads who had all talked about their family. Before he had slipped into sleep last night it had been lodged in his mind again.

"Mum," he said, suddenly feeling like a teenager asking to go to a party. "Can you tell me about Dad again? I know what you've said before, that he was killed in the war and all that, but tell me about him. What he was like as a person?"

Mash's mother was washing dishes at the sink; she paused with her hands in the water. Mash looked at her back and could see the tensed muscles. She was always like this when he asked about his dad. But he wanted to know.

Suddenly his mother started vigorously washing the dishes again.

"Well, your father was a wonderful man," she said briskly. "Kind, thoughtful and generous."

She stopped talking and Mash wondered if that was all he was going to get. But she put down the sponge and picked up a tea towel. She carefully dried her hands and then sat down in the chair opposite him and took his hand.

"I see a lot of him in you," she said.

Mash felt a stab of pride.

"I'm sure you'll grow to be as good a man as him," she continued, squeezing his hand with her own.

She paused and smiled at Mash, but he saw something behind her eyes, something that he always saw when she spoke of his father. He had used to think that it was sorrow, but he could not tell anymore. It was sorrow and something else.

"I also see what war has done to you both," she said. "He came back on leave with that look in his eyes, and now you have it too."

She paused again and swallowed.

"Only this war is just starting, who knows how long it's going to go on," her voice cracked and she suddenly stood up from her seat.

Mash heard her make a noise like she was trying not to sob. He was going to get up to comfort her but she turned back to him and looked at him rather fiercely.

"Whatever happens, remember that I love you very much and that your father would be so, so proud of you."

Her eyes brimmed with tears that she would not spill. Mash gripped her hand and nodded, finding he could not speak. Then he got up and hugged her, feeling tears prick at his eyes as he was sure they were in hers.

The next day was Mash's last in Hull. He and his mother had decided not to discuss the war, Colette or anything else. Instead they went for a long walk through town and out into the countryside. Mash suspected that his mother was rather pleased that she could show off her boy and she missed no opportunity to introduce him to friends she met along the way. Once out in the fields they stopped for a picnic overlooking the Humber and talked about anything and everything. Mash found himself laughing for the first time in a long time. As they walked home he felt lighter, not better again but on the way.

And then all too soon it was time for him to leave. Together he and his mother walked in silence to the station. He went through the motions of getting the ticket and waiting for the train, his mother a silent shadow by his side. It got to the point where he could do nothing else but get on the train. The station master blew his whistle. He turned to his mother and tried to put into words all the things that were crowding to get out of his mouth. But before he could speak she grabbed him and hugged him close.

"Don't say anything," she said into his ear as her slim arms gripped him like a vice.

"Keep yourself safe and remember that I love you," she took his head in her hands and kissed his forehead as she had done all through the years when he had been a boy.

"Now go before I make a fool of myself."

He did as he was told and got on the train just in time for it to start pulling away. Mash watched her until she was just a dot in the distance then pulled himself inside. As he took his seat he wondered if he would ever see her again and knew that she was thinking the same thing.

★ ★ ★

After a very long train journey and a brisk but pleasant walk from the station Mash found himself standing at the gates of Greystone Manor. The sun was still in its prime and the heather just beginning to bloom, earlier than normal due to the warm weather, giving the hills a faint touch of purple. Mash stood soaking up the sun and the view. He loved this place; it was the Highlands at their best, with the hills and lochs running side by side with the forests and rivers. He could remember standing by the same gates several years ago when he had first come for the job. His mother had managed to find him the position of junior keeper at the manor through an old Army friend of his father's. It was a blessing as the job prospects in Hull were not good. But that had not stopped him almost quaking as he stood before the imposing gates, feeling homesick already though he did not want to admit it, and so terrified of the impending job that he had not even taken in the surroundings. But slowly they had insinuated themselves and he had grown to love them as well as a born and bred Highlander.

He walked down the winding drive, looking out for the first sign of the manor. And then, as he rounded a corner, there she was. To his eye the manor was still the most beautiful building he had ever seen. Half country house, half castle, it sat in the glen as though it had been there for all time. In awe he paused as he saw the building again, taking in every feature. After a few minutes he continued down the drive. Instead of going to the front of the house he followed it round to the back and on to the gamekeepers lodge. The small but cosy cottage was really little more than a hut but its unpretentious air seemed to welcome Mash.

As he walked in the first thing he saw was old Jock Macgregor sitting in his favourite chair by the now empty fireplace.

"You look as though you haven't moved since I left," said Mash.

Jock almost dropped the pipe that he had been in the process of lighting.

"Well I'll be buggered," he said, his keen eyes squinting out from under his huge grey eyebrows. "If it isn't young Edward."

Jock got up from the chair with difficulty and came over to him. Mash thought he looked older, but then Jock had always looked old; he seemed to be still going only through steely determination.

The man surveyed Mash.

"Looks like you've got some stories to tell," he said.

"Perhaps I have Jock," replied Mash.

"Well you'll have to wait if you want an audience bigger than just me, the others won't be back until this evening and they'll want to see you."

And with that Mash was back in the fold, just like Jock in his chair, as though nothing had changed. Soon he was in the kitchen, diving into a huge meal with the others, no danger of rationing shortages on an estate of this size, and Mash was warmed to see so many familiar faces come to say hello.

All the keepers wanted to hear his news. Mash described St Valéry and his escape but did not tell them about Colette; it was enough that Rod and his mother knew.

The assembled keepers saw the change in him. The older ones, those who had served on the Western Front, recognised the far away stare and the awkward silences.

The next few days flashed past. Occasionally Mash would help one of the keepers with a job, but most of the time he wandered alone around the estate. He was still shattered by the events in France but he found that the perfect weather and the wild but beautiful countryside had a calming effect on him. However, though the landscape brought him moments of peace his mind was still unsettled. It was not just Colette's death, the shock and unfairness of which still sometimes took his breath away, but it was wondering who had done it and who had knocked him out that kept Mash's brain from resting and recovering. The thoughts consumed him. It was like an itch he could not scratch.

Eventually, after hours of endless torture he came up with a scenario that seemed to fit the facts. The Germans were swarming everywhere so one of them had to have come into the house, found Colette in her room and raped and killed her. He then must have left when he heard Mash return and call for her. From there the only explanation was that Colette's father, attracted by the same shouts, had come out of his hiding place in the cellar and hit him thinking he was the one who had attacked her. The facts fitted but Mash had an empty feeling about it. Yet he could not come up with a better explanation. The knowledge that he would never know for sure haunted him.

On the day before his leave was over, Mash stood up from his favourite spot overlooking the manor. He had been going over the events for the thousandth time when there was a shout from behind him.

"You there, what are you up to? Stand still," came the voice.

Mash jumped up and quickly rubbed his red eyes.

Two Labradors came into view, one chocolate and one golden. Mash gulped. He immediately recognised them as belonging to the earl. Frantically he tried to straighten his clothes, smarten his hair and give his eyes another wipe before standing rigidly to attention. A moment later the earl came round the corner of the bushes, resplendent in his summer tweeds. He stopped when he saw Mash.

"Oh, I recognise you," said the earl. "It's Mr James, one of the keepers isn't it?"

Mash had seen the earl a number of times before, at church, shoots and various gatherings or social occasions. He had even once loaded for His Lordship when his usual loader had fallen ill just before a drive. He remembered fondly how nervous he had been at the beginning but had soon got into the rhythm of the shoot and quite enjoyed himself. He had even been given a shilling by the earl at the end so he must have thought Mash did OK.

"Yes my lord, I hope I didn't cause you offence."

"No, not at all. I saw someone up here on my walk and just thought for a moment it might be someone up to no good. Mr Couttie tells me that the salmon poachers are about and I thought you might be a scouting party."

He wiped his brow while looking at Mash, who prayed that he would not see his red eyes.

"If I remember correctly you're home on leave after France, is that correct?"

"Yes, my lord," replied Mash, wondering at the way no

gossip escapes such a small community. The earl straightened his cap, walked round behind Mash and looked out over the view.

"A wonderful view, is it your favourite spot?"

"Yes my lord," replied Mash, still firmly at attention. He did not add that he loved how the manor looked as though it had grown out of the land itself.

The earl smiled and gazed out for a moment before looking back at Mash.

"Oh for goodness sake, don't stand there as though you're on a parade ground, man. I'm not a sergeant major you know. Come and enjoy your view."

Mash, rather nervously, turned and joined the earl.

"I hear things were pretty dreadful out in France," he said. Mash nodded.

"We're just beginning to hear about our beloved Highland Division and I think that'll devastate the community."

He paused for a moment and glanced again at Mash before carrying on in a more hushed tone.

"You know a lot of us saw some awful things in the last war and lost people we cared about. You don't get over that sort of thing quickly."

He was talking quietly but staring out at the view, his face curiously impassive.

"It's a bit of a cliché but time is a great healer. You never forget them, but the pain does eventually go."

Mash looked at him to find that the earl had focused his eyes on Mash's face. Mash saw for a second understanding in his expression. But then the earl quickly looked away again.

"Still it doesn't do to reflect on these things," he said, turning away from the view.

"I'll not disturb your leave any further Mr James, have a good day." With that he resumed his walk, with his Labs hurrying to catch him up.

"Yes my lord, the same to you," said Mash after the disappearing earl who simply raised a hand in farewell without looking back.

★ ★ ★

The following evening Mash made his way back to Inverness barracks. By now all the billboards and newspapers were full of the disaster at St Valéry. The surrender of the Highland Division and the loss of almost 6,000 men had touched most families in the small catchment population. There was an overwhelming sense of sorrow which, over the coming weeks and months, would harden into anger and a burning desire for revenge on the Germans.

Rod was already back and so the friends swapped stories about their leave and any other gossip they had. Mash felt better after his break and was able to chat with Rod amiably.

"By the way," said Rod. "I've got some news for you. It looks as though we're two out of 1350 or so men to have escaped from St Valéry, plus the Ark Force lot. The rest aren't coming back. The division and the battalion have both gone so there's a lot of reorganising going on and everyone's in a flap. Word has it that they're going to recreate the division out of the Territorials. It also looks as though we're going to join a new battalion as the 4th is no more. We'll still be in 152 Brigade along with the 2nd and the new 5th Seaforths, but our home now is the 5th Battalion, Cameron Highlanders."

Whilst the original Highland Division was gone, fortunately the lost division had a ready platform for its replacement. The Territorial 9th (Scottish) Division was a duplicate for the 51st Highland Division and was formed in 1939 under the command of Major General Cunningham. Its role was to undertake coastal defence duties and to supply fresh troops to the 51st. Cunningham, seeing there was a need for a new Highland Division, had no hesitation in offering his command to become the reborn 51st Highland Division.

Over the next few weeks order started to form out of the chaos as the new division was formed and the returning men were amalgamated into the new battalions. Mash was not surprised to find that Mitchell had survived; he knew Mitchell would have weaselled his way through somehow. Mash had not seen him in the last days of St Valéry; the word was that he had managed to talk his way to Le Havre as part of Ark Force and had been taken off by the Royal Navy. It would be typical of him to leave his comrades to ensure his own safety. Worse, he had been promoted to corporal. Mash was just thankful he was not in Mitchell's section. Luckily he was still with Rod; both had been promoted; Mash to lance corporal in a section with Rod as corporal, which he felt duly grateful for.

The rest of his new unit were mainly from the Outer Hebrides; they all seemed to know each other or be related somehow; Ross Hamilton, or Gasman as the others called him as he had serviced so many old boilers of both kinds, was Gordon Macdonald's cousin's husband's brother. And Niall Stewart, a farmer who, if you believed what he said, owned half of the Hebrides, once courted Ross' sister. The ringleader of this group was Gordon Macdonald, a short, wiry man with the pent-up energy of a spring and a shock of red hair. He was a mechanic in his previous life and it was rumoured that he had a magic touch in repairing engines. His young cousin, Finnean, a gangly eighteen-year-old, was also in the section. He was a taller, stretched out version of Gordon; he looked like a long-legged Irish wolf hound compared to the small, terrier-like Gordon. Gordon guarded him just as fiercely as a terrier does its catch.

The other members of Mash's new unit were Hamish Crawford, commonly known as Kipper due to his previous occupation with the Navy, despite chronic seasickness, and

Callum MacKenzie, a labourer from Stirling who had huge arms from hauling bricks but a laidback disposition. Finally there was Malcolm Macrae, or Drillbit as the others had already come to call him. Mash discovered the reason for this nickname when, in the first five minutes of meeting him, Malcolm told Mash where he had been born, the name of his school, mother and his first girlfriend. His monotone drone did seem to drill into Mash's head.

Mash and Rod were the only two who had seen action. The ill-fated St Valéry action had taken on legendary status and Mash could sense the curiosity of the rest of the section. But it was a conflict of emotions. Those who had not been in action wanted to know what had happened and what it was like. At the same time Rod, Mash and the others who had made it back were very conscious of the hurt in the community and felt that somehow they had let them down.

It took them a while to ask but eventually Kipper, the most confident of the group, came forwards with the question they all wanted to know.

"What was it like?"

Kipper had freckles that converged over his nose and a ready smile, but Mash could see the apprehension beneath the jovial exterior. The others had gathered behind him, none of them could conceal their interest. Even Gordon MacDonald, who Mash could tell was not particularly pleased about having an Englishman in his section, showed curiosity.

Mash wondered how to sum up the experience for them; the constant noise of battle, cowering in trenches, knowing that you could be killed any second but fighting on anyway. He could not put it into words.

"Oh it was a barrel of laughs," said Rod. "Sunbathing all day, occasional shooting practice and as many women as you want."

"Really?" said Gasman. He was a thin figure with a

scruffy moustache which he probably thought made him look debonair but was in fact just slightly disturbing. Mash saw Gordon roll his eyes.

"He's being sarcastic," said Callum.

"Show them your leg," said Mash.

They all looked at Mash then back again to Rod who grinned and rolled up his trouser to reveal the scars from his shrapnel wound. The wound looked much worse than it was. Rod had been lucky in that his puncture wounds had been from small pieces of shrapnel that had been relatively easy to remove. However, a larger piece had made two large half-moon-shaped incisions right the way down his calf but without seriously damaging the muscle and bone underneath.

"Caught this in France gentlemen," he said. "Followed by a very pleasant hour having the still-burning shards removed with no anaesthetic." He gave a monstrous wink to Mash which none of the others saw.

Mash smirked to himself.

Gasman muttered something under his breath and stroked his moustache, a habit Mash noticed he did when he was nervous.

"But it's alright boys," said Rod. "At least I've still got the leg."

Young Finnean was staring at the scars as Rod rolled his trousers back down.

"You just have to get on with it," said Mash, to no one in particular.

They all turned to look back at him.

"Don't think too much about what you're doing," said Mash again. "Just kill and kill again or else you'll be mad or dead or both."

They all stared at him and Mash realised that that was not what they wanted to hear. He tried to think of something else to say, something comforting. But nothing came to mind and he decided that he could not be bothered.

His new section was not a bad bunch, but Mash did not have the energy or the inclination to make friends. He was civil but did not go out of his way to be more than that. He had not always been so; one of the best things about the Army was the camaraderie, but since Colette and St Valéry it was different. Kipper and Callum were the friendliest and tried to engage him in conversation a few times. Mash answered them politely enough but kept them at arm's length. The majority of the section did not make much more of an effort with him; Gordon and his cronies tended to ignore him and speak Gaelic whenever he was around. Although they did not say anything openly, Mash knew they did not trust an Englishman, especially one in the Highland Division. This feeling was especially rife with the defeat at St Valéry; in a manner typical to the Scots, a great defeat always seemed to increase the sense of patriotism, rather than a great victory. St Valéry was being compared to the battle of Flodden. Mash felt the need for revenge just as much as the others, though his was not driven by patriotism. In the time he had been back in Britain his anger over Colette's death and the loss of the division had merged into one. He threw himself into training. He did not know how else to cope with the loss of Colette and the constant question that swarmed through his head: who had killed her? Most of the time he could avoid these thoughts by keeping busy, but they waited, until the moment he fell into bed, then swooped and tormented him until he slipped into fitful dreams.

Initially it was as though the Army were not quite sure what to do with them. In the stalemate brought about by the defeat in France, followed so soon by the Battle of Britain victory, the Germans could not invade but the British did not have the strength to attack either. To the Camerons it meant months and months of guard duty along the Scottish coast interspersed with periods of training. In the beginning the lack of equipment was laughable, with pretend tanks, artillery and trucks being a common feature of the training. But very gradually equipment started to arrive and the shortages were made good. The training also took a dramatic change, especially when Major General Wimberley was brought in as the new commanding officer in May 1941, eleven months after the St Valéry disaster. He was a Cameron man and very keen on there being only Highlanders in his division. Wimberley, or Lang Tam as he was known to the troops due to his tall, gangly frame, was passionate about getting the men to the top level of readiness for the days ahead. Under him, the training became more intense and 'realistic'; it was designed not only to get them fit and efficient but also to give them a taste of what war was really like.

The months progressed and in April 1942 the division was sent to Aldershot in Hampshire. The training was now as realistic as it could be made with the aim of making the troops ready for deployment. This involved having machine guns fired over their heads to get them used to the sound of battle. Even though Mash had experienced it before, and was quite used to the sound of gunfire from his work as a gamekeeper, he still winced at the sound and the feel of the air as the bullets rushed past his head. He was reminded that death could be a matter of inches. He and the others also had to sit in a trench as tanks drove over them. Again, for Mash and Rod it was horribly familiar, but the others had never experienced it before. Mash watched them as they sat hunched in the mud and felt the weight of the tank above. Callum sat quietly, Kipper cracked jokes but his hands twitched nervously. Mash was rather amused to see that even a tank could not stop Drillbit talking. Gordon sat still with his eyes wide open the whole time. When it was over he stood up shakily. But, as they were clambering out of the trench, he teased Gasman.

"You've had heavier things lying on top of you haven't you Gasman."

The others laughed, rather more than they would have done in normal circumstances, even Gasman. They all needed a stiff drink after that, including Mash, who normally avoided the joviality of the NAAFI bar.

★ ★ ★

As the months of intensified training had passed by, it hardened the men and threw them into each other's company more. Though most still kept to themselves around him, Callum and Kipper still tried to be friendly to Mash and he gradually thawed. He could not help it; the environment pushed them together. In the forces the men became your family, even in the way that you sometimes want to throttle family members, he felt close to it with Drillbit, but you would still kill to protect them. He would sometimes go for a drink at the NAAFI bar with the rest of the section. Though the others saw it as a chance to socialise, Mash still held back and kept his own company.

It came as a surprise when, one day, Mash realised that it had been nearly two years since Colette had been killed. The initial swells of despair had died down, only rearing their heads occasionally to catch him off guard. But he was left with a general numbness; when he tried to look forwards he could see no future. Without Colette there was nothing to look forward to after the war so he focused solely on the training and the present.

But the day came when he had to think about the future when he and the section were issued with tropical kit. This set off a flurry of rumours as to where they were going. Mash went to the NAAFI that night with Callum, Kipper and Rod to discuss it.

"I reckon Japan," said Callum.

"Most likely the Middle East," said Rod, gazing into his pint.

"Shit," said Kipper. "Why does it have to be so far away?"

"What's wrong with that?" asked Callum.

"It's going to take ages," said Kipper. "Ages on a boat."

The others laughed, Mash smiled into his drink.

"They say the further you go the more jabs you get," said Rod. "I reckon after today we're going to the bloody moon."

"That woman was vicious," muttered Callum.

Earlier that day they had all been given inoculations, though Mash considered the time spent with the seemingly malicious nurse and a blunt needle more as a form of torture than a safety precaution. His arm still ached.

The others were rolling up their shirts to compare bruises but Mash could not get into the mood. He swallowed the dregs of his beer and decided to leave. Ignoring the calls of the others to stay, he pushed out of the crammed bar. The fresh air hit him as he stepped outside. He paused for a few minutes to breathe it in, and then turned to walk back to the barracks. As he passed the alleyway by the building he heard muffled sounds, thumps and voices. He paused and looked into the gloom. He could just make out a tangle of limbs and bodies. He heard more thumps and recognised the sound of flesh hitting flesh. He stuffed his hands in his pockets and looked towards the lights of the barracks. He did not want to be a Good Samaritan; if someone was brawling that was their business. But he did not move.

He squinted back down the alleyway and, as his eyes adjusted to the light, he saw the mass of shadows as separate people; it looked like two large men were holding a smaller one while another figure pummelled it. A sudden image flashed across Mash's mind, of Colette being held down by someone stronger than her, intent on inflicting pain. He jerked his head and blinked his eyes, trying to disperse the picture, but his mind was set. He stalked down the alley, keeping to the shadows. He was right; some poor sod was being beaten. As he got closer he saw that the man had red hair; it was Gordon Macdonald. Mash squatted behind a bin. Gordon may not be his favourite person but he was in his section, and you looked out for your section. His mind was firmly decided when he saw who was doing the beating.

Mitchell paused to catch his breath; he surveyed his bloody knuckles and smiled. He was about to resume his pummelling when a sudden blow to the side of his face knocked him to the ground.

Mash knew he had seconds before the two brutes holding Gordon could react. He recognised them as the ever present Douglas Campbell and Wallace Smith. Once he had whacked Mitchell across the face with a dustbin lid he caught Douglas with the rebound, before planting his hobnailed boot into the groin of Wallace. Wallace sank slowly to his knees as Douglas staggered backwards letting go of Gordon who dropped to the floor and lay unmoving. Mitchell had collapsed as well. Mash knew he must deal with the dazed Douglas first and flew at him, throwing punches at a face already bleeding from the edge of the dustbin lid. He landed a haymaker and felt the man's nose explode under his fist, showering blood. Mitchell tried to stumble to his feet so Mash kicked him in the stomach. He needed to get Gordon out but he did not want to get boxed in the alley. Holding the dustbin lid like a shield he dashed towards the form on the ground.

"Mash, what the fuck are you doing," snarled Mitchell as he clutched his stomach.

"I don't like bullies."

"Jesus Christ, do you have to be so fucking saintly," Mitchell screeched, his usually laidback persona gone.

Mash ignored him and tried to lift Gordon's inert form, but suddenly Mitchell lunged across the ground, grabbing him by the ankle. Mash fell, dropping Gordon back to the floor. He rolled over and kicked back hard at Mitchell's face. Mitchell managed to twist away so the boot just caught him a painful sliding blow on the ear, but then he yelped in pain as Mash's boot came down on the fingers still holding onto Mash's other leg, forcing him to release his grip. Mash jumped up and grabbed Gordon, dragging him to his feet. Mitchell was still on the ground but starting to get up and both the heavies were recovering from the shock of the attack and moving back into the fray. One circled round to block his exit. Mitchell, leaning against the wall wheezing, realised that Mash and Gordon were stuck. His face split into a vicious grin. Mash wondered why the hell he had got involved, he was going to be ripped apart just because he tried to help some ginger bugger he did not even like. The three men closed in on him. Well if he was going to go down then he would go down fighting. Mash left Gordon propped against a wall, starting to regain consciousness but still very groggy, and dived at Douglas blocking the exit, head-butting him in the solar plexus. The man went down like a sack of potatoes, the breath knocked out of him. Mash took the opportunity to grab Gordon and dive down the alley, towards freedom. If he could get out where people could see them then Mitchell would not follow. He turned back to see Mitchell charging towards them.

"You fucking bastard," he was screaming. Wallace was behind him, joining in with the chase.

"Come on Gordon," Mash shouted.

He managed to force Gordon into a run and they stumbled out of the alley and into the street with Mitchell close on their heels. Mash's heart fell as he realised there was no one around; they were alone and Mitchell was closing in fast. In desperation Mash ducked back towards the NAAFI entrance, but Gordon was slowing. They were not going to make it. He turned to make his last stand as Gordon crumpled to his knees.

"What's going on?" a familiar voice roared. "Come on lads the boys are in trouble."

Rod appeared out of the darkness, quickly followed by the rest of the section. Mash's body flooded with relief as Mitchell and his minder skidded to a halt and fled the other way. Rod and the others sprinted after them.

Mash dropped to the floor next to Gordon. Both panted heavily then Gordon rolled over, wretched loudly, and vomited onto the ground. Mash did not even care, he sat panting and felt the adrenaline slowly leave his body. Gordon spat on the floor then sat back up, wiping his mouth on the back of his hand. In the moonlight Mash could see that his face was a bloody pulp. They both sat, breathing deeply, too tired to move. Eventually Gordon looked up and squinted at Mash through his already swelling eye.

"I would have had them if they hadn't crept up on me from behind, fucking cowards."

"That's how Mitchell likes to fight," said Mash.

"I reckoned I was done for," said Gordon.

"So did I," said Mash. "I thought you were dead."

"Just needed to get my breath back," Gordon grinned at him, blood lining his teeth. "That was very brave of you," he said it as though it was a question.

"It was fucking stupid of me," said Mash.

The other man nodded. They both sat in silence for a little longer then Gordon quietly said; "I'm sorry about your girl."

Mash looked at him.

"Rod told me," said Gordon.

"What did he tell you?" asked Mash through clenched teeth.

"Just that you had a girl who died, think he told us to explain why you were such a grumpy bastard."

Mash did not say a word; he felt he should be angry with Rod, but he did not feel anything.

"I guess that's a fair reason to be a grumpy bastard," Gordon conceded.

Mash did not say anything again, he ached all over, his knuckles were bloody and stinging. He was trying to summon the energy to stand when Gordon suddenly turned to him.

"You may be English but you're as brave as a Scot, I reckon I owe you my life."

Mash tried to interrupt but Gordon stopped him.

"You ever need anything you call on me or my family, alright? I don't leave a favour unpaid."

He held his hand out. Mash felt slightly ridiculous but Gordon looked so serious that Mash shook his hand. Gordon winced.

"You need to get to the medical unit," said Mash.

Mash pulled himself to his feet. As he did so, the others returned, out of breath but laughing.

"We weren't able to catch Mitchell, he's quick when he's running for his life, but we did manage to teach Wallace a lesson," announced Rod.

From the look of his raw knuckles and the smiles on the rest of the section's faces it would be a lesson the heavy would not forget for a while. Finnean went and knelt down besides Gordon, the others gathered behind him.

"They've ruined your pretty face Gordon," said Callum.

Gordon tried to smile, but winced as it tore at his split lip.

"Come on we've got to get you help," said Mash.

He and Finnean managed to drag Gordon to his feet.

Together the group made their way back to the barracks, practically carrying Gordon most of the way. Despite being bloodied and beaten, Mash felt a full part of the section for once and felt the last of his standoffishness leave him.

# CHAPTER SIX

# THE ROLLING DUCHESS

Gordon was luckily only in the medical unit for a couple of days and then returned to light duties. Normally he would not have sought medical attention at all in case it landed him in trouble, but he was sure he had broken at least one rib given the pain in breathing, making any exercise out of the question. By some miracle the butcher's bill was not as bad as he had feared: two cracked ribs and only his nose and a couple of fingers broken. The rest of him was just very battered, "like a tenderised steak" said the doctor. He and the platoon officer, Lieutenant Wilson-Brown, had tried to get Gordon to tell them who had beaten him up, but Gordon insisted it had been too dark to see. Wilson-Brown, or WB as the men called him, had frowned; he, as well as everyone else, had seen Mitchell's flunky walking around with a broken jaw and a black eye, it was not hard to put two and two together. But still, no one talked.

Mash went to visit Gordon the day after the fight. Gordon, who had barely acknowledged Mash's existence before, now seemed ecstatic to see him. He made him sit down and chat to him; he wanted to know everything about him. And he seemed to want to share as much with Mash. Lying in the hospital bed, Gordon told Mash all about his upbringing in Stonoway on the Isle of Lewis. He had spent his time tinkering with cars and had been driving tractors since he was nine, often without permission. He had been an engineer before he joined the

Army and proudly told Mash that it was said he could get any motor started. At first Mash just listened politely, but he could not help getting drawn in. He discovered that Gordon could talk as much as Drillbit, but his stories were not as mind-numbingly dull and involved a lot more Gaelic swearwords.

Gordon was also curious about Mash; he seemed to find him fascinating and fired questions at him: where was he from? Who was his Ma? What happened to his Pa? When Mash answered that he had never met him Gordon replied that he could have his one. He asked all about the 'toffs' at Greystone Manor and the action he and Rod had seen. Mash was a little surprised by the onslaught of questions but found that he was happy to answer them. After keeping to himself for so long he actually felt it a relief to talk. That was until Gordon asked about Colette. They were talking about Gordon's home and Mash asked him if he had a girl there.

"Not likely," said Gordon. "There's barely a decent-looking woman for thirty miles and if there is I'm most likely related to her."

Mash smiled.

"What about you?" said Gordon. "Tell me about your girl."

Mash was caught off guard.

"I don't want to talk about her," he said.

"You have to," said Gordon. "Can't keep stuff like that inside."

"What are you, one of those psycho doctors?" snapped Mash. He suspected Gordon had been planning to ask him about Colette for a while.

Gordon ignored his tone and shifted himself in bed, wincing as he pushed himself up with his injured hand.

"There was this farmer back home," he said. "Married a young girl, they were happy and everything for a year or two. But then she died suddenly of pneumonia. It was terrible. He never spoke about her again. Just sat silent up in that farmhouse. Then one day he put his gun in his mouth and shot himself dead. No one found him for over a week."

Mash tried not to picture the man in the lonely house. "I reckon some nice German will blow my head off before I get a chance," he said, with an attempt at levity.

"Come on," said Gordon. "You don't have to tell me, you know, about her dying. Tell me the good stuff. What was her name?"

Mash clutched the side of his chair; he had the urge to break Gordon's nose again.

"Why are you so interested?" Mash asked.

Gordon shrugged. "I suppose I'm nosy," he said. "Plus, you saved my life; I don't want you to top yourself before I get a chance to return the favour. I saw that farmer once you know. He came down to the town occasionally to buy supplies. He looked as though he was walking in a different world, like he was already a ghost. I reckon that's what you look like sometimes."

"Christ," said Mash. "You're intense."

Gordon shrugged again.

"I'm not going to top myself," said Mash.

"Glad to hear it," said Gordon.

"And I don't reckon I saved your life, I just saved you from looking even more like minced meat than you already do."

Gordon grinned and then swore as the cut on his lip split open again.

Mash let out a breath.

"Colette," he said

"What?" said Gordon as he blotted his lip on his bed sheet.

"That was her name, Colette," said Mash.

"Nice," said Gordon. "What is that, foreign?"

"French," said Mash.

"A French girl?" said Gordon, with the tone of someone who believed that anyone who was not a full-blooded Scot had horns and cloven hooves, but then saw the look on Mash's face.

"French, very nice, like Greta Garbo."

"I think Garbo is Swedish," said Mash.

"Well, one of those other countries," said Gordon. "Tell me about her."

Mash was quiet, how could he describe her? Get across all that she was to Gordon?

"She rode a motorbike," said Mash finally.

"A motorbike?"

"Yep," laughed Mash. "Couldn't believe it when I first saw her on it. She was pretty great," he finished.

"Sounds it," said Gordon.

"I wasn't the only one who thought so," said Mash. "Mitchell tried it on with her."

"Mitchell liked her?"

"Yep, he asked her out and she turned him down," said Mash, trying but failing to hide the pride in his voice.

"She was a good judge of character then," said Gordon. "That's why he doesn't like you much."

"Among other reasons," said Mash. "We just don't get on."

They continued to talk about Colette. Gordon did not ask Mash about her death and Mash did not offer up the information. Ever since the day he had found her in the house, all Mash's memories of Colette had been tainted with her death. But as he talked to Gordon, she came back into his memory, not as a body but a living person.

When Mash got up to go he paused at the door.

"Thank you," he said to Gordon, then he turned and left.

Outside he looked up at the darkening sky. After a dry start to the month it had rained a lot over the last week and the evenings were cooler. Mash adjusted his coat and tucked his hands deep into his pockets. Strolling towards the barracks he felt lighter than he had in a while. On the way he passed the

NAAFI bar and saw that Mitchell and a group of his friends were outside. Mash paused, the lightness evaporating. They had not spoken since the fight; Mitchell seemed to be taking the approach of pretending Mash and his friends did not exist. Framed in the light of the window and standing in that infuriatingly over-casual pose he had, Mitchell was the centre of the group and, judging from his gesticulating arms, was in the middle of telling a story. Mash bunched his fists in his pockets and was about to move on when Mitchell glanced over and saw him. He paused in his story and looked at Mash, then waved in a faux friendly manner. The men around him laughed sycophantically. Mash resisted the urge to sprint over there and pummel his sneering face. He wished he had done more damage to him in the fight, but at the time he was just glad he and Gordon had got out alive. With great self-discipline he turned away from Mitchell and continued walking.

\* \* \*

Gordon was discharged from the hospital just in time to join the preparations for the visit of the king and queen. It was scheduled for the 1$^{st}$ June but before that there were countless rounds of inspections and hours of drill to polish the troops' skills to a peak of efficiency. Throughout the Highland Division drill sergeants stomped up and down hurling abuse at soldiers who made the slightest error. The drill square rang out to comments, such as "Hamilton, swing your arms properly or I'll tear them off and beat you to death with the soggy ends."

Mash was surprised to see the change in both the section and in himself. At first they hated every bit of the practice but slowly, as they started to get more proficient, a pride was also apparent in them. Mash was interested to see the reaction of the men to the royals. They were held in high esteem, especially the Queen who was seen as "one of them, a true Scot."

On the big day the event was over in the blink of an eye. Fortunately, the weather was kind, sunny but not too hot, making the inevitable wait between everyone forming up and the arrival of the king not too demanding. During the wait Mash squinted at the men in the sunshine; they looked immaculate, perfectly cleaned and pressed tunics above the regimental kilt with rifles gleaming in the light. On their heads they wore the Tam-O-Shanter beret, all worn at the same jaunty angle, and boots polished so highly you could see your face to shave in them.

*Well at least we look like a fighting unit.*

And then they were off. Orders shouted in the clear air were responded to with crisp, clean movements. Gone were the days when an order would be responded to with what sounded like gunfire as boots came down at different times up and down the line. Now they had been practised and honed so that every hobnailed boot came down at exactly the same time with a satisfying crunch.

What surprised Mash the most was the buzz of excitement and pride when the king was seen to be wearing a Cameron Highlander kilt and it was with an extra swagger that the troops marched past. Even Mash found himself feeling a swell of emotion at being part of the Highlanders and the unexpected pride in seeing the king wearing 'their' tartan.

After the visit there was more excitement when rumours started to circulate that the division was due to depart on June 20th. Whilst troop movements were meant to be a matter of secrecy the rumour mill was in top gear and, in this case, accurate. The section discussed it in the NAAFI bar one evening. It was June and, though it was mild, it had drizzled persistently all day.

"Hopefully it'll be somewhere dry," said Callum, looking out of the window at the heavy grey sky.

"Judging by our kit it'll be somewhere baking," said Rod.

"I really hope it's not the Far East," said Gasman.

"Maybe it'll be Africa," said Finnean. "They've got lions there."

"Yeah, "said Gordon. "They'll likely be armed with guns and shooting at you."

Mash was quiet; now that the time for despatch was near, he was not sure how he felt about it. Until the war he had never even been overseas. Africa and the Far East sounded like places from a story, lions like fairytale creatures. He supposed though that wherever they were sent it would not matter; they would still be on the front line, lions or no lions.

The time passed all too quickly and it was soon the day of departure. The section found themselves, with hundreds of others, gathered on a dock in Liverpool, waiting to board their ship. The section was on the CPR *Duchess of Richmond*. Mash could not believe how huge it was; it looked even bigger than Greystone Manor. They boarded and made their way to the tiny mess they would call home until they got to wherever they were going. They rushed back up on deck to see the ship leave port.

"I thought there'd be crowds and people cheering us off!" said Niall.

"Aye, me too, where are the bands and the streamers?" agreed Finnean.

But there was nothing, only the sights and sounds of a busy port hard at work under a grey and threatening sky. Too many troops had departed to too many distant shores for this to be seen as anything other than business as usual. Somewhat deflated they turned and left. All except Mash, who continued to stare out as the ship pulled away from the dock. He felt a twinge of something close to excitement, like he had as a boy reading about heroes setting off to exotic places on adventures. Even though he had seen enough fighting to know the reality of adventure, he still could not keep down a feeling of buoyancy.

At first life on the ship seemed like a holiday. They still had to train every day but there were several amusements laid on for them, including various sports and competitions. There was also an inexhaustible supply of cards and they often played poker in the evenings. This was when they were not watching the latest films, which were shown most nights. The Pipes and Drums were played at various times throughout the day, which Mash thought pleasant at first but soon grew sick of. Gordon, however, always stopped to listen and would often hum along with the tune.

Mash was worried he would feel seasick as he had rarely been on boats before. He did feel a little queasy at first and it took him a couple of days to get used to the fact that he was not standing on solid land, but overall he did not react too badly. That was until, three days into the trip, they reached the Bay of Biscay. Situated off the west coast of France, the bay was famous for being one of the roughest crossings in the world. Nothing could have prepared Mash for it. Soon after they entered the area the winds grew stronger and started to rock the ship. In no time at all it seemed to Mash the boat was heaving and rolling beneath him, dropping like a rock suddenly and taking his stomach with it. He had never felt so sick, he tried to keep it down but he could not. He vomited until he had nothing left in his stomach and still he felt nauseous with every roll. He desperately wanted to go on deck; if he could feel the cool air and sea spray he thought he might feel better. But the troops were banned, it was too dangerous. The already cramped atmosphere below deck was made almost unbearable, the smell of vomit was thick in the air and the temperature gradually built. They had been told that the important thing was to stay hydrated and keep eating, but water never seemed to quench their thirst and the thought of eating made them feel even sicker. Mash thought it would never end as he sweated and retched. But eventually they were on calmer seas. Mash, dragging himself up on wobbling legs like a baby deer, made his way up to the deck where he saw the sun was shining in a blue sky and the sea lay like a velvet blanket all around, as though it could never be ruffled. He spat over the side.

The trip through the Bay of Biscay earned the ship the nickname the Rolling Duchess. Most of the men settled back down afterwards, only feeling the occasional jolt of sickness when the seas were particularly rough. All except Kipper. Mash had often suspected that Kipper exaggerated his departure from the Navy, but as soon as his foot had touched the deck he had been a nauseous shade of green and could barely keep any food down. He could most often be found throwing up in the toilets, cursing boats and whoever invented them, cursing the Army, the war, the Germans and generally working his way back to Hitler, who he held personally responsible for his wretched situation. He spent so much time in the toilets that Niall pinned a note to the door reading 'This stall is reserved for the use of Kipper.'

The others tried to encourage him to do something to distract himself, such as sports or darts, but Kipper declined. Back on land he was one of the most sociable of the group, but on ship, as soon as he had dragged himself through training, he took himself away to a corner of the deck with a pack of cards and played solitaire over and over again.

The only thing Kipper was looking forward to was the King Neptune ceremony. This happened when a ship crossed the equator; all those on board who had not crossed before had to undergo the ceremony, which seemed to involve sitting in front of 'Neptune's' court to face punishment. Kipper, having been in the Navy, had undergone the ceremony already. He would not let on to the others what was going to happen, but he worried them by saying how glad he was that he was not going to have to go through it again.

The first few days on the ship and the Bay of Biscay were overwhelming. But after a while a routine became established and Mash started to feel restless. The Duchess, which had seemed so huge in the dock, felt claustrophobic. Below it was like a rabbit warren and on deck, though the expanse of sea and sky spread ever onwards, Mash felt trapped. He realised that the entertainment was laid on to keep them occupied, like small children on a long journey.

He was not alone; Gordon did not take to sea life, he had rarely been on a ship before and he claimed he could barely stand up, even on the stillest of waters. He did not trust how something so heavy could float.

"It ain't natural," he could often be heard muttering.

Rod, on the other hand, had spent a lot of his youth sailing. He would often lecture the others on nautical terms and would irritate Gordon and Kipper by standing on the deck, taking a deep breath and loudly saying, "Is there anything better than sea air?" This was usually answered by a groan from Kipper.

Mash tried to keep himself occupied, but he felt like a rat in a cage. He had excessive energy; the fact that he could not go for a long run made him want to. He played a lot of sports to try and tire himself out. He also tried to distract himself with the frequent lectures they were given.

Unfortunately, he was struck down for a few days with a stomach bug. While the others were learning how to navigate by compass and the stars in the desert he was in the sick bay trying to keep down food. He did not think he had missed much; the others said they were bored to tears by the officer giving the talk – apparently he could outtalk Drillbit and for once Drillbit did not disagree. This and the fact that the boys said it was impossible to work out which bit of the night sky he was referring to in the middle of the day convinced Mash not to bother with any future lectures on the subject. Once he was well again he did attend other lectures though; they were mainly about desert life, including graphic descriptions of the many insects they would encounter and the effects of the heat.

In the evenings Mash usually played cards with the rest of the section. Cards were popular, especially with Mitchell and his friends. True to form, Mitchell had established a gambling den almost as soon as they had set sail. Mash and a lot of others avoided Mitchell's games; most people had seen the beating Gordon had taken. But some of the troops were not so wary, especially the newest recruits. They were drawn to the high stakes and Mitchell's jack the lad persona. Mash would watch them play, looking eager and afterwards walking a bit taller as though they were part of something important. But Mash knew it would not be too long until someone could not pay up and the trouble would start.

★ ★ ★

The convoy continued southward and the weather grew warmer. Day after day the sky was clear and the sea calm. While there was a cooling breeze on deck, the cramped conditions below made the heat and humidity almost unbearable. Eventually the troops realised that their course had changed and that they were on a more easterly heading. Rod tried to explain the particulars to Mash but he could not understand it. But Rod said he thought they would reach land soon. Eventually they were greeted with the smudge of darkness on the horizon with the tell-tale covering of cloud. Kipper was beside himself at the thought of leaving the ship. The others were just as excited, they did not know where they were but they did not care, if they could spend a few days on land they would be happy.

However, this was not to be the case. The convoy had reached Freetown in Sierra Leone and the danger of malaria was very real. The powers that be did not want troop numbers severely diminished by a preventable disease, so no shore leave was granted and the ships anchored well away from the land. The troops stayed on board and were dosed with tablets and ointments to protect them.

The section, along with most of the other men on board, gathered on deck and looked longingly at the shore. Kipper was desolate, cursing everyone and anything that came to mind as he gazed out onto the forbidden land. They had only been there a short while before the water between them and the land began to fill with dark specks. As they grew closer the men could see that the specks were small rowing boats heading towards them. As they got within hearing distance the men in the boats started shouting and waving at them. They were holding up food of all descriptions, carved souvenirs and anything that they thought they had a chance of selling. One had a boatload of fruit.

"What's that?" asked Finnean.

"I don't know but don't even think of trying it," said Rod. "It can make you sick."

"Looks better than what we've been getting," said Niall.

Some of the other soldiers were shouting to the traders and holding out money, others were trying to stop them.

Niall was eyeing the colourful wedge of fruit the trader was holding up; it dripped juice which looked delicious in the overpowering heat.

"Anyone dare me to try it?" he asked.

No one answered; they all knew he would do it anyway. Mash suspected that even if it made him ill Niall would like having the story to tell.

"They warned us not to eat it," said Drillbit eventually.

Niall did not listen.

"I'm getting some," he said.

He beckoned the boat with the fruit over and, to everyone's surprise, Finnean leapt forward to do the same.

"What are you doing?" said Gordon.

"I want to try it," said Finnean.

"Don't be stupid."

"I'm not stupid," said Finnean. "I want to try it, alright."

Gordon looked as though he was going to say something else, but instead he shrugged his shoulders and let Finnean pass.

"Don't come crying to me if you get poisoned," he muttered.

Finnean and Niall declared that the fruit was delicious and that everyone else was a coward for not trying it. They felt fine for the rest of the day and into the evening until, almost at exactly the same time, they both lurched to the latrines.

Mash was later walking past the toilet blocks and found Gordon standing outside, grinning evilly.

"I wouldn't go in there," he said to Mash. "The stupid buggers are sick, got it coming out of both ends."

"I'd better tell Wimberley that you're not able to come and chat," shouted Mash before lowering his voice and continuing to Gordon, "Aye, Lang Tam's aboard, come to pay us a visit."

"Told you that heathen fruit was bad," Gordon yelled through the door, barely listening to what Mash said.

In between the sounds of retching Mash could hear Finnean cursing Gordon in Gaelic.

★ ★ ★

The *Duchess* continued her journey, drawing nearer to the equator. The excitement for the King Neptune ceremony grew. Mash was actually wishing for it, he wanted something to happen, anything to break the monotony and distract him from the heat. It grew hotter every day; below deck it was cramped; hammocks slung everywhere and crammed with men who severely needed a wash.

Most of the men had never crossed the equator before and so were to face the ceremony.

"What exactly happens?" asked Finnean the evening before the event. They were in their sleeping quarters, preparing for bed.

"I think it's pretty harmless," said Rod. "They'll be someone dressed up as Neptune and we'll be dunked."

"Harmless?" said Niall. "I heard someone got killed in a crossing."

"No you didn't," said Gordon, who was getting tired of Niall's stories.

"I swear to God," said Niall, emphasising his point with hand gestures, which he always did whenever he wanted to hammer something home. "Part of the ceremony was to drag the men in the surf behind the ship and one man got stuck under for too long." Niall paused to ensure he had everyone's attention. "And he drowned," he finished.

"No one's going to let that happen," said Rod into the silence that followed.

"Why don't we ask Kipper?" said Gasman. "He's the only one who's done it before."

"Certainly have," said Kipper, who was lying in his hammock. "Got the certificate to prove it." He waved a rather tatty piece of paper at them.

"Let's see it," said Drillbit, grabbing for it.

"No way," said Kipper, holding it out of his reach.

"Why do you get a certificate?" asked Finnean.

"To prove that you've been through the ceremony," said Kipper. "I'm part of the initiated."

"Good grief," muttered Gasman.

"Well come on Kipper," said Callum. "Let us know what's going to happen tomorrow."

"Can't," said Kipper, smiling at the ceiling. "More than my life's worth."

"Well you're smiling more than I've seen you do on this whole trip so I'm guessing it's going to be bad for us," said Mash.

"Can't say," said Kipper again, but he grinned even wider.

Despite the rest of the section questioning him, Kipper would not give anything away. They all eventually went to sleep, Kipper still clutching his certificate like a talisman.

Mash was brought unceremoniously to wakefulness the next morning by Kipper and a number of others clanging pans together. He squinted in sleepy stupefaction at Kipper, who was wearing an eye patch, striped trousers and what looked like a stuffed budgie on his shoulder.

"You're not a pretty sight to wake up to Kipper," he said.

"Silence Pollywog!" shouted Kipper.

Rod snorted with laughter.

"What on earth's a Pollywog?" said Gasman, who had fallen out of his hammock and was trying to find his glasses.

"You are," said one of Kipper's crew. "Pollywogs are the uninitiated and we're Shellbacks, those that have crossed before."

"You're to stay down here and get dressed in these," Kipper threw a bag at them then he and the other Shellbacks left, clanging their pans all along the corridor.

Rod opened the bag and pulled out a selection of flowery dresses and a black lace bra.

"This is going to be interesting," he said.

They dressed to great amusement. Mash donned a floral red tea dress and some matching red lipstick. Callum wore a blue spotted dress which strained over his arms.

"Jesus Callum," said Niall. "You look like the sort of girl Gasman goes for."

Gasman smiled amiably as he pulled on a pair of stockings.

"Finnean's actually quite pretty," said Rod. "You've got good legs."

"Shut up," said Finnean, throwing a bra at him.

After what seemed like hours they were allowed up on deck. They were herded along by the Shellbacks, some using ropes and paddles to coerce them. There was much laughter on deck as everyone gathered, dressed in drag.

A Shellback called them all to attention. Mash recognised Shelton, one of the ship's crew, beneath his bandana and eye patch. He informed them that they were all to be judged by King Neptune's court, but not before they had visited the barber and doctor.

The 'barber' was another of the ship's crew dressed in a white coat with, Mash hoped, fake blood on it. They all went to the chair to get trimmed. Mash had all his hair shaved off, as did Callum. Gordon had an elaborate swirl pattern shaved into his ginger hair. Particular hilarity was reserved for Gasman; the barber managed to shave his moustache off and Gasman stroked the bare, pale skin above his lip with a look of desolation. Everyone found this amusing, more so than they would normally have but the spirit of the day made them all slightly hysterical.

Next up was the doctor. They queued to see the man dressed again in a white coat spattered with scarlet. One after another they were inspected, rather roughly, and then the doctor tried to force them to take their 'medicine'. Mash did not know exactly what was in the concoction, except for raw eggs and pepper, and he did not want to know. The doctor did everything he could, both physical and psychological, to get the men to open their mouths to get the liquid down.

"There's no way that vile stuff is going in my mouth," muttered Gordon as he watched a corporal retch over the side of the ship.

Mash silently agreed with him.

Rod went first and despite a rather brutal handling and teasing he kept his mouth shut with a slight smile splayed across his lips. The doctor eventually let him go and moved onto Gordon. He determinedly kept his mouth closed, ignoring all the doctor's taunts, that was until the doctor asked him where he was from.

"He's from Stonoway," shouted Kipper who appeared beside the doctor. "He's an inbred with the IQ of a potato."

The men roared with laughter and Gordon, unable to help himself, leapt up, opening his mouth to shout at Kipper. The doctor took the opportunity to shove the spoon in. A cheer arose as Gordon staggered to one side, gagging and cursing Kipper who was laughing just out of his reach.

Mash was next; he determinedly kept his mouth shut through punches and taunts.

"It seems we can't get this one to open his mouth," said the doctor to the crowd.

"Make the English bastard," said a voice. It was Mitchell. He seemed to have managed to avoid having any of his hair shaved off and the only concession he had made to dressing up was to don a silk scarf round his neck.

There was a boo and shouts of laughter from the crowd.

"English!" shouted the doctor theatrically, enjoying his moment. "This calls for drastic measures."

Before Mash knew what was happening the man had grabbed his nose and was holding it shut so he could not breathe. Mash held on for as long as he could as the doctor acted up to the crowd, looking at his watch, but eventually he had to gasp for air and the spoon was shoved into his mouth with some force.

The doctor let him go as Mash lurched away coughing and spluttering, the mingled taste of raw eggs, pepper and God knows what else mixing in his stomach. He looked up to see Mitchell roaring with laughter. If it was anyone else but Mitchell, Mash knew it would have been in fun. Mash forced himself to stand up and take a little bow to the crowd then joined Rod and Gordon, still coughing.

They next went to see King Neptune himself and his Queen Amphitrite. They seemed to have got the costumes the wrong way round; the king of the seas was played by the slight petty officer Grant while his wife was played by the large, bearded boatswain in a blonde wig. Mash and the rest appeared before the court to be judged and were eventually dunked, rather vigorously by the pirates. Having passed out of the pool they were given their certificates and declared Shellbacks.

They spent the rest of the day drinking the extra ration for the crossing ceremony while getting involved in the games, sketches and countless other distractions that had been laid on. Mash felt that for the first time on the ship that he had let go; he could tell the others did too. Everything was overly funny and they enjoyed themselves into the night without thinking about the consequences.

The day after the ceremony they were greeted with more than just a muzzy head. They were brought harshly back to reality when they were gathered on deck to be told that Tobruk, the bastion that Rommel had never been able to take, had fallen. The mood of the rest of that day was in stark contrast to the one before; Tobruk had stood in their minds as a symbol; undefeatable, small but holding firm against the enemy. But it had fallen under.

For the first time Mash started to worry about whether they would actually lose the war. It had always been fairly certain in his head that they would win. It was to everyone; they were going to teach Jerry a lesson, like they had last time. That is what everyone believed, what the radio said and, most importantly, what Churchill said.

But Mash began to worry about what would happen if the Germans took over. If he lived to see it, then life would change as he knew it.

He voiced his worries to Rod and Gordon one evening. They were on deck enjoying a smoke.

"What'll happen if we lose?" Mash said, not looking at either of them but staring out at the sun as it sank into the sea.

Rod took a puff on his cigarette; "Then we'll all be speaking Kraut and munching on wiener schnitzel," he said.

"No way," said Gordon. "No way are we going to speak that hacking spitting language in the Highlands."

"Yes, we can barely understand you as it is," said Rod.

"I mean it," said Gordon. "We've always fought against tyranny, stopping the bloody English from putting us down, 'scusing your presence," he said to Mash.

"If Hitler turned up on our shores we'd war up old style, kilts, body paint and screaming," Gordon continued.

"Well that'd certainly put him off," said Mash.

At that point Callum wandered over to join them. He took a rumpled cigarette out of his pocket.

"What're you lot talking about?" he asked as he lit it.

"Mash's asked the question no one should ask," said Rod. "What if we don't win?"

Callum blew out a plume of smoke, "I guess we just have to hope someone high up knows what the hell they're doing."

"Do you really think they know what they're doing?" asked Gordon.

"No," said Callum, leaning against the rail. "But we just have to hope."

At that moment they heard muttered voices and Mitchell came walking around the corner. He was in deep conversation with a young squaddie called Peterson who Mash recognised from around the ship. The boy had a prominent Adam's apple and wide eyes. Mitchell had his arm round the boy's shoulders, in a seemingly friendly gesture, but Mash could see that he was clutching Peterson's shoulder tightly.

They all turned to look at Mitchell, who had not yet noticed them.

"Looks cosy," muttered Callum.

"Going for a romantic stroll Gavin?" called Rod.

Mitchell jerked his head up; the boy made a move as though he wanted to flee, but Mitchell had a tight grip on him. Mitchell quickly hid his surprise and pasted his normal crooked smile on his face.

"Just having a quiet chat," he said. "A private one."

"Looks friendly," said Gordon.

"You alright kid?" asked Mash, who was watching the boy; his bulging eyes were darting between them and Mitchell.

"Oh look, the boy scout jumps in again," said Mitchell, his smile slipping. "You going to rescue someone else from my evil clutches?"

"In a fair fight Mitchell it's you that'd need rescuing," said Gordon.

"Look who's piped up," said Mitchell. "You know Gordon, we've got a game on tonight if you want to join in. We'll give you great odds. I know you like to bet."

Mash could feel Gordon tensing up next to him. He shifted on his feet.

"I'm done betting with the likes of you," snarled Gordon.

"You should watch your mouth, Yeast," said Mitchell.

Mash was not quick enough to stop Gordon; he launched himself at Mitchell, sending them both flying. Peterson scuttled to one side as Gordon, who was on top of Mitchell, landed a punch square on his nose. Mitchell yelled.

"That's for breaking my nose you bastard," shouted Gordon.

He grinned at Mitchell but that changed to a grimace as Mitchell got his foot free and booted Gordon in the stomach. Mitchell tried to wriggle away but, despite being winded, Gordon would not let him go and continued to land blows on his body. Mitchell scrabbled to get him off, managing to get his hands free and round Gordon's neck.

This was when the others thought it was time to step in

before anyone saw. Rod and Mash ran forwards to prise them apart but Callum was too quick for them. Callum very rarely got into fights, his relaxed, laidback manner not allowing him to grow heated enough, but he often found himself breaking them up. He pulled Gordon off, who Rod and Mash grabbed and hauled backwards. With the other hand he picked Mitchell up and slammed him against the bulkhead, holding him by the throat. Mitchell struggled, but Callum's arm was immovable.

"What was that he called him?" asked Callum, speaking to the others but not taking his eyes off Mitchell.

"Yeast," laughed Rod. "It means inbred."

"That's actually quite clever Mitchell," said Callum.

Mitchell tried to wrestle Callum's arm away but he held firm.

"Your gorillas aren't with you now Mitchell," he said quietly.

Mitchell's eyes flicked from the tensed muscles of Callum's arm to Gordon, who Mash and Rod were still struggling to restrain.

"Fine," he choked, "Let me go, I'm done with him."

Callum released him. Clutching his throat, Mitchell dropped to the floor. But he quickly pulled himself up and smoothed his hair down. His bleeding nose belied his air of nonchalance.

"Remember our conversation," he said, pointing at Peterson, who had stood to the side, gaping, for the whole fight.

"Evening lads," said Mitchell, in the faux jovial manner that jarred Mash, and he skulked off, holding his nose.

They watched him walk away then Rod and Mash let go of Gordon.

"You should've let me pummel him," said Gordon as he clutched his stomach.

"Maybe next time," said Rod.

"You got in a few good blows," said Mash. "I reckon that nose will ruin his not so pretty face."

Gordon turned to the boy. "You alright?" he said.

Peterson nodded.

"You want a cigarette?" asked Rod, holding his pack out.

Peterson edged towards them, he reminded Mash of a rabbit stuck in head lights. He had an overwhelming urge to give the boy a clip round the ear and tell him to get a grip. But, looking at his bulging eyes, he recognised that the boy was terrified.

"I ain't gonna bite," said Rod.

"You be careful kid," said Gordon. "You don't want to get mixed up with Mitchell, he's bad news."

The boy stopped, a few inches away from the proffered cigarettes. Then he set his jaw.

"I'm not a kid," he said, his wavering voice belying his bold words. "I don't need your help."

With that he turned and ran off. They watched him go.

"Nervy little thing isn't he," said Gordon.

"I think I've seen him with Mitchell before," said Callum. "Playing cards."

"Christ," said Mash. "If he owes Mitchell money no wonder he's nervous."

Gordon leant against the rail, clutching his stomach.

"Bastard got his boot in alright," he wheezed.

"Come on," said Rod, putting his arm round Gordon in a mockery of Mitchell. "Let's have a drink."

# CHAPTER SEVEN

# Cape Town

The troops finally got to go ashore when they reached Cape Town on July 18th.

As they got ready to depart Lt. Wilson-Brown had a word with them.

"You'll be granted leave for two days," he told them.

There was a chorus of cheers and clapping. WB waved his hands at them, "Yes I know, I'm eager to be off this tin can too, but for the first three days we've a few engagements, inspections and the like. But the last two days will be your own."

There was another cheer and WB nodded along with the men. He held up a hand again for quiet.

"Just please remember you're representing the British Army and the Highland Division, so please try to be on your best behaviour."

The men mumbled in agreement; they would have agreed to anything WB said just to get off the boat.

Slowly the convoy entered Table Bay and the excitement as they gathered on deck was palpable; Kipper was practically hopping from foot to foot. The port of Cape Town was laid out before them. The famous Table Mountain looked down on the port, bathed in sunshine and surrounded by green country. A wreath of white cloud sat over the top of the mountain.

"The mountain's got its table cloth on," said Rod

They all looked at him as if he had gone mad.

"The mountain's called Table Mountain because it's so flat on top. The mix of air currents means that there's often a layer of cloud lying on top of the mountain and people say it's Table Mountain's table cloth," explained Rod.

"How the hell do you know that?" asked Gordon.

"I don't know," said Rod, looking momentarily perplexed. "I'm just full of useful information."

As the ship drew closer to the shore they passed small boats and ships in the bay, shouting and sounding their fog horns. Soon these were joined by the sight and sound of cheering from the quay as crowds came into view.

"Is this for us?" Mash said quietly.

"I've never seen anything like it," replied Gordon in equally hushed tones.

Slowly the ship docked. Mash held himself still as they prepared to disembark, though he felt like he was vibrating with impatience. Finally the Pipes and Drums started up and they filed off the ship. They were to march through the streets to the civic hall. They were amazed to see that people lined the streets to cheer them through. Mash gazed at the sea of faces and hands and listened to the roar of the shouting and felt it fill him up with energy. Slowly he began to smile and wave at the crowd. Fruits, cakes and cigarettes were thrown at them, which they grabbed with eager hands.

"This is more like it," said Gordon taking a huge bite out of a cake he had just caught and waving at a group of pretty girls.

Mash noticed that there were a lot of women lining the streets, a lot of attractive girls waving at them.

As they marched they turned down a different street and almost immediately the faces watching them changed from white to black.

"Did I just miss something?" whispered Gordon.

"They're not allowed to mix," said Rod.

"Bloody hell they've got that very neat haven't they," said Gordon.

"Decent of them to come out," said Rod. He waved back and so did the rest of the unit. Though Mash noticed some of the troops did not wave, including Mitchell.

They marched all the way to the civic hall, where there were even more people. Mash smiled so much that, as he lay in bed that evening in the barracks he and the rest of the unit had been stationed in, his cheeks ached. He fell asleep, thankful to be in a bed that did not sway.

The first couple of days were spent in marches and inspections from Cape Town and British dignitaries. They mainly spent a lot of time standing in the sun while interchangeable old men exchanged pleasantries and compared medals.

On the third day they visited a local school as part of a press drive. On the way to the school Mash was amazed by the contrast of rich and poor; not far from the fancy hotels were the townships, cramped huts made of corrugated iron that looked like they would fall down with one breath of wind. He saw black faces of scruffy-looking children watching them as they went by. Mash, who had expected South Africa to be flooded with blacks, had only seen them on that first day when they had been on their own street. It was like they were kept locked away in their townships.

The school they went to had no black faces either. It was clearly a well-to-do one, private, Mash could tell. The section was not particularly looking forward to visiting the school. They were champing at the bit to be free and they could not be bothered to kick a ball about with a few kids. But in the end they were won over, mainly by their own vanity; the children looked at them like they were heroes and asked them all about battles and the ship they had been on. They were especially fascinated by their accents and Gordon busied himself teaching them Gaelic swearwords until WB caught him at it. They then played a few games of football while the photographers snapped away. Aware of the cameras, Niall showed off, making flamboyant kicks and usually missing them. Drillbit, having talked the ears off the rest of them about his prowess on the football field, proved to be terrible, barely able to make contact with the ball. The kids found it pretty amusing, thinking he was doing it deliberately.

When they had finished at the school they headed over to a veterans club. It left them with a different feeling to the school; with the children they had been able to believe their own hype for a while, but here, whilst the welcome was still very warm, they could see a different side.

They stood awkwardly in a large, light room, immaculately clean, filled with armchairs of various styles and ages. Sitting on nearly every one was a man, usually in their mid-forties although some were older.

"I don't think any of them have the right number of limbs," Kipper whispered to Mash.

He was right; most of them had some kind of injury. Mash had a vision of himself sitting in one of these rooms in thirty years' time, maybe missing a limb, being made to talk to the latest recruits about some new war.

They were urged to take a seat, have a cup of tea and a chat. Mash was reminded of a time when he was a child and his mother had taken him to see his great aunt and her family, who Mash had never met before in his life. He was ushered into a sitting room, much like this one, with, what seemed to him, a group of ancient men and women. He was advised to sit and talk, to recite what he had been learning and generally perform for a group of people he was supposed to have a connection with.

Slowly the men filtered forward and awkwardly availed themselves of chairs. Niall, always happy to have an audience, was chatting away with three old boys in under a minute. One man, who was missing an arm, was ambushed by Drillbit and Gasman, as if he had not already suffered enough, thought Mash. He could see the old man listening to Drillbit with a glazed expression which Mash recognised only too well. Gasman sat to one side and let Drillbit do the talking, while absentmindedly stroking the down on his lip where his moustache was starting to grow back. He caught Mash's glance and rolled his eyes at him.

Gordon had marched Finnean over to meet "a real hero" and Mash could see that under Gordon's enthusiastic encouragement the man was showing them his medals.

Kipper and Callum were sitting with a group of three men; Callum perched on a tiny stool that he dwarfed while the short Kipper was curled up like a cat in a huge armchair.

Mash stuck with Rod; they took their time pouring tea from the large canteens then finally made their way to a couple of tapestry chairs by the window where an older man was sitting. They introduced themselves awkwardly. The man was hunched over and had a patch on his eye. That seemed to be his only injury, but he had a weariness about him which seemed to seep from him and infect Mash, making him slouch in the chair. Yet, when they shook his hand, though his skin was papery and thin, his grip was firm. He introduced himself as Frank.

"So you've come to entertain me have you?" he asked, his accent strong.

"So we've been told," said Rod. "Though I don't know how entertaining we are."

"Or maybe I'm supposed to regale you with stories of my war days," said Frank. "Would you like to hear a story?"

"If you'd like to tell us," said Mash.

Frank looked at him with his one eye, which seemed to Mash as though it was extra strong, as though taking up the gaze of the missing one.

"You boys seen battle yet?" he asked.

"Yes Sir," said Mash and he explained about France.

The old man nodded. "Thought you didn't look quite as bright-eyed and bushytailed as some that they send in here. You know what it's like – that makes it harder."

Rod and Mash both nodded.

"Well then," said Frank. "I don't need to tell you anything."

"What regiment were you with?" asked Rod, eager to get the conversation going.

"I was in the 1st South African Brigade, 2nd Infantry Regiment," Frank replied quietly. Rod and Mash glanced at each other. From the countless lectures on the Camerons' history and their briefing before the visit, they knew that the Camerons had been with the South African Brigade on the Somme. The 2nd Regiment had been in the lead when the South Africans had advanced into what was to become the Battle of Delville Wood, a battle so vicious that it was to become known as one of the most brutal engagements of the Battle of the Somme, which in its own right was engraved in the memory as a bloodbath. The fighting, much of it hand to hand, was so intense that the wood was reduced to a lunar landscape. Of the 3,200 South Africans that went into the battle only 600 came out. Frank had survived one of the most appalling engagements of World War One.

Rod and Mash were both quiet. Mash looked out of the window at the sun-filled garden. He had the same feeling he used to have on the last day of school before the holidays. The jumpiness to get away, yet the hours seem to deliberately slow down, trickling by heavily, while all the time the sun taunted him.

"I don't normally come to these things," said Frank. "They bring back too many unpleasant memories. But when I heard that the 5th Camerons were coming I knew I had to make an exception. Back in July 1916 when we were going forward we had guides from the 5<sup>th</sup> Camerons to lead us to our start points. That was the first engagement any of us had ever been in and, whilst we wanted to do SA proud as the only contingent in France, we were all scared out of our wits. Our guide could see I was terrified and said some kind words – not much, just 'Be safe' and a handshake – but it meant the world to me and I never forgot it. When I heard you were coming I wanted to return the favour."

Mash instantly felt remorse at wanting to get away. This was very personal and clearly important to Frank.

"I'll tell you one thing," said Frank. "The war, it was the worst time of my life."

Rod and Mash glanced at each other.

"But," continued Frank, "it was also the best, the best damn time I've ever had." Frank clenched his fist to make his point.

"That's strange isn't it?" he said. "One second you're exhausted, in pain, usually sick from some damn illness and the next you're laughing until you can't stop with your friends, who're like your family."

Frank's eye looked away into the middle distance.

"I'd a really good group of lads in my section," he said.

Then he turned his gaze back on Rod and Mash.

"I was the only one that came back though," he said.

Mash looked down into his cup of tea; his finger barely fit through the delicate handle, which was decorated with pink roses. He did not want to look at Rod.

Frank's eye flicked between the two of them, then he leant back in his chair.

"I could tell you how I lost my eye," he said.

"Is it gruesome?" asked Rod as Mash looked up.

For the first time Frank cracked a grin, which made him look like a buccaneer pirate.

"It's horrible," he said.

"Go ahead then," said Rod.

They spent the rest of the time listening to Frank's story, which was truly grisly, involving a German soldier, a bayonet and a fight to the death. When they had to leave, Rod and Mash both got up from their chairs, leaving their now cold cups of tea. Frank pulled himself out of his chair as well, with some difficulty which Rod and Mash pretended not to see. He shook their hands.

"Be safe," he said.

Rod and Mash nodded.

Outside in the sunshine they blinked their eyes, like moles emerging from the earth.

"Christ," said Rod as he took a cigarette from his pocket. "That didn't half give me the willies, do you think that's how people are going to look at us?"

"If we survive," said Mash.

Mash could not stop thinking about what Frank had said about being the only one left alive. He could not help looking around at the rest of the section as they slouched along in the sun and wonder who would be left by the end of this. He knew that it was very unlikely that all of them would make it home. Mash could not help think if he was to be one of them, one of the many who die. Or, possibly worse, what if he was the one that survived?

"I think it was an honour to have met them." Gordon appeared beside them, Finnean trailing in his wake.

"Yes it was," said Mash quietly. "Still doesn't stop me being scared shitless."

"Fair point," Gordon conceded.

At that moment they were tackled by Kipper.

"Come on boys," he yelled, one arm round each of them. "We're free, and we're on land! I'm going to party while I've still got all my limbs!"

Then he ran off after Callum, leaping on his back.

"He's cheerful," said Rod.

"He's right though," said Gordon. "I suggest we find the nearest bar and set up camp."

They did find the nearest bar, and after several drinks in there they moved on to the next one, and then several more. They found, to their delight, that their uniforms got them in everywhere. And the uniforms were everywhere; all over the city the Army swarmed, let loose. Mash did not remember much of that night, he just had patches of memory: Finnean drinking five shots of whiskey one after the other, Finnean vomiting profusely in the street as Gordon slapped his back and shouted, "Get that out boy," Gasman pulling the fattest woman Mash had ever seen (they had been curled up together like Jack Sprat and his wife). There were more shots and he remembered Rod dancing with a girl; he believed he danced as well, which meant he must have been drunk. The last thing he remembered was the whole section walking through the streets, trying to find their way back to the barracks, struggling to hold each other up. Callum had an unconscious Finnean over his shoulder and they were all singing 'The March of the Cameron Men' at the top of their voices.

The next day they took the opportunity to sleep in, but Mash still woke up with an awful hangover, as did the rest of the section. He just wanted to stay in bed but they dragged themselves up and went to look at Table Mountain.

They all agreed that it looked very table-like as they squinted at it in the glaring sun.

"Let's go up it," said Niall.

"Fuck that," said Kipper.

"We can't come all this way and just look at it," said Callum.

"Yes we can," said Kipper. "I plan on looking at it from that little bar over there while I have a refreshing beer."

"Christ," said Callum. "How can you drink anything else?"

"Hair of the dog," said Rod. "However, I reckon I'm going to go up it, got to say you did it haven't you."

"Me too," said Drillbit. Mash saw Rod's good-natured smile flicker.

"Well I'm staying here," said Kipper.

"Me too," said Finnean, who was drooping like a parched flower. "But I'm not drinking anything, I'm not drinking alcohol ever again."

They eventually split up into two groups: Kipper, Finnean and Gasman stayed at the bar while the others walked up the mountain. It took them longer than they thought, the path zigzagging its way upwards, which Mash was quite thankful for; he did not think he could have coped with a steep climb. Only a few feet up he was wishing he had stayed at the bar with the others, but by the time he reached the top he had sweated most of the alcohol out. At the top they all stood and looked at the view; the city spread out below them, turning into green then melding into blue. However, it was quickly obscured by cloud. They were in the very clouds themselves and the columns and patches drifted around them eerily. They walked along the top, but after a while they realised the only thing they could do was to go back down again.

After the mountain they made their way to a market where they were assailed by stall holders pressing all kinds of items on them; Mash could see it was mostly tat. Callum stood at one stall looking at necklaces; he held a wooden one in each hand. Callum was the only one of the unit who was married, albeit only for a year, and he seemed determined to bring his wife home some trinket from everywhere they went.

"Which one do you think Anne would like best?" he mused out loud to Mash.

Almost immediately he turned to Mash.

"Christ I'm sorry," he said. "That was insensitive."

"No it's alright," said Mash. "But honestly I have no idea, pick either."

He walked away, leaving Callum clutching both necklaces. Whatever he said to Callum, he had been thinking about Colette. He imagined if she was still alive and he was writing her a letter. He would tell her that he had the hangover from hell, but that he had climbed Table Mountain. He would tell her about the clouds that you felt you could touch. He would buy her a necklace that she probably would not like but that she would treasure because he had bought it for her from Africa. He would tell her all about Gordon and the others. How, when they had come down from the mountain, Finnean, who had sworn he would never drink again, was on his third pint and was tucking into a steak and chips.

Mash went and sat in the shade and waited for the others. He lit a cigarette. Suddenly the sun seemed too bright, the crowd too loud and he longed for somewhere dark and quiet. He rested his forehead in his hands and closed his eyes.

"You alright Mash?"

He looked up to find Gordon standing in front of him.

"Yes I'm fine," said Mash as he rubbed his eyes. "I just need a drink."

"Great idea," said Gordon.

That started another night of drinking. They ended up in a club that they had been at the night before. There was a long bar that ran the length of the room and was crowded with people. The backdrop to this was a pair of red velvet curtains which were designed to give the hall a theatrical glamour, which only worked if you did not look too close to see how moth-eaten they were. No one cared what it looked like though; they all drank, topping up the levels already in their systems.

Gasman's voluptuous conquest appeared again and brought some of her thinner friends with her. Finnean was making fine headway with a young blonde girl who was giggling at everything he said.

He was not the only one; Callum spent a large part of the evening chatting to a pretty brunette. Mash thought it was fairly innocent until Gordon grabbed him by the arm and pointed to the door. Callum was leaving through it with the girl.

"What the hell's he doing?" said Gordon. "He's married."

Mash shrugged; he was pretty surprised at Callum, but he was too drunk to think about it properly.

About half an hour and two more pints later Callum came walking back through the door. He stalked straight up to the bar and ordered a double whiskey.

Gordon turned on him.

"You should be ashamed," said Gordon. "You're a married man."

For once Callum looked like he was going to lose his temper.

"Yes Gordon," he said. "I'm a married man, a very married man. I'm very aware of this right now because I just had this pretty girl, totally up for it and all I did was walk her home."

Mash smiled to himself as Gordon slowly pieced together what Callum was saying.

"So you didn't do nothing with her?"

"No I didn't do nothing with her, because I love my wife, the bloody cow," said Callum. The barman passed him his drink and he immediately poured it down his throat.

"Same again," he said as he wheezed.

Gordon grinned and put his arm around Callum.

"You'll be rewarded in heaven," he said to him.

"I'd rather be rewarded now," mumbled Callum. "Let's drink until we can't see."

"Yes!" shouted Gordon.

Mash, who was leaning against the bar, turned so he had

his back to it and surveyed the room which was crowded with people. He was at the stage of drunkenness where his thoughts clouded together and he struggled to separate them out, but he was not yet disorientated or sick. The room seemed to be filled with women. It may have been his imagination but there seemed to be at least three to every soldier. They were all South African, mainly blonde with tanned skin and that good health that seemed to emanate from them. I'm in a room full of beautiful women and I'm not doing anything, thought Mash. He glanced over at Callum who was having his ear bent by Gordon, probably about the status of his soul. Callum was not doing anything either, but that was because he had a girl waiting at home for him. No one was waiting for Mash.

At random he turned to one of the women next to him at the bar.

"Can I buy you a drink?" he asked.

She seemed a bit taken aback to suddenly have the silent soldier talk to her but she nodded and asked for a gin and tonic.

Mash summoned the bar tender and placed their order. He looked out of the corner of his eye at the girl. She was fair, obviously, and quite short. She was curvaceous, teetering on the edge of plump, probably the type to go to fat in a few years but at that moment her curves were perfect.

"I'm Harriet," she said.

"Mash."

The girl crinkled up her tanned brow.

"That's an odd name," she said.

So Mash had to launch into the explanation. This took them through one drink and he bought them another and they continued to talk. He found out that she was a college student who had been born and raised in Cape Town and shared a house with two other girls. Mash found it surprisingly easy to drop back into the chat-up; it had been an age since he had last done it. He was sure it was helped by the vast amounts of alcohol he was consuming. As the crowd grew, he leaned in closer to talk to her; the band was so loud that they had to practically shout in each other's ears. He could smell her skin and the delicate floral fragrance of her perfume. It made his head swim. Eventually he asked her to dance, though he was not very good at it, but the dance floor was so crowded they really just held each other up. They were crammed close together and Mash could feel every curve of her rather generous body through her dress. He noticed she blushed a little, but when the crowd thinned slightly she did not move away.

"I should probably get home soon," she said; it was past one o'clock.

Mash looked down at her face; she was looking at him blankly, but he could see the promise.

"I'll walk you home," he said.

He did not bother saying goodbye to the others; they were either too drunk to notice or were off with their own women.

Outside the club the night air had a chilling touch to it. Mash helped Harriet into her coat then they set off to her house. In contrast to the club, they walked a little apart, not touching. Talk was stilted and after only a short time they reached a terraced house.

"This is me," said Harriet.

She took out her keys from her bag but stayed where she was. Mash looked at her.

"Thank you for walking me home," she said.

Still she did not move, but fiddled with the keys in her hand. With sudden decision Mash crossed the gap between them and kissed her.

He kissed her with the enthusiasm of someone who had been celibate for two years; tangling his hands in her hair and pressing her closer. She responded with equal fervour. If he had been thinking at all Mash would have thought that he was surprised how naturally it came back to him.

Finally they broke apart. Mash was breathing heavily.

"Do you want to come in?" asked Harriet.

Mash wanted to say yes, he did very much want to come in. But something stopped him. He looked at the house then he looked back at Harriet. She was so pretty, her blond hair coming undone. Blonde hair, thought Mash, Colette's was dark brown. He shut his eyes and felt the world shift; he was not sure if it was from alcohol or lust.

"I'd really like to come in," said Mash.

Harriet smiled.

"But, I don't think I can."

"Oh," said Harriet, her smile slipping. "That's OK."

"No," said Mash. "It's not that I don't want to, I really want to. And part of me is wondering why the hell I'm saying this."

Harriet looked at him as he rambled and rubbed his hand through his hair.

"It's just that…" Mash continued.

"Is there someone else?" asked Harriet.

Mash dropped his hand and looked at her.

"Yes," he said. "There's someone else."

Harriet nodded.

"I'm really sorry," said Mash.

"It's alright," said Harriet. "I understand."

"Thank you," said Mash.

Harriet kissed him once more softly on the lips.

"Good luck Mash," she said, then she walked to the door and went inside without looking back.

Mash stood staring after her. His heart was still pumping and for a moment he wondered about running after her and hammering on the door. But he did not, he stood still and let his heart slow down. Weariness overtook him and he started to realise how drunk he was. Slowly he turned around and started to walk.

The barracks must have only been about ten minutes away, but it took him almost an hour to get back. He staggered through the streets, not recognising anything, the dark buildings all merging into one. Eventually, by pure luck, he found himself outside the barracks.

He just wanted to pass out and he was hoping that none of the others would be back so he could slip into bed without seeing anyone. However, Rod and Gordon were sitting on their bunks talking. An unconscious Drillbit was on his own bunk.

"Only damn time he's quiet," said Rod, smiling at Mash.

"You make it with that girl Mash?" asked Gordon. "She was fine."

Mash walked over to his bed and collapsed on it head first.

"Not exactly," he said into his pillow.

"What does that mean?" asked Gordon.

"I don't want to talk about it," Mash said.

Although he could not see them, he could feel Rod and Gordon look at each other.

"What happened?" asked Rod.

Mash was quiet for a moment then he rolled over onto his back and stared at the ceiling.

"I couldn't do it," he said.

There was silence, then Gordon spoke.

"You mean that you, erm, couldn't rise to the occasion?" asked Gordon.

"What? No," said Mash. "I mean there she is, asking me to come in, this gorgeous woman, gorgeous," he repeated. "And I feel guilty. I feel like I'm betraying Colette."

Rod and Gordon were both quiet. Mash could practically hear them racking their brains for something to say.

"Oh Christ," said Gordon. "I don't know what to say

Mash, except, well, are you just never going to be with another woman again? That's no way to live."

"That's no way to live," repeated Mash, he closed his eyes and he felt the room swim around him. "I'm only bloody human, can't do that."

"You can't beat yourself up Mash," said Rod. "It's, well it's a tragedy what happened, but you can't change it. And you can't act as though you're dead as well."

Mash opened his eyes and blinked several times; the lights on the ceiling were multiplying before his eyes. He gripped his head with his hands.

"I can't think about this now," he mumbled. "This bed's rocking as much as the Bay of Biscay crossing."

"Bet whatever bed young Finnean is in is rocking too," Mash heard Rod say.

"Shut up," came Gordon's retort. "I'll string the bugger up when he gets back."

Mash listened to them bicker as he drifted off to sleep, a swirl of blonde and dark-haired girls dancing through his mind.

The next day they all remained in bed until past noon. No one suggested a trip, no one had the energy. However, later in the day a few of them, including Mash, ventured out to buy essentials like food and cigarettes. Gordon and Rod were watching Mash warily, but Mash assured them he was OK. In truth most of the previous night was a blur and he felt so ill he could only concentrate on not being sick. He focused on his hangover, finding it preferable to thinking about Colette.

They went to another pub that evening, all except Finnean who had a date with his conquest of the night before. Most of them could not handle another big night and just had a couple of pints and played darts. All except Gasman and Niall who carried on drinking into the early hours.

They severely regretted it the next day when they had to

return to the ship. Everyone was in a bleak mood; the break had made them feel human again but now that they were back on the ship a blanket of depression settled over them. Finnean was mooning around about his girl and Kipper practically had to be dragged back on board.

Mash lay in his bed that evening, back in the cramped quarters of the ship, listening to Kipper groaning and thought about what Rod had said. He was not dead, he was alive. Maybe he should start acting like it.

★ ★ ★

A few days later, on the 26th July, the *Duchess* arrived off Durban, as did the rest of the convoy, reformed ready for the next part of the journey.

Mash joined the section on deck to watch the sight of the convoy forming, with its escort ships fussing about making sure everyone was in their rightful place. He pulled out a cigarette and turned to light it, cupping his hand round the match. As it caught, he looked up and scanned the rest of the deck. His eyes settled on a figure, amidst all the others who were gathering around the rails; he was going the opposite way. From his profile Mash could tell it was Peterson. Mash inhaled a deep drag of the cigarette as the boy walked slowly away from the crowd, trying but failing to disguise a limp. Mash blew out his plume of smoke. He would lay bets that it was Mitchell's handiwork; he had learnt from the fight with Gordon to hit where bruises could not be seen. Mash made a mental note to try and talk to the boy again, though he did not know how much help he could be.

At that moment Gordon's voice tore through him.

"For the love of Christ," he said. "You only knew her for two days, stop moping around."

Mash turned back to see Gordon berating Finnean, who was slouched against the rails, staring blankly at the water.

Finnean muttered something Mash could not hear and Gordon exclaimed again.

"He reckons he's in love," said Gordon. "I ask you, love, doesn't know what he's talking about."

"Shut the hell up Gordon," shouted Finnean suddenly. "What the hell would you know, the only woman you seriously courted was Maggie Young and she was dumber than a bag of hammers."

The section snickered whilst Gordon, unsurprisingly, bristled. He squared up to Finnean, who was almost a foot taller than him.

"What's that, you get your willy wet once and you think you're a man?"

With the ensuing argument and the time it took to talk each of them down, Mash was completely distracted from Peterson and all thoughts of talking to him had gone from his head.

The next morning Gordon, who always woke with the dawn, had already gone to the shower block whilst the rest of the unit were attempting to drag themselves out of bed. A few minutes later he came rushing back in.

"You're not going to believe it?" he said.

"What?" yawned Rod.

"They reckon Peterson has thrown himself overboard."

They all froze and stared at Gordon. Mash felt his stomach jolt as though he was going to be sick. Finnean, who had managed to sit up, fell back onto his bed and stared at the ceiling.

"He left his stuff all packed neatly up on his bed with a note," said Gordon.

"How do you know?" asked Mash.

"Heard it from Malcolm Stuart, who heard it from Anderson who only sleeps a few feet away from him. He's shaken up, said he didn't hear a thing in the night."

"Is he sure?" asked Gasman.

"Apparently the ship's being searched," said Gordon. "But Malcolm said he left a note with his stuff, it said to tell his mother he was sorry."

"Jesus," Rod said.

"Shit," said Mash.

He sat down on his bed. "Shit," he said again. "It was Mitchell. The kid was terrified of him, I saw him limping yesterday, I reckon he'd already been worked over."

"Couldn't bare another go," said Callum quietly.

"Anderson said Peterson had been hanging around Mitchell, thought he was in with the big boys. Until he got in too deep," said Gordon.

"Poor little sod must've been terrified," said Rod.

No one said anything else. They got dressed in silence then sat waiting for the search of the ship to be completed.

They waited for over an hour, listening to the footsteps overhead; even Drillbit was quiet and sat on his bunk picking at his shoe laces. Mash knew they would not find anything. He kept picturing the skinny boy setting his possessions to rights before creeping out, past the sleeping men, up to the deck. He must have climbed onto the rails and stood on the edge, looking into the dark depths which he saw as more inviting than his own life. Mash tried to imagine how he must have felt as he stood there. Did he do it swiftly? Or did he stand, staring into the water, trying to make the leap? He must have been desperate.

They were finally called on deck to be told what they all already knew, that Peterson had gone overboard. They had a minute's silence to remember him. Mash suspected that most of the men had no idea who Peterson was. During the silence, when everyone's head was hung, Mash glanced over at Mitchell. His face was expressionless, but his two mates were standing next to him, one was shifting from foot to foot and the other one was staring down at his shoes, a look of confusion on his face. Mash wondered if Mitchell felt any guilt at all. He stared at Mitchell, willing him to look over, to move; anything to acknowledge what he had done. But Mitchell stared stonily at the ground. Mash looked back at the floor himself. He wondered if he could have done anything; he meant to speak to the boy but he never got around to it. If he had would Peterson still be alive? Mash closed his eyes; he could not let thoughts like that get hold of him. There was only one person to blame and that was Mitchell.

The death of Peterson seemed to lay heavy over the ship, some even claimed to have seen his ghost standing at the railings. But the ship still carried on moving towards its unknown destination. Bets were starting to be taken on where they would end up. India was a popular choice.

On 6th August the convoy reached the coast of Saudi Arabia and put into Aden for refuelling, but with no shore leave. The convoy separated again, this time apparently for good, with some ships going to Basra and others onto India. The moment was sealed by the escort HMS *Frobisher* steaming past with all hands lining the deck, giving the troops three cheers as the ship's horns 'whooped' over their heads.

After a few more days at sea they reached Port Tewfik (now known as Port Suez) in Egypt. This, they were informed, was where they would be disembarking. So it was to be Egypt, thought Mash. The news did not make that much difference to him; Africa, India, they were all foreign lands to him. The only thing he knew about Egypt was that it had pyramids and it was hot. Now that the time had come, Mash was not even sure he wanted to leave the ship; he did not know what lay ahead, only that it was not going to be pleasant.

Not everyone felt the same; there was almost a stampede to get ashore. Kipper actually lay down and kissed the ground. Mash did feel good to be standing on ground that did not shift beneath his feet, but the heat soon stripped him of any pleasure he found in being on land. It had been hot on the ship, but it seemed to hit him like a fist when he went ashore. Through this heavy heat they were herded from the bustling dock to the train station. They were left to wait, for how long they did not know. At first they were formed up, trying not to stare obviously at the alien world around them, the dry landscape and the dark-skinned men and women looking at them with blank curiosity. As time dragged itself slowly on they started to droop. An hour went by and then another. They fought over the smallest piece of shade, desperately trying to get cool.

Finally, after three hours, the train arrived. It was not much cooler than the station but at least it moved. As they travelled across the countryside the men looked out of the windows, their noses pressed against the glass like curious children. Most had never seen a landscape like it before. The sky seemed to sit right on top of the dusty ground and there was no sign of any green. The people were swathed in cloth, apart from the children who ran around practically naked. When Mash saw his first camel he could barely believe it; it did not look real.

"It must be pot luck picking a woman here," said Gordon to Mash. "They could look like anything underneath those sheets."

Finally the train reached Quassassin Station where they were greeted by their guides. The men had only been in Africa for three weeks but their skin was already a ruddy brown and they looked with amusement at the dishevelled, sweating troops. They took them in trucks to El Tahag, where they would be based, for how long Mash did not know.

They disembarked, exhausted and sweltering, to look on the bleak stretch of sand where they would be staying. The only things that punctuated the landscape were the scabby tents and latrine blocks. The unit stood staring at the place where they would be living, bugs flying lazily around their heads.

"Christ," said Kipper. "I miss the ship."

★ ★ ★

After a few days in El Tahag Mash decided his first impression was wrong; El Tahag was not bleak, it was worse. The expanse of insect-filled dust left him as flat as the landscape. The sand got everywhere and the ground always seemed to be moving because of the multitude of bugs, Mash jerked and twitched so much that he felt as though he had a nervous tick. But the worst thing was the heat; Mash could not believe the strength of it, it was like a physical presence. It was inescapable during the day, with no let up or breath of wind. It made him want to scream, but somehow he managed to keep it in, dragging himself through the day until the night came when it was blessedly cool, though still full of dust and insects. He was sure he would not have been able to cope if the nights were hot. He honestly thought he would have gone mad.

The others were not handling it much better. Daily they forced themselves through training, learning how to live and fight in the desert, whilst pouring with sweat and feeling as though they were going to pass out. The rest of the time they just dropped like flies, lying wherever they could. Being mainly Scottish, they were used to grey skies and drizzle, after a day or two of the incessant glare they could not stand it. Mash swore everyone walked around with a permanent squint.

Mash did not know how the locals could live in it. There were quite a few of them living around the camp, they would often do small jobs for the men, including washing their clothes or dhobying as it was called, which miraculously freed them of any dirt and dust until the troops donned them again. The locals did not seem affected by the heat at all, apparently the clothes they wore kept them cool, though they looked baking to Mash. The Egyptians would watch the troops, sweating in their topees and socks, as they went through their training, and spoke to each other in what Gordon referred to as "damned gobbledygook." They all seemed to gather especially when the division were going through their 'sunburn drill.' For ten minutes each afternoon they would parade with their shirts off and at mercy to the blaring sun. The idea was to gradually tan their skin and get them used to the heat. It worked for most of them, they slowly grew darker, all except Gordon. He suffered terribly from the sun; his pale skin and red hair were no match for the rays. In the brief ten minutes of the sunburn drill he would turn a bright lobster red. He was soon raw and blistered. Whenever he had free time he would lay in whatever shade he could find with his eyes closed. When Mash asked him what he was thinking of he answered snow-covered mountains.

On their third evening in El Tahag, Gordon and Mash sat outside their tents, making the most of the cool night coming and smoking their Victory V's, the strong cigarettes they were issued which were rumoured to be made of Indian tree trunks. They had both taken their hated topees off and Mash's hair was plastered to his head with dried sweat. They sat panting like dogs, feeling the first fingers of coolness as the sun lowered on the horizon. Gordon examined his peeling arms.

"I reckon this is what hell's like," he said. "Hot, painful and unrelenting."

"Why couldn't we have been stationed somewhere cold?" asked Mash.

"Like the Arctic," said Gordon.

"Yes," said Mash. "Except I don't think the Arctic is involved in the war."

"I don't care," said Gordon. "Imagine snow right now."

"And ice," said Mash.

Jackson, one of the soldiers who had been in El Tahag for several weeks, heard them as he walked past their tent. He stopped and grinned at them.

"You boys think this is hell?" he said. "Just you wait until you get gyppy tummy. And you will get it, everyone does. Then you'll realise this is just a warm up."

The man walked away.

Mash and Gordon looked at each other; ever since they had reached El Tahag all the talk had been of gyppy tummy. It was a form of dysentery that was carried by insects and was said to be atrocious. None of the section had caught it yet but it was only a matter of time.

Mash managed to avoid it for a few more days. Not so lucky were Drillbit and Gasman, who succumbed the next day; they were swiftly followed by Callum and Kipper. Mash was starting to hope he was immune; he had seen the look of the other lot and did not fancy catching it. But on the sixth day it got him.

He woke in the middle of the night, sweating and nauseous and with an overwhelming urge to empty his bowels. He had to sprint for the latrines and only just made it in time. He stayed in the cubicle for the whole night, feeling as though all his insides were being ejected from his body. He was so weak he could barely move and whenever he did he thought he would be sick.

He was not the only one afflicted; Gordon and Rod eventually caught it as well. One evening he, Gordon, Rod and Kipper were in latrines next to each other. The smell coming out of the stalls was evil.

Mash leant his throbbing head against the wall. He could hear Gordon groaning in the other stall.

"I feel like my whole stomach is trying to come out of my arse," said Gordon. "I must have done something terrible to be punished like this."

"We must all be sinners then," Mash called through the wall.

"I didn't think anything could be worse than the seasickness," came Kipper's weak voice.

"We should set up house in these damn things," shouted Rod from the other stall. "We spend enough time here."

It lasted for four days; four long days mainly spent looking at the toilet wall. Mash was so thirsty all the time; he felt dried up from the inside out, but the water ration of one and a half gallons a day each never seemed enough. He had no appetite for food but he tried to smoke; unfortunately the illness made the cigarettes taste disgusting.

Finally, after what seemed a lifetime, the illness passed. Mash felt as though a devil had left him.

He felt better just in time because they had to be present for a number of inspections. The first was for a visit from General Wavell on the 19th August, who marched up and down the row of dusty, sunburnt soldiers and announced them raw but promising. The next inspection was from none other than Winston Churchill himself on the 22nd. They were lined up as neatly as possible again and waited for Churchill. Finally, he arrived with General Alanbrooke. He was sitting in an open-top car which drove up and down the lines. He waved his famous victory sign and puffed on his usual cigar. The men cheered as he went through. He was smaller than Mash thought he would be. It was odd to see the familiar face there in reality. It was like when he had first seen the London Bridge after seeing so many pictures of it, he could not quite believe it was real. But he cheered with the rest, all the while remembering what Callum had said back on the *Duchess*, about how he hoped somebody knew what they were doing. Mash sure hoped Churchill did.

# CHAPTER EIGHT

# CAIRO

After ten long days at El Tahag they were finally transferred again. At HQ there was concern that Rommel, who by this time was only fifty miles from Cairo, would use the upcoming full moon to launch an attack. As part of the defensive measures Wimberley was given responsibility for the defence of Cairo itself and as a result he moved the division to positions covering the south and west approaches to the capital. The Camerons found themselves moved to a patch of desert lying astride the main Mena – Cairo road. After the featureless desert of El Tahag the view was stunning; by day they could see the pyramids reaching to the sky in all their glory whilst by night, as they were only five miles from the city of Cairo itself, they were treated to the spectacle of the city lit up in a way that British cities had not been for three years. To Mash the pyramids seemed too big to be real. Cairo had always held a fascination with him; the whole country of Egypt conjured up romantic adventure stories and tales of mummies from his childhood. But so far Egypt had only brought him heat stroke, bugs and dysentery. Common sense told him that Cairo would be much of the same, but he still gazed at the pyramids and the lights of Cairo whenever he had a spare second, daydreaming about hidden treasures. The others were the same; they were desperate for leave.

Mash did not know when, if ever, they would be allowed time off. As usual they spent most of their time training. Mash did not think it could get any more intense but he was wrong, they were immersed in desert survival. Given the division was new to the desert and, unbeknown to them, would fight between Australian 9th and New Zealand 2nd Divisions, both of whom were very experienced in desert fighting having been part of the desert war since the outbreak of hostilities, they found themselves partnered with their ANZAC colleagues so that they could pass on their knowledge. It was an immediate success and the Highlanders naturally clicked with their teachers, particularly the Aussies.

In addition to ongoing field exercises they started to learn from the Aussies about desert survival skills including how to live on the minimum of water by only drinking in the morning and evening, to use a Benghazi burner – a fire made from sand and petrol, to check for scorpions before putting your boots on in the morning, that if your weapon was to fire it had to be completely free of oil and that the British four-gallon non-returnable tin petrol container had many uses but carrying petrol was not one – for that a captured German 'Jerry' can was infinitely better. These tricks of the trade were vital lessons not taught as part of the military manoeuvres but which were essential to living in the desert. It was also just the beginning of the relationship between the Highlanders and the Aussies, one that would stretch to the battle and beyond and which was critical in bringing the Highlanders up to speed in as little time as possible.

Another change was in the colour of the Highlanders. Mash soon found that he was acclimatising to the heat. His skin had become a golden brown thanks to the sunburn drills, even Gordon's red and white body was slowly turning to a tanned colour and his burns were easing.

Mash longed for leave more than ever now that he did not feel like fainting from heat exhaustion all the time. The fact that they were so close to Cairo seemed to taunt him and the lights seemed to draw him in. He had heard great things about the city from the Australians; they talked of the bars, the alcohol and the women all the time.

Women, they soon found out, were easy to acquire with only a small amount of money. Gasman came in to the barracks one evening, his moustache quivering with excitement.

"I've just been talking to Norton, one of the Aussies, and he told me about the brothels in Cairo," he said in a stage whisper, despite the fact that it was only the section in the room.

"Lovely," said Rod.

"Norton is almost as much of a dirty bastard as you Gasman," said Mash. He was writing to his mother and was trying to make the strain of desert life sound appealing.

"No seriously," said Gasman. "These places are great, there're hundreds of girls and it hardly costs anything to have a go."

"Must admit," said Niall. "It's been a while."

"Some of us managed to get some in Cape Town," said Rod, clapping Finnean on the back. Finnean kept his eyes lowered. Gordon signalled at Rod to be quiet; Finnean was still moping about leaving his girl behind and if anyone suggested that what they shared was not the purest of love then the usually laidback boy bristled for a fight.

"Still a long time though," said Kipper, changing the subject.

"A very long time," muttered Drillbit, who had not managed to bag a girl in Cape Town, nor any other time since Mash had known him.

"We should definitely pay one a visit," said Niall.

Gordon, who had been growing steadily redder in the face, could not restrain himself any longer.

"You lot shouldn't go anywhere near those places," he said. "They're disgusting."

"Oh, leave off Gordon," said Niall.

"And it's a sin," said Gordon, with a sense of finality.

"Christ," muttered Gasman.

"So you're saying you're a pure, clean, untouched virgin are you Gordon?" said Niall.

The others laughed and Gordon went even redder.

"I think what Gordon is trying to say is that there's a difference between going out and paying for it, and losing control when rolling around in the hay with... who was it again Finnean?" asked Rod.

"Maggie Young," said Finnean.

"I'm pretty sure that's what God meant," said Rod.

"Alright, alright," said Gordon, cutting through the laughter. "But you're basically right, those places are... are..."

"Dens of iniquity?" said Mash.

"Yes," said Gordon.

"Well you can find a nice Bible group to join Gordon, the rest of us will be sinning our hearts out," said Niall.

"Not all of you, you're not bloody going," said Gordon, pointing viciously at Finnean who rolled his eyes. "Callum won't be going either."

"You are the voice of my conscience Gordon," said Callum who had been listening to the exchange with an indulgent smile on his face.

"And Mash won't be going," said Gordon.

Mash looked up from his letter to find everybody staring at him.

"You won't be going will you Mash?" said Gordon.

Mash did not say anything.

"I'm not sure he's as convinced as you are Gordon," said Gasman.

"Mash, you can't be serious," said Gordon, staring at Mash as though he had just punched his grandmother.

"Don't look at me like that Gordon," said Mash. "I don't know what I'll do; I only know it's been a very long time."

"Leave him be Gordon," said Kipper. "He's only human."

Mash was desperate for the subject to change. What he did not tell the others was that the unfinished evening with Harriet in Cape Town had awoken something in him that had been dormant since Colette had died. In short, he was as horny as a bull in a cow field.

"None of this who's doing what matters as we haven't been told we're getting leave yet," said Rod.

"They've got to soon," said Drillbit.

"Please God," said Kipper.

In fact it was only a few days later that leave was announced. Whilst the threat of attack from Rommel still remained, it was decided to grant limited leave for a small number of troops at a time, some to Alexandria and some to Cairo. The section was ecstatic when Rod told them they were to be one of the first groups to go to Cairo.

In the hours until their leave they were like children waiting for Christmas. They dragged themselves through training and found themselves shouted at a lot more than usual as their minds were fixed on the city. All the talk was of Cairo and what they would do, where they would go and how much they would drink. They had built it up to such high standards in their minds that Mash worried slightly that the real Cairo could not compete with the one of their imagination. But it was only a minor worry, he was just keen to get away from the desert and, if he was honest with himself, he was seriously considering visiting one of the many brothels.

Time eventually dragged itself round to the evening of their leave and they bundled into desert trucks before being driven into the city. The blaring sun was starting to lose its heat and Mash hung out of the truck, trying to catch a breath of air.

The scene changed as they drove; shacks started to sprout in the never-ending flatness of the desert, single at first then gradually they grew closer together. Soon these buildings changed to brick and they doubled, tripled in number until there was no sand to be seen, only buildings, everywhere, packed as close together as possible. But there seemed to be even more people than houses, they covered the city, talking, walking, living. Vendors shouted at them as they went by, waving their wares at them. Trams rushed past, oblivious of pedestrians. The smell of the city was overpowering, it was not one scent but several; meat, Mash was not sure what kind, people and animals. And over all of that was the smell of the Nile; the great river oozed with life and sewage. The stench infiltrated the whole city, mixing with the other scents to create the smell of Cairo. It was not pleasant, but it was not repulsive. It stamped itself on Mash's nasal hairs; it was a smell he would never forget.

Eventually the trucks pulled up and they were let loose on the city. They wanted to go to the pyramids but they decided it was too late. Gasman and Niall suggested finding the brothel straight away, but the others wanted to relax and most of all get clean. Mash felt as though he had been covered in sand for centuries, sand that the pathetic showers at the barracks could not shift. The Australians had all told them to go to one of the public baths. Mash did not particularly like the idea of stewing in hot water when the heat was still strong, but his mind was soon changed when he sank into the steaming liquid. It seemed to relax every tired muscle in his body.

The bath made Mash's limbs heavy and he fought the urge to sleep; he had not come to Cairo to sleep. He and the rest of the section, now clean, combed and in their best gear, set out in search of a bar. Gasman and Niall were chomping at the bit to go to a brothel, but Mash felt he needed several very strong drinks before he ventured there. He was still not sure he wanted to do it; on the one hand he had Niall egging him on and on the other he had Gordon bristling with silent disapproval, like his own personal angel and devil. He just did not know which one was which.

★ ★ ★

Like moths, they headed towards the brightest lights. Mash had practically forgotten what neon lights looked like after blacked-out Britain. Everywhere they flashed, advertising alcohol, dice and girls. The lights fired the men up, there seemed to be an energy pumping through the town, one with a slightly desperate tinge, people trying to pack living into the short days they had spare, and other people trying to make as much money from them as possible.

First they ate, not caring how much money they spent. Mash ordered steak, or at least what the menu said was steak but Mash suspected that a donkey or camel that was getting too old had paid the ultimate price. It did not matter, anything was better than Army rations and he wolfed it down. After they had paid, tipping generously, they headed to a bar. Mash did not register the name; he just wanted to get a drink inside him.

The beer was delicious; everything seemed to taste better in Cairo. He was on his second one and was chatting to Kipper when he noticed that Gasman had left the group and was talking in an undertone to an airman, who was also on leave. As he watched, Gasman patted the man on the back and walked back to Mash and the others. He signalled to them all to gather round in a furtive manner that Mash felt drew more attention to them than if he had just spoken normally.

"The Brylcream boy told me the best area to go," he whispered to the others.

"For what?" asked Finnean.

"You know," said Gasman, opening his eyes wide.

"He means brothels," said Niall.

Gasman shushed him.

"Gasman, you're happy to go plough some obliging lady of the night but you can't say the word brothel out loud," said Rod.

The others laughed and Gasman smiled amiably.

"There's a street called Berka which has the best ones," said Gasman. "And the cheapest," he added; Gasman did not like to spend a penny more than he needed to. Mash was actually surprised that he was prepared to part with any cash at all on this venture; clearly he was desperate.

"Well I'm more than ready," said Niall. "Who's coming?"

"Count me in," said Kipper, who was practically bouncing on the balls of his feet.

"Me too," said Drillbit who, already drunk, was sniggering uncontrollably.

"I'm going to sit this one out," said Rod, "I don't particularly want my willy to shrivel up."

Niall rolled his eyes. "That's just a rumour."

"Lover boy and I are staying here," said Callum, clapping a hand on Finnean's shoulder.

"Me too," said Gordon, as though anyone had ever been in doubt.

They all turned to look at Mash. He felt their gaze on him like a heat. He looked around at all of them until he reached Gordon; he quickly pulled his eyes away, though he could still feel Gordon's glare steady on him.

God knows he wanted to go, but, apart from the ever present memory of Colette, he was also worried about disease. They had all been given a rather graphic leaflet about VD and he did not fancy catching it.

As though reading his mind, Niall patted his pockets and winked at Mash.

"Got you covered," he said.

Mash was relieved, but he still felt like a schoolboy being

pressured into something. But that was a part of it, he did not want to come all the way to Cairo and not visit the famous brothels, he wanted to at least say that he had seen them.

"Oh screw it," he said. He downed his drink in one swallow and slammed the glass on the counter.

"I'm in."

Kipper and Gasman cheered while Niall grabbed him and steered him after Drillbit who was already out of the door. Mash grinned, but he did not look back at Gordon, though he could imagine his expression.

They walked through the streets, guided by Gasman, who was following directions that the airman had given him. Mash walked quietly among the others. He had only had two drinks and, though he could feel them starting to take effect, he was not sure it was enough to go through with it. He had wanted to go with the others, it was all a big joke that way, but now they were going he wished he was by himself. It did not mean anything to the others, but though he tried to convince himself that it was not a big deal, he knew he was kidding himself. This would be the first time he had had sex since Colette. He felt guilt rush over him. In his head he tried to justify himself to Colette; it was better this way, a meaningless coupling, he was just fulfilling a natural urge. He thought about turning back and going to the brothel at another time. But when could he do it when there was no one around? Sneak in during the day for an afternoon session? He doubted the places were open during the day, the girls needed their rest. Plus, he could not do it in the light of day, it seemed much seedier.

Mash was jarred out of his thoughts by Niall clamping his arm around him.

"You look like you're being dragged to the hangman's noose," said Niall.

Mash smiled apologetically. Niall, who was already fairly drunk, continued.

"It's alright Mash," he said, his grip like steel. "It's been too long for all of us. We all need to get our end away."

"Amen to that," said Drillbit, who looked positively feverish.

"If we ever get there," said Niall to Mash. "Hey Gasman, you're getting us lost," he yelled.

Gasman was looking up at the buildings around him as though there would be a giant arrow pointing the way.

"Maybe we shouldn't have turned down this street," he muttered.

"For Christ sake," said Kipper. "Just ask someone."

"We can't ask a member of the public the way to a brothel," said Gasman in a high-pitched whisper.

"Why not?" said Kipper. "It's probably where everyone's going anyway."

"Because, because you just don't talk about it," said Gasman, looking around him warily.

"Christ Gasman, you sound like an Englishman," said Niall. "No offence Mash."

"None taken," said Mash.

"I'm asking someone," said Kipper. He walked away before Gasman could stop him and approached a couple of nearby soldiers. Mash watched with amusement as Gasman pretended not to know Kipper, while Kipper spoke, gesticulating emphatically to show where he wanted to go. Eventually he sauntered back again, grinning at them.

"I know where we're going," he said.

"Lead on MacDuff," said Niall.

With Kipper navigating they managed to backtrack and find the place. Mash was surprised; he did not know what he had expected but not the large, four-story house. It was clearly quite old and had probably once been a grand and impressive structure. But now most of the windows were boarded up and there was a general air of decay. It would not have looked out of place in a horror film. This contrasted with the flashing fluorescent lights on the outside, advertising to everyone the wares within.

They walked through the front door and into a long corridor. The damp smells of mould and urine immediately hit Mash, filling him with anxiety and distaste. He wrinkled his nose and looked at the others.

"Don't worry about the smell," said Niall.

"I do worry Niall," said Mash. "I worry very much, why does it stink of piss?"

"Don't be such a prude," said Niall.

"It does reek," said Kipper.

Niall held the bridge of his nose in the manner of a despairing teacher.

"Who cares about the smell," he said. "It's an old house, it smells funny. There are naked girls upstairs!"

He gestured along the corridor where there was a narrow staircase at the end with a light glowing at the top and the sound of voices.

Mash glanced at Kipper, but they followed Niall anyway; as he said, there were naked women, and they tended to outweigh most things. The staircase complained with a loud creaking that sounded like the groan of a dying soldier as they walked up. Mash was worried his feet would go straight through the floorboards.

At the top of the stairs they came out into a dimly lit hallway. There was a small desk with what looked like photographs scattered across it. Behind it stood a woman who seemed to be as wide as she was tall. Mash could not see much of her except for her enormous and rather drooping chest which flopped on the desk.

Beyond her, the corridor stretched on into darkness, Mash could not see the end. There were several doors leading off it and there were dozens of men, nearly all soldiers, standing in queues outside the doors.

The large woman on the reception brought a chunky arm up and took a pull of a cigarette. Her mouth and eyes were caked in makeup and tracks of orange foundation ran into the many folds in her neck.

"She's just your type," Kipper whispered to Gasman and they all sniggered like school boys until the woman stared them down. Such was the power of her gaze that they quietened and shuffled up to the desk in silence.

The woman's scowl suddenly broke into a wide smile, showing tobacco-stained teeth and creating several extra cheeks.

"You here for good time," she said. It was not a question but a statement.

They nodded, no one speaking.

"You pick girl," she said and gestured at the photographs. Mash looked down and saw that the pictures were all of naked women. He presumed these corresponded with girls behind the many doors. They were all standing full on, so everything was displayed. Some were attempting to pose in an alluring manner, others just stood straight, their faces expressionless. The men pored over them. Mash had expected them all to be young and look like pin-ups but, although some did, most were fairly ordinary-looking. A few were out right podgy and there were a couple that were quite clearly past their prime. Mash was drawn to the younger, pert ones.

While they were looking at the pictures one of the doors opened and a couple of women came out. One was only wearing a very thin and grubby-looking negligee and the other was completely naked.

Out of nowhere a little scrap of a girl, only about eight years old, scuttled up to them with a cigarette packet. The women both took one without looking at the girl, then chatted in their language, looking for all the world as though they were gossiping over the garden fence. Mash watched the little girl scurry back away, her dirty feet picking up more dust on the floorboards. She paused just before she reached the door and Mash caught a glimpse of her face; it already had the expressionless look of the girls in the photos.

Mash's eyes lingered on the door where the girl had disappeared. Her presence had shocked him, though he remembered that some of the other men had told him about children like her. They served in the place, taking messages from the madam, towels, disinfectant and cigarettes to the girls. In a few years, Mash did not want to think how few, they would become one of the earning girls. He felt a prickling of unrest in his stomach; it irritated him; he did not want to think about the plight of these young girls, he was there to get some satisfaction and that was all he wanted to think about.

Mash looked again at the two women who were now sitting quietly, one picking her fingernails while the other blew smoke at the ceiling. Mash was taken aback by their stark nudity, especially as all the women he had seen so far in the country were covered in layers. The women did not seem to care; they completely ignored the men around them. Mash presumed they must be on a break and did not blame them for wanting to ignore the clients. Mash stared at them, for some reason their bare flesh was not arousing. It was too blatant.

One of the girls slowly turned her head in his direction and Mash quickly snapped his gaze away. He wondered why he did not want to be caught staring; of all places this was alright to do it in.

Mash turned his attention back to the photographs and the others who were bickering over who the best-looking one was.

"God Gasman, I thought you only went with dogs because you couldn't get the lookers. Why are you picking one of the old birds?" said Niall.

"I'm going for experience," said Gasman. "The older ones know all the good tricks."

"I don't care which one," said Drillbit. "Let's get going."

Drillbit picked his woman, one of the better-looking ones, and paid his money. He went to queue up at the appropriate door. The others did the same and scattered to their individual doors but still called insults to each other across the room. Mash picked a girl at random, luckily a looker, and paid the woman. He went to the appropriate door. He did not pick the same one as any of the others; even though he knew the girls would have seen dozens of men before him already that night, there was something unsavoury about going straight after someone he knew. Still, he could not help notice that the man before him was very tall. He shifted on his feet and stood a little straighter. Did these girls compare? Probably. He told himself not to be so stupid. He was here to get his rocks off with an attractive girl and that was it.

Mash looked around the rest of the room. He was not an overly cleanly person but the building seemed ingrained in dirt. He could not see into the corners as the lights were so dim, but what he could see of the floorboards was covered in dust and grit that just got moved about as people walked over it. The place stank of damp, plus a mix of stale sweat, disinfectant and the overwhelming smell of sex. Mash felt the lust leaking out of him. When he saw something small scuttle into one of the dark corners he shuddered.

His door opened and a man came out, avoiding everyone else's eye. The tall man in front of him walked into the room.

"You're up next Mash," Niall called over to him.

Mash attempted to smile back. He suddenly really wanted to be anywhere else. He did not know why but he felt as nervous as he had as a gangly seventeen-year-old with his first time with Flora Mackintosh in her parents' garden shed. Unfortunately, the teenage lust that had powered him that day did not seem to be rearing its head. As the door shut behind the man Mash caught a glimpse of a woman sprawled on the bed; she heaved herself up on her elbows and wiped the hair out of her face, barely getting a breather before the next customer. Mash kept looking even after the door had shut. He continued to look until his attention was caught by the sound of laughter. He turned to see a group of men by one of the doors, gathered around something on the wall. They seemed to be clamouring to see. One of them moved and Mash saw that one man had his eye to the wall; he was peering through a hole.

"What are they looking at?" asked Gasman.

"What do you think?" said Kipper.

The others snickered and Mash realised that the men were watching their friend through a hole in the wall. A couple of them were cheering.

"Jesus," Mash muttered to himself. He looked around the corridor and realised that there were holes next to every door. There was no way anyone was going to watch him.

As Mash was making plans to block the peep hole, a man came out of the door in front of Drillbit. Drillbit, smiling smugly, entered the door. Kipper, Gasman and Niall cheered him and Mash tried to join in.

Drillbit had barely been in there a minute when Niall snuck over to the hole by Drillbit's door.

"Oh don't," said Mash.

"You know you want to look," said Kipper, who followed Niall, pushing him out of the way. He put his eye to the peep hole then let out a guffaw.

"He gets stuck in quickly," said Kipper.

Gasman followed them over, pretending to be disapproving but really wanting to get an eyeful.

"Christ he's skinny," said Niall. "Come and have a look Mash."

Mash did not know why he stepped forwards, perhaps

because he was hoping to catch some of the others' casual amusement. He put his eye up to the wall; he could not see much at first but then, swivelling his gaze, he caught the full sight of Drillbit's scrawny behind bobbing up and down.

Mash pulled away from the wall; whatever trace of lust he had had left was obliterated by that sight.

"I can't do this," he said.

"Don't take it so seriously Mash," said Kipper, laughing at Gasman peering through the hole.

From the corner of his eye Mash saw his door open and the tall man walk out. He turned to see the man go and join his friends, grinning. As the door swung shut he saw the girl sit up on the bed again. She grabbed the sheet from the mattress, calmly wiped herself between the legs, then arranged herself on the bed again.

"I definitely can't do this," said Mash.

He turned and headed for the door. The others shouted after him.

"Come on Mash," said Niall. "If Drillbit can do it then you can."

But Mash just waved at them as he headed towards the stairs. As he passed the reception desk he glanced at the woman and saw she was grinning at him with ill-concealed distain.

"No refunds," she said.

Mash, who had not been going to ask, ignored her and hurried down the rotten stairs.

He walked out of the door as fast as he could and carried on down the street until he was far away from the urine-soaked house. Once he had turned a corner and was on a main street he stopped outside a building and leant against the wall. He watched for a couple of minutes at life passing him. Soldiers swarmed the streets, like ants, everywhere you turned you were bound to step on one. The Egyptian vendors were shouting their wares at them and trying to tempt passing men with their roasted meats.

Mash fumbled in his pocket for a cigarette. Pulling one out he lit it, took a deep drag and closed his eyes. The bricks were cool through the fabric of his shirt; he let his shoulders relax. He stared up at the sky, illuminated with the fluorescent glow, and the corner of his mouth twitched once, then he broke into a smile.

*Christ, how precious am I? The lads will never let me forget this.*

But he had no urge to go back into the building. Still smiling to himself he slowly walked along the road, heading in the direction he hoped the rest of the section was.

Gordon did a double take when Mash sauntered into the bar and sat down beside him.

"Christ," he said. "That was quick."

Mash signalled to the barman.

"I didn't do it," he said.

He did not look at Gordon but he could feel his friend's face break into a smile.

"Well done," Gordon said, clapping Mash on the back with surprising strength. "I knew you'd see the error of your ways."

"It wasn't that," said Mash. "The place was like a conveyor belt and it was filthy."

Gordon's grin slipped a bit.

"Well at least you didn't go through with it," he said. "I'll get you this." He pulled out his wallet to pay for Mash's beer.

Mash took a long pull of the cool liquid then let out a belch.

"It was the sight of Drillbit's bare arse that turned me right off," he said.

"What?" asked Gordon.

Mash explained about the peep hole.

"Bloody backwards country," muttered Gordon.

"Drillbit's arse must be enough to put anybody off sex," said Callum who had been listening. "He's going to be strutting around like the bloody cock of the walk now."

"Stick with us celibates Mash," said Rod, who appeared at his elbow with Finnean in tow. "We may be frustrated as hell but we'll all go to heaven."

Mash grinned and downed his drink.

"Another," he said to the barman.

They had more drinks then moved on to another bar down the road. Mash could not really see the point but the others wanted to visit as many places as possible. Mash just wanted to get drunk. He felt a strange energy in him. He was not usually one to start a fight, but that evening he felt a force pulsing through him that was putting him on edge; everything seemed more in focus than normal, everything was more funny, more exciting but also more irritating. It was frustration he knew, from not going through with it at the brothel. He found himself getting irritated by the crowds, especially the RAF boys who were out on mass. There was always a rivalry between the Army and RAF. Mash did not usually get involved in it, but that evening when Morgan, a bloke from another unit, shouted insults at the RAF lot, Mash joined in the jeers.

"Calm down Mash," said Gordon. "Isn't it usually you telling me to chill out?"

"I don't know," said Mash, looking down into his drink. "I just want to get annihilated."

"Well you're well on the path to it," said Rod.

"'S'cuse me," said a voice. They turned to see an Australian leaning against the bar addressing them. Mash vaguely recognised him from the base but he had not trained with him.

"Couldn't help overhearing," he said, his accent lifting the ends of his words up. "If you're wanting to get that drunk you should try Zebeeb."

"Christ, I've heard of that," said Rod.

"I haven't," said Gordon. "What is it?"

"It's a bit like Ouzo," said Rod.

"I'm still none the wiser," said Gordon.

"I've had it," said Mash, he only remembered the lingering liquorice taste from a party five years ago as he had been so hungover the next day.

"It's lethal," he said. "It's perfect."

"Five Zebeebs," he said to the barman. "Do you want one?" he added, turning to the Australian.

"Kind of you thanks," he said. He had a wide grin, the sides of his mouth seeming to be elasticated, and he had the ruddy skin of all the Antipodeans Mash had seen. He was tall and slim but wiry, with a mop of black hair on top.

Mash passed them all drinks.

"Thanks," said the Australian again. "I'm Jack by the way, Jack Williams."

Everyone introduced themselves and shook hands.

"Bottoms up," said Rod.

They all downed their glasses.

"Jesus," said Gordon. "It tastes like aniseed. I want another."

They had several more Zebeebs, each time the liquorice taste getting easier to swallow. Jack joined them and so did some of his friends, but by that point Mash was too far gone to remember names. They stood, buffeted by the sea of people around them. Mash and the others were constantly knocked about by the crowd but Jack was like a reed; he rolled with the waves but he stood grounded. Mash was not sure how Jack did it; he himself was a few inches taller than Jack and definitely broader, but Jack seemed to remain unbuffeted. Mash liked him immediately, he seemed so laidback; a reeling drunk bumped into him and slopped his drink down Jack's front, and instead of taking this as a reason to start a fight Jack righted the man and patted him on the head. The bemused man stumbled away.

Gordon liked Jack too; he seemed to take to all the

Australians, believing them to be "practically Scottish." Mash felt a slightly childish annoyance that Gordon took to Jack and the rest so quickly, yet it had taken a lifesaving event to get him to like Mash. But then, thought Mash, he had not exactly been friendly, unlike Jack who seemed to ooze easiness. I used to be like that, thought Mash, I was not always so resistant. He realised how bad he had been, how introverted when he had first joined the unit. He had not wanted to interact with anyone, it was only really Rod he had made any effort with, and that was because Rod had not given up on him. He looked at Gordon and the others and realised that, without knowing it, he had been getting better. It was easier to be amongst people, not the tiring effort it had seemed before, when Colette had died.

He was not sure how long they stayed there or how many drinks they had but he gradually grew drunker, as did the others, especially Rod; the Zebeeb seemed to affect him the most. Soon he was slumped in a corner, his eyes glazed over and his words running into each other.

"We should probably get him back," said Callum, who was swaying himself.

"Yeah, I think I'm done for the night too," said Finnean.

"Don't go yet," said Mash. "It's only one o'clock."

"I'm done in mate," said Callum. "And he can't stand." He nodded at Rod who had his head on the bar.

Jack's two friends wanted to go too.

"I'm still awake," said Jack.

"Me too," said Gordon. "Let's go somewhere else."

"Good plan," said Mash.

Callum and Finnean got Rod up between them, taking an arm each, and supported him out of the bar. Rod's legs scrabbled, trying to gain a hold, like a spider on roller skates. Jack's friends left after them, in a similarly unsteady manner.

Jack, who did not seem in the least tired and had only got

a slightly glazed look from all the alcohol he had consumed, suggested they went to the Blue Nile Cabaret.

Even Mash had heard of that place, it was legendary amongst the Australians. Luckily, it lived up to his expectations.

As soon as he walked in to the place he was blinded, by sequins. There were so many girls in tiny costumes; the little surface area they had were covered in sparkles.

"Jesus," said Gordon. "They should name this place temptation."

"Hold on to that crucifix Gordon," muttered Mash.

Mash did not usually enjoy those types of places; he very much liked the girls but he was not fussed about the over-the-top glamour, but he still had that hyped-up feeling and he wanted to do something. This place seemed right, it was the centre of everything and he wanted to be in it. The warmth, the music and the sparkles melted away the memory of the dank brothel. Watching the girls dancing on stage, their lined stockings leading up to paradise, he felt the lust come flooding back. He did not know if it was the Zebeeb but he felt confident. Maybe he could even get lucky without the aid of money.

They got drinks from the bar and were soon joined by a gaggle of showgirls. Deep beneath the layers of drink Mash knew the women were paid to talk to them, but he did not care. This is what he had wanted when he went to the brothel, not dead-eyed women with questionable hygiene habits, but smiling, interested girls wearing just enough to excite.

He made the acquaintance of a blonde standing next to him. The alcohol had loosened his tongue and he was soon explaining what it was like to be the only Englishman in a Scottish section and other nonsensical inanities that he would later forget. The girl seemed to find him incredibly funny and Mash had to stop himself from staring at her chest as she giggled. Gordon was faring much the same; he was talking to a dancer almost twice the height as himself and he looked like a puppy eyeing a bone. If he had a tail it would have been wagging.

Mash was chatting away to the girl, the sweet and above all clean scent emanating from her skin making him dizzy, when he saw something that threw a bucket of icy water over his libido. Through the blur of faces behind the blonde's head he saw one that was completely still and looking directly at him. It was Mitchell. He was standing a few feet away from him and was with a couple of his goons. Mash did not know how long Mitchell had been there; he had not seen him come in. Mash looked back at him, neither man moved, neither smiled.

Mash's concentration was broken by a tug on his arm.

"Do you want another?" Gordon shouted over the noise of the crowd.

Mash nodded distractedly then looked back towards Mitchell, but he had turned away and was talking to Douglas.

"What are you staring at?" asked Gordon.

"Mitchell's here," said Mash.

Gordon stood on his tiptoes and peered in the direction Mash was looking.

"Ah Christ," he said. "I can't be arsed with him tonight. Just ignore him."

Mash nodded and turned his attention back to the pretty girl, whose name he had already forgotten. He tried to engage with her but it was as though he could sense Mitchell's presence. It was like an irritation, an itch that he needed to scratch. Though he tried to ignore it, it throbbed painfully in the background. He thought of Gordon's bloodied face after Mitchell and his thugs had finished with him, and Peterson's limp. The energy that had been pulsating within him all evening quickened. He stood a little straighter, flexed his knuckles and felt his senses heighten. He knew something was going to happen and he wanted to be ready.

He and the others were standing in front of the bar, not a great place as they were constantly jostled, but none of them suggested moving. As he watched from the corner of his eye, Mash saw Mitchell and his group making their way closer to the bar and to them. Mash pretended to listen to the girl but he really watched Mitchell's progress. He shifted on his feet, squaring up. Mitchell and the others were pushing through the crowds, coming right by them. It looked like they were passing them. But then Douglas rammed into Jack's shoulder. Mash bristled but Jack just steadied himself.

"Everyone wants to dance with me tonight," he said.

Jack smiled but Mash and Gordon did not.

"Watch where you're going," said Douglas.

"Piss off Douglas," said Gordon.

"Yes, run along Dougie," said Jack, still smiling; he seemed to find the situation hilarious. This just seemed to anger Douglas. Mitchell was stood a little behind Douglas, he was not saying anything, just standing with his arms crossed, watching the situation unfold. Mash knew how it was going to end, he could tell from Mitchell's face, he could tell from Gordon's tensing beside him, he could tell from his own fists clenching.

What Mash was not prepared for was Jack's swift upper cut to Douglas' jaw. Neither was Douglas; the blow knocked him backwards and he stumbled to his knees.

"Stay down mate," said Jack, still smiling.

For a moment everyone stood still, all staring at Jack. Then Douglas launched himself into Jack's stomach. Jack dodged and caught him a blow again. Douglas howled and swiped at Jack, catching his ankle and causing Jack to stumble. Gordon leapt on Douglas's back to stop him from rushing Jack, but Wallace grabbed Gordon by the scruff of his neck. Mash rushed forwards to help Gordon but he was blocked by Mitchell. His usual seedy smile was gone, his face serious; he was spoiling for a fight. Perfect, thought Mash. The energy that had been building in him broke and he shot forwards like a coiled spring released. He went to hit Mitchell but Mitchell caught him in the jaw and Mash went reeling backwards. He was only stopped from falling by the sheer number of people in the bar. He pushed himself away from the bodies, ignoring the curses and shouting, dodged under Mitchell's right hook and ran headfirst into his stomach. He felt Mitchell collapse on top of him and they barrelled into the crowd. Mash barely noticed the screams around him, he just focused on Mitchell, who was hammering on his back. He did not realise that their fight, like a spark to a powder keg, had set off the whole bar. Everyone was either throwing punches or trying to make a run for it. The chorus girls were screaming and scrambling away, though some were joining in the fight. But Mash did not care about anyone else, he just wanted to hurt Mitchell, really wanted to hurt him like he had not hurt anyone before. He was acting on pure instinct and his instinct was to fight. Mitchell was the same; they were vicious; wherever they could get a blow they landed it. Mash managed to get on top of Mitchell and slammed his head against the ground, but Mitchell jabbed an elbow into his stomach. They both rolled away, then launched again for another attack. Mash barely felt the pain from his wounds. He felt Mitchell's knee in his ribs and he planted his fist in Mitchell's face again. Not pausing to savour the sweet sting, he lifted his arm for another go, Mitchell struggling, when he felt a hand tugging at his shirt and heard a voice shouting incomprehensible sounds into his ear. He shook the hand off and blocked Mitchell's wild hit. But then he was yanked backwards, away from Mitchell, and this time he heard the voice.

"Mash, for Christ sake, they've called in the military police."

Mash turned his head to see Gordon standing beside him.

"The police Mash!" shouted Gordon. "We've got to go."

Mash looked at Mitchell who was on the floor just a short distance away; he was gathering himself up but he too had realised that something was wrong. Around them there were a lot of men still grappling with each other, but there were now an awful lot trying to head for the door too.

"Come on Mash!" yelled Gordon.

Mash and Mitchell looked at each other again.

"Damn it," said Mash. He scrambled to his feet. Mitchell did the same and in a second he melted into the crowd.

Standing up, Mash could see what looked like hundreds of military police pouring through the door.

"There's got to be a back way out," said Jack, who was behind Gordon.

"Try behind the bar," said Mash.

They pushed towards the bar, each keeping a firm grip on each other. The heat and noise were building. People were now fighting to get away from the police, throwing others in the way to save themselves. Bodies pressed against Mash as he pushed onwards, he fought to get through, using his elbows mercilessly. They finally reached the bar only to find the few barmen left were holding bats. Mash tried to approach one but the man took a swipe at him.

"We just want to leave," Mash shouted, trying to be heard, but the man brandished the bat at him like a sword.

"Shit!" Mash shouted.

He turned to the others, only to see that Jack had been grabbed by a policeman. Jack struggled but the man clubbed him in the stomach and he doubled over.

Gordon made a lunge at the policeman, shouting obscenities. Mash thoughtlessly jumped after him. He later realised that there was no way they were going to fight their way out, they should have just gone quietly, they may have sustained less bruises. But the adrenaline was pumping and Mash felt a rage, fuelled by alcohol, that was animalistic.

He and Gordon fought the police as fiercely as they would the Germans. But they were majorly outnumbered and the military police had truncheons that they used without mercy. Gordon got cracked in the ribs and the back of the leg. Mash saw him go down and a huge policeman literally picked him up and threw him into the back of a van. Mash tried to reach him but he got a clout round the face from another officer's bat. He fell to the floor and hit the back of his head on the road. He yelled in pain but the officers ignored him. Two of them picked him up and forced him into the van; he was closely followed by Jack who was being held by the scruff of his neck. The door clanged shut behind them.

★ ★ ★

Almost immediately the van careered off the kerb. They were all slammed against the side as it turned a corner and Mash swore loudly as he hit the back of his head again.

Gordon groaned on the floor, clutching his ribs.

Mash heard him mumble something.

"What?" said Jack.

"I said they're bastards," said Gordon as he sat up slowly, spitting blood on the floor. "They'd better not have cracked my ribs again."

They were flung around another corner and Mash almost ended up on Jack's lap.

"Where are we going?" said Mash, trying to peer out of the tiny barred window.

"Don't know, the Australian base is probably the nearest," said Jack.

"Shit," said Gordon. "What do you think our punishment will be?"

Mash exhaled deeply. "I feel punished already."

"That was just a light beating," said Jack. "The military police don't usually hold back that much."

Mash clutched his forehead; it did not feel like holding back.

"What do you think we'll get then?" asked Gordon, driving them back to the point.

"I don't know," said Mash. They went round another corner and Mash gripped on to the seat. His stomach rolled with the van and he started to feel the adrenaline drain out of him.

"It's not fair, they can't do this," said Gordon.

"I reckon they can," said Mash.

Gordon suddenly sprang up from the floor and launched himself at the cabin of the van.

"You can't do this," he shouted through the bars. "We're British citizens!"

Mash looked at Jack, who rolled his eyes.

"Leave it now Gordon, alright," Mash called.

"They can't cart us off like this," said Gordon.

"Why?" asked Jack. Yawning widely, he leant back against the side of van.

Gordon looked round at him, "What do you mean why? They just can't."

"I see," said Jack.

Gordon squinted at him, trying to figure out if he was taking the piss or not.

"We were fighting," said Mash, rubbing his fingers across his forehead. "It's not like we were innocent bystanders."

Gordon pushed himself away from the wall and came to sit next to them, swaying slightly as he landed.

"They started it," he said. "We were minding our own business."

"I believe I threw the first punch though," said Jack through another yawn.

"Yeah but Douglas was winding you up," said Gordon. Then he turned to Jack, his tone changing. "That was an impressive punch, I didn't see it coming."

"Neither did Douglas," said Mash.

"The expression on his face," laughed Gordon.

"I do what I can," said Jack, smiling.

"No, seriously," said Gordon. "Where did you learn to hit like that? You don't look like you have it in you."

"Well no offence but neither do you," said Jack.

Mash laughed and Gordon gave a reluctant smile.

"Small but powerful," he said.

"You're punching above your weight," said Mash to Jack.

"I grew up on a sheep farm in the outback," said Jack. "A hard life and I learnt a lot."

Mash nodded but then leant his head back against the wall; he felt sick but he tried to swallow it down.

"You were off like a rocket," said Jack, turning to Mash. "Looked like you and that fella had some previous."

Gordon snorted.

"You could say that," said Mash, pressing his palms to his aching eyes.

"The man's a tosser," said Gordon.

Mash and Gordon related their dealings with Mitchell to Jack. This took some time and by the end all three were flagging in energy and spirits.

"We're going to be for it," said Gordon. "And it's all Mitchell's fault."

"I bet he got away," said Mash. "He always squirms out of everything."

Gordon agreed but Jack did not say anything. They turned to see that he had drifted off to sleep, his head lolling on his chest.

"How on earth can he sleep at a time like this?" said Gordon, staring incredulously.

Mash squinted at Jack; he envied him; all he wanted to do was fall asleep; the adrenaline had seeped out of him and his whole body felt heavy. But he was worried he may have a concussion; if he slept he might not wake up again.

Suddenly the van came to a halt, the shock of which woke Jack up and caused Mash to hit the back of his head again. The doors were flung open and the officers stood with their truncheons brandished, but neither Mash nor the others had the energy left to fight. They got out quietly and shuffled as fast as they could as the officers herded them into what Mash supposed was the Australian MP's base. Mash wondered if the punishment would be more or less brutal than one they would have got from their own forces. But he could not think properly, nor did he particularly care about the punishment. He was starting to feel very sick and it was taking most of his energy not to let it come up.

He was unceremoniously frogmarched in to see the duty officer, Gordon next to him, swaying slightly with a bruise growing around his eye. Jack lagged behind them, trying to keep his eyes open. Mash wondered how bad they looked and tried to care.

They stood before the desk. The duty officer was on the phone, talking earnestly into the handset. The man was probably about Mash's age and had thick black hair that was oiled down close to his head; he was clearly very proud of it. However, at that time his hair seemed to be the last thing on the man's mind. He barely glanced up when they walked in, but continued muttering into the phone.

Mash, who was expecting to get laid into, wondered what had happened. But he only cared in a far-off way; the nausea was rolling in his stomach and the lights in the office seemed to be swirling above his head. He prayed he was not going to throw up; that would probably make his punishment much worse.

The man put the phone down. He sighed deeply and ran

his hands over his oiled hair. Without looking up he beckoned the duty clerk and said in a whisper that barely registered in the befuddled heads of Mash and the others.

"General recall. Get round all the usual hangouts and find everybody you can. All leave cancelled and get them back to their units, I don't care what state they're in!"

The duty officer finally looked up at the motley group in front of him.

"Not another damn bar fight?" he said.

"Yes sir."

The duty officer rubbed his hair again, he could not seem to leave it alone.

"Why does a general recall have to happen on my night?" he muttered to no one in particular.

Mash watched as the man felt around his desk, finally locating a wodge of forms. Mash tried and failed to force his body to stand to attention. He could feel the sweat beading on his forehead.

"You boys have really picked a perfect time," the duty officer said, his pen racing across the papers. "What've you got to say for yourselves?"

Mash tried to answer, but he was terrified that if he opened his mouth he would be sick. But he was saved the trouble.

"To be honest I don't need to know – someone said something or knocked into you before launching an unprovoked attack from which you were forced to defend yourself, I've heard every variation on the theme," the duty officer said almost immediately. "When will you gentlemen realise that there is a war on and that we have better things to do than to clean up after your playground squabbles?"

He continued scribbling so fast that Mash was sure that whatever he was writing was not legible.

It took a while to occur to him but Mash noticed that there seemed to be an awful lot of activity, more so than there normally would be in the small hours of the morning. There were several men about and there was a general sense of activity, even if it was going on behind closed doors, he could sense it.

The duty officer stabbed a full stop on the page then threw his pen down. He finally looked directly at them.

"Well the good news gentlemen is that you could not have timed it better."

Gordon shot a side-long look at Mash; neither of them knew why. But Mash was getting a squirming feeling in his stomach that was separate to the nausea. He sensed that the bad news was going to be very bad.

"The Germans are coming," said the duty officer.

He looked at them all.

"I thought that would sober you up," he said, grinning briefly.

"Looks like Rommel's making his move so the proverbial has hit the fan. All leave is cancelled which means I don't have the time or inclination to deal with you as your behaviour warrants. Get back to your units and get ready to face the Nazi hoards. I can only hope that you make as good a job of fighting the Germans as you do of fighting each other".

Nobody said anything. Mash tried to process the news, but he could barely concentrate. He was sweating all over; he was either going to throw up or pass out.

"You're dismissed, get out of my sight and back to your outfits."

Mash was spun around and marched out of the room and the building. He was not sure how his legs were working; they did not feel connected to his body. His head felt tight and the world was spinning around him. They were halted outside, but the sky still span and he felt the bile rise up his gullet. Throwing himself to one side he just managed to miss the well-polished shoes of the military policeman as he vomited profusely onto the floor.

CHAPTER NINE

# Going up the Blue

It took Mash a while to recover from the night in Cairo. He did not have much memory of getting back to camp or saying goodbye to Jack; in fact, he did not have much memory of the night at all. However, his head and body carried the evidence of the fight for several days. Even when the physical signs disappeared, he still felt the aches and bruises.

Mash and the others did not have much time to reminisce or catch each other up, which Mash was quite glad about; there were a few remarks made about him not being able to follow through at the brothel but not as many as he had expected. The men were too busy packing up and journeying 'up the Blue' to El Hammam.

"Why's it called 'up the Blue'?" asked Finnean as they were bounced and shaken in the back of a lorry, all of them covered in a thick, clay-like dust which had been thrown up from the vehicles further up in the convoy.

"The proper desert is totally featureless, no hills, nothing," answered Rod. "So all you can see is the flat yellow of the desert with a massive expanse of blue sky. Hence the nickname."

"What do you mean 'proper desert'?" said Finnean. "Haven't we been in the proper desert?"

"That was improper desert," said Gasman, chuckling at his own joke.

Rod smiled. "Apparently the desert is going to get a lot more 'proper'," he said. "Which, roughly translated, means a lot worse."

They were quiet the rest of the way, each wondering how it could possibly get any worse, until they finally came to a halt. Once they had clambered out of the trucks they could see what Rod had been talking about. They were awed, and not a little intimidated, by the bleak, endless rock and sand, topped by what felt like a never-ending sky from which the sun beat down on the shelterless ground.

Mash had thought he had been in the proper desert before, but he had been fooling himself. He had not thought it was possible but the insects at El Hammam were worse than any he had encountered yet.

"Can you believe this?" said Mash as he futilely attempted to ward off what felt like a hundred flies and insects.

"If you told anyone back home they'd never believe you," said Rod.

"It's bloody meal times that get me," agreed Gordon. "There're so many of the buggers that they get in your mouth and up your nose. It's impossible to eat anything without getting a mouthful of flies."

"They're rapidly becoming the main form of protein," quipped Mash, although even he did not find it funny.

"I found a scorpion in my boot this morning," grumbled Gordon. "Imagine if I'd put it on without looking. I'm glad the Aussies drilled it into us to check your boots without fail before putting them on."

"It seems to have got even hotter if that's possible," continued Rod, as though it was a game to see who had the most complaints. "I feel like an ant under a magnifying glass."

"And yet tonight we'll freeze our balls off as soon as the sun goes down," added Mash, who still hadn't come to terms with the fact that it could be scorching during the day but freezing at night. "We'll all be wrapped in greatcoats and woollen jumpers, gathered around the nearest fire."

"If it wasn't for the sand, bugs and heat in the day, you'd

think it was late autumn in the Outer Hebrides," said Gordon.

Still, Mash and the others were getting better at keeping cool in the day and warm at night. They were getting better at desert survival in general. When they had first reached Egypt their water allowance had been a gallon and a half a day. With that, most thought it impossible to do all their cooking and washing. If someone had told Mash that he would be surviving the desert heat up at the front with only two pints water ration a day and a diet of hardtack and bully, he would not have believed it possible. They learnt to only drink in the morning and evening. To drink in the heat of the day would mean that they instantly sweated away any fluids and felt worse than before they had drunk anything. The first couple of weeks had been hell on earth, but now he was hardening to desert life, they all were, even Gordon. Not, Mash thought, that he would not dearly love a gallon of water to drink, a break from the flies and a decent latrine, but he was surviving. He only had the occasional bout of gyppy tummy now, which was still just as bad as it had been the first time, but he could cope with it.

They had to persevere. Along with the heat and flies the training had intensified even more. In a war of movement and one dominated by tanks, mines were one of their main activities and they quickly became skilled in laying and lifting them. Their whole camp, known as 'boxes', sat like a small island encircled by a sea of minefields. The only other surroundings were old German tanks and the debris of war from what proved to be the high watermark of the German push east. The tanks lay like shipwrecks, some half sunk in the sand where the wind had blown dunes up against them, and were useful targets during training.

They trained a lot with the Australians of the 9th Division cementing their friendship. This was at all levels and was even recognised by Montgomery who mused "they got on very well, maybe because both of them are slightly uncivilised, and could be trusted." This liaison had major practical benefits as the Aussies brought the Highlanders up to speed on how to live and fight in the desert. One example saw each Highland brigade in turn move into the Australian sector for a week so that they could learn first-hand about being on the front line. Lessons were absorbed on patrolling, creating and camouflaging defensive positions and the need for silence at night along with a complete blackout. In early October it was Rod's section's turn.

They all felt like they were right at the sharp end of the war, there was nothing between them and the Germans but sand and empty space. Mash particularly felt this when he was on guard duty. A couple of days into his week on the frontline he was on guard in a forward position looking out towards the west. It was about two in the morning and he was staring out into the blank desert. He had mixed emotions; part of him was alive to the fact that in front of him was the enemy and the first person he would come across would be trying to kill him, the other part was exhausted from the endless exercises and continued rigors of living in the desert. Trying to keep his heavy eyelids from falling he stared into the night, looking for any sign of movement, but it was difficult to make out anything in the inky darkness. He was intensely relieved when Drillbit came to take over. Drillbit clearly wanted to chat, as usual, but Mash managed to cut him off before he really got going, and set off towards the camp. All he wanted to do was sleep.

The night was cold, as it always was in the desert. There was a slight light from the half-moon overhead and the many stars, just enough to see a few feet ahead. Mash squinted into the gloom and walked forwards. The camp was only a few minutes away and he just had to go in a straight line. He ambled onwards, thinking of nothing much but his bed. But he was irritated by something in his boot. He paused and shook his foot, trying to dislodge it. But the pebble, or whatever it was, stayed resolutely beneath his sole. Cursing quietly to himself he bent down and undid his laces. He fiddled about and managed to pull out the stone. Chucking it to one side he did up his laces then set off again. He continued onwards, his arms wrapped around his body to keep warm. He expected the dark shadow of the camp to loom up before him, but it did not. He continued walking. He must be almost there by now, he thought. But he kept walking and the camp never materialised. He slowed down and looked around him. The flat desert, silvery in the moonlight, spread out from him in every direction looked exactly the same. He could not have gone the wrong way, he thought, he had not been walking long enough.

It did not make sense. How could you get lost walking in a straight line in good weather? Yet he had to admit he was lost. He looked around him but the desert gave no clue as to which was the right way to go. He started to feel a slight panic, a fizzing in his fingertips.

*Maybe when I stopped to get the stone out of my boot I set off a different way.*

He had not thought that he had, but he may have just turned slightly; a few degrees can become miles in the desert. He reached into his pocket to get the compass he had been issued with for times just like this, but when his hand closed over empty air his heart thumped in his chest. He carefully went through every other pocket, but he knew it was not on his person. He remembered he had been looking at it while he was on watch. He must have left it there. He closed his eyes. How could he be so stupid? They had had it drilled into them to have the compass issued for their guard duty with them at all times. Mash had always thought they were exaggerating, but, standing in the empty desert with no idea where he was, he understood completely.

He looked up into the sky and was confronted by a plethora of stars scattered across an unending darkness. If he had not been ill on the ship he would know how to navigate by them, but to him they were just a collection of dots.

*Why didn't I catch up on the lecture, or ask one of the others to brief me?*

He took two deep breaths and tried to calm the fear that now had a tight grip on his stomach. He had not been walking for that long so he could not be too far out of the way. He tried to work out how he had gone off course, if it had been when he was tying his boot then he had only turned slightly. But which way? It was his right foot, maybe he had ended up turning a bit to the right. Was that possible? He felt panic rise. He stood still, frozen to the spot by indecision. Should he just wait and hope someone found him? But he knew he should not just stand still. Again he looked up at the sky and silently prayed that the mess of stars would somehow make sense. But they revealed nothing. Mash stood, staring at the sky, and contemplated the thought that he could die, not from a battle, but from being stupid enough to leave his compass behind in the desert night.

He looked back down at the ground. He had to at least try and get out of this.

If he had turned right then he should just turn a little left and hopefully he would end up going in the right direction. So he turned slightly back and set out with more resolution than he felt.

He carried on forwards slowly. He kept staring into the dark, desperate to see a denser patch of darkness that would mean there was something ahead. He thought he saw something, but he did not know if he was imagining it. He walked closer, it looked like a person.

"Mash?"

Mash froze. He recognised the whispered Australian

voice from somewhere. He dredged through his mind and remembered the tone along with the taste of Zebeebs and a thumping headache.

"Jack?" he said.

"Shhh, keep your voice down or Jerry will want to join in," said the voice in hushed tones.

The dark shape came nearer and developed into the figure of a man. Mash could see in the dark that it was indeed the Australian from the night out in Cairo. Mash felt relief overwhelm him; he had the urge to fling his arms around Jack but he resisted.

"Thank Christ," whispered Mash.

"What are you doing out here?" asked Jack.

"What are you doing out here?" replied Mash.

"I'm on guard duty," said Jack. "It was a good job I recognised you, me mate there was ready to plug you one. We've been following you stroll about for a while."

Mash squinted into the darkness and saw that a few feet off there was a dark figure, another soldier on duty with a rifle that was still pointed towards him. He tried to work out where he was; if he had come over to the Australian side then he must be way out from his camp.

"I got lost," said Mash. "I was heading for camp after guard duty and somehow went the wrong way."

Jack smiled. "You really are lost," he said. "You're heading into enemy lines."

Mash stared into the darkness. "Shit," he said. "I didn't think I'd gone that far off course. I don't understand how it happened."

"Don't you listen to anything they drum into us?" said Jack, lowering his rifle. "One wrong move and you're in the middle of nowhere."

"I know," said Mash. "God, I never really believed it before. I left my compass behind as well."

Jack stared at him.

"I know, don't look at me like that," said Mash. "I'm a bloody idiot."

Jack let out a low sigh.

"I don't think you're getting the best opinion of me," laughed Mash. "You first meet me and we end up in a bar fight, now I almost got myself lost in the desert."

Jack smiled.

"Look, you can find your way back by the stars," he said, pointing up to the sky. "There's nothing to it when you know what you're doing and it can be a lifesaver. The easiest way up here in the northern hemisphere is to find the North Star. Once you've found it you just follow it down to the ground with your finger in a straight line and that's north. From there you can work out wherever you need to go. It's a bit trickier for those of us in the southern hemisphere but there you have it."

Mash looked up at the myriad of stars above him. His despair at ever being able to find a single star amongst all the others must have been written across his face as Jack quickly continued.

"Just look up into the sky. Do you know what the Plough looks like?"

Searching back into his memory Mash could remember being asked a similar question by one of the gamekeepers on the estate. But at the time he was too young to pay attention and, as he grew to know the estate like the back of his hand, he had never needed the skill. It had also made him blasé to the lectures on the ship out. Now, gazing up, he wished he had paid more attention.

"Do you see those seven stars up there," said Jack, pointing to a group of brightly shining stars. "That's the Plough as you pohms call it or the Big Dipper as the Yanks say."

Staring up Mash could clearly make out the constellation

and saw that it looked like an old-fashioned plough, or a ladle with a curved arm.

"Follow the two stars that make up the front edge of the plough about five times their distance and you come to the North Star."

Mash followed where Jack was pointing and it all became clear. The Plough was an easy-to-remember landmark in the sky, from there the North Star was simple to find.

"So that means my camp is over there," said Mash, pointing out into the night.

"Reckon you're right – exactly opposite to the way you were going," replied Jack.

"I owe you a very big drink," said Mash.

Jack grinned, his teeth glinting in the moonlight.

"I'll hold you to it," he said.

"Have you finished teaching your pommie girlfriend the facts of life or are you going to walk her home?" came a gruff voice from behind Jack.

"Don't mind him, he's always cranky when he's cold," said Jack. "Still, I'd best be getting back. Good luck to you."

With a wave he returned to his guard duty. Mash waved back before retracing his steps, using his newfound knowledge to guide him. It was not long before he felt a blast of relief when the camp finally came in to view. He vowed to himself that he would never leave his compass behind again.

Mash slept deeply as soon as he reached his bunk. He was glad for this as Rod briefed the section the following morning that they would be conducting their first patrol by themselves that night: a mine clearance patrol. It was vital to know where the enemy had planted mines, what type and in what numbers. In the never-ending game of cat and mouse, each side would probe the other's minefields whilst the other constantly changed, improved and laid traps for the unsuspecting.

Once dark, the section started to make its preparations.

During the day there was minimal activity as any movement could be seen from miles away and was sure to bring a response. However, at night the balance of the senses changed. Sight was no longer the key as the darkness cloaked movement. Instead, sound became the best form of detection. With no hills, trees or greenery to absorb it, sound carried for miles.

The Aussies had taught the Highlanders the need to make sure that nothing rattled or clanged when they were on patrol. A sort of unofficial uniform had developed over time to reduce the risks; most wore several layers under a jumper and the regulation baggy shorts. This, along with activity and adrenaline, would be enough to keep them warm. Tin helmets were exchanged for a woollen cap, partly so that there was no danger of a metallic noise and partly because the British tin helmet made it difficult to hear if there was any wind blowing. No webbing was worn in case of rattles, so spare ammunition and grenades were stuffed into pockets. Finally, faces and hands were blackened and nervous men jumped up and down to check that they made no noise.

At the appointed time Mash and the others silently made their way out into no man's land. As the Aussies had taught them, they moved forwards in stretches of no more than 20 or 30 yards before crouching in all-round defence to listen. They searched for the slightest noise or whisper that would betray the presence of the enemy or warn of their discovery.

Mash soon found himself with the rest of the section, lying on his stomach in the sand, probing for the explosive devices. Everyone was quiet; all commands were given by hand signal. Again, Mash was overwhelmed by the feeling that the enemy was close. He tried to ignore that thought and probed with his bayonet gently into the sand. Mash frequently found himself holding his breath whenever he lowered the blade, not sure if he would hit a rock or a mine. The biggest fear for all of them was of triggering an anti-personnel S-mine, which would spoil their day very quickly. Mash sweated partly from the effort and partly from the knowledge that every moment could be his last. In France it had been different; the countryside had been like the estate, he felt in control and hidden even when out on patrols such as this. Here, with no cover at all, he felt bare and vulnerable.

From the corner of his eye Mash noticed Gordon signal. He had found something. Together they started to brush away the sand. Slowly a round, dustbin-lid-like metal object appeared out of the sand. Mash held his breath as, very gently, they cleared the sand to reveal the edges and smoothly lifted it out of the sand. It was a Teller mine, painted Gledbraun or Afrika Korps tan and it had a large handle on one side. They passed it back and covered over where it had been before carrying on. Slowly they worked on and completed their mission without incident.

When they returned to camp later the men were jovial, cracking jokes about what parts they did not want blown off. Rod was proud. For most of them it had been their first venture into enemy territory and, having returned unscathed, they were jubilant, even though Mash had seen their pale, terrified faces only a few hours before.

A few days later Mash, Rod and the others were sharing a meal with their Aussie instructors. After the usual light-hearted banter the conversation had turned more serious and the Highlanders had asked the Aussies about the desert war.

"You gotta understand that we've been up and down this coastal road more times than a whore's draws," said the first Aussie, Stan, "first we push them back and then they do the same to us."

"Yeah, but I reckon this time's different," his mate Frank replied. "The Auk's picked a bloody good spot this time. El Alamein might just be a railway stop in the middle of nowhere but it's got the Mediterranean to the north as always, but this time we've got the Qattara Depression in the south."

"What's that and what's the Auk?" asked Finnean

"The Auk is what we call General Auchinleck. As for the depression, it's an expanse of sand, salt lakes and marshes that make it impassable to tanks and vehicles. So, for the first time the only way the Desert Fox can win is to smash through the forty-mile gap between the sea and depression. He can't loop round the open flank as he's always done and give us an Afrika Korps 'right hook'," explained Frank.

"Still don't understand why the top brass can't see that coming," grumbled Stan, "they've done it so many times."

Mash looked around him and was amused to see most of his colleagues staring at the Aussies like children being read a story. He glanced at Rod, who winked, but the Aussies had them all spellbound.

"I've always wondered why Rommel's called the Desert Fox," said Niall

"He's got a good brain and a cunning that means his attacks always seems to surprise us."

"And we can never catch him," interrupted Stan

"I guess he's a worthy opponent," Frank admitted.

"We know that first-hand, we've got our own score to settle with him," said Gordon.

"You'll get your chance soon enough. You see the Auk was able to stop Rommel this July but it meant that we're in a stalemate at the moment and when we go on the attack all the advantages we had in stopping them will now be helping the Jerries."

"Mind you it'll be this new bloke Montgomery in charge, the Auk got his marching orders from Churchill," Stan chipped in.

They were quite a good double act thought Mash as he watched the interchange, as enthralled as the others.

"We don't know what he's going to be like in battle," continued Frank. "He must've come about the same time as you boys got here. Mind you he's made a bloody good job of it so far. He seems obsessed training and ensuring we've got everything we need."

"Sounds a bit like Lang Tam," laughed Gordon.

"Well, I've heard tell that we've got nearly a two-to-one advantage in men, tanks and artillery. He's also taking his time. He ain't going to be rushed. But the bit I like best is that he's always out with us, inspecting, giving us pep talks and the like, we've never had that before. Strikes me as though he's his own man and can stand up to the likes of Rommel."

"He's also booted out anyone who he doesn't think is up to it," chimed in Stan, "if we're not careful we might stand a chance."

"That's a first coming from you, you pessimistic old bastard!" his friend retorted.

"Yeah, but it ain't like Jerry's being doing nothing in the interim," came the reply. "Rommel's been making his line as impenetrable as he can with the supplies he's got. He knows that a desert war is all about movement and tanks, so his first line of defence is mines, by the bloody thousand. Rumour has it that there're two bands of mines in front of their positions, over 500,000 in total! Most of its anti-tank, Teller mines, but scattered about are those bastard personnel S mines which spring a charge up before exploding and peppering the unfortunate bastard who triggered it and his mates."

"You gotta understand these minefields are only the first line of defence and they're five miles deep. Don't forget that behind the minefields you've got the main defences with infantry, artillery and anti-tank guns forming a defensive belt over a mile deep. We know from our patrolling that they're a mix of the 164th Saxon, Trento and Bologna Divisions of infantry who were dug in with the minefields surrounding them, supported by machine guns and mortars. Finally there're the tanks of the 15th Panzer and Littorio Armoured Divisions."

He paused for dramatic effect and was rewarded with a look of amazement and dismay on the faces of the Highlanders. Before he could go on, Frank jumped in again.

"Before Stan convinces you that it ain't worth the effort, we've got quite a few things in our favour. Rommel's in trouble; he's no longer the priority for supplies, it's the latest push on the Eastern Front now. The supply convoys he's got are being smashed to buggery by the Navy and R.A.F. out of Malta. Those that do get through unload onto lorries, only for them to have to drive across the desert to the front line, which burns up a lot of fuel. These fuel shortages mean that Rommel has to spread his tanks along the line rather than have them in a mobile unit ready to plug any holes. Plus the Eyetie tanks are no match for ours, only the Kraut ones are any good."

Frank paused and was rewarded by seeing the faces in front of him looking more positive before continuing.

"Remember, Rommel has to stop us on his defensive line, if we break through into the open then our numbers and the lack of Jerry fuel means he's done for. Remember the Krauts don't trust the Eyetie infantry and have inter-dispersed German and Italian units so that Jerries can keep an eye on them; they call it 'corset staves'."

"That's true," admitted Stan, almost as though he was as convinced by Frank's argument as the audience were. "We've got short supply lines and we're well stocked. I heard we've got 300 of those new Sherman tanks from America."

"God bless us," cried Frank with mock theatrics. "Don't tell me I've turned a whinging old bastard like you into a believer!"

★ ★ ★

Their week on the frontline with the Aussies drew to an end. They had been out on further patrols and their skills had grown immensely. The Aussies had been kind and patient instructors and had done much to hone the Highlanders' skills. Mash wished he could search out Jack and thank him again, but he knew it was not possible and that even if he did find him Jack would laugh it off in his typical laidback way.

The section then moved to El Halfa where the training stepped up once more. Mash told himself that he really had to stop being surprised by the intensity; every time he thought that they were doing the most serious training yet, they would be moved on and it would step up once again. This time their training was more realistic; the division had created mock German positions mimicking the ones they were to face. They did exercise after exercise against these. They also started working with live ammunition, not just with bullets but also with artillery and they had to learn how to move behind a rolling barrage.

Even before the shell landed there were noises and sensations to get used to.

"What's that funny noise?" asked Finnean as they practised with their first barrage. "Sounds like a load of geese or something."

"It's the shells as they go overhead," replied Rod. "They make that whirring noise. Now shut up and keep in line."

Some of the others giggled but the smile was instantly wiped off their faces when the shell exploded with an enormous bang on the hard desert floor, throwing up huge plumes of dust and assaulting their senses with the concussion of the blast.

After their time in France Mash and Rod were used to the assault on the senses that close proximity to exploding shells brings, but even they were intimidated by the rolling barrage. It was an act of faith to walk as close as they could to a wall of explosions, relying on the accuracy of the gunners and the belief that the shells, due to their trajectory, would throw their deadly shrapnel forward.

But there were reminders of how dangerous the task was; all around them as they advanced were spent pieces of shrapnel, some as big as a man's arm.

"Can you imagine being hit by that?" said Gordon, staring at a particularly big piece as he and Mash rested after one exercise.

"You wouldn't know much about it if it did," replied Mash.

"You just don't realise that lumps of metal that big are whizzing about."

Over the coming days there were more reminders of the danger as they were pushed to get ever closer to the barrage. It was a paradox – the closer to the barrage they were the less time the defenders had to react to the attack, but there was a higher chance of being hurt by friendly fire. As the training pushed them ever closer to the barrage men began to get hit by spent shrapnel. Callum had a close call when a good-sized spent piece hit him in the shoulder. The massive purple and red bruise was a timely reminder of the game they were playing.

They were progressing well, until one day the practice became a little too realistic. They were practising walking behind the barrage as usual when a shot fell short. The first thing Mash knew about it was the sound. They had grown used to the noise and had started to understand the sounds that the shells made. This one was different, a screech like a runaway express train before a very loud explosion. They had instinctively ducked and crouched. Then there was another sound, a yelp, almost like an animal in pain. There were shouts and Mash looked round to see that the men had stopped walking and were gathering around something.

"Shit," said Gordon. "Was someone just hit?"

"I don't know," said Mash.

None of them knew what to do so they all came to a staggered halt. There was a shout for the medics and they came running. As the other men moved aside Mash saw a body on the floor. The man's head looked untouched with almost a look of surprise. But below his head all the skin had been peeled away from his chest to reveal his ribs as you would see in an abattoir. Below that there was nothing, just lumps of bone, flesh and gut. Beside him Mash heard Drillbit retch and felt his own stomach jolt. In front of the still-smoking shallow crater where the shell had landed there were other body parts, none very big, just abstract parts of what seconds before had been a man – or men, as it was impossible to tell how many had fallen victim. Elsewhere men were alive, some screaming, others quiet.

Mash saw another man lying on the ground near to him, not moving. He cannot be dead, thought Mash. But as the medics hurried past them Mash got a clear view of the man; Fletcher was his name though Mash did not know him very well. He was still not moving, but Mash could see from one look that he was not going to make it. His chest had been torn open. Medics helped another man past; he was screaming and clutching his face, which seemed to have a chunk missing. Yet another man was carried by on a stretcher; his leg was in pieces, hanging on by a few inches of singed skin. Mash looked away; he felt nausea rise but swallowed it down.

He heard Gordon swear loudly under his breath. He glanced round and saw that the section were all staring, just like he was. Callum had gone very pale and Finnean was staring at them with his mouth open; the others did not look much better. Mash looked at Rod; they both had the same thought: this was the first time the section had seen death and suffering. Rod nodded at Mash then bellowed at the rest of them, causing them to jump out of their skins.

"Who told you to stop walking?" he shouted. "Keep moving, keep up with the barrage. Come on let's go!"

Mash obeyed and chivvied the others along with him.

Around them, other NCOs were shouting similar commands at their men, moving them on and away from the injured bodies. Mash noticed that everyone was progressing much more gingerly than before. Mash did not blame them; to get injured in battle was one thing, but to get killed on a practice. It was almost ridiculous. Mash tried not to think of the dead and wounded men and carried on, pretending it was a real battle. He had been taught to leave the injured and keep going.

Each second dragged out but they finally completed the exercise. When they were finished they were sent back to base where everyone was asking questions about the dead and injured men. Rumours were whirling around, there were three injured, five, ten. They had all died, most were maimed, some would never walk again. In the end it turned out it was three dead and another five injured, to varying degrees. The one who had lost a leg and the one with the injured face had both survived, though they were forever maimed. Fletcher had died, almost immediately after Mash had seen him. With the torso he had seen that meant that the splatter of body parts was only one man.

"To die in an exercise," said Kipper later on as the section was eating dinner.

"I know," said Mash. "Bad enough having Jerry blow you to pieces but to have your own side do it." The futility of it made his chest swell. He tried to ignore the feeling, worried that if he followed that train of thought the futility of the whole bloody war would become apparent. Everyone was scurrying around in the desert trying to kill everybody else. What mattered was that the shot came from in front of you not behind you.

"What happened?" asked Finnean.

"A round just fell short lad," said Rod.

"How does that happen when all the others go where they're meant to?" continued Finnean as he tried to make sense of it all.

"We don't know. Maybe one of the gun's wheels sank an inch or two in the sand, maybe when the girl in the factory spilt a few grains of powder she carried on and hoped no one would notice. We don't know and there's no point in trying to work it out. It's a lottery and when it happens there's often no logic to it."

They were quiet again.

"That face on the torso just looking at you," said Callum.

"That's something I really wish I hadn't seen," said Niall.

"I just didn't realise that it would be so... bloody," said Gasman.

They all stared at him.

"What do you think was going to come out, pixie dust?" said Gordon.

"I don't mean that, I knew there would be blood, I just thought it would be a bit," he raised his hands up, as though searching for the words. "Neater," he said eventually.

Mash knew what Gasman meant, though he did not verbalise it well. When Mash had first seen a body hit by artillery fire he had been shocked by the way it had been torn to pieces, it was not a simple and tidy bullet hole, it was shredded. Often men were reduced to small pieces of bloody meat, sometimes they just disappeared with only a boot or a bit of kit to mark where they had been.

"I know," said Kipper. "That poor guy had his leg just ripped off. It was pretty much in pieces."

"'fraid that's what it's like lads," said Rod.

They were all quiet again; the only sound was the slow chewing of their food, though most of the men seemed to have little appetite. Mash and Rod on the other hand ate their bully beef quickly. Mash did not think this made them less affected by the injuries, but he and Rod had learnt from experience the need to keep their strength up.

"That could be one of us," said Gordon.

Mash swallowed a lump of bully beef and looked at him. Gordon was staring at his hands.

"You've always known that was possible," said Rod.

"I know," said Gordon. "But now it's become more…"

"Real," finished Callum.

"People die in wars," said Rod. "Usually on your own in a ditch somewhere. My job is to try and keep as many of you alive as possible. But death is something that's going to happen to us and the sooner you get your heads round that the better."

Mash looked at Rod, expecting him to say something comforting to take the sting out of the realisation. But he had no words; he simply finished his food then got up and left. Slowly, everyone else did the same.

# CHAPTER TEN

# PATROL

On 18th October the section moved to the front for the last time in readiness for the battle.

They undertook more patrolling, but it was different to what they had done before.

"We're doing a snatch patrol," Rod explained to them as they lounged around in the cool dusk of the dying day.

"What's that?" asked Finnean.

Niall laughed.

"What is it, you ain't half thick sometimes Finn."

"Like you know what it is," said Gordon, who as usual jumped to Finnean's defence.

Niall's expression flickered for a moment as it did when he realised he had been caught out. But it was just for a second then he smiled patronisingly at Gordon.

"The clue is obviously in the title," he said.

"So we're snatching something?" said Finnean.

"Of course," said Niall.

"And do you want to tell us what that is," said Gordon.

"I think Rod's about to do that for me," said Niall.

"Christ you are full of shit Niall," said Gordon.

"Alright," said Rod. "That's enough bickering. To put it bluntly, we go over to the Jerry trenches and bring back one or two of them for questioning. We get to check who's up against us and it gives them a chance to sing like canaries to the intelligence boys."

"Shit," said Callum.

Niall opened his mouth to say something but Gordon threw a clod of sand at him.

"Don't even," he said as Niall lunged at him.

"Would you cut it out," said Rod in a manner so like a teacher that Gordon and Niall stopped fighting straight away and sat back down.

"Did you not hear what I said?" asked Rod.

"Aye," said Gordon. "We're capturing some Jerry."

"Great, time to actually do something real," said Kipper.

"If we manage to catch any," said Drillbit.

"Don't be such a pessimist," said Kipper.

"For Christ sake," snapped Rod, who was unusually crabby. "This is not something to make light of, it's going to be difficult and we have to be on top of our game."

Everyone was quiet, dually chastised.

"Plus," he said slowly. "It won't be just us. It's a two-section patrol."

"Who will we be with?" asked Gasman.

"We will be paired with Mitchell's section," said Rod quickly, avoiding eye contact with everyone.

Mash heard Gordon's exclamation of anger at the same time that he expressed his disbelief. The others groaned.

"This'll be fun," said Callum.

"Right," said Rod, clapping his hands. "I dislike the little turd as much as the rest of you. Having said that, we are professionals. What's more, the number one rule in a battle scenario is that you have to work together. This is going to be dangerous and I don't want the danger made worse by infighting."

Mash felt Rod's gaze briefly fall on him. He frowned.

"Mitchell and his section are going to want to have a quick and successful patrol too, so we will work together to complete it, OK?"

There was a muttered affirmative and Rod let out a breath.

"Right," he said. "Lecture over. Someone make us some tea."

As the others bickered over whose turn it was to make the tea, Gordon whispered to Mash.

"No matter what he says, there's no way I feel safe with that weasel next to me."

Gordon had summed up Mash's thoughts perfectly and, Mash suspected from Rod's continued irritable air, that Gordon had got a handle on Rod's thoughts too.

Later, while everyone else was relaxing, playing poker, writing letters and generally taking advantage of not having to be anywhere or do anything, Mash noticed Rod separate from the rest of the group and head off in the direction of Mitchell's gang. Mash hurried after him.

"What are you doing?" he said when he caught up with him.

Rod turned around and frowned at him.

"I'm going to talk to Mitchell," he said.

Mash did not say the words 'are you mad' but he thought them, and Rod could clearly tell.

"I wasn't exaggerating when I said this was serious," said Rod.

They had stopped a few yards away from a group with Mitchell in the middle. Over Rod's shoulder Mash could see that Mitchell had noticed them. His expression was impossible to read in the darkness.

"Mash," said Rod, drawing his attention. "All this petty fighting…"

"It's not petty," said Mash.

Rod held up his hand.

"None of that matters when we're out there in the field. I don't want to have to be worrying that I can't trust the men around me."

Mash knew that this was a completely sensible approach, and with anyone else it would work. But Mash just did not trust Mitchell.

"Whatever Mitchell's like, he doesn't want to cock this up either. I'm just going to extend an olive branch, explain that we need to work together so we have to put whatever bitterness there is behind us."

Mash shifted his feet irritably in the sand. He could not fault Rod's logic.

"I just don't trust the bastard," he muttered.

"Neither do I really," said Rod thoughtfully. "But we've got to work together, so that's that. Now, would you mind buggering off? I don't want you hovering around like a fly on shit while I'm trying to talk."

Mash smiled slightly.

"Alright," he said, glancing towards Mitchell again. "Go and be grown up."

Rod smiled then walked towards Mitchell. Mash backed into the darkness, but instead of returning to the others, he crouched down in a fold in the ground. He watched as Rod raised his hand in greeting and Mitchell walked slowly towards him. For once he left his goons Douglas and Wallace behind, but they glowered at Rod to let him know they were still there.

Mash continued to watch as they spoke. Rod did most of the talking, occasionally gesticulating with a lit cigarette. Mitchell stayed quiet and still. He could imagine how Rod would approach it, in the same way that he had just explained it to Mash; he would not try any phony ploy at friendship, he would come straight out with it. We do not get along but we need to work together, so let us put a lid on the hostility and get the job done. It was typical Rod, and it was the right and sensible thing to do. Mash knew this; he just did not trust Mitchell.

Mitchell eventually replied to Rod. Mash could not tell

what he was saying and his stance did not give anything away. Then Mitchell looked up and gestured over to where Rod and Mash had just been standing. Rod turned to look too and Mash quickly ducked down, scared he had been caught out. But when he looked up they were speaking again. Rod seemed to be standing slightly straighter than before. Mash knew they were talking about him.

Finally, Rod and Mitchell seemed to come to an agreement. Rod held out his hand. Mash held his breath as Mitchell looked at it for a second too long, but took the offered hand and shook it briefly. They parted and Rod turned and walked back towards the section. Mitchell watched him go. Mash waited a second but then melted into the darkness as Rod approached. He returned to the section a minute before Rod. Both pretended that nothing had happened.

★ ★ ★

It seemed that Mitchell had taken Rod's conversation to heart; he was professional and worked well with Rod as the two sections set out on their mission. Rod smiled a little smugly at Mash, which grated on him; he did not want to think of Mitchell as a reasonable human being. He was also irritated to see that Mitchell was actually a good leader of his group; all his men listened to him, he only had to give one of them a nod or a single word and the men would carry out his orders as though they had read his thoughts. Mash reasoned that this was because most of them were as twisted as Mitchell was, but Mash had to admit that they were not a bad outfit.

Mash could not focus on Mitchell's leadership technique for too long because he had to pay attention to the mission. They worked their way out towards the enemy lines, stopping and listening every thirty or so yards as they had been trained. The atmosphere was intense. On mine patrol the intent was to probe but stay undiscovered. Now they were looking for the enemy and it made it much more personal.

Mitchell's hand went up and they all went to ground. For what felt like an eternity, but was probably no more than a minute, they listened in silence. Then the faintest sound of voices came on the wind.

*God, Mitchell was good to hear that.*

With crisp and succinct hand signals Mitchell pointed the way ahead, gave the unit its dispositions and moved the attack forward. They still had no idea of where the voices were or how many there were but they followed the sounds onwards. The voices gradually grew louder. It sounded like there were three voices. German. Mash supposed that if there were three of them then it was probably a four-man trench with one on guard.

Mash could not understand what was being said but from the rhythm of the voices it sounded like any conversation he and the others would have in their own lines. The voices were talking in whispers but the sound carried clearly. It was an eye-opener to him; it could so easily be him and any of the others in the unit obliviously talking and not realising how far sound travels.

They crept closer, expecting the lookout to spot them at any moment and the silence to be ripped apart by gunfire, but nothing happened. They were so close that they could hear the men eating and the noise their utensils made in their billycans. Again Mitchell held up his hand and they all went to ground.

Part of the deal between Rod and Mitchell must have been that Mitchell would lead, Mash reasoned. Rod had kept that quiet, but then he would probably have had a mutiny if he had told them Mitchell was leading.

Mitchell signalled for the team to stay still while he and another of his section very carefully picked their way forward to do a reconnoitre. As they closed in Mash watched Mitchell;

he seemed completely focused on the mission. Mash chastised himself. Maybe he was being childish and letting his dislike of Mitchell cloud his view of him as a soldier.

After a good few minutes Mitchell returned. He quickly communicated that the target trench did have four people in it. He gestured that there were two other trenches close by and that they had machine guns. He then called the snatch squad to him and deployed the remainder to give covering fire.

The snatch squad was made up of five men. Mitchell was leading and he had two of his section with him. Mash and Gordon had previously agreed with Rod that they would go from his section. Mash had not been looking forward to it but in the light of recent events he was feeling more relaxed.

They knew surprise would be the key. It was essential that they hit the men in the trench before they had a chance to make a noise. The first the Germans would know would be when four men literally dived on top of them. The fifth man in the squad would stay above the trench ready to lay down immediate fire if needed or to deal with any unforeseen issues. The plan was for two of the Germans to be quickly killed whilst the remaining two would be taken back to the British lines. If it went well then they would be in and out before anyone knew they had been there.

Mitchell efficiently and quickly communicated how they would approach. He then assigned roles; he and Mash would take the prisoners. Mash was surprised Mitchell had picked him but he did not let on. With a quick check and a thumbs-up all round they were off.

They made their way forwards painstakingly slowly, inching across the sand towards the blind side of the trench. After what seemed like an age they were in position and could see the trench whilst remaining unseen themselves by the other two. There was a guard at one corner who was only half paying attention to his duties; he was clearly trying to listen to the conversation of his colleagues. The other Germans could not be seen, only fleeting glimpses of their heads as they moved. Mash and the others paused for a second, bayonets at the ready in sweaty hands, just long enough to ensure they would co-ordinate their strike. Then they dived into the trench.

Gordon disposed of the guard quickly and efficiently with a hand round the mouth and a knife in the back. The other three dropped onto their targets. Both Mash and Mitchell timed their jumps perfectly and the two Germans where winded with a hand over their mouths and a bayonet at their throats before they knew what was happening. The last, a man named Macpherson, timed his jump well but was barged sideways by the bodies next to him. His target was knocked against the end of the trench and let out a muffled cry before Macpherson's bayonet caught him under the chin, driving up into the base of his brain. He was dead before he could make another sound.

The attackers all paused, listening, waiting to see if they had been detected. Mash held his breath, but there was no sound. They got to their feet, hands still over the captives mouths and bayonets still firmly to their throats. Just as they started for the lip of the trench out of the darkness a hushed but alarmed voice called out.

"Helmut, was war das? Ich habe etwas gehört."

They froze. Again the voice came from the other trench with the same question only with more urgency. Mitchell, glaring at the German and pushing the bayonet as hard as he dare into his neck, slowly removed his hand and twitched his head towards the other trench. They needed a reply and this man was going to give it.

"Kein Problem. Alles in Ordnung," said the German, trying to sound as natural as possible.

There was a pause whilst the answer was digested and then:

"Wo ist Helmut?" came the slightly guarded response.

The German looked at Mitchell and felt both the bayonet at his throat and the small trickle of blood it had already drawn. He closed his eyes and swallowed hard, then opened them.

"Tot," he said with a laugh.

Nothing happened and there was no answer. After a few minutes, time enough for the other trenches to resume their daily routine, Mitchell signalled for the snatch squad to withdraw. The first man, who had remained outside the trench, rose into a crouched position and turned to go.

The two machine guns ripped into life, literally cutting the man in two. From that distance the ferocity and power of the guns was awesome and it stunned the others as though they had been punched. The muzzle flashes lit up the area. Both trenches were fifteen or so yards from the trench they were in, with soldiers lining the lip.

Mitchell was the first to recover. He pressed the bayonet even closer against the German's throat.

"What the fuck does tot mean," he snarled.

The German was shaking, but he smiled slightly and said one word.

"Dead."

Mitchell stared at the smiling German, then suddenly thrust his bayonet forwards, skewering the German through the throat. His mouth gaped open as his life's blood spurted out and he sank to the bottom of the trench.

"Fucking Jerry," Mitchell growled before looking round to assess the situation.

From behind them Rod's voice could be heard shouting "return fire" an instant before their fire crashed out.

"Go, go, go," shouted Mitchell

Macpherson was the first out. Behind him Mash struggled to get his captive up and out behind Macpherson. He put his shoulder underneath the German's backside and heaved him out of the trench. No sooner than Mash had raised the German up there was another burst of machine gun fire and both Macpherson and the German collapsed backwards. Mash and Gordon were knocked to the floor of the trench by the dead weight of the men.

Desperately Mash and Gordon fought to untangle themselves from the bloody bodies. Quickly looking around they could see they were on their own.

"Where's Mitchell gone?" cried Gordon

"He must have bailed out from the other side of the trench when Macpherson went over this side."

"The bastards left us," cursed Gordon.

"Be fair he said to go, it was every man for himself," admonished Mash. "Anyway, how the fuck are we going to get out, they've obviously got a bead on us despite the covering fire."

Gordon looked like he had been wrongly told off by a teacher. But they were in a serious problem. Sand and pieces of rock showered down on them as the machine guns constantly raked the top of the trench.

"There's no way we're going to be able to get out into that," groaned Gordon.

"The only thing we can do is to stay here and hope Rod and the others can knock those guns out," replied Mash.

With every passing minute the Germans were waking up to the fact that there was an assault on their position and the enemy fire was increasing. Mortars were now starting to fall and it would not be long before they found Rod and the others.

Mash was not sure what the Germans would do with them, but he knew that if it was him he would throw a grenade in the trench to make sure there was no one living.

"Shit," Gordon swore as a bullet skimmed the lip of the trench, right near his head.

"That bastard," he said as the realisation that they were alone finally dawned on him. "That stinking little bag of rat shit. We're dead. We're going to die because of bloody Mitchell."

"No," said Mash fiercely. "No, I refuse to die in this stinking trench. And stop going on about Mitchell, that doesn't help us now."

"You know why this is," said Gordon, his anger battling with his fear. "It's for the fight outside the NAAFI back in Blighty. He's never forgiven us for getting away."

"Will you fucking shut up about Mitchell and let me think!" shouted Mash.

He knew that their only chance of survival was getting out of the trench, but he had no idea how they were going to do that. He desperately looked around him and the answer presented itself. Already the fire from the rest of the raiding party was starting to die down. They had no other option. The Germans were gaining in strength with every second and if they stayed there they too would become casualties. There had been no movement from the trench and they could only presume that none of the snatch party remained.

"This is a long shot but it's our only chance," Mash said. "The others have got to go. The Jerries will then make sure we're dead by throwing a grenade in here. Our only hope is to get under the bodies and play dead. You've got to get enough bodies on top of you to stop the grenade. And for fuck sake keep your mouth open when it goes off."

Gordon looked around him in a daze. There were five bodies in the trench, the four Germans and Macpherson. They already had to stand and crouch on them given the restrictive space of the trench. Then the idea caught hold and he and Mash feverishly grabbed at the bodies and pulled them on top of themselves. It was a dreadful, disgusting job as the bodies dripped blood and gore onto them. It was also hard work as the bodies were heavy and awkward, but they managed to pull and wriggle their way to the bottom of the pile.

Outside the gunfire had died down and the silence was only interrupted by the odd burst as the Germans shot at shadows. Mash waited, tensed for the grenade, the smell of blood in his nostrils.

The stick grenade arched in the night's sky and fell into the trench. They were lucky. It caught the back of the trench and wedged between the wall and the back of the German Mitchell had killed. There it sat fizzing for a brief second. Mash opened his mouth and braced himself for the explosion. He prayed Gordon was doing the same.

In such a small area the explosion was ferocious. The dead German literally disintegrated as the body took the full force of the grenade. Remaining shrapnel and bits of bone and flesh fired out but the bodies on top of Mash and Gordon absorbed their force. But as deadly as the shrapnel was, the concussion of the blast was equally as dangerous. Again the bodies absorbed the force, whilst opening his mouth meant that the pressures in Mash's head were equalised and he did not burst his eardrums. Despite this he was completely deaf to any sound as his ears buzzed from the shock.

Mash kept rock-still. The only movement he allowed himself was to half open one eye. Above him a group of Germans peered down, their rifles pointing at him. He knew the scene must look like one of total devastation.

Mash and Gordon lay completely still, both listening to the Germans, though they could not understand what they were saying. Mash guessed that they were planning to fill the trench in as a grave.

"Andreas, warten sie hier. Wir werden bald wieder zurück sein," Mash heard. Then he heard the men walk away. He guessed they had gone to get shovels. This was the time to escape; they only had a few seconds.

They stood up and looked at each other; each of them looked like a zombie, covered in blood, gore and brain matter. They nodded to each other to indicate that they were unharmed, before clambering out of the trench.

In front of them stood a young German. His eyes were bulging out of his head and his mouth gaped open, but no sound came out. Quickly Mash grabbed his bayonet and held it to the German's throat.

"Ssshhhh!" he whispered into his ear.

But the effect was only to compound the man's fear and he began to shake uncontrollably before he was roughly pushed forwards and away from the trench. They reached the spot where the raiding party had gone to ground. No one was there, just the empty casings in the sand. They tried to listen for any sign that they had been spotted but their ears still buzzed, although it was beginning to subside. In the dark they could see nothing. While Gordon held a bayonet to the German Mash bent down and removed one of his boot laces. He quickly tied the man's hands behind his back and pushed him forward again. The combination of having his hands tied and the difficulty in running with a boot coming off would slow the man if he tried to make a break for it.

Mash had no idea where he was or where he was going. But his first priority was to put some distance between them and the Germans so they moved quickly in a direction that Mash hoped was back towards their lines. After he thought they had made good their break they came across a small fold in the ground and stopped. The buzzing in Mash's ears was subsiding; he could hear his boots on the sand so he knew it was nearly back. He listened intently for any sound but there was nothing.

Beside him Gordon's breathing came in rasps. Mash whispered to him.

"I think we may've got away with it."

"Christ I hope so," said Gordon.

"We've got to get back before the sun comes up," said Mash.

"Shit," said Gordon as he rifled in his uniform. "I don't have a compass."

"Neither do I, but we can use the stars," said Mash.

"I thought you didn't go to those lectures when we were on the *Duchess*," said Gordon.

"I didn't, but Jack told me," said Mash.

They both looked up at the sky.

"We've got to find the North Star, haven't we," said Gordon. "They all look the bloody same."

But Mash was quiet; he was looking for the plough as Jack had taught him. Finally he saw it and he followed the stars to the large, bright one.

"There it is," he said, pointing. "The base is to the east of our current position."

"So, we need to keep the star on our left," said Gordon, sounding more positive.

They set out, keeping low and pushing the German out in front of them. They were both exhausted and starving and made slow progress, but they kept going. They marched on in silence; just pausing to check the stars and make sure the German was not going to break for it. But he seemed resigned to his fate and blindly did as he was told.

\*\*\*

"Don't fucking move!" came a growled challenge.

The menace in the voice was such that even the German was stopped in his tracks.

"Two of the raiding party plus prisoner returning," said Mash with his arms wide out.

"Advance and be recognised," came the whispered reply

which was followed a moment later with: "Jesus Christ, look at the state of you!"

One of the benefits of being covered in blood and gore was that it spoke more loudly than words that someone was coming back from a fight rather than looking for one. The guard relaxed.

"The rest of your party were through here a while back, although they didn't say there were any more to come."

"Thank fuck," muttered Gordon.

"They don't think we made it and they were nearly bloody right," answered Mash.

A man was quickly found to cover the prisoner and guide them back to camp. Off they set again before finally they saw a patch of solid darkness appear out of the gloom and they realised they were back.

They were taken to the platoon HQ. There Wilson-Brown and Sergeant Robertson were debriefing Mitchell and Rod on what went wrong with the raid. It was obvious that the atmosphere was tense. As they walked in with their prisoner Mash was amused to see the reaction their appearance made. At first there were looks of horror that quickly turned to relief, particularly from Rod.

"Christ!" shouted Rod. "Mash, Gordon. Where the hell have you been?"

He grabbed both of them by their arms and stared at them as though he had not seen them for years. They both felt his fingers tighten round their arms.

Mash looked at Mitchell. His face showed surprise but nothing else. Nothing to say whether he had left them on purpose or if it was an accident of war. Once the German had been taken away under guard, WB turned to the two.

"So what happened?" he asked

"Mitchell left us to it," blurted out Gordon before Mash had a chance to say anything. "He was gone in a second and never came back."

Mash took a long, slow in-breath. Accusations of desertion and cowardice were not something you made in the heat of the moment to an officer, especially when they were not sure if it was true.

WB's eyebrows were knitted together.

"What are you saying?" he said.

"That's not bloody true," said Mitchell. But WB held up a hand to silence him.

"I'm saying Sir that he left us there deliberately. We barely made it out of there or back here," said Gordon, trying to keep his voice level.

"That's a very serious accusation," said WB. He looked worried, as well he might. Mash felt he was alright for an officer; he was fair, but he tended to try and avoid emotion and conflict wherever possible. He was not much older than Mash himself but had a different background. His voice had the clipped tones of the upper-class Scot and spoke of private school and a top university education. He was clearly uncomfortable.

"It's true Sir," replied Gordon.

"What's your take on it," said WB as he turned to Mash.

Mash's brain was a whir. He was not sure if Mitchell had deserted them. If he had then that was something they would sort out in the dark of the night rather than have a full-blown court martial with officers and lawyers involved. So he gave a dispassionate and objective summary of what had happened and how they had made their escape.

"So you are saying that Mitchell ordered everyone out of the trench, but he went out a different way to the way you were intending. You were then knocked back into the trench by which time Mitchell had gone as had the opportunity to escape. Is that correct?"

"Yes, Sir."

WB paused for a moment.

"Macdonald, I don't understand why you think Mitchell deserted you. Any of you could have got out of the trench in a different way and you wouldn't have known who else made it until you got back to the others."

"Sir," said Gordon, his eyes still blazing at Mitchell.

"Sergeant Robertson and I know that everything between you and Mitchell isn't rosy but don't use that as an excuse to throw very serious allegations about, understood?"

"Sir," repeated Gordon, but this time his gaze was turned upon Mash. Mash knew Gordon felt he had let him down.

"We're not here for you to fight personal vendettas so sort it out. Given what you've been through I'll overlook it this time."

With that he turned to Mitchell.

"It strikes me as though you owe these two a word of thanks. Before they came in you had lost four men out of the party and failed to bring a prisoner, not a very good outcome. Thanks to these two, while it's not a glowing reference, it's a success. So I'm looking for you to play your part in burying the hatchet."

"Sir," replied Mitchell.

"Right, go and get cleaned up and no more playground stuff from either of you."

As they were leaving WB gave a short nod to Mash as though to say well done. Once they were away from the platoon HQ Rod turned to Mitchell.

Before he could say anything Rod had leapt forwards with the speed of a cat and was standing an inch from Mitchell's face.

"Understand and understand good. I trusted you and I gave you a chance. If I ever find out that you deliberately left two of my men out there to die because of some petty personal vendetta then you'll pay."

Mitchell opened his mouth as though to say something

but then thought better of it; the look in Rod's eyes spoke volumes. With a glance at Mash and Gordon he turned and slowly and walked away.

As soon as he had gone Gordon turned on Mash.

"You fucking let me down!" he shouted.

"No he didn't," interrupted Rod with a voice like thunder. "You can't throw allegations like that around, especially as it would have been easy for him to dodge out of it. Mash did you a favour in defusing the situation otherwise you'd have been the one in trouble."

Gordon did not say anything. He glowered at Rod but he seemed too afraid of Rod's mood to say anything further.

"Look, I dislike Mitchell just as much as you," added Rod, his tone more conciliatory. "But you can't argue that he had handled the raid pretty well up to that point and he did tell you to go. If the roles were reversed I probably wouldn't have hung around either. If we find out he did leave you intentionally then I promise you Mash and I'll hold him while you kick the crap out of him."

"I'm sorry if you think I let you down," said Mash. "I hate the bloody bastard too but I just couldn't be sure."

Gordon thought for moment then let out a breath; he seemed to deflate like a punctured balloon. All the bluster ran out of him.

"It's alright I suppose. If it wasn't for you I'd never have made it out of that trench."

"And while we're all kissing and making up, I'm sorry I didn't come and look for you," said Rod. "Before Mitchell came back I saw Macpherson and the German get shot. When Mitchell turned up he said he didn't know if anyone else got out alive. We waited for as long as we could but the mortars were getting just too close, we'd have lost a lot of men. I know it was the right decision but I promise you I was beating myself up about it until you appeared like a couple of ghosts."

"That's OK," Gordon said for both of them.

The three smiled at each other.

"Now bugger off and get cleaned up, you both stink to high heaven," said Rod.

Over the next few days the training continued but Mash barely saw Mitchell. When they did it was professional and the interchange to a minimum. Mitchell gave no sign or hint about the raid and Mash was still left in two minds.

The thing that had surprised him most was that WB and Sergeant Robertson had known about the feud. Thinking about it, Mash realised that it was impossible to keep something like that quiet, especially from someone like the sergeant who was a wily old fox and knew how to keep his ear to the ground. Mash wondered if this was why Mitchell was being so careful.

Mash knew that Mitchell was an unpleasant piece of work, but he also knew how much he himself had changed since returning from France. Should he give Mitchell the benefit of the doubt and think he too had changed? He did not know and only time would tell.

There were changes in the mood of the men as a whole. It was impossible to hide that there would be a battle and that the Highlanders would be playing an attacking role; the training they had undergone spoke volumes. What they did not know was when, only that it would be soon. Bets were constantly being taken on when and where, and it left everyone with an empty feeling in the stomachs.

Thoughts amongst the men turned to home. Letters were written, photos of loved ones stared at for hours, agreements made with friends and pals that each would look after the other's loved ones if the worst happened. So, when they finally were called to a briefing, it could mean only one thing. Mash was actually relieved that the wait was over.

★ ★ ★

Lieutenant Wilson-Brown gathered them together to brief them. He walked into the middle of the circle of men and stood still. As the desert night was its usual all-encompassing black and the blackout restrictions meant there was no man-made light. What little reflected light there was from the moon barely illuminated WB and so his features were blurred and his teeth flashed. He looked to Mash not like WB, the mild-mannered commander, but as a nameless leader with none of his foibles.

"Blimey, you could cut the tension with a knife," Gordon whispered.

"I know," said Mash. "This is the first battle for most guys. Mind you that includes WB and he's going to have to play it carefully if he isn't going to lose the boys."

WB calmly cleared his throat and the men fell quiet.

"Gentlemen, tomorrow night we're going to assault Inverness."

There was a stunned silence for a second before one wit in the dark said, "That's a bloody long way!"

"Careful mind, my mother-in-law can put up a good fight," said another voice.

This immediately brought a muffled roar of laughter from all present, quickly followed by other, more ribald, comments on the defensive qualities of the townsfolk. The atmosphere had changed; it was like someone had burst a balloon and released all the tension of a minute before.

"All right you lot, quieten down and listen in," said WB.

He began to outline the plan of action, the plan that Montgomery and his staff had been working on since his arrival in mid-August and for which the Highland Division had been training intensively for over the last six weeks.

"153 and 154 Brigades are going to attack down an 8,000-yard corridor, through ours and the enemies' minefields and take a number of objectives currently manned by our

German and Italian friends. Each objective has been given the codename of the home town of the battalion attacking it, and that, gentlemen, is why we're attacking Inverness.

"The Camerons are supplying two companies, B and C under Major Davey, to 154 Brigade and we're going to form the extreme left of the division's push. To our north will be the recce and tank boys of 154, beyond them the 7th Argylls. To our south is the 2nd New Zealanders."

"Once we've got through the mines and taken our objective we're then to stop on the green line just beyond Inverness and allow the 7th Black Watch to pass through our position as they go on to attack their objective which is not surprisingly called Kirkcaldy and is on the blue line. Any questions so far?"

"Yes, Sir," replied one strained voice. "How're we going to get through the minefields before the Jerries know we're there?"

"I was coming to that; we're going to enjoy the pleasures of a firework display laid on by the artillery boys. They're going to blast away at all known enemy artillery positions before we kick off. Once done they're going to lay down a rolling barrage for us to follow, all very similar to what we've trained for except I'm told it will be on a scale that we can't dream of."

"Are we going to have time to clear the mines if there's a rolling barrage, Sir?"

"No, we're going to advance right over the top of them. We know from our training that the weight of a man isn't enough to set one of the Teller mines off, not even the weight of Macgregor there."

A round of subdued laughter and a few well-chosen comments followed.

"And it's for this reason that some bright spark in HQ has christened the attack Operation Lightfoot."

There was a groan but at least it showed that the men were still with him.

"I bet some stuck-up Sassenach officer with a silver spoon up his arse had to spend all night thinking of that one," growled Gordon, using the derogatory comment all Highlanders reserved for Englishmen. WB went on.

"Once the 7th Black Watch and others have captured their objectives and the sappers have managed to clear lanes though the minefields, then Lumsden's armoured X Corps follows up through the gap we've made, beat off any counter attacks and emerge into the enemy's rear."

"We'll be moving up to our kick-off point later tonight and you need to be well bedded down for the morning as there'll be no movement for the whole of the 23rd."

"What do you mean no movement, Sir?" asked Robertson.

"I'm afraid exactly what it says – nobody is to move about under any circumstances. We don't want Jerry to suspect a thing and that means everyone stays in their trenches all day until nightfall. If you need to go to the loo you do it in your trench, so pick your partners well."

"NCOs I need you to enforce the no-movement order to the letter. I know it will mean a horrible day in the heat but it's in all our interests that Jerry doesn't know that we're coming."

"How's your tummy?" Mash asked Gordon with a grin. "Because if you so much as fart you're out of that trench regardless of the Jerries."

"That's for me to know and you to worry about," said Gordon with a chuckle.

WB then went on to describe the expected defences and outline all the movement orders and minutiae that facilitate an attack of this nature.

At the end he said, "I know this is the first battle for most of you and you know it's my first too. However, we've trained hard for this and we're as well prepared as we can be, Lang Tam and Monty have seen to that."

There was a murmur of approval through the men.

"We've grown together as men and we know we're ready as are the others of the Highland Division. And with the Aussies on one side of us and the Kiwi's on the other then we know we can trust them."

He then drew himself up and looked around at his men.

"I don't want to give you motivational speeches; I simply need to remind you gentlemen that this is the first time the 51st has been in action since that fateful day at St Valéry. Opposite us is Rommel, the same man that took 6000 of our friends and countrymen into captivity and brought shame on our division and country. Now is the time that we avenge that shame. Now is the time we restore the good name of the division. Gentleman in the name of Scotland, go out there and remind Rommel why we were called the Ladies from Hell."

Calling on the name the Germans had given the Highlanders in the Great War did not bring a roar of approval; it was more serious than that. To a man all had felt the suffering from the St Valéry disaster and to a man they wanted to avenge it. Therefore the response was more a communal grunt of approval as the men focused on the task ahead with a steely determination.

"Sergeant, dismiss the men and ensure those not here are briefed," said WB and then he turned away, back to the platoon truck that he called home.

Around him the men dispersed, returning to their trenches, talking in soft but determined voices and readying themselves for the trials and tribulations that lay ahead.

# CHAPTER ELEVEN

# INVERNESS

On the 23$^{rd}$ October 1942, as night fell over the desert of El Alamein, figures rose up from the ground, seemingly climbing out of the earth itself. The Camerons took the opportunity to clamber out of their grave like trenches and stretch their legs. They had been confined to the cramped holes since before first light, waiting for the enemy's dawn reconnaissance flight. They had then sat for thirteen hours in the full heat of the day, not allowed out under any circumstances in case the movement alerted the enemy to the forthcoming battle. They had been plagued by flies and had only basic rations of hard biscuits, a tin of bully beef and water to sustain them for the long hours.

But boredom had been the hardest part, it had made the time drag and given them time to think, think about the oncoming battle and their own mortality.

But now, finally, dusk had fallen and the men emerged.

"Thank Christ that's over," said Gordon. "I spent all day wondering if I might be in a similar hole by the morning."

"I kept thinking about what that old South African soldier we met in Cape Town said: 'it was the best and the worst of times but I was the only one to come back'," said Mash.

"I wonder how many of us will be left when this battle's over?" Gordon almost whispered.

"Come on you two," cut in Rod. "I know it was hard but secrecy's the key and the enemy can't know we're coming."

Both Mash and Gordon muttered wordless grunts; they knew he was right but it did not make it any easier.

The mood was temporarily broken by the arrival of the cooks who brought up hot stew and milkless tea, which the troops fell upon.

"Best rations I've had in a long time," said Gordon, hungrily wolfing down the stew.

"A good meal for the condemned man," replied Kipper.

"These crosses on our backs are a bit spooky," said Finnean, he seemed unable to concentrate on his food.

"You'll be glad of those in the confusion," answered Mash. "At least you'll know who's on your side."

Each man in the division had a St Andrews cross made out of rolls of rifle cleaning patches on his back. The idea was that it would allow others some form of instant recognition in the heat of battle.

Finnean nodded, though he did not look the least bit comforted.

Now that they were out of the trenches the time quickened its pace until they were almost ready to commence their first battle. In the gathering cold the men huddled together and spoke in hushed tones. Cigarettes were smoked; occasionally a joke was cracked and answered with slightly forced laughter as the soldiers tried not to focus on the coming events. All around men were showing their nerves. Endlessly, compulsively checking and rechecking their weapons and equipment. Slinking off to relieve themselves for the countless time or to be sick in a trench somewhere.

Mash stared into his mess tin. He did not speak much, he was too busy thinking; the same thoughts that every soldier had on the eve of battle. Would he survive the night, let his mates down, prove himself to be a hero or coward? War had ever been such and the thoughts were the same over the generations – although this made it none the less real for

Mash and the other men of his section as they awaited their fate. This was different from France. The scale was huge and everyone knew the battle would be pivotal.

Mash looked up from his tin and peered round at the men in his section. Rod was trying to keep the men's spirits up. Gordon and Finnean sat quietly together and Mash knew Gordon was probably worrying more for Finnean's safety than his own, especially as his aunt, Finnean's mother, had threatened him with grievous bodily harm if he did not 'bring her boy back alive.' The rest of the section were in huddles, awaiting their fate. They and all the other men knew that at 22:00 hours they would leave their start lines and advance into the unknown, preceded by an artillery barrage that was supposed to be something special.

Still they waited, staring out at the flat and featureless landscape; the almost full moon gave them a pale sheen, like they were already ghosts.

The first hint of activity was the faint hum of engines, lots of engines. The sound grew in intensity as the Wellington and Halifax bombers grew closer, on their way to pound the enemy lines.

Rod looked at his watch. It was a few seconds before 21:40 hours.

"Not long now," he said.

At that moment there were flashes in the east.

"That's not very much," exclaimed Mash. Scarcely were the words out of his mouth when all hell broke loose.

The first impression was that someone had switched the lights on; men, trucks, guns and tanks were all lit up as clear as day. It was later said that you could read a newspaper, the light was so bright. Then, a second after the lights came the deafening crash as guns of every calibre fired their opening salvo. The men recoiled as though hit by an unseen fist and some ducked down again in their holes. The earth shook and the light show amazed, but it was the noise that had the most impact; the incessant thunder of hundreds of guns which was soon joined by the whine of shells as they poured overhead on their way to seek destruction on the Axis forces.

"That's more like it," spluttered Mash as he recovered from the shock of the assault on his senses.

What he did not know was that the onslaught was part of a carefully planned and orchestrated barrage. The first flashes were the big 5.5-inch guns firing from behind the lines. They had opened up seconds earlier than the rest so that their shells hit their targets at exactly the same time as those fired from smaller-calibre guns closer to the front. Even the aircraft had been dispatched early so that they would be overhead with their bombs falling to their targets as the first shells landed. The idea was to try and gain complete surprise so that as many of the Italian and German troops as possible would be out of their trenches and exposed to the devastating bombardment.

For fifteen minutes the guns exclusively pounded the enemy's artillery, whose positions had been gleaned from hours of patrols and reconnaissance flights over the preceding weeks. 880 guns opened up that night, spread across a front of some forty miles. The barrage was intensified in the north; covering the seven-mile front of XXX Corps, of which the Highland Division were part, there were no less than 480 guns of all calibres pounding the Axis positions, one every sixty yards.

Then, as suddenly at it had started, the barrage stopped.

For five minutes the guns were silent.

Mash knew that this time was for the gunners to adjust their sights for their next task – a rolling barrage to cover the advance of the infantry. The tension of waiting was unbearable; the silence of the guns seemed to make it worse. Behind Mash someone vomited, his evening stew erupting on the man beside him.

"Och you bastard, fucking puke somewhere else will you," was the curt response.

"Shit the Jerries and Eyeties will smell us coming now," came a comment from further back.

Normally this would have raised a laugh, but not now.

Mash was waiting for the signal to go; he felt like a racehorse on the start line.

"Steady lads, not long now," said Rod firmly, trying to calm his section. "Remember what Lang Tam said – Scotland forever and second to none – we've trained and we're ready. Now let's bloody do it."

They did not have to wait long; at exactly 22:00 hours the guns opened up again. The rounds screeched overhead and landed in front of the troops, starting the rolling barrage.

"Here we go," whispered Mash.

Gordon, who was standing next to him, nodded and shifted his feet.

All along the line the men emerged from their holes or huddles where they had been waiting. They quickly formed up, as they had practised countless times. Two searchlights reached into the sky before lowering to form a St Andrew's cross behind them. They advanced to the skirl of the pipes. Wimberley had insisted that every company go into battle with the sound leading them. So Pipers Macpherson and Campbell, resplendent in tartan and armed only with their instruments, led the Camerons into battle like the pipers of old. Part of Mash wanted them to fight in their tartans, as their fathers had done in the Great War, but they were in their baggy desert shorts or trousers; only the unarmed pipers would have that honour.

Behind them the men advanced at fifty yards a minute, nothing more than a stroll so that they would not hurry into the rolling barrage. They were spaced five yards apart to try and lessen the casualties from the expected fire, weapons held at the high port in a way that their fathers would have recognised.

Mash surveyed the scene about him as he slowly progressed. Ahead was the piper, looking as though he was performing at Edinburgh Castle, striding forward with military precision. He was playing a tune that Mash did not recognise, although he was sure the others would be outraged by his lack of knowledge. Mash clutched his rifle; he thought that he would not have the courage to be out front and defenceless like the pipers. He glanced left and right. The terrain was absolutely flat, no cover at all. If the enemy came to their senses it would be a killing field. They were lit up by the full moon, walking in an extended line as though on a Sunday afternoon amble. But their faces were strained as they waited for the first contact that would show them the enemy had woken up.

"This is weird," said Mash.

"Perhaps the guns have got all of the bastards," replied Niall hopefully, his usual aura of confidence gone.

"Not bloody likely," said Rod. "Now shut up and concentrate on keeping in line."

As if to reinforce the point, megaphones sounded above the din, cajoling and reprimanding as men got out of position. This gave the proceedings a slightly comical air, making many feel as though they were on some sort of strange parade ground exercise.

"Still no return fire," said Mash quietly to Rod.

"I know," replied Rod. "Part of me's really happy about it and the other part's very disturbed."

"Let's hope it stays quiet all the way," said Mash. He meant to say it out loud, but it came out like a whispered prayer.

Then the enemy woke up and men started to die.

★ ★ ★

To Mash, a number of separate events seemed to happen in a relatively short time. First they entered into the dust thrown up by the rolling barrage. The scene became blurred instantly; men who a moment ago could be seen clearly, became vague shapes. They stumbled forward, finding it difficult to keep the line. Mash could now see the reason for the St Andrew's crosses on their backs, anything helped.

Next was the arrival of the first enemy shells. There were not that many, and his section was not affected, but Mash could feel the explosions and knew that men were falling. He imagined the mangled bodies, the screams and the blood. He was glad he was not being targeted but he wondered for how much longer it would last.

In front of them, the surviving Axis artillery were coming around from the shock of the initial barrage and were reorganising themselves to reply. At first they targeted the artillery that had been pounding them. Soon they started to receive news of troop movements and their fire orders changed accordingly.

Mash tripped on a white post stuck in the ground, he had not seen it in the dust and confusion. He knew immediately what it was; a marker to give the defenders an accurate range of the advancing troops. Mash knew that they were usually set 300 yards or so from the enemy position; they were getting close.

Suddenly the rolling barrage stopped. The silence that followed was unnerving and played with the senses; they had gone from seeing clearly with the comforting racket of shells shrieking towards the enemy, to limited vision and total silence. The only exception was that the bagpipes grew more audible. The effect was unsettling.

"What the hell's happening? Why've our guns stopped now?" asked Kipper, his nerves making his voice much louder than he had intended.

"Don't worry, they have to stop. They think we're getting close to our target and they don't want to shell their own side," replied Rod, trying to sound as reassuring as he could.

It did little to calm Mash; if they were that close to their objective and the enemy was now awake then they were in for a hard time of it.

As if on cue, the first of the enemy machine gun fire ripped through the ranks of the advancing soldiers. Mash started to hear the screams of men along with the flat, slap-like noise of bullets hitting flesh. He could feel as well as hear rounds passing close to him, sounding like angry bees. This was a lottery, no cover, no way of dodging death.

Mash heard the crack of Italian Breda machine guns, but also the distinctive noise of the German Spandaus. So it could be Italians or Germans they were facing; only one way to find out.

As if this was not enough he heard the crump of mortars falling around him.

"Keep moving, keep moving, don't stop!" bellowed Rod

At that moment, as if in accord with Rod, the piper changed his tune. Even Mash recognised the new one; 'The Cameron Men' was their song and it gave them fresh heart. Mash even heard Gordon whistling along.

The music made Mash feel more positive until he was brought back to reality with a jolt when he caught his foot and stumbled. Looking down he realised with horror that he had tripped over a man. The soldier was badly wounded in the stomach and the blood was pooling around him. He was not screaming or writhing; instead he was quietly sobbing. The old adage was that the noisier the man, the less seriously hurt he was; if he had the strength to scream then he was not badly injured. Mash knew the man did not have long to live and felt uncomfortable being a witness to his dying moments. Although Mash's senses told him to stop and help, he had seen enough fighting to know that if men stopped to help a fallen comrade the attack would stall. It was too late for this man and the best chance of survival was for the living to keep going. So he quickly moved on, leaving the man to his fate.

Whilst the casualties were now coming thick and fast, the Camerons were also close to their objective.

"Come on lads, let's be at them," shouted Rod as he broke into a run.

The others followed, firing from the hip as they ran in an effort to keep the enemy's heads down. The first thing Mash saw as he sprinted through the gloom was the outline of a machine gun and crew. He immediately grabbed for one of his grenades and threw it at the machine gun nest. He saw it explode right by the gun, lifting it over the trench towards him along with the body of the loader whilst the gunner sank backwards. Mash was aware of other heads and shoulders appearing out of the ground. Confusion reigned. Some men had their hands in the air and were clearly trying to surrender, whilst in the trench next to them others put up a stiff resistance and were firing for all they were worth.

The first trench Mash came to was on his right; the two men in it were both shooting at attackers coming at them from the front. Immediately Mash aimed and fired at the nearer man, hitting him in the neck. The man was flung to one side, blood spraying from the wound. The round continued through the first man and into the one beside him. He was thrown against the far wall of the trench where he made laboured efforts to get to his feet again, only for one of his frontal attackers to hit him with a round to the head. He sank down, leaving a bloody smear on the trench wall.

"Keep moving, drive through the position!" someone was shouting in the din of gunfire.

Mash's training had kicked in and any nerves he had felt at the start were now a distant memory. He was focused on destroying the enemy, only vaguely aware of his exertions and oblivious to the lives he was taking. He did not even know if the others were with him or if he was on his own.

*Here's the next trench. Men firing, shoot back. One down. On top of the trench now, a man is in front, use the bayonet.*

As he stabbed forward he remembered to twist the rifle sideways, going for the chest, aiming the blade between the bones. He felt the bayonet jar as he hit a rib, but then it slid between them, deep into the man, who screamed as he was driven back onto the far wall by Mash's momentum.

*Twist and pull, break the blood seal and pull out the bayonet. Onwards, here's the next trench, men with their hands up, no weapons visible.*

Mash hesitated, he had heard of men who surrendered only to pick up their weapons and start shooting again once the attackers moved past. But he could not shoot the men in cold blood. He left them and ran forwards onto the next threat. He saw a man out of his trench, retreating. But he was carrying his rifle and turning to fire at the Highlanders. Mash shot from the hip as he ran towards him. His round missed but it made the man turn to face him and raise his gun.

*Shit, I'm not going to get there in time.*

At the very same moment that Mash expected the bullet to pierce his flesh the man was hurled to one side, blood exploding from his chest.

*No time to see who fired, just keep going.*

Rounds buzzed and zipped around him, kicking up the sand in front of him. The next trench loomed up to his left, only a matter of yards away. It was a more open trench with a mortar in the middle. The crew, now that the enemy were so close, had stopped firing the mortar and were shooting at the Highlanders from the rim. Mash fired at the man on the far side, who sank back down into the trench, then sprang forward towards the rest of the occupants with his bayonet at the ready. The German closest to Mash turned to engage him, but at that moment a grenade thrown from an unseen hand landed right in the trench. The man hesitated but Mash instinctively ducked down behind the outside lip of the trench as the explosion ripped into the defenders. In an instant he was up and into the trench. There were no survivors; if the grenade had been thrown a second later Mash would have been with them.

*No time to think. Forward, forward. Where's the next threat?*

And then there was nothing. Mash halted, breathing heavily, unsure of what was happening. There was no one in front of him; only the bleak desert. Then it occurred to him: he was through the position.

A sharp crack and a wall of hot air hit him on the side of the face like a punch. He turned to see a German with a gun aimed at him.

*Get him before he can fire again. How did he miss from this range?*

*Rifle up, aim centre body. Bang, kick in the shoulder. The man falls. Bolt action another round. Empty casing ejects onto the sand.*

*Look for the next target. How many have I fired?*

But instead of the enemy, he saw his comrades. Other familiar faces started to appear next to him.

"Don't stop, keep going right the way through the position."

Whoever had said it was right; you do not stop immediately once through, you carry on in case there is more enemy in support of the position you have stormed. But there were none and the adrenaline that had been powering Mash started to abate.

"Jesus that was unreal," said Gasman as he came to a stop beside Mash.

"I thought I'd bloody had it several times," replied Callum.

"Did you see Mash get that machine gun with the grenade? Hell of a throw," added Drillbit.

"All right everyone, we still have to press on to the red line," said Rod, sounding every bit like a school teacher gently rebuking his pupils, whilst simultaneously glowing with pride at how they had performed. At the moment there was still enough adrenaline for them to think it was a game. Plus, by incredible fortune all of the section had survived. Soon, however, the full realisation of what they had done would hit home; that they had taken human life, that they had watched their friends die and seen sights no one should have to see. Still, they had to reach their final objective and it was best to keep the men as occupied as possible. So they formed a line again and advanced the couple of hundred yards until it was decided they were at the red line.

"Right, is anyone hurt? No? Good. Make sure your weapons are fully loaded and working, then start digging, all-round defence," ordered Rod.

And from somewhere nearby a message was sent.

★ ★ ★

Wimberley waited restlessly at Tactical Divisional Headquarters for the first news of how the attack was progressing. He had done all he could and, like a football manager, had to sit back and await events. This was not something that came easily to him.

He knew that any plan was the first casualty of battle and wondered how he and his men would react to the changing events. All the years of rebuilding the division, the training and preparation had come down to this. It was time to see what fate had in store. He thought of the desert war and the events that had brought the two sides to this bleak and unforgiving place.

Montgomery had come up with a simple plan. Its main features were a feint in the south and a broad infantry assault in the north, where they would punch holes in the enemy's defences for the armour to pour through. It was a rehash of exactly the kind of WW1 horror that the desert generals had endured as young officers and tried so hard to spare another generation.

First there was the deception, called Operation Bertram. In September the Allies dumped waste materials and discarded packing cases under camouflage nets in the northern sector, making them appear to be ammunition or ration dumps. The Axis naturally noticed these but, as no offensive action immediately followed and the 'dumps' did not change in appearance, they were subsequently ignored. This allowed the $8^{th}$ Army to build up supplies in the forward area unnoticed by the Axis, by replacing the rubbish with ammunition, petrol or rations at night. Meanwhile, a dummy pipeline was built, hopefully leading the Axis to believe the attack would occur much later than it did and much further to the south. To further the illusion, dummy tanks consisting of plywood frames placed over jeeps were constructed and deployed in the south. In a reverse feint, the tanks destined for fighting in the north were disguised as supply trucks by placing removable plywood superstructures over them.

The battle plan was as simple as Montgomery could make it. The infantry would lead the attack. As it was known that the weight of a man was not sufficient to set off a Teller anti-tank mine, the troops would simply walk across the minefields. The initial barrage was designed to neutralise the enemy artillery. The infantry would then engage the defending troops, who would be in a state of shock after the rolling barrage. Immediately behind the infantry, the sappers would clear paths through the minefields so that the tanks and anti-tank guns could be quickly brought up. The initial emphasis was to be on destroying the enemy's infantry as that would draw the Axis tanks into rescuing the infantry by counter attacking. They would be engaged and destroyed by the Allies' tanks and anti-tank guns that had been brought up. The Allied tanks would then be free to break through into the rear of the enemy.

All simple enough thought Wimberley. He was pleased that the division would have the Australian 9th Division closest to the coast on one side of the Highlanders with the 2nd New Zealanders on their left. After that came the South Africans and finally the Indians, showing the multinational makeup of the Allies' forces. Behind the infantry were the 1st and 10th Armoured Divisions of X Corps with tanks, armoured cars and truck-borne infantry. If all went to plan Montgomery estimated that it would be a "dog fight lasting about twelve days".

To direct the advance Montgomery had created a Manhattan-style grid system in the northern sector. Laterally and running parallel with the coast were six 'streets' of which those named Sun, Moon and Star were in the Highland sector. There were then 'avenues' running north to south. The first was the green line, known as Bombay, then the red line – Springbok, followed by the black line – Qattara, and finally the blue line – Oxalic. The infantry would advance along the streets, with their objectives and progress measured by when they crossed the avenues. Oxalic, the last avenue, was meant to have been reached by 03:10 hours on the 24th. If all went to plan it would mean that the infantry had crossed the minefields, destroyed the infantry emplacements guarding them, the sappers would have cleared paths in the minefields and the tanks and anti-tank guns would be in support of the infantry, ready to destroy the remaining Axis tanks when they counter attacked.

That's all there is to it, thought Wimberley, but the risks were obvious. The deception had to work, the artillery had to subdue the Axis guns and keep the defenders' heads down, the infantry had to overcome the enemy and the sappers had to clear lanes quick enough for the tanks to arrive in time to repulse the expected counter attacks. A lot could go wrong and, if it did, the effect would be devastating.

The first indicator of whether things were going well or not would come from the Camerons. Their objective, codenamed Inverness, was closest to the start line and so, in theory, they should be the first to give good news or report back problems.

Wimberley, a former Cameron himself, absentmindedly fingered the Cameron cap badge that he always wore as he waited for news. He knew the perils that the men faced and he was desperate for success. He also hoped beyond hope that his own Camerons would be the first indicator of that triumph.

"Excuse me Sir."

Wimberley dropped his hand from the badge and turned to see a staff officer holding a message. Wimberley took it with a word of thanks. He waited for the officer to leave then opened it. There were only two words printed inside – Camerons, Inverness.

Wimberley beamed.

★ ★ ★

Their night's work done, the Camerons dug in and prepared to defend their position in case of an enemy counter attack. The battle plan said that the next event to happen in this sector was for the 7th Battalion of the Black Watch to pass through the Camerons' position on their way to their objective, codenamed Kirkcaldy, which was on the blue line, Oxalic. Its capture would mean that Operation Lightfoot would have been a success on this part of the front.

The feature at Kirkcaldy lay on the end of Miteirya Ridge and was an oddity on the El Alamein battlefield in that it was a hill some thirty feet high. It may not have seemed much, but on a featureless desert that was as flat as a billiard table it was highly useful. It presented a difficult nut to crack but it would be worth it as, once taken, it would provide a bird's eye view of the battlefield. The thirty-foot hill had earned itself the nickname of 'the Ben' from the Highlanders.

Once the trenches and scrapes were dug, arcs of fire assigned and communications established, it was possible for one of the men in a trench to prepare a hot drink and something to eat whilst the other stood guard, watching for counter attack from the front and the arrival of the Black Watch from the rear.

It gave the men time to reflect on the night's activity.

"That was a short, sharp action," said Rod. He stood on guard while Mash got a brew going in their two-man trench.

"It was weird. In France the fighting was drawn out over days and weeks but here it was one event," replied Mash.

"Well, that's it for us for tonight. But I think the battle will go on for some time. You never know, Jerry may still put in an appearance."

"The boys did well though, didn't they?" said Mash as he stirred the tar-coloured tea.

"Aye, I was proud of them. They'll be feeling it now though," Rod accepted the mug from Mash and wrapped his hands around it. "We'll need to keep an eye out in case any react badly now that they've had time to think."

Mash was quiet for a second.

"It was a bloody miracle that the whole section got through unscathed. Though I heard we got off pretty lightly in attack, although this shelling's going to add to that if it gets any harder."

Rod nodded. The enemy fire was slowly growing in intensity as they came to their senses.

"I think the reason was the rolling barrage," he said, as logical as ever. "Without it then it would have been a different story. Also, you knocked out that machine gun before he'd clocked we were there. Nice throw by the way."

"Thanks, I was in the first eleven at school," said Mash with a grin.

"I don't know how many we killed but we seemed to have quite a few captured. I saw them being rounded up. There must have been at least fifty of them," mused Rod.

"Well we've done our bit. I hope it goes OK everywhere else."

"I'll second that."

"Men coming up from the rear," shouted Kipper. "Must be the Black Watch."

"Don't take any chances; make sure it's them before you relax," said Rod.

Men started to appear out of the gloom. They were definitely the Black Watch. It was clear that they were up for a fight as they shouted out battle cries and curses, as was their tradition.

"They do know it's us, don't they?" asked Mash.

"Maybe not," said Rod. "We'll be the first people carrying weapons that they see."

At that point, from further down the line came a booming voice.

"Halt, who goes there? Stand and be recognised!"

No response, the Black Watch kept coming. Mash could feel the tension rise. It was easier for the Camerons in their trenches to see than be seen. There was the distinct danger that the Camerons could be attacked by their own side.

"Uncle, I repeat Uncle," shouted the voice. Uncle was the password until midday on the 24th when it would be replaced by 'Harper'. Uncle Harper had been the nickname of the 51st Division's commanding officer in the Great War.

There was nothing in return.

"Shit, what are we going to do?" exclaimed Mash.

Before Rod could answer there was a familiar sound; the skirl of the pipes and a jaunty tune echoed across the desert.

"That's Pibroch o' Donald Dubh!" shouted Gordon

"Trust you to come up with that now," Mash shouted back.

"It's Black Donald's March to you ignorant Sassenach," replied Gordon with a grin on his face.

"I don't care what it is, it's working," said Mash.

The effect was instantaneous; as soon as the Black Watch heard the pipes the battle cries stopped, the attitudes relaxed and communication started. Slowly the Black Watch advanced through the Camerons on their way to Kirkcaldy.

"You had us worried there for a moment," shouted Gordon to a passing man.

"We thought it was strange that the Jerries and Eyeties had learnt to play the pipes," came the reply.

"You were right to be worried though, we'd stuff a Cameron any day of the week," came the comment from the next man in line.

"In your dreams laddie, in your dreams," replied Kipper. "Best of luck, give them hell."

A relative peace returned to the Camerons once the Black Watch had passed through. The rolling barrage was continuing, covering the Black Watch advance. But the amount of return artillery and mortar fire was continuing to increase, both on the advancing Black Watch and on the Inverness position.

As the minutes passed the men became aware of a lot of small arms fire from their front. All sorts of explosions rang out in the night.

"Sounds like the Black Watch are having a tough time of it," said Rod

"I wonder how things are going – for them and in general," replied Mash.

"No idea," said Rod, sipping his tea and wincing at the

scalding liquid. "It could all be going fine and we're going to be bored out of our wits. Or the next person we see could be Jerry wanting his patch of desert back."

"Nothing to do but wait I suppose," said Mash.

# CHAPTER TWELVE

# THE BEN

"Movement to the front," came the hushed but urgent call from Callum.

"OK, stand to everyone and be ready. Pass the word on to HQ," replied Rod. Everyone was up with their weapons at the ready, scanning for any sign of movement.

"There, I saw something straight ahead," said Gordon excitedly.

"Keep calm and don't fire until you're told to," said Rod.

"What the hell is it?" asked Kipper.

"It could be anything; Jerry, our own boys or a stray camel. Don't be too jumpy," calmed Mash.

Every eye strained into the darkness. The seconds ticked by, whatever was out there was not moving quickly. Mash worried that they were gathering for an attack. At that point there was the sound of scuffling boots close behind. Mash and Rod, who had been concentrating to the front, swung round quickly at the same time that a man dived into the trench.

"Evening gentlemen, what've you got for me?" said Platoon Sergeant Alastair Robertson as an introduction.

Rod and Mash relaxed.

"Movement out front, Sarge. Not sure what it is but they seem to be moving slowly," answered Rod.

They all peered out. Gradually, lit up by distant explosions, men started to come into view. They were crouching as though advancing and expecting trouble.

"I think they're Germans," said Mash.

"I'm not so sure," replied Robertson as he squinted at the shapes. "They're not formed up. If they are an attacking force I would have them out practising every day for a fortnight. Let's give them some time to get closer. If they're Jerry then they'll be walking into a killing field. If it's friendlies then it will do no harm."

Again they waited, watching men emerge out of the gloom. Robertson was right; there was no order to them, they were spread out in irregular clusters. Finally the challenge went out.

"Halt, who goes there? Uncle I repeat Uncle," shouted Robertson.

"Harper, Harper, it's alright we're Black Watch," came the faint reply.

"Advance and be recognised."

Slowly one of the men came forward. It was indeed a soldier from the Black Watch. He was clearly wounded and in pain; the blood across the whole of his stomach bore witness to the fact.

"Are you all wounded Black Watch men? No tricks now." asked Robertson

"Aye, we're Black Watch, it's just us. It's bloody murder up there, so many dead and injured."

"Alright laddie, you're safe now," said Robertson.

He turned to Rod.

"Get half your section up there to help them in, they look on their last legs. Keep a good eye out in case there're any Jerries tailgating them."

More men filtered back. If they said anything at all it was to confirm the bitter struggle going on up ahead and the dreadful casualties being taken. For those who did not say anything the look in their eyes spoke for them, along with their hideous wounds. As they appeared they were helped to a makeshift dressing station so that their injuries could be tended to before being sent to the rear.

"Jesus, it looks as though our boys are taking a pounding up there," said Finnean, the fear and worry clear on his face.

"No need to get jumpy Finn," counselled Gordon. "Let's just wait and see what the powers that be want to do."

After a short while word was sent for Rod, who quickly disappeared to find out what was happening. The rest of the section waited, helping stragglers as they came in and wondering what the future would bring.

★ ★ ★

"Alright lads, listen in," Rod looked at the section and started his briefing.

"It's clear that there's been a very stiff action up ahead that's still going on. We know from the casualties that the Black Watch have taken their first objective, Dundee on the Black line. They'll press on towards Kirkcaldy after they've had time to regroup. We also know that they were taking casualties all the way during the advance. It sounds like the Jerries were well awake by the time we finished here and there was constant artillery, mortar and machine gun fire all the way. There're also reports of lots of S mines and booby traps. What we don't know is what happened after Dundee. It might be that the Black Watch were able to drive through and take Kirkcaldy or that they were repulsed. Any questions so far?"

No one said anything. The same thought was in all their heads – if he is telling us this then it is going to involve us.

"OK. So everyone wants to know what's going on and that's where we come in," continued Rod. "As we're one of the few sections untouched by the assault on Inverness we've been chosen to make a rapid reconnaissance forward. We're to go onward and attempt to make contact with the remainder of the Black Watch. If they've taken the position and are in good shape then we help the wounded come back and report. If they need help in taking the position then we do all we can. If all we find are Jerries and Eyeties then we hotfoot it back here and report. Any questions?"

Again no one spoke. To a number this seemed like a tough job and they felt that they had already done their bit. But no one was going to say so. Plus, if part of the Highland Division was in trouble then they were going to help.

"Make sure you've got all the ammo you can carry, "said Rod. "Leave anything you don't need here and expect to be knackered by the time we get there – we've got a lot of catching up to do. The rolling barrage will have paused to allow the Black Watch to regroup after Dundee but it'll then have moved forward again with the remainder following it. We have to catch them up so we're going to have to move fast. Now get ready as we're going straight away."

Everyone rushed off to re-arm and drop anything that might slow them down.

"Anything I need to know?" Mash asked Rod as they prepared themselves.

"No, I think I covered it all. The key is to get there as quickly as possible without running straight into trouble. I reckon there won't be any opposition this side of Dundee so my plan is to get there on the double then progress more gingerly after that."

The men were ready in seconds. They quickly formed up in an arrowhead and set off, as Rod had planned, at the double. Whilst it was the most dangerous position, Rod had put Mash at point; he needed someone who had been in battle before and knew what to look for if they were going to be advancing quickly.

The dust from the rolling barrage had now started to settle so visibility was improving. The moonlight was returning and with it came the ghostly appearance of the dead flat desert. They had several miles to travel, with Dundee almost exactly half way along.

To begin with they made rapid progress. The light was sufficient to see the ground ahead and avoid any obstacles. The men had been worked hard since arriving in Egypt and they were fit, plus the cool night ensured that they did not get too hot. The rolling barrage had only created shallow craters. The mixture of sand and rock may not have provided any cover and did create a blinding dust screen when the shells landed, but the shells had barely made a mark on the surface. It was enough though to expose some of the Teller mines that had been laid. They looked like someone had scattered dishes all over the battlefield. Mash remembered from one of the lectures when they had been sailing out to Egypt that 'Teller' was the German for plate. But he also knew that each one contained over five and a half kilograms of TNT, enough to blow the tracks off any of the Allied tanks.

Immediately he also thought of the S mines. At this speed there would be no chance of seeing the trip wires that set them off. They were running on blind faith that either the barrage or the earlier advance of the Black Watch would have set off any S mines in their path. If they were wrong then the first they would know about it would be the snap of the initial charge as it threw the mine up to six feet into the air. And that would be the last they knew as they would then be showered by 360 ball bearings, each one as capable of killing a man as a bullet. Mash gritted his teeth and kept moving, hoping that this was not his unlucky night.

It was not long before they saw more evidence of battle. Bodies started to appear; to begin with they looked to have been killed by artillery. In some cases the men seemed to have just fallen down with no obvious marks. In others, the body had literally been blown apart.

"Keep going, don't stop," shouted Rod.

Some of the men slowed as they looked aghast at the bodies. They knew they were getting close to Dundee as the casualties started to have bullet wounds from the machine guns. The walking wounded had all gone, leaving only the dead and those in their death throes. Out of the corner of his eye Mash would see a movement, swing to engage, before realising that it was a man in agony trying to summon help. He forced himself to look away.

Soon they came across the first objective of the Black Watch, Dundee. In many ways it was the same as the Camerons' objective of Inverness and it was plain to see that a frontal assault had been driven through the position. Allied and Axis troops lay dead beside each other, often in tangled masses. It was clear that there had been a lot of Black Watch casualties, but they had taken the position.

"Take a quick breather, but maintain an all-round defence," said Rod. The section, glad of the chance to rest, slumped down on the ground.

"It looks as though the Black Watch had a hell of a time," said Mash.

'Aye," said Rod, panting slightly with exertion. "It makes me think they'll have problems at Kirkcaldy; it's more difficult than here and I'm not sure they've got enough men left."

At that moment they both swung round, weapons in the shoulder, as they spotted an arm slowing moving just feet away from them. It belonged to one of the men Kipper and Gordon had spoken to when the Black Watch had moved through the Cameron position. It looked like he had been caught by a burst from a machine gun as there were several wounds.

"Water," he whispered, almost so quietly that they did not hear.

Mash got the man's water bottle out and held it to his lips. The majority of the liquid fell down his tunic but Mash managed to get a few drops into his mouth.

"Thanks," he sighed.

It was clear that the man could not be moved and did not have long left.

"I'm sorry but we can't stay," said Rod gently.

"Don't let me be stopping you."

They made him as comfortable as possible and left. After a few yards Mash looked back. The man's head had already rolled to one side. If not dead then he was very close to it. They moved more carefully now, weapons at the ready and alert to any danger. The sound of battle grew closer, along with the thickening dust. They were catching the rolling barrage up and, with it, the Black Watch. Navigation at least was easy. The Ben was at the end of Miteirya Ridge and, given its height, was easy to find. As they drew closer they were also guided by the enemy fire coming from the position.

"That means that it hasn't been captured yet," said Rod. "Go carefully, we're either going to run into our boys, who'll be jumpy, or into the enemy. Either way they'll be trigger-happy."

In the event, contact with the Black Watch was a casual affair. They were challenged and provided the password, but it was clear that there was a lot of confusion and reorganisation going on. All the time they were under fire and the barrage was moving ahead. Rod grabbed a man and asked to be taken to the commanding officer. The man simply pointed to a group and dashed off. Rod found Lt Col Oliver and reported to him, who briefed him in return. Mash was standing nearby so overheard most of the conversation.

"We've taken a bit of a pounding getting up here. I reckon our leading companies have been reduced to a third of their starting strength and we've had six navigating officers killed or wounded," said Oliver.

That explains the casualties moving back to the rear thought Mash.

"We're currently pulling together two scratch companies that are going to do the assault and I want your section to join them, we need every able-bodied man. I'll send one of our walking wounded back to update everyone with what's going on," continued Oliver. "Captain Cathcart is going to lead the assault, you'll find him over there."

Rod went over to Cathcart to report while the others got their breath back. On his return he briefed them on the attack. With the nature of the Ben there was little alternative but to do a frontal assault. They would approach as close as possible behind the rolling barrage before making the final charge. Given that the enemy were thoroughly awake and aware of their presence, it was not going to be easy.

★ ★ ★

The Germans and Italians had occupied their positions for two months. In that time they had built some formidable defences in key places, such as Miteirya Ridge. They had managed to build trenches in the tough terrain, with additional support and communication trenches off them. There were artillery observation posts and anti-tank gun emplacements as well as mortars and machine gun nests. The Ben was a fearsome obstacle. In addition, whilst the rolling barrage was frightening and lethal to those in the open, the Germans and Italians soon learnt that if they were in a properly prepared trench they were relatively safe.

The main advantage to the Highlanders was that the barrage threw up so much dust that visibility was at a minimum; this meant that the Axis gunners only had a limited time to see their targets. The key was to keep close to the rolling barrage to give as little time as possible for the enemy to recover and the dust to settle. Fortunately for the Black Watch, Oliver and his officers had done an excellent job in keeping up with the barrage, despite the horrific losses sustained in the advance.

The Black Watch, along with Rod's section, were crouched down as they moved forward as close as they could to the barrage. They had to get as near as possible before charging and making the final assault. There was very little, if any, cover as they made their way forward towards the hill and the enemy.

"Christ they must see us any second," said Rod. "If they do then it's up and forwards."

Mash knew that to take cover when the enemy discovered them would be to die. If they stayed where they were then, with so little shelter, it would only be a short time before the machine guns found them. The only answer was to sprint into the fire and hope that they got to the enemy before they got them. It took a rare form of courage to stand up and run into enemy fire when every sense in your body was telling you to try and bury yourself into the ground.

Moving further forwards they encountered dense barbed wire, only partially destroyed by the barrage. They rapidly cut gaps in the remainder and pushed on. All of a sudden there was the bark of machine gun fire to the right. The advancing Highlanders had come across the first line of defences; strategically placed machine gun nests at the base of the ridge. A short but intense fire fight flared up briefly before the position was overrun. Mash wondered why they had not tripped a similar nest. He was still wondering when they came across the remnants of one. They had been very lucky; the nest had taken a direct hit from the barrage, totally destroying it. Had the barrage missed by a few feet either way then Mash and the others would have had a much warmer welcome.

The hill rose before them and they paused briefly at its base as they worked out the best way up. It provided a little more cover than the flatlands as the rocks and sand were weathered into shallow gullies and rises. Rod used hand signals to indicate that they were to follow a slight depression that ran to the left. It was only inches deep but at least it gave some form of cover.

As they advanced the dust and smell of cordite grabbed at the back of their throats. Even though it was very cold Mash was sweating, partly from the effort but also from the tension of waiting for the first contact. Moving up the hill was not difficult and the depression gave the small feeling of cover, but each yard brought them closer to the enemy.

They came across more and more barbed wire through which a corridor had to be cut. Whilst waiting for this to be done Mash glanced around and, even at the low height they had reached, he could see the reason that the position was so important. At only ten feet or so it felt like he was suspended in the air. On such a flat landscape any height would have a remarkable view, even if for now the amount of dust still in the air blanked it. He could only imagine what it was like from the top in clear daylight.

A burst of machine gun fire, sounding very close, made Mash jump. It was followed almost instantaneously by a scream as the bullets struck home. They had been seen and now it was every man for himself. Already Mash could hear the battle cries of the Black Watch as they charged. A split second later Rod too was on his feet.

"Go, go, go!" he shouted as he leapt forward.

The others immediately charged, screaming at the top of their voices. Mash's nerves vanished as he sprang into action. It was clear that they had woken up a hornets' nest; small arms fire was pouring down from the Ben. Up ahead a machine gun was firing, close enough for the gunners to be outlined by the muzzle flashes.

"Callum, Finnean, covering fire!" Rod shouted. "The rest of you, on that machine gun."

Callum and Finnean immediately dropped to one knee and began putting as many rounds on the target as possible. The gunners, sensing the attack from their right, turned to engage. Rod ran forward, firing his Tommy gun from the hip. Alone in the section the corporal carried a Thompson sub machine gun and it was very effective at this range.

One of the Germans had been hit and the other was frantically trying to swing back towards Rod. He was too late, the Camerons were on him, and he fell back with a round from Kipper in his chest.

Some of the men fanned out to either side of the trench whilst others continued over the top. All around was the din of close-quarter fighting; gunfire, screams and shouting. Rod and Mash went over the top and almost fell over the next position in the dust and confusion. There were three Germans in the trench who looked as surprised as Mash and Rod. Instantly Rod raised his Tommy gun and fired. The noise was deafening in the enclosed space. The burst killed one of the Germans and wounded another in the shoulder. He was swung round by the force and before he could recover Rod was on him, reigning blows onto his head with the butt of his Thompson. The man's head burst open like a ripe melon, showering everyone with blood. Rod beat the man until his skull was caved in and he was reduced to a twitching wreck.

Whilst Rod was fighting Mash was engaged with the third German. The man reacted before Mash and thrust out with his bayonet at Mash's stomach. In the restricted trench Mash could only just deflect the blade away and to his right with a defensive parry. He then drove forward as hard as he could, thrusting the stock of his rifle in to the face of the man. The German was caught off balance and fell backwards, blood streaming from his nose. In the separation this created between them Mash was able to lower his rifle and bayonet the man in the stomach. The man grunted as it pinned him. Mash twisted and pulled to release the blade.

Mash had no time to dwell on how close he had been to death. He and Rod peered over the trench and saw another machine gun firing at the attackers. A couple of grenades soon put paid to them. They moved up and over the trench and onto the next target, moving right to try to follow the line of the position. As they did so they came across a group firing at the Highlanders. Rod and Mash were on the inward side of the position so they came up behind and to the right of the firing men. Mash threw a grenade and Rod opened up with his sub machine gun. But he only got a few rounds off before he was out of ammo, having fired most of his twenty rounds in the earlier engagement. Mash heard him begin cursing the Army for not using the fifty-round drum magazine made famous in the gangster movies and berating himself for not keeping a count of his rounds. He was desperately reaching for another magazine when the grenade went off, drowning out the rest of the tirade.

The grenade killed and injured some, but at least five angry Germans had focused their attention onto Mash and Rod. Mash was able to fire two shots before the Germans were on them. He did not know where the rounds went but it was difficult to miss in the cramped quarters and he thought he accounted for two.

One of the Germans confronted Rod, who was still reloading and at a distinct disadvantage. The other two came for Mash, firing as they closed the gap. Mash instinctively ducked down and felt the blast of air as the rounds zipped past. One missed his head by fractions whilst the other passed through his tunic without touching him. The move had saved him from the rounds but crouching down he was off balance and the Germans barrelled into him. His rifle crashed away out of his grip as he went flying. He landed on his back, spread-eagled, with the two Germans towering over him. They raised their rifles, the bayonets angled at Mash's chest and stomach.

*Christ, this is it.*

He instinctively clenched his muscles, ready for the stab wounds that would drive into his unprotected body and, in the split second before the bayonets came down, he thought of Colette.

Then the head of one of his attackers exploded. One moment he was looking down at Mash ready to stab, the next his blood and brains spattered Mash and the other German who, glancing up, was just in time to see a bayonet hit him in his chest. The force of the blow drove the blade all the way up to the muzzle. The bodies of both Germans fell on top of Mash. He looked up to see Gordon staring down at him before turning a second later towards Rod.

Rod had done the only thing he could; he had got inside the arc of the rifle and bayonet of his attacker so that he could not be stabbed, but he had lost grip of his empty gun in doing so. He had grabbed the man and swung him round violently enough to dislodge his weapon. It meant that they were locked in a hand-to-hand brawl and the German was considerably bigger than Rod. In the preceding seconds the German's weight and power had told. Rod was on his back with the German on top of him. His forearm was across Rod's throat and the combined force of his weight and strength meant that Rod was choking. His eyes bulged with fear as he realised the fact. But suddenly the German went limp and slowly toppled forward onto Rod. Their faces met and in another world it looked like the two were kissing. Only Rod could feel and smell the blood as it bubbled up out of the dead German's mouth. In shock, with the weight of the German holding him down, Rod glimpsed Gordon above him. In his hands was his rifle, the blade covered in blood.

Gordon reached down and pulled the German off Rod and then turned to do the same for Mash.

"I think that makes us even," he said before giving Mash a wink. With that he was off, back to re-join the fight.

Rod and Mash lay stunned for a moment, both coughing and retching. They staggered to their feet, stumbling like drunks on a night out.

"Remind me to buy Gordon a beer," croaked Rod as he picked up his weapon and immediately reloaded it.

"Never thought I would be so pleased to see the little bugger," stammered Mash as he too retrieved his rifle.

★ ★ ★

It took them a few seconds to regain their composure before they went forward once more. Mash tried to wipe the fact that he had almost just died from his mind. It was too big to comprehend and he did not have time to try. The Highlanders' assault had descended into a hand-to-hand slugging match. It was reminiscent of a medieval battlefield as men beat each other with whatever came to hand, the action rarely opening out to more than a few yards. Men cursed, screamed, called for their mothers and died. It was a battle of attrition and, with the loss of numbers getting to the Ben, the result was in the balance. Glancing around, it was clear to Mash that a command blockhouse was forming the backbone of resistance in their area. There must have been twenty or so Germans firing continuously at the Highlanders. At either end of the position there were machine guns adding their weight to the defence. In front of the position was a pile of dead Highlanders, a statement to the strength of the defence.

"The only way to destroy that position is to loop round to the left and take that machine gun out first from the side," said Rod, thinking out loud. "Then we can roll up along the line and the machine gun at the other end won't be able to fire in case he hits his own side."

"Also, by rolling them up they'll be limited in how many can front up to us at one time," replied Mash.

"Round up as many of the boys as you can find quickly and let's see what we can do," said Rod.

Mash managed to find Gordon, Kipper, Callum and Finnean. He tried not to think about what had happened to Gasman, Drillbit and Niall.

He tried to express his thanks to Gordon for saving his life, but Gordon just brushed him away.

"Later," he said.

They all crouched down next to Rod who quickly briefed them.

"I want Callum and Finnean with me, we'll put down suppressing fire on the machine gun from that trench." He pointed to an abandoned stretch of trench in front and to the left of the machine gun nest. "The rest of you circle round and be ready to assault the position from over there." Again he pointed to a trench, this one further out to the left and in line with the German position. "As soon as you're in the position give us covering fire as we come up to join you and then we'll roll them up. Any questions?"

No one said anything so he continued.

"OK, we go in two minutes so get a move on. We'll start with three grenades so charge when you see them. Good luck."

They split up and quickly moved to their start positions. The distances were not great but there was no guarantee that the starting trenches were unoccupied. There was no fire as Mash and the others approached. Mash reached the lip and cautiously peered over the top. It had been a mortar pit and there were both German and Highlander bodies in the bottom. It had obviously been the site of a tough fight, but now it was unoccupied by the living. They climbed in and, stepping over the bodies, moved along to the point closest to the machine gun and waited. The gun was firing intermittently. It had stalled the advance and was now scanning the front, shooting at anything that attracted its attention. The seconds ticked by, each one feeling like a minute, whilst Gordon, Kipper and Mash crouched in the trench, ready to charge. Eventually three grenades arched over and fell round the nest. Rod and the others were throwing blind from within their position, but the grenades were close enough to the target and the gunners ducked when the explosions showered them with dirt and rocks. Instantly Mash heard the sound of Rod's Tommy gun, supported by Callum and Finnean's rifles.

Mash and the others leapt over the top of the trench and raced towards the machine gun. Mash was aware of rounds passing around him but, crucially, they were not from the machine gun. They reached the gun pit to find three men; one was unconscious and had been hit by either the grenades or, more likely, the suppressing fire. The other two were frantically swinging the gun round to meet them, but they were too late; Kipper shot one whilst Gordon bayoneted the other. In the pit they immediately started to fire at the troops in the adjacent trench. Mash grabbed the German machine gun, an MG34, and started to shoot, hugely increasing their firepower.

Out of the corner of his eye Mash saw Rod and the others spring up and run to join them. The troops in the trench had realised that they were being attacked from their right and were facing up to the threat. Rounds started to come towards the three as they ran, but there were not many and they were off target. Finnean was the first across and dived into the bottom of the gun pit, closely followed by Callum. The machine gun nest was getting full, what with five men in it plus the bodies of the Germans. Mash was engaged so he did not see Rod hesitate on the lip to spot a place for himself.

It was Finnean's shout that alerted him and the others to Rod's fall.

Mash swung round to see Rod lying draped over the body of a German. His head had turned as he had landed and he was staring with lifeless eyes at Mash. A trickle of blood ran out the side of his mouth.

The bullet had caught him just under his ribs on the right side, smashed its way through his lungs and heart before exiting near his left armpit. He was dead before he hit the ground.

Mash scrambled over the bodies towards Rod. He grasped Rod by his shirt and shook him. But Rod's head lolled backwards. Mash sat back on his haunches, trying to comprehend the sight before him.

"It can't be true," was all he could whisper.

But it was true, Rod was gone. Mash crouched, transfixed, staring at the body that had been his friend and companion. The others were all frozen too. They had never lost anyone in battle before and they looked in disbelief at the crumpled body that a few seconds ago had been leading them.

Gordon was the first to react. While the Highlanders had paused, the Germans were responding to the threat. The amount of fire had increased, although restricted by the limited front, shooting down the length of the trench. One or two had dared to leave the trench and move to the sides to get a better shot.

"For fuck's sake wake up you lot!" screamed Gordon. His voice wavered slightly but he started to return fire.

A grenade bounced into the pit. Just in time, Finnean was able to scoop it out of the trench to safety but it served its purpose in galvanising the others to return to the fray. All except Mash, who continued to look at Rod. He did not make a sound but tears slowly fell down his face, carving a track through the grime.

Another shout from Gordon snapped him out of his daze. He looked up to see the Germans attacking and he felt something break inside him. He leapt up, grabbing the MG34, and dived over the trench towards the Germans. With total disregard for his own safety he ran towards the enemy trench, firing for all he was worth. In his fury he had chosen well; the MG34 was the best machine gun in the world, combining a mobility that meant that one man could carry it along with an incredible rate of fire of over 800 rounds per minute. In the hands of a driven man like Mash it was a killing machine.

Bullets buzzed past him and he sensed one graze his shoulder and another hit his webbing, but he was in another world where pain and fear did not exist. Fire poured from the MG and soon found its mark. Men at the side of the trench facing him were flung backwards, impeding others and allowing Mash to progress. At the top of the trench Mash paused and poured a long burst into the trench. From that range it was carnage. Men were torn in two, limbs blown off and heads pulverised. Having disintegrated the first line of men the rounds passed through them into the next, wreaking the same slaughter on them. The effect was devastating. Germans not touched by the wall of lead panicked and turned as they saw what happened to their comrades. Some were leaping out of the trench to run to the rear, whilst others backed as far away down the trench as they could, all intent on getting away from the mad man. Mash continued along the top firing down into the trench below, which was becoming a mass grave of dead and dying.

Knowing they were going to be attacked, the German defenders had joined belts of fifty rounds into a long snaking trail of ammunition. But with the MG's rate of fire, Mash was getting through them rapidly. He fired the remaining shots at the far machine gun emplacement, before throwing the MG to one side and grabbing a dropped German Mauser. Seeing that all resistance had ended from the trench below him he ran towards the machine gun. From nowhere a German appeared in front of him. He had probably got out of the trench when Rod had died. The man stabbed forward with his bayonet and Mash did not have time to fully deflect the thrust. He felt an intense stab of pain as the bayonet entered his right forearm. It tore through the skin before immediately jarring against the bone, then it slid onwards for six inches before it exited short of his elbow. Mash's forward momentum pushed the blade away from him and the two men collided like players on a rugby field. Mash rolled over the top of the German as he fell and ended lying on his back, winded. Behind him the others of the section were close on Mash's heels; as the German struggled to get up he was dispatched by Kipper.

The others swept past onto the machine gun nest, quickly killing the occupants. The momentum had swung and all around the Highlanders were making progress and the Germans started to withdraw, some turning to fire as they pulled back, others dropping their weapons and running rearward. There were also men standing up with their hands in the air, ready to be taken prisoner. It was over, Kirkcaldy was theirs.

★ ★ ★

Mash remained lying where he was, staring at the stars and getting his wind back. He gulped deep breaths of air and felt the pain build in his arm as the adrenaline left him. He reached round for his first-aid kit. He managed to get the lint along the wound before trying to hold it in place with the bandage, which proved difficult as he was using his left hand. He cursed as it slipped and had to start again. By the end it looked a mess but it was all he could manage.

After a couple of minutes he pulled himself up and joined the others. They had pursued the fleeing Germans, only stopping when they came under fire from enemy positions behind the Ben as they started down the other side. Exhausted, they returned to the summit and started to consolidate the position. The Highlanders took over the German trenches, only this time facing west. They started to move the prisoners away, rearmed, cared for their wounded and prepared the fortifications along with the myriad of other things that needed doing. Eventually they collapsed into their positions.

Mash was joined by Gordon in a trench.

"For Christ sake let me sort that arm out for you, that dressing looks like the first attempt of a ten-year-old boy scout."

Mash let Gordon get to work. He had been lucky in that the blade had peeled the skin back without cutting into muscle or breaking the bone. It still hurt like hell but Gordon made a much better job of bandaging it.

"What time is it?" Mash asked Gordon.

"About quarter past six," came the answer. "It'll be sunrise soon, I reckon we must have taken the place at about four."

Gordon was quiet, then looked at Mash from the corner of his eye.

"Are you OK?" he asked.

"I'm just numb now," said Mash. His fury of earlier had left him and his senses felt deadened.

Gordon nodded and Mash turned to look at him. Gordon's face was pale beneath the sunburn. Gordon had not lost anybody before; this was the first time he was feeling this sort of pain and shock. Unfortunately Mash knew the feeling only too well. His thoughts turned to Colette and, as always, the image of her lying in a pool of blood, just as Rod had been.

He pressed his hands to his eyes and pushed, trying to dislodge the image.

"Shit, I suppose this means that I'm in charge of the section now," he said, attempting to distract himself and Gordon.

"Aye it does," said Gordon. "Don't worry, we'll be behind you. I hate to admit it but for a Sassenach you're not bad," said Gordon with a smile, hoping that the humour would lighten things.

Mash gazed out from the top of the Ben. Behind him the first hint of dawn was starting to creep over the horizon. Mash shivered in the desert night. He was dog-tired and his mind was a whir of thoughts. On top of everything he had to get his head around being in charge of the section. This was a momentous time for them as well as him and Gordon was right to make him realise his responsibilities, but he had big boots to fill. He thought bitterly about how proud his mother would be to hear he was in charge. He himself had wanted to rise to a position of authority. But not like this.

"Thank you by the way," said Mash into the silence.

"For what?" said Gordon.

"You saved my life," he said. "And Rod's," he added.

Gordon shook his head as though it had been nothing.

"I told you, we're even now," said Gordon.

Mash rolled his eyes.

"I saved you from a beating, I was about to be speared by that German. So thanks."

"Well," said Gordon.

Mash waited for him to finish, but that seemed to be all he could come up with. Mash did not feel the need to say anymore.

He and Gordon continued to sit, not speaking, and watched the sunrise. It illuminated the landscape of the battlefield, spilling colours into the day; pinks, oranges and yellows, as well as forming darker shadows on the desert. In the clear morning air, still cool before the heat of the day, the scene laid out before Mash was a truly beautiful one. He could see for miles in crisp detail and he even briefly forgot about his exhaustion and pain to drink in the view.

He realised that the battle was going to be fought over this ground and he could start understanding the topology of it. Ahead and to his right, a couple of miles distant, was Kidney Ridge, which was not a ridge at all but a depression. Further back in the distance, running north/south, was the Rahman track which formed the backbone of the Axis defensive line. He drank in every detail, all the subtle contours and landmarks, until he felt he knew the land well. It was what Rod would have done.

Later that morning the section were released from their duties at the Ben and told they were free to re-join their unit. They wearily made their way back to the other Camerons at Inverness. As they went they had their first indications that the battle had not gone according to plan. There was a horrendous traffic jam of armour all the way back. Every so often a tank or other vehicle had hit a mine at the very edge of the cleared lane, probably because the driver had lost sight of the lane marker, or the vehicle had broken down or been hit by enemy first. The lanes were so narrow that if one stopped everything else piled up behind it. Men sweated as they tried to push trucks out of the way or get them towed; sergeants shouted and voices were raised.

"This is going to take hours to get sorted," said Gordon.

"The lanes aren't wide enough," replied Mash. "Though given the problems of last night it's a miracle to get a lane cleared at all."

At that moment a salvo of enemy artillery fire came over and they all dived for cover. A lorry was hit, although its driver had time to take cover and was not injured. But the fire and explosion from the wrecked vehicle added to the already chaotic scenes.

"Christ, if the German artillery zeros in or their planes put in an appearance then they'll be sitting ducks," said Gordon.

None of the section were in any state to help, so they moved on and eventually linked up with the other Camerons. Mash went off to find Lt Wilson-Brown to report back and to tell him of the fight and the loss of Rod. They had only just got back in time; the Camerons were in the process of moving to be in reserve for 154 Brigade. Mash made his report to WB, who listened mainly in silence while Mash delivered his report, only asking the odd question for clarification. When Mash had finished they were both quiet for a moment, then WB exhaled deeply.

"Look, I know you and Rod were close and had been through a lot together," he said, shifting his eyes around the room, focusing anywhere but Mash's face. "But that's war and what we're about. It sounds like it was over for him instantly and that's a blessing. The best thing you can do is not to dwell on it and move on. This battle is a long way from being won and we need everybody to be on top of their game."

His eyes finally came to settle on Mash. He was more comfortable now they were talking about the fighting.

"I want you to take over the section going forward from here. Now I suggest you go and get your arm seen to at the dressing station. You're going to need a few stitches to say the least. Take one other with you and afterwards see what you can scrounge up in terms of ammo, dressings and anything else that you think might be of use. Not sure you will get anything as everyone is in short supply after last night but no harm in trying. Now carry on."

Just as Mash was leaving WB spoke again.

"Well done for what you did out there. It sounds as though it was a hard fight and you boys did a good job."

Outside, Mash made his way back to the section. He called them together to brief them on the conversation with WB.

"Sorry to tell you lads, but WB's told me to take over the section."

"Bloody hell, these English bastards are taking over everywhere," came the ribald response from Gordon.

"It's been that way for centuries, we do all the fighting and they get all the rewards," chipped in Kipper.

"He'll have us doing drill on the parade ground and morning inspections every day," added Callum.

"Have I told you about the time I had an English sergeant at basic training?" started Drillbit before he was drowned out by jeers and catcalls from the others, just as they always did when he started on one of his monotonous stories.

The banter was somewhat forced but it made them feel better.

"Well I only hope I can do as good a job as the last man," said Mash.

The others murmured their agreement. He looked at them to see that most of their eyes were red. Callum, the largest and strongest man in the section, unabashedly had tears running down his face, whilst Niall, usually the centre of attention, was quiet and withdrawn. Mash realised that he could not dwell on the past and that these men were now his responsibility.

"But this does mean that I get first night rights over you lot," he added.

There was a roar of protest at the mention of the ancient right that the English lords had been given by the hated King Edward Longshanks to bed a Scottish bride on her wedding night.

"Mind you, looking at some of Gasman's conquests I think you would be bloody brave," piped in Gordon.

All the section, including Gasman, laughed. Mash smiled then left them to it. He and Gordon set off to go to Divisional HQ.

★ ★ ★

Throughout the previous night, reports had continued to reach Wimberley. After the good start from the Camerons the news had been mixed. At dawn on the 24th Wimberley knew that about half of the allotted objectives had been achieved. Even where they had not, a big bulge had been made into the Axis lines. There was still work to do in taking all of the objectives on the Oxalic line but, overall, Wimberley was pleased and proud of the performance of the Highland Division.

But the wider battle was not going well; the early morning reconnaissance flights by the RAF had shown that the main

Axis battle lines were little changed from the previous morning. In Wimberley's mind this was down to the armour and he was still fuming at the arguments that he had been having with his opposite numbers. Whilst the infantry had managed to achieve many of its objectives and make a substantial bulge in the line, the armour had not exploited a single opportunity. Nowhere had they broken out beyond the Axis defences to protect the infantry from the expected enemy tank counter attack. With only one exception they were all still in the minefields. To Wimberley and the other infantry commanders the armoured units lacked the aggressive spirit required and were in need of determined leadership. Brigadier Fisher's 2nd Armoured Brigade had refused to move forward as they said the Highland Division had not cleared the way, despite the fact that their orders were to fight their way through even if the infantry got stuck. Both Wimberley and Morshead, the Australian divisional commander, were adamant that, as a whole, the Armoured Division, under Brigg's command, had missed opportunities to break out. The tank men were accused of seeing an 88mm around every corner and lacking any drive. Fortunately for the infantrymen, Montgomery was of the same opinion and gave Lumsden, Brigg's and Fischer's commander, a dressing down and said that if they hung back any more he would replace them.

Wimberley was still dwelling on the problems with the armour as he clambered into the jeep that was to take him to see the Black Watch early on the 24th. He mused that they had lost the element of surprise and it would now become a slow grind from here on out. The vehicle bounced its way forward. Wimberley sat in the passenger seat with his gangly legs tucked into the confined space so that his knees were under his chin. He saw the same traffic jams that Mash had seen. On the one hand this made him fume even more as he thought of the missed opportunity whilst, on the other, he could begin to understand the difficulties the tank men had. He knew of the problems with the time it had taken and the fact that the sappers were having to probe for the mines under shelling and machine gun fire, plus the hindrance that the bottlenecks caused.

"That's all well and good," thought Wimberley. "But if my boys were stopped by every problem then they would never have moved from the start line. The tankies have got to drive through."

Wimberley was thinking on this problem when there was suddenly a blinding flash. He felt a roaring heat then a jolt as he was thrown from the jeep. A second later he slammed into the earth, his body crumpled like a ragdoll.

"Are you OK Sir?" were the first words Wimberley heard as he came round. His eyes struggled to focus on the faces above him. For a minute he had no recollection of where he was. As the faces came into focus, so did his memory of the explosion.

"I'm fine," Wimberley replied, but he did not recognise his own voice.

As his head cleared and he regained his senses, he saw beyond the men the thick black smoke billowing up from the pile of wreckage that had so recently been his jeep.

"What happened?" he croaked. Every part of him was aching but especially his head. He reached up tentatively and felt the wet warmth of blood in his hair.

"You hit a mine," said one of the men.

"You were thrown at least twenty yards then you hit your head on a rock when you landed Sir," said another one.

Wimberley's grip on consciousness was loose for the next couple of hours but eventually he pieced together that when the mine had gone off he had been blown clear of the devastation. He had been incredibly lucky to survive without major injury, escaping with only a concussion. Unfortunately, the same could not be said for the other occupants in the jeep. His driver and a soldier acting as his personal protection had been killed and the officer he was travelling with was seriously injured.

He spent the rest of the morning being brought back and checked out by the MO. He had a cracker of a headache but apart from that he was fine. The MO had made it very clear to him how lucky he had been and the need to take it easy. But as he arrived at his HQ he was confronted by a full-blown disagreement between his own officers and those of the Armoured Brigade about the positions they had reached.

Relations between the infantry and armour officers were already at a low following the row about the lack of a breakthrough by the armour. Against this heated background, agreement could now not be reached on something as simple as map reading. The problem was that in a barren and featureless desert with no natural landmarks, it was incredibly difficult to accurately pinpoint the locations of men and objectives. As Wimberley was embroiled in the argument it became clear that the infantry and armour maps differed by as much as two-thirds of a mile. To make matters worse, even the two divisional artilleries could not agree on the matter. The potential for a calamity was huge if the infantry and armour did not know where each other were and both were in danger of being shelled by their own side. To Wimberley's mind the argument descended into farce when the realisation was made about Kidney Ridge being a depression. Apparently someone had misread the map symbol for a depression some time ago when the position was first analysed and the name Kidney Ridge had stuck.

Wimberley thought on the stupidity of this as his head pounded. The argument was going nowhere and the HQ was hot and stuffy.

"Gentlemen," he said in a raised and irritable voice. "I'm

not prepared to sit here and listen to this squabbling on something as basic as whether a depression is a ridge or not when the outcome of a battle and men's lives depend on it. Get out now and don't come back until you all agree where Kidney Ridge is and any other position we might feel like attacking to win this battle."

In silence the officers filed out, each feeling that they were in the right but had still been told off. As soon as they were outside voices were raised again as each continued to push their point.

# CHAPTER THIRTEEN

# SNIPE

Mash was sitting on a low wall outside the hospital, where he had just had his arm stitched up properly. He sat in the sun immersed in thoughts; now that he had slowed down the reality of Rod's death was creeping up on him. He was trying to keep his mind focused on the unit and what he should do next but his grief was threatening to overflow.

His thoughts were interrupted by a sharp pain in his wounded arm and he was jolted out of his reverie.

He turned to see that Gordon was digging him in the ribs and had accidently caught his arm.

"Get off my bloody arm!" Mash snarled at Gordon who, instead of stopping, continued his assault on his ribs whilst pointing off to an alley down the side of the hospital.

"Come and have a look at this," said Gordon, oblivious of Mash's confused state.

With difficulty Mash dragged his thoughts back into the present and focused on Gordon.

"I went to have a leak down this alley. It leads on to the Divisional HQ area and just as I'm about to pee I hear these raised voices coming from between some parked-up trucks. You'll never guess what it was – come and have a look."

Reluctantly Mash followed Gordon and, soon enough, he could hear raised voices. Like a couple of schoolboys they peered round the corner of a truck and saw two officers, one from the Highland Division and another from 1st Armoured Division.

They were clearly arguing, though they were trying to do so in hushed tones. It was very rare for Other Ranks to see officers having a disagreement, even if the officers had tried to get out of sight. But here they were, at one moment consumed by events and not far off a slanging match, whilst at the next moment conscious of their surroundings and trying to talk in hushed tones and act as though nothing was amiss. The sight was enough to shift Mash out of his reverie; he found the sight almost comical.

"What's wrong with them?" asked Mash.

"They're arguing over a map. Seems like they can't agree where any landmarks or positions are. With a bit of luck this could end in a punch-up, a shilling says the Highlander wins."

They continued to listen as discreetly as they could.

"I thought I heard them say Kidney Ridge a moment ago," said Mash. "We know where that is, we were looking at it from the Ben."

"Now don't you start get any stupid ideas," counselled Gordon. "When the elephants are mating, keep out of the long grass."

"What?" said Mash. "That's a bloody weird saying."

Gordon shrugged.

"I'm just saying you don't want to get involved when officers are arguing – it can only end up bad."

"Anyway," said Mash. "I'm sure they're talking about the ground on the western side of the Ben. We know that ground. I spent a long time looking at it this morning."

As he was speaking the argument was coming to an end, though by the looks on the officers' faces an agreement had not been reached. Both men turned to walk in opposite directions; as they did so Mash walked round the corner of the truck and, before Gordon could stop him, approached the Highland officer. He saluted smartly.

"Excuse me, Sir, but I couldn't help overhearing your conversation."

"You what? Do you make a habit of listening to other people's conversations?" snapped the officer, clearly still up for a fight. Mash lowered his gaze to look him squarely in the eye.

"With respect, Sir, it was difficult not to overhear. Anyway, I think I can help you."

The officer blustered and looked down.

"You say you can help?" he asked contritely.

"Yes Sir, I heard you talk about Kidney Ridge and the difficulty in locating it when there aren't any features to help. My section was on the Ben last night helping out. This morning we got to see the ground laid out in front of us and from the top of the ridge. I was able to make a detailed study of the terrain. I reckon I know it well and I certainly know where Kidney Ridge is."

The officer was somewhat taken aback.

"Are you telling me that you know unequivocally where Kidney Ridge is? Do you think you'd be able to guide troops to it, at night?"

"I'm sure of it in daylight, Sir. Night will be much more difficult but I'm willing to give it a go."

Behind him Mash heard a faint but distinct groan from Gordon. Mash was volunteering himself, but he knew that Gordon would consider himself part of the team. This was lost on the officer who was deep in thought. Suddenly he made up his mind.

"Right, come with me," he said and set off at a fast walk which took both Mash and Gordon by surprise. They quickly gathered their kit and dashed off after the officer.

Minutes later they were in front of a map. There were the positions of various units marked out but Mash did not spend time looking at those. Instead he quickly orientated himself to the area shown on the map. There were surprisingly few landmarks but Mash was able to see the Ben and from there get his bearings.

"So where do you think Kidney Ridge is?" asked the officer.

"By my reckoning it's here," replied Mash, pointing to the map. There was a moment's silence before the officer reflected.

"That's where we think it is but I'm afraid there are many who don't agree."

He paused again and looked at Mash. Eventually he seemed to come to some decision.

"You two wait here and I'll be back shortly."

Mash and Gordon sat themselves down in a couple of chairs and looked nervously around them.

"Why the bloody hell did you have to open your mouth?" Gordon whispered. "There we were, ready to go and re-join the boys and you have to start volunteering, what's got into you?"

"I didn't like the way that tanker was having a go at our man."

"Well from where I was standing he was giving as good as he was getting, and in any case why do you feel the need to put your nose in where it's not wanted?"

"That's not what you said when I turned up behind the NAAFI and disturbed your party with Mitchell," retorted Mash. "Anyway, I didn't include you, why did you feel the need to tag along?"

"Tag along?" Gordon bristled, but he could not go any further because Major General Wimberley strode into the room. He was followed by the officer from outside. Both Mash and Gordon leapt to their feet and stood rigidly to attention.

"OK, stand easy. Now which one of you professes to know the countryside?"

"Sir," said Mash with as much conviction as he could. He was now wishing that he had done exactly what Gordon had suggested and kept his nose out; he never imagined he would be called up in front of Wimberley himself.

"So tell me how you are able to, in our opinion, accurately identify key positions when half the Army thinks you're wrong?"

Mash started to tell the story of the Ben as he had done earlier. All the time he stared at an invisible point somewhere over Wimberley's head, not easy given his height, but sufficiently close to Wimberley to see a frown run across his brow when he heard Mash's accent.

"So," said Wimberley once Mash had finished. "We have an Englishman in the midst of my Highlanders who helps out the Black Watch in what, by all accounts, was a very hard but successful action, and then appears by magic ready to solve our problems. All sounds a bit strange. So how did you come by him?" said Wimberley, staring at the officer.

He blinked and glanced at Mash and Gordon, who kept quiet.

"Ah, heard them talking outside about what had happened on the Ben and how they had a good view of the place, Sir," he said.

There was a moment's silence whilst Wimberley glanced at Mash and Gordon who stood transfixed, looking over his head with the thousand-yard stare.

"Don't you know that careless talk costs lives?" said Wimberley to Mash but staring at the officer, who flushed red and looked away. Wimberley turned his attention to Gordon.

"And why should I trust an Englishman? Is it too much to ask for a Scot in a Highland Division?" Then looking directly at Gordon, "I suppose you're another Englishman too?"

"Gu dearbha chan e!" said Gordon, which meant 'Indeed I am not'. "Stornoway born and bred, Sir." Gordon summoned his courage and continued, "Begging your pardon, Sir, but he's lived and worked in Scotland long enough for him to be a pretty good Mash man, Sir!"

The corner of Mash's mouth twitched as he held back

a smile; it said a lot that Gordon would defend him against Wimberley of all people.

Wimberley looked at Gordon closely who, in return, continued to stare intently at the imaginary spot somewhere above Wimberley's head. It was well known that Wimberley was a furiously proud Scot who had tried hard to ensure that only Highlanders were allowed into the Highland Division. In this he had failed as various detachments and replacements had, in Wimberley's eyes, continued to corrupt his division.

Wimberley thought for a moment and looked intently at both before speaking.

"Alright gentlemen, sit down and listen in."

Mash and Gordon glanced at each other before doing as they were told. This was one of the many things that made Wimberley so popular with his troops, the ability to communicate with the ordinary ranker and put them at ease.

"We've made a good start with the battle and you boys have done well," started Wimberley. "But in order to win we have to get the armour through Jerry's lines and into the desert. We want to create a couple of forward positions to act like the hinges of a door that the armour can pass through and into the enemy's lines. The problem is that the armoured boys and ourselves seem to have come to an impasse over our ability to read maps. At the moment we seem to be the best part of a mile apart in our understanding. The artillery are using our maps and will be firing in support on objectives where we think they are. Given this could be a very long way from where the armoured boys think they are then the possibility of hitting the wrong side is enormous and could be catastrophic to the mission. We've been getting ourselves in a tizz all day over it."

Wimberley paused and looked at the two of them, as if wondering whether to continue. Without realising it both Mash and Gordon leaned forwards a little in their seats.

"What I want to do is to attach you two to the 2nd Rifle Brigade under Lt Col Turner's command; you can guide him to a point just to the south of the western edge of Kidney Ridge. Let me tell you two things up front. Firstly, as 2RB are part of Brigg's Armoured Division I suspect they will be less than happy to have you aboard and telling them they can't map read for a toffee. In fact it's by no means a done deal that they'll agree to have you along. The second point is that this could be a very risky operation as I don't suspect Rommel will take having these forward positions too kindly. So I'm sorry but you may well have trouble from Jerry and from our own side. Have I sold it well enough to you, are you in?"

"Yes, Sir," replied both Mash and Gordon immediately, totally seduced by the way in which Lang Tam had taken them into his confidence. Wimberley looked hard at them.

"Alright gentlemen, thank you for your help. I'll speak to my opposite numbers and see where we get to. I suggest you return to your unit. If I don't call for you then you'll know that the armoured boys want to keep the party to themselves. Otherwise you'll get orders attaching you to 2RB for the duration of this operation. Any questions? No? Right, carry on."

With that he was up and away, closely followed by the officer, leaving Mash and Gordon looking at each other.

"That did just happen didn't it?" said Mash.

"I'm not sure," said Gordon, letting out a long breath.

★ ★ ★

Lt Col Turner sat in senior company, surrounded on all sides by generals, but he was not a happy man. After a false start on the 25th he had been summoned to Brigade HQ on the 26th where he had been ordered to capture and hold an objective called 'Snipe'; a spur to the south-west of Kidney

Ridge. He had immediately done a recce of the approach and had quickly discovered the disconnect over the exact location of the objective and the differences in map reading. He had returned to HQ to try and find some answers but instead had found himself sat with generals Wimberley, Lumsden and Briggs as well as his boss Brigadier Bosvile. It was clear to him that the disagreements stretched right the way to the top. He was becoming increasingly frustrated that both sides were convinced they were correct and not prepared to come to an agreement, without which they were putting the lives of his men at risk. In a pause he coughed loudly and all eyes turned to him. Turner was aware he needed to tread a narrow line. After a moment's pause he came up with the astute and politically wise way forward of telling them that he would assume that the Armoured Division were correct until proved wrong, then he would follow the barrage. The meeting broke up, but as they went outside Wimberley asked if he could have a word.

"Look, I understand your position and I know you were frustrated in there. I can assure you we all are. I just wanted to tell you that I've got a couple of men who know where the objective is and the lay of the land very well. They can help guide you to the objective if you think it'd be of use. I've spoken to them personally and can vouch for them. I hope it's of use to you."

Turner was taken aback but tried not to show it. While his face remained blank his mind ran over the proposition; part of him thought that the last thing he needed was a couple of Highlanders confusing things; on the other hand it was the first offer of help to solve the navigation issues he had received.

"Thanks for the offer," he said slowly, "I'll take them. But please understand that I'll do as I said; I'll follow a bearing which assumes my chain of command is correct and only deviate if the barrage goes in a different direction."

"That's understood. Hopefully there won't be an issue but it might help if you have someone who knows where they are. I'll get them sent over to you. The very best of luck."

Mash and Gordon reported to Lt Col Turner in the afternoon of the 26th. A short, stocky man with a moustache, he calmly and professionally finished going about his business before he turned to Mash and Gordon. He then reiterated what he had told Wimberley about his strategy, plus he explained that two scout platoons would lead the way in their carriers with the rest of the recce platoon following on foot. They were to accompany him and that kick-off would be at 23:00. Once the advance party was in position they would call forward the anti-tank guns and the vehicles, which would remain at the start line until the position was taken. With that they were dismissed.

"He didn't seem all that happy to see us," said Gordon.

"What do you expect?" said Mash. "I reckon he'd have had a job to turn down a request from Lang Tam. Still he seems to know what he's doing."

"Aye, and it looks to be an interesting collection. From what I can see there're a load of anti-tank guns with transport, jeeps and Bren gun carriers."

"The anti-tank guns look to be the new six-pounders so that'll add to the fire power. They all look a tough lot as well, as though they've seen a bit of action."

"That should mean we've got a good chance. Let's just hope they listen to us when it comes to the navigation."

With that they settled down and waited for nightfall.

★ ★ ★

"We're going to head off on 233 degrees, any comments?" said Turner to Mash without looking up. Mash swallowed.

"I would suggest further to the west, Sir," he said and pointed in the direction he thought was right.

Turner shot him a glance that at once made Mash feel like he was back at school and had made a basic error with his maths.

"Well, that may be but we'll be heading out on 233 degrees until I deem otherwise," said Turner in a quiet tone but one which left Mash in no doubt as to the merit of his proposal.

At that moment the barrage opened up and the column set off with the carriers in the lead. However, it soon became clear that the barrage was not following the same line of advance as the 2RB. With every second the barrage moved to the right of their line, more than thirty degrees to the west. Turner gave the order to turn to the west to follow the barrage. Turner looked at Mash and gave a small nod followed by a stare which, at the same time, conveyed his recognition of Mash's accuracy and a warning not to look smug. Mash felt he had won a mini victory but made sure his face wore nothing but a deadpan expression.

"Jesus, this is heavy going," muttered Gordon. The sand they were walking in was soft and every step was an effort. They also kicked up so much dust that they could not see very far ahead.

"This dust and the shifting sand will make it hard for the guns to come up. I hope they make it," said Mash.

"How far do you think we've gone?" asked Gordon.

"I would guess about a thousand yards," said Mash, trying and failing to see behind him. "It's difficult to tell. I started counting my steps but it's not a realistic measure in this sand. The only good news is that there's still a lot of moonlight so I've been able to keep a rough idea of where we are."

At that moment there was a burst of fire from one of the carriers and a flurry of activity as men jumped from the carriers and went forward. There was the sound of shouting, then everything died down again quickly. Soon after, Mash saw an officer come to report to Turner. He shifted forwards to eavesdrop.

"What's going on?" whispered Gordon.

"Apparently we came across a group of Germans. They were totally surprised by our arrival and they've taken the majority as prisoner. Some got away though."

"I bet they're telling their powers that be we're here," groaned Gordon

"I doubt it, they probably haven't stopped running. Anyway come the morning it'll be clear enough where we are."

On they pressed again. After another thousand yards Mash was summoned by Turner.

"How much further do you think we need to go?" asked Turner. "I've been using the milometer on the jeep and I reckon we've gone 2000 yards which means we must be nearly there."

"I reckon we still have the best part of a mile to go Sir," said Mash only to receive a piercing glance from Turner. Mash wondered why Turner had brought him on the advance if he was not going to listen to him. But then Turner's brow furrowed as he considered his options.

"All right, the barrage is continuing so they obviously believe we're not there yet. We'll press on for another thousand yards but I think that'll be far enough, I can't believe it's further than that."

On they pressed through the sand. Mash could see that Turner was concerned but also knew that they were away from the objective. He too was starting to question himself; judging distance was difficult and they were now well away from the front lines. Finally they came across an oval depression. Turner called a halt and Mash was summoned once more.

"I think we've got at least a half mile to go Sir," answered Mash to Turner's question.

"Well I'm not sure; we're past where I thought the objective would be and this depression looks promising. The barrage is still coming down though. Tell the FOO to come up will you." This last comment was to his adjutant. Seconds later the forward observation officer for the artillery joined them.

"Tell your gunners to fire a single smoke shell on where they think the objective is will you," said Turner. The FOO disappeared to give the order. A short time later they saw the smoke shell burst about 300 yards in front. It made up Turner's mind.

The depression turned out to measure 900 by 400 yards and was, at most, three to four feet deep. It had been occupied by the Germans, of whom the corpses of some remained, and had been used as a store depot with a small bunker at one end which was taken over as the HQ. Turner then sent the word 'Cotswold', the success message, back to the remainder of his force to start the process of ferrying the guns and ammunition up to the position. Now that they had arrived at the position, although Mash was still sure that they were short of where they should be, Mash was no longer required.

"There's no point in you making the return trip," Turner had said. "So pick yourselves a bit of perimeter and make yourselves useful."

And so he and Gordon picked a stretch of perimeter in the south-western corner and made themselves at home.

"We need to dig in but it's going to be difficult in this sand," said Mash. "At least this depression gives good cover along with these bushes and the camel thorn."

"Aye, I was talking to one of the Rifles boys and they were telling me that a six-pounder will just peer over the top, a natural dug-in position."

"Good, hopefully we won't have too long to wait until they come up."

Unbeknownst to them the guns were having a hard time of it. Soon after Turner and the others had left they had been hit by a stick of bombs from a bomber and had then been subjected to artillery fire. In the chaos the medical officer ended up being left at the start line as he looked after the wounded men. Once the guns and transport got going they continued having difficulties; constantly having to dig or tow vehicles out after becoming bogged down in the sand and struggling to find their way in the dust. Eventually they made it to the position and deployed an all-round defence around the perimeter at just before 04:00. In total thirteen of the battalion's guns made it plus another six from the Royal Artillery's 239 Anti-tank Battery attached to 2RB for the operation, somewhat short of the planned twenty-seven.

Whilst the guns were being positioned and stores unloaded Mash and Gordon saw a section of Bren gun carriers set off towards the enemy.

"I wonder what they're up to?" mused Gordon

"Checking to see there's no one just in front of us I'd imagine," said Mash.

A short time later the relative calm was shattered by sustained gun fire only a mile or so to the west. Rounds zipped through the night and soon several vehicles were on fire. At first all the fire seemed to come from one direction but soon it was answered with an ever growing barrage of return fire that included tank rounds, highlighting that there was a large enemy force out there.

Mash and Gordon watched the flames.

"I'm not sure what we've got ourselves into," said Gordon as he pulled on a cigarette. "There seems to be a hell of a lot of fire."

"Look," said Mash. "The fire from our side's dying down so they must be withdrawing."

It was not long before the carriers rushed back to the depression and the crew spilled out, all full of the engagement they had just been in.

"What happened?" Mash asked one of the men from the carriers, offering him a cigarette which he gratefully took.

"We only got about 750 yards before we spotted a lot of tanks and the like. Our boss decides to have a go as they're hankered down for the night. So in we go shooting at anything that moves, including the tanks. Mind you we've collected a fair number of extras over the years so we can lay down a fair bit of lead. Anyway, it doesn't take Jerry long to wake up and he spots us by the light of the burning lorries and now it's our turn to start fretting. The boss thinks we've stirred it up enough and so we beat a hasty retreat, we lost one of the carriers though."

"Sounds like you had a night of it. There were lots of tanks you say?"

"Yup, loads of them, it was like some sort of holding position for them and they were being refuelled and rearmed."

At that moment there was a shout to stand to and they all took up their positions on the rim of the depression. Out in the dark was the unmistakable sound of tanks, their engines gunning as they manoeuvred, along with the constant squeak and screech of tracks. From the light of the earlier engagement they could make out two groups, one coming straight for them whilst the other headed further north.

"What do you reckon?" said Gordon as they watched the tanks roll forward.

"Not sure if they're chasing the carriers or not. If they are then why split the force, if not then they're heading straight for us," said Mash as he watched the tanks advance.

"Won't be long before the guns open up," said Gordon as though to sooth his own nerves.

"Aye, but I doubt they're fully dug in and anyway they can't aim in the dark," said Mash.

"Go on, cheer me up why don't you?"

"There seem to be a lot of them; I reckon about twenty to thirty all up. Look at that one in front, it's twice the size of the others."

A burst of gunfire cut the conversation short as both sides made their presence felt. In the darkness they were like blind men, neither side having any form of night sight. But some rounds found their mark and Mash heard a scream as a machine gun raked a six-pounder. The gun was silent and the lead tank kept coming on.

Mash felt himself sweating as the tank continued its slow advance. No one was shooting at it. It was now very close to the depression and Mash thought it must break into the position.

Then at no more than thirty yards' range the gun that had been silent, fired. With an almighty clang the tank ground to a halt as though stunned by a punch. Seconds later another round from the gun hit it and the tank exploded.

"Christ, look at that," said Gordon. "That thing's just about inside the depression. Whoever fired that must have nerves of steel."

"Look there's an Eyetie tank lit up by the explosion."

Like an aircraft caught in the searchlights the Italian tank became the focus of a number of guns and soon it was also knocked out. The remaining tanks, seeing their lead tank knocked out and aware that they had stumbled on a well-defended position they could not see, started to pull back.

"They're legging it," said Mash excitedly. "Christ, that was too close for comfort."

"Aye, but we only got two and that means there're still loads out there, they're like sharks circling just outta sight," muttered Gordon.

It was clear that nothing further was going to happen until dawn. The Germans knew they were there but could not see where or in what strength. For 2RB the mission was to hold the position until the armour could come up and move forward into the Axis front line. Now that the position was established Turner used the lull to send away all the vulnerable transport and they all waited to see what the morning would bring. Turner's list of problems was growing. The FOO had earlier left the depression to try and find a good observation point, ready for his fire orders in the day. He had not come back and Turner was acutely aware that he now did not have a way of communicating with his artillery.

In the quiet after the action Mash and Gordon got talking to one of the gun crews.

"What was that big bastard that was leading the Jerries?" asked Gordon.

"He was a prize beastie," replied the gunner. "It was a Mark IV Special: the biggest, baddest thing the Jerries have got. Do you see that gun? It's a long-barrelled 75mm and it makes the Special the most effective tank in the battle. The good news is that the Jerries don't have many and now they've got one less."

"Good news but why did you guys let him get so close?"

"Well I'm not sure I would've held my nerve that well but up to now we've only had the two-pounder and they had an annoying habit of bouncing off the better tanks. So the gunner was letting him get close to maximise his chances. Mind you we've been really pleased to see what the six-pounder can do. We haven't had the chance to try it in the field and it's good to know it packs a punch. Jerries don't usually catch fire as they're diesel-powered, unlike our petrol-driven tanks which go up at a moment's notice. So for him to go up like that means we've got some serious stopping power."

"I think we're going to need it," said Mash as he looked out. "You know, I'm starting to think we've been bloody lucky."

"How do you work that out?" asked Gordon

"It's getting close to dawn. Look out there, every second I see another enemy tank revealed by the light. There're loads of the bastards."

Sure enough, as the dawn's first rays started to creep over the desert, an apparently never-ending number of tanks and self-propelled guns were becoming visible out of the gloom. The men all looked in fascinated horror at a desert that seemed to be a car park for enemy tanks.

"It looks as though we're on the edge of the whole German Army," said Gordon.

"I'm sure we're short of where we should be but if we'd gone to where we should be we'd be eating breakfast in a PoW camp," said Mash. "This position is a God-send, providing cover for the guns so that the Jerries can't see us until they're on top of us."

Mash was right. 2RB were right amongst the 15th Panzer and Littorio Armoured Divisions. As the dawn light revealed more and more tanks, the guns started to open fire. Confident in the stopping power of their new six-pounders they were firing at targets no more than 800 yards away and side on – perfect targets. It was as though the Germans and Italians had not recognised the events of the night and that 2RB were in their midst. Tank after tank was hit and disabled; as their crews bailed out they were chased on their way by machine gun fire from the depression. Mash and Gordon cheered and jeered with the others as another target was hit and its crew scuttled away. In a short time the guns accounted for sixteen tanks and two self-propelled guns along with an 88mm anti-tank gun and a staff car.

"Did you see that?" shouted a jubilant Gordon. "It's like shooting ducks at a fairground."

Mash grinned in reply. But the celebrations were short-lived. The Germans now knew they were there and it was not long before their artillery started to reply.

The enemy were firing high explosive air burst rounds and the effect on the exposed men at their guns was devastating. Screams rang out as men were hit. Mash and Gordon tried to bury themselves as far into the sand as possible, but they could not just let wounded men lie out and bleed to death. They and others crept from their hiding places and started to carry the wounded back to the dressing station.

"Where's the Doc?" panted Mash as he carried in one man who was almost unconscious and covered in blood.

"Sorry, I'm all you've got," replied a rifleman medical orderly. "The Doc was left at the start and never got here. Now ease him down here."

Mash lowered the man and the medic quietly started to assess him.

"Are you really the only one?" Mash asked. The medic nodded.

"But the casualties are coming thick and fast."

"Then you'd better get out of my way and let me work," said the medic levelly, but Mash could sense his panic. Mash did as he was told and got out as the medic started to assess the man's wounds.

On the way back Mash passed a gun that had been put out of action.

"They've taken out one of the guns," he said to Gordon as they reunited.

"Aye, there're another two over there that have also gone. What time do you make it?"

"Coming up on 07:30. It can't be long until the tankies come up and take them on, at least I hope it won't be much longer, there's only one medic."

"Let's hope there're not many more casualties," said Gordon. He peered into the distance. "But I think help is on its way," he said, pointing over to the east. "I saw that dust cloud when I got back here."

Mash looked round and sure enough there was a cloud of dust thrown up by 24th Armoured Brigade.

"Thank God," he said. Before he could say any more a tank round came crashing in twenty or so yards to his left. They all dropped to the ground.

"What the fuck was that?" shouted Mash.

"They're firing at us!" said Gordon. "Don't the daft bastards know that we're here?"

More shells were fired by the tanks as they came into sight and a scream rang out as one found its mark.

"They're killing their own side! Why don't they tell them to stop?" yelled Gordon.

As if in answer a carrier shot out of the depression and headed for the tanks.

"Looks like they've not got any radio contact," said Mash. "That poor bugger's been sent to stop them."

Fascinated, they watched the carrier make its way towards the tanks. They expected it to be hit at any second.

"I can't watch anymore," said Gordon, covering his eyes after a near miss.

Mash kept watching as it somehow reached the tanks. It managed to stop one squadron of tanks from firing. However, the other kept on going.

The gun crews around Mash and Gordon started attending to their guns.

"Do you think they're going to fire back?" asked Mash

"No, they're not turning to face them. Wait a minute, look over there."

Gordon pointed to about twenty-five enemy tanks that had seen the approach of the British tanks and were forming up to attack. Soon the first of the guns started firing at them and scored hits. In total, three enemy tanks were hit and the others withdrew.

Mash and Gordon sat in the relative quiet.

"That was sort of lucky," said Gordon. "The Jerries backed off and those dozy bastards over there have realised who we are."

"It was getting bloody uncomfortable," said Mash as he lit a cigarette. "Being attacked from both sides." He took a deep draw on the cigarette and relished the feeling of the smoke burning his lungs. "It's a good job they weren't as effective as those air bursts from earlier or we really would've been for it."

"I'm going to give them a piece of my mind when they get here."

"Don't bother. They probably saw all the Jerry tanks around us and our barrels sticking out from a defensive position and thought we were the bad guys. It happens."

"Tell that to the mother of one of the poor bastards who just got shot by their own side," muttered Gordon in reply.

Half an hour or so later the tanks pulled into the depression. Gordon glared at them, giving them the evil eye, as did a number of the others. One tank commander noticed.

"Hey Jock, what're you looking at?"

"Some daft bugger who doesn't know what a Scotsman looks like."

The commander leaned forward out of his Sherman's turret ready to let fly with an obscenity when his turret burst off the chassis of the tank in a terrific explosion and cartwheeled away. Gordon was flung to the ground and the body of the commander was literally cut in half. The severed top half fell out of the tank and landed near Mash. The tank burst into flame and screams came from within. A hatch opened and a man tried to get out but sank slowly back into the tank as the flames consumed him. Gordon stared transfixed. In the space of a couple of seconds a Sherman and all its crew had gone.

"Fuck me," he stammered and tried to struggle to his feet.

"Get down you daft sod!" shouted Mash as more rounds cracked through the air. A few seconds later another Sherman was hit. This time it did not explode, just caught fire. They heard another scream come from inside and the hatch flew open and the men struggled to get out.

"Let's help them," shouted Gordon as he ran forward.

Mash paused for a second as the flames licked higher, then

he too ran towards the burning tank. Together he and Gordon climbed up onto the tank and pulled the driver out. His clothing was smouldering but they got him to the ground and quickly smothered the flames before carrying him as rapidly as they could to the dressing station. They went back but the tank was engulfed in flames; one other man had managed to get out.

Within fifteen minutes seven tanks had been knocked out along with three anti-tank guns in the depression.

"They're starting to pull out," cursed Gordon. "They're going to leave us."

"Don't worry, it'll probably take the attention away from us. The Shermans have such tall sides that they stick out over the top of the rim and make brilliant targets for the Jerry 88mm," said Mash.

The tanks were pulling back behind the ridge, their advance decisively repulsed. 2RB was on its own and the enemy knew exactly where they were but, for about half an hour, calm returned to the outpost.

Mash and Gordon had almost been lulled into a false sense of security when there came a shout.

"Movement to the south!"

"Can you see them?" Mash asked Gordon.

"Aye, a bunch of Eyetie infantry are going to give it a go."

"This could get interesting, there may be few of us but a lot of men are on the guns and the like, there aren't all that many riflemen."

As if Turner had been reading Mash's mind, the platoon of carriers that had caused so much damage at the outset of the engagement were soon charging forward to engage the Italian infantry.

"Cor, they're making mincemeat of them," said Gordon. The extra firepower gathered by the recce platoon during its time in the desert was having a major affect again.

"I can see them running and it looks as though they've lost

a couple of vehicles with no losses to the carriers, a nice job," continued Gordon.

"Aye, but it looks as though we've got a bigger problem. Have a look at all those bloody tanks."

The Germans were keen to counter attack 24th Armoured Brigade that had been hit so hard whilst in the depression. They mobilised thirteen Italian M13 tanks to suppress the Snipe position whilst another thirty or so German tanks went to attack 24th Brigade, making their way to the south of Snipe whilst the Italians attacked them. In the depression the gunners were moving two of the six-pounders to face the new threat. This was not easy in the sand. Fire from the advancing Italians started to take its toll; two men were hit on a gun near Gordon and Mash. They ran over to the gun to help.

"What do we do?" shouted Mash to a very red-faced, sweating gunner.

"Just push like fuck, grab hold of anything. We've got to get it up with that other one ahead," the man yelled back.

The two put their shoulders into it and heaved with all their might. The gun bogged down in the sand at every turn and they had to manhandle its dead weight to move it forward. All the time enemy fire reached out for them. The six-pounder had armour but it was small and unable to protect all the crew, especially as they were moving the gun. Soon the fire started to take effect and several lives were lost on the two guns.

Mash and Gordon were soon as red-faced and sweaty as the gunner, but eventually they got the gun up.

They collapsed back down behind the parapet, panting.

"That was as unpleasant as I'd like to see," said Mash. "If being peppered wasn't enough it's got to be over 100 degrees in the shade already. Too bloody hot to be hauling lumps of metal around in a sandpit."

"Bloody knackered," agreed Gordon. "I hope they give those Eyeties what for after giving us that peppering."

Behind them a loud crack announced the first of the answering fire from the six-pounders. Very soon the gunners found their mark and the first of the Italian tanks was put out of action.

"Got it lads," encouraged Gordon. "Look, there's a second one gone," he said to Mash.

All the time the Italians blazed away. From their vantage point they could see very little of the 2RB position given the barrels were only just over the top of the rim and well camouflaged by the bushes and camel thorn. So they were firing blind whilst the six-pounders continued to take their toll.

"That's four," said Mash. "And it looks like the others have had enough."

The remainder were pulling back, leaving the German tanks that were counter attacking 24th Brigade.

"Looks like all me Christmases have come at once," came a cockney voice on one of the guns.

The attacking German force was now side on to the Snipe position and well under a thousand yards away. Soon the six-pounders were onto them. A cheer went up every time one of the tanks was hit.

"It's a bleeding shooting gallery," came the cockney voice again as the gun barked out its defiance once more.

In all, eight more tanks were hit before the Germans disengaged and pulled back. For a moment there was relative calm, apart from some sniping between the riflemen and some enemy infantry. But everyone knew that though the attack had stalled, the shelling would soon resume its pounding of the position.

Turner used the calm to try and get the worst of the wounded out in a couple of carriers, aiming to have them bring a doctor and more ammunition on the return. Unseen by Mash and Gordon, they made their break for it and were instantly engaged by enemy artillery. A shell hit one carrier although the other managed to get through unscathed. It was clear though that the resupply force could not get to them. 2RB were cut off.

## CHAPTER FOURTEEN

# ATTRITION

Mash and Gordon tried to find out how they were doing. They got into conversation with a couple of gunners, one of which was the cockney voice from earlier. They grilled them on what they knew.

"We must be in a good defensive position," said Gordon as he offered his cigarettes around.

"You're right there," said the cockney, "and I reckon we've taken out near thirty tanks and guns."

"Great," said Mash.

"I think we've helped push back the Axis counter attack," said the cockney's friend, another Londoner.

"That's right, we're pissing them off good and proper, being a thorn in their side," said the cockney.

"Yeah but we've been hit haven't we," said Mash.

"Yep, by all counts we've lost a few guns and most of the carriers have been knocked out by the shell fire. I bet we're going to start running out of ammunition soon."

The men all drew on their cigarettes.

"We're on our own now aren't we," said Gordon. "24th Brigade has gone."

"They should get some more supplies to us," said the cockney, who was clearly an optimist. "I heard there's a resupply convoy on the way."

"They'll never make it," said his friend. "You saw what happened when they tried to get those two carriers away. Jerry's got the gap well covered, nothing's going to get through that."

"Well, we're all going to have a hard time of it if this continues," said Mash. "I don't know how much longer we can stay here."

The enemy artillery certainly knew where they were and Mash knew it would not be long before the shells and mortars started again. Outside the sand was already churned up by the earlier incessant shelling, making further movement of the guns impossible.

"There's no way we can move," said Gordon. "Not until nightfall at least."

"What's the time now?" asked the cockney.

"Only 11:00," said Gordon. "I feel like we've been fighting for a week."

"How are you two getting along, enjoying the fun?" a voice interrupted. Looking round they saw they had been joined by Turner. He often patrolled the perimeter, always checking up and helping out, but none of them had heard him arrive.

"Sir," replied Mash immediately and after a hesitation. "Looks like we're punching above our weight."

"I agree, we're doing a grand job," replied Turner, before carrying on. "I wish we could communicate with the guns though. I'd love to engage Jerries' artillery and some of the other plum targets in front of us."

The other three looked at him.

"Very glad of this position though," said Turner. "We would have been in for a pounding if we hadn't found it."

Mash was not sure if Turner was making a point or not. Before he could reply Turner added,

"Mind you, I have to say I think you were right in that we're short of where we should be." With a wink he was off to see the next gun in the line.

"That was decent of him," said Mash. "He didn't have to do that".

"Aye, for an English officer he's alright," said Gordon.

The cockney was about to say something when there came a shout.

"Incoming!"

A second later artillery and mortar rounds started falling on the depression.

"Jerry clearly thinks we've had enough of a breather," sighed Gordon and took cover. But Mash did not join him.

"What are you doing?" said Gordon.

"I hate just sitting here and taking it," replied Mash. "I'm going to join those guys over there having a shooting contest. If I've got to go then I'd prefer to be shooting back."

★ ★ ★

The shelling lasted almost two hours; Mash spent most of it shooting at the enemy. When relative quiet resumed he went back to find Gordon.

"Did you enjoy your shooting practice?" asked Gordon.

"Aye, there was a young lad out there, built like a brick outhouse, who was a very good shot. A few of us were hiding under the wreck of that big tank that was taken out early on and knocking them over without trouble. It felt good to get my eye in again."

"I'm glad you enjoyed it because here comes the next attack!"

Coming straight for them were eight Italian M14s supported by a Semovente self-propelled gun.

"They've picked a good spot," said Mash. "I can only see one gun left covering that sector and these Eyeties seem to be made of sterner stuff."

Mash and Gordon watched as the tanks came on, spraying the area with machine gun fire.

"Bloody hell, there's only one person at that gun," said Gordon.

"Bugger," muttered Mash as he realised that Gordon was right. "We'd better get over there."

Unbeknownst to them, Turner had gone to the gun to help too, along with the platoon commander, Lieutenant Toms. They helped Sergeant Calistan, the only one left, to work the gun. Together they fired time and time again with a cool, calm precision and the single gun managed to hit five of the tanks and the self-propelled gun.

Mash and Gordon were a short distance behind the gun. But the edge of the depression was very low and, with a ferocity not seen before, the Italians were advancing, firing continually with their machine guns and cannons.

"There's no way we're going to get to them," shouted Mash. He ducked down as another shell burst close to them.

"They can't hold out for long, we've got to do something," said Gordon. "They must be running out of ammo."

Mash looked round to see others also desperate to get to the gun but also pinned down.

"We can't get to them through this fire," yelled Mash and then: "Jesus, look at him."

Toms had leapt from the gun and was sprinting towards his jeep some hundred yards away.

"What the hell's he doing?" said Gordon.

"He must be trying to get more ammo," said Mash.

The Italians saw him and immediately focused their guns on him. Bullets buzzed and whizzed all around him, kicking up the sand as Toms ran desperately on. Mash found he was holding his breath watching him, willing him to make it safely.

"He's made it," yelled Gordon, punching Mash on the arm.

Sure enough, Toms had somehow reached the jeep unscathed and had leapt into the driver's seat. They watched as he started to drive back to the gun.

"He must have ammo in the jeep," said Mash.

"Mad bugger's gonna get blown up," said Gordon.

They both kept their eyes on the jeep, making its way under heavy fire. Gordon was muttering "come on" over again under his breath.

"He's been hit," said Mash as the jeep was slammed across the sand. However, Toms carried on driving and evidently the ammo had not been hit.

"Christ, I think he might make it," said Gordon, who was unconsciously clinging onto the sleeve of Mash's shirt and shaking it. Mash barely noticed; he was trying to will Toms to the gun.

"There are flames," said Mash. Fire was erupting from the jeep but Toms did not stop.

"Almost there," said Mash.

But then, about ten yards away from the gun another burst hit the jeep and it gave up the fight; flames spurting out all over the vehicle.

"Shit!" both Mash and Gordon yelled at once.

"Did he get out?" said Gordon, squinting his eyes.

"I don't know but, if he can do it so can we, let's make a run for it," said Mash.

Gordon swallowed briefly before nodding, then they both ran for the gun.

They were joined in making a dash by a corporal who had also been willed on by Toms' heroic display. They moved as fast and low as they could, trying not to be seen even though they knew they must be obvious. Mash's heart seemed to be beating at double the rate as he sped through the sand faster than he had ever ran before.

Maybe the Italians were stunned by Toms' actions or they were starting to lose heart but all three managed to get to the gun. Mash did not have time to rejoice in his survival, or be surprised by the presence of Turner, as he immediately rushed to the remains of the jeep. Turner and Toms, who had miraculously survived, were dragging the heavy wooden boxes containing the rounds to the gun. Mash and Gordon joined them and together they managed to move the boxes over and start to feed the gun.

"Bloody brave, Sir," Mash managed to say to Toms. Toms just shook his head and carried on hauling the boxes. Turner briefly placed a hand on Toms' back.

Meanwhile, Calistan and the corporal who had braved the enemy fire waited whilst the tanks grew ever larger in their sights.

Suddenly there was a cry and Turner, his helmet spinning away, fell to his knees. Mash and Gordon rushed over to him to see blood pouring down his face. He had been hit by a round that had gone through his helmet and into his skull. Somehow he pulled himself up and staggered towards the gun. But then he stumbled and Mash grabbed him. Through the blood Turner's expression was of disbelief; as though he could not believe that his body would not do what he told it to.

"Sir, you've got to take cover," said Mash.

"I'm alright," said Turner, pushing Mash's hand away. He tried to struggle to his feet again but he made it one step before collapsing again. Toms ran up to them.

"You must get into cover," he said to Turner.

Reluctantly Turner nodded and Toms and Mash helped him to a patch of cover behind the gun.

"I want to know what's going on," he said, blood still pouring from his wound.

"Yes, Sir," said Mash, then he and Toms ran back to help. Mash glanced round to see Turner staring at his own blood-covered hand.

Calistan was watching the three remaining tanks through his sights. They were almost on top of him. He waited until they were at 150 yards, point-blank range for the enemy gunners, then he opened up on the tanks. Mash watched as, cool as you like, Calistan traversed, aimed and fired, hitting all three tanks with successive shots. All the time bullets bounced and ricocheted away only inches from him and cannon fire exploded all around. Toms was relaying the information back to Turner in a calm, matter-of-fact way.

"Good work – a hat trick!" Turner yelled out when Toms announced that the third tank had exploded in a sheet of flame.

In the shocked silence immediately after the action, Calistan quietly stood up from behind the gun and leisurely poured some water into a billycan before placing it on the burning jeep.

"Anyone fancy a brew?" he asked.

★ ★ ★

With all of the Italian tanks knocked out there was a lull in the fighting, which allowed Mash and Gordon to get back to their trench and Turner to get to the first-aid tent. Before he was carried off he gave a short "well done boys" to the two of them.

The lull did not last long, very soon the German artillery fire started again.

"Here it comes again," said Gordon as he hunkered down in the bottom of the trench.

They were both quiet as they listened to the sound of the guns and felt the earth shake.

"I think the shelling has been the worst part of this," said Gordon.

Mash shook his head.

"Those bloody tank attacks have it for me," he said. "I can't wait for nightfall when those bastards will have to stop. Mind you, you have to take your hat off to those gunners; that Calistan was so cool, just picking them off one by one."

"Aye, and the officers are good, the way that lieutenant got that ammo, that took guts," added Gordon.

"I can't believe he made it," said Mash.

Gordon opened his mouth to agree but at that moment there was a sound like a roaring express train followed immediately by an ear-splitting explosion. Mash just caught a glimpse of a spray of sand before he felt the walls fall in around him. He tried to jump up but it was too late, sand poured over him. He tried to reach up but the weight pushed him down, it was in his eyes, his ears and his nose. He gasped for breath but sand filled his mouth. He felt himself going under as a drowning man would and he flailed with his arms, trying to get a grip on something, anything. His lungs were stinging, he desperately scrabbled but there was nothing. Just as the world was going black he felt a hand grab his arm and start to pull him up, then another hand reached down and grabbed him by the scruff of the neck and jerked him up. Mash helped push himself up and he finally felt the surface of the sand break and the air hit him. For a while he could not hear or speak, he just gulped great breaths through a sand-grated mouth. He coughed up sand as though it was water. His eyes burned with all the dust so that tears rolled down his cheeks. Finally, he started to breathe a little easier and his vision began to clear. He saw Gordon in front of him, looking like an Egyptian sand mummy.

"Are you alright? I thought you were a goner," panted Gordon

Mash shook his head, he could not speak. He coughed again, almost vomiting sand onto the ground. Eventually he managed to gasp a few words.

"What happened?" he croaked.

"Shell exploded close to your end of the trench and it caved in," said Gordon, who was watching him closely. "This soft sand is bloody useless for trenches; you were under before

I knew it and I was about waist-deep. Here, swill your mouth out with some of this."

He handed over his water bottle. Mash took a mouthful of the tepid water and swilled it round his mouth. He then spat it onto the ground; it was full of sand and grit.

He sat up and tried to breathe deeply.

"That was close," he stammered. "You may have a point about the shelling being the worst thing."

★ ★ ★

The enemy continued to shell the outpost and the casualties mounted. One shell caught Major Bird, the second in command, talking to Lieutenants Toms and Flower, injuring all three. Bird was eventually put next to Turner who, once he had been bandaged by the overworked medic, Burnhope, had tried to continue his circuit of the guns until he had grown weak and begun to hallucinate.

Mash and Gordon were exhausted. The battle had gone on all day and as soon as one attack ended the artillery resumed its fire before the next attack began.

"I'm not sure how much more of this I can take," said Gordon, who was sitting with his hands over his ears.

"Hold on a bit longer," said Mash, his eyes half closed. "It's just on 16:00, we've only got three hours of daylight and then we'll get a breather."

"Thank God for that," replied Gordon before turning quickly at a shout from close by. "Look at that, it's the bloody cavalry!" he said.

"Bloody marvellous," said Mash, jerking awake and looking in the same direction. "Maybe we won't have to wait until nightfall".

Tanks were emerging over the ridge behind them to the north-east. Moving cautiously the 2$^{nd}$ Armoured Brigade edged forward. Like 24ᵗʰ Brigade that morning they were trying to use Snipe as a lever to get into the Axis lines. Unlike the 24ᵗʰ Brigade they did not shell the Snipe position – but their supporting artillery, 105mm self-propelled guns called Priests, did. The cheers of the men who thought they were about to be relieved were short-lived as the HE air bursts cracked overhead.

"Not a-fucking-gain!" shouted Mash as the air was shattered by round after round, all aimed to burst before impact on the ground to fling lethal shards and chunks of shrapnel over a maximum area.

"Over there," shouted Gordon, pointing to where two men had just been torn apart by a shell from their own side. "The sods are making the same mistake, they think we're Jerries."

They ducked as low as they could in their remains of their trench. Shell fire burst all around and more screams were heard. It was not long until the Priests were called off, but the short period was deadly. After all they had endured, it was the low point for all at Snipe.

Gordon was incandescent with rage.

"Those bloody bastards, if they fucking well shelled the Jerries with as much bloody enthusiasm as they do us then we'd have won the fucking war by now. Just when you thought it couldn't get any worse they bloody well have to make the same mistake again. Christ I can't wait to get my hands on the bastards." After pausing for breath he continued the tirade in Gaelic for several more minutes.

"Are you calling on all your ancestors to shrivel their balls to dust or something similar? If so can you ask them to do something nasty to them for me," said Mash once the tirade started to falter.

"To have your hopes raised like that and then to see good men cut down by their own side is more than man can take," said Gordon, glaring at Mash as though he was somehow involved.

"Stand to!" The shout cut across their conversation.

Mash and Gordon looked around to see a massive enemy tank formation massing to the west.

"There're loads of the bastards," shouted someone close by. He was right; it seemed the whole horizon was full of enemy tanks.

"I reckon there're at least seventy of them out there," said Gordon. "This is it; we can't hold this lot off."

"They're going for our tanks on the ridge," said Mash.

The two watched in horrified fascination as the enemy tanks formed up some 1,200 yards in front of them. They made two groups, one with about forty Italian and German tanks whilst the other group of thirty was all German.

"Things are starting to happen," said Gordon as the larger group moved.

The tank group thundered forward, getting closer to their position with every second. Mash watched the tanks, but something seemed to be wrong.

"I don't understand it," he said. "They seem to be heading just to the north of us, as though they don't know we're here. But they've been pounding our position all day."

"Perhaps they haven't been told about us," replied Gordon.

"Well you'd have thought they'd got a hint by all the knocked-out tanks around us."

"If they keep coming as they are then they'll be side on to the 239 Battery boys," said Gordon.

The 239 Battery, on the north-east of the depression, had not seen much action but had lost a couple of guns in the fighting and were now down to four operable ones. Slowly from left to right the enemy tanks came on. Mash was right about them not knowing that the British were in the depression; the tanks were from 21$^{st}$ Panzer Division which had only just been moved up from their original position in the south by Rommel in order to counter the ever increasing pressure in the north. In a most un-Afrika-Korps-like breakdown in communications they had not been told of the enemy guns in the depression and, ignoring signs to the contrary, thought the only threat came from the British tanks to their front.

From their position Mash and Gordon watched as the gunners held their fire until the tanks were only 200 yards away and with their vulnerable side armour exposed. The first gun fired and instantly knocked out a tank. The others joined in and soon all four guns were firing as fast as they could.

"I see six out of action already," beamed Mash. "They don't know what's hit them!"

"Look, they're clocking we're here," cried Gordon as other tanks halted and started to turn to face the cause of their losses.

"Aye, but that just leaves them side on to the tanks they were supposed to be attacking," grinned Mash as yet another machine exploded, this time as a result of fire from the British tanks up on the ridge. "It's a killing ground, they don't stand a chance."

One German, in another long-barrelled Mark IV Special, desperately charged towards the depression, firing continuously as he came on. 100 yards from the guns it erupted in flames as it was hit by two of the six-pounders at the same time.

However, it was not all one way traffic. An HE round took out one gun, killing all the crew but for the sergeant who, somehow, was untouched. But the German group commander could see he was trapped and to continue was to invite annihilation. He ordered the withdrawal and the enemy tanks backed away.

"Well that was one for us," said Mash.

"Aye, by my reckoning there's twenty tanks knocked out," replied Gordon. "And of those I think we got nine of them."

"They haven't given up though. Look, they're not going

all the way back, just out of range and then getting into hull-down positions."

"More and more of the guns are being knocked out, they've got to have noticed," said Gordon.

He was interrupted by a shout and they looked round to see the next attack forming. Fifteen Panzers were closing from the north-west, attacking a stretch about 400 yards away from Mash and Gordon.

"Doesn't look like we've much left to stop them," said Mash. "I can only see two guns left covering that sector."

"We've got to hold out. It's not long until nightfall and then we can take stock. We've got to repel them."

The tanks started firing as they came on. They were supported by the other tanks from the earlier attack in their hull-down positions, some of which had found a position on a ridge that was not covered by any of the surviving guns.

"Christ, they've got one of the guns," shouted Gordon.

One of the first rounds had knocked a six-pounder; its crew were either wounded or diving for cover.

"He didn't even fire a shot. Fifteen against one, we're in trouble again," said Mash.

He saw black smoke start to emanate from the command bunker; he knew this meant that all the confidential codebooks were being soaked in petrol and set on fire.

"Looks as though you're not the only one to think we're buggered," said Mash nodding towards the smoke.

"Aye, and these Krauts seem to know what they're doing. Do you see the way they're covering each other, one in a fold in the ground or some form of cover firing, whilst another moves?"

Further behind the remaining gun, men were desperately trying to turn another to face the threat, machine gun fire chewing up the sand all around them. Eventually they managed to turn it despite the soft sand and opened fire.

"At least we're back to fifteen against two," said Gordon. "Bugger me, look at that!"

A figure was running towards the knocked-out gun. In an instant the German gunners were on him, firing for all they were worth.

"He's down," cried Gordon, narrating the man's journey. "No wait, he's OK. Go it man!" He shouted as the man, who had thrown himself down to throw off the fire, got up and resumed his race to the knocked-out gun. By some miracle he made it and, though he was alone at the gun, this meant that there were now three against fifteen in the fight.

"Why are they holding fire?" asked Mash.

Gordon just shrugged. Unbeknownst to them, the guns were down to their last thirty rounds between the three of them. The gunners held their fire, letting the Germans get ever closer, knowing they had to make every round count. At 200 yards they opened fire. Immediately tanks burst into flame and ground to a halt. The remainder of the six-pounder crew, many of them wounded, then joined the lone figure of Sergeant Swann to bring the gun back to its full compliment. On they fired and one tank was hit simultaneously by all three guns. But the tanks were getting closer, machine gunning and firing as they came. One tank got within 100 yards of the position before it was knocked out, but it was as far as they got. With six out of the fifteen tanks knocked out the Germans had had enough and retreated. What they did not know was that the guns were down to their last nine rounds between them. If they had pushed on they would have broken into the depression. Instead they withdrew but continued to fire machine guns into the depression from hull-down positions until the light started to fade.

Mash and Gordon had watched it all.

"That was bloody close," said Mash. "I thought we'd had it."

"Aye, if they'd got into the depression then none of the

guns would have been able to bear and they could have driven round and round taking us all out."

Mash glanced at the sun, which was starting to sink below the horizon.

"Hopefully that's it for today," he said.

"I bloody hope so," said Gordon. "I don't think we can take anymore."

Slowly the dusk descended. The German machine gun fire was still heavy but they were firing blind at the depression.

Mash and Gordon had just managed to relax slightly when they heard the six-pounders open up.

"Why are they firing, are the Jerries attacking again?" asked a concerned Gordon.

"No, look over there," answered Mash, pointing to a patch, some 1,200 yards away, that was clearly lit by the last of the sun's rays and showed the German tanks finally pulling back. The gunners, knowing they did not have enough ammunition to beat off another attack and seeing the enemy withdrawing, were firing the last of their ammunition in a last act of defiance.

"Bugger me, they got one," said Gordon. Away in the distance, beyond any normal range for the six-pounder and with almost no light, a tank slewed to a halt as it was put out of action, the cheers from the successful gun floated out on the evening air.

As the night closed in around them the firing died down from both sides. Thoughts turned to food and, in the quiet, men started to prepare a meal. They were in desperate need of sustenance having been in constant action since before dawn and on the move for much longer. Just six of the nineteen guns that started that morning were still operable and they were out of ammunition. Word came round that they would be relieved at 21:00.

"Thank Christ," said Mash. "I'm that bloody tired I'll sleep for a week."

"Perhaps this'll stop you from volunteering next time?" replied Gordon with a wry look.

"Just at the moment I think you can take that for granted."

They ate then waited to be relieved. 21:00 came and went.

"Where's the bloody relief?" said Mash "Don't they know we're out of ammo and completely buggered?"

But no one came. On and on they waited and finally they were told that they would withdraw at 23:00 and abandon the position.

"After all we've done," moaned Mash.

"Aye, it doesn't feel right," replied Gordon as he looked out across the battlefield. "Hang on, I can see movement."

Almost instantaneously the shout to stand to went up and they stared forward.

"Look over there," said Gordon. "I can see quite a few of them."

"Do you think they're going to have another go with a nighttime infantry advance?" whispered Mash. "If they do we don't have anything left to stop them with."

"If they attack when we're meant to be pulling out, that'll cause all sorts of confusion."

They watched the Germans for several more minutes.

"They're not forming up," said Mash eventually. "I don't think they're going to attack."

"You're right, look they're collecting their wounded."

"And there's a recovery unit hitching up a tank over there."

Exhausted and without the means or desire to oppose them, the British left the Germans to their recovery efforts and at 23:00 started to withdraw. Of the six remaining guns only one could be recovered and was dragged back towards the British lines by a very shot-up and sole surviving truck. The breeches and gun sights of the remainder were destroyed to render them inoperable. Of the seventy or so casualties, the worst of the wounded were loaded on the three remaining jeeps and six carriers whilst the walking wounded would need to be helped back by their comrades. The dead were buried at the depression and left. The troops began to withdraw by companies. They made slow progress back, moving at the speed of the wounded. Throughout their way back there was intermittent shelling and machine gun fire which further reduced their numbers. Mash and Gordon remained until the end. Quietly they watched the riflemen move back whilst, in front of them, the Germans came ever closer as they recovered their wounded. Neither side made any attempt to disturb the other.

"Do you think this will be seen as a victory or a defeat?" asked Gordon as they savoured the cool night air.

Mash, whose thoughts were slowing with the need to sleep, shrugged.

"Do you think it's a defeat?" he asked.

"Well, we've had to abandon the guns and withdraw, plus the armoured boys haven't made their breakthrough."

"Yeah, but look around you at all the knocked-out tanks; apart from the handful that were hit when they joined us this morning, all of them are Jerry or Eyetie."

Gordon made a noise of assent but did not say anything.

"There must be the best part of seventy tanks out there," continued Mash. "If this is meant to be a battle of attrition and Rommel's short on tanks and fuel then I think that's a trade Monty would make any day of the week. I reckon this little outpost has put a considerable hole in Rommel's ability to hold out. So, for my money, it's a bloody good victory."

"You're becoming an optimist," said Gordon.

A noise behind them made them hurriedly look round.

"It's that gunner who was as cool as a cucumber earlier on," said Gordon.

"Eh up Sarge, what brings you back here?" asked Mash.

Calistan looked rather sheepish.

"I was carrying one of the casualties back but we got caught by a burst of machine gun fire and he copped it, so I've come back for another," he replied. He was quiet for a second but then blurted out: "Thing is, now I'm here I wanted to say goodbye to me gun. I know it sounds daft but there you are."

"Given what you did today it doesn't sound daft at all," said Mash.

"Don't mind us," added Gordon.

Calistan nodded then continued to his gun. Both Mash and Gordon pretended to be busy but neither could help watching as Calistan looked down on the gun for a moment, then patted the breach. He turned and made his way to help one of the last of the wounded.

"Brave man that," said Gordon. "Not sure I would come back, under fire, for another wounded man. Especially if the first had been shot dead on my back and I had the chance to get out of here. And that's on top of what he did to those Eyetie tanks before."

"Very brave," said Mash. "Come on, it's time we were making tracks as well."

They picked up their equipment and stood up. Less than a hundred yards away a German, who was searching one of the tanks hit close to the depression, must have heard or seen them and stood up, staring at them. The German was standing over the body of one of the crew from the knocked-out tank. The tank was still burning so Mash could see him clearly. He paused for a moment as he and the German looked at each other. Eventually the German simply raised a hand in greeting. Mash hesitated for a moment then raised his hand in reply. The German then bent down and carried on with his work whilst Mash turned and hurried to catch Gordon up.

CHAPTER FIFTEEN

# SNIPER

Wearily Mash and Gordon made their way back to their battalion, only to find that it had moved. It took them some time to discover that 152 Brigade had gone north-west into the Australian sector to release troops for the ongoing push the Aussies were making up near the coast.

"You would've thought they'd have let us know where they were going," grumbled Gordon. "I'm knackered, I don't want to chase around after them."

"At least it'll be quiet for a while," said Mash.

The two men were exhausted, both physically and mentally. It was the thought of having some time to sleep and eat that made them start to pick their way through the mass of tanks, infantry and trucks that were still clogging the approaches to the front. Finally, they were able to hitch a ride on an ammunition truck heading north to resupply the Aussies. They huddled in the back, surrounded by ammunition of all calibres and sat down on boxes of hand grenades. The lorry pulled away and they were just starting to relax when there was a crash as the lorry dropped into a hole. They stared at each other in horror.

"Well at least we wouldn't know much about it," whispered Mash as the lorry pulled itself out of the hole and bucked its way forward.

"Makes you wonder why the other lorries don't give them a very wide berth," replied Gordon.

They spent an anxious five minutes getting used to the movement of the lorry and the realisation that a bump did not mean instant death. As they started to relax Mash was in a reflective mood.

"You know, it strikes me that we're winning but we aren't making a very good job of it," he said after a while.

"What do you mean?" asked Gordon, who was trying hard to find a comfortable position to sleep in.

"The bravery of the boys is without question, just look at how the Black Watch took the Ben and the guts of the Rifle Brigade at Snipe. And we've pushed a large bulge into the line. But we've failed to exploit because no one seems to be able to map read for a toffee and there's no teamwork between the tankies and the infantry. We think that they're no use and I'm sure they have the same opinion of us."

"Not sure why they would say that," mumbled Gordon as he squirmed into a comfortable position. "It's not us who couldn't make the breakthrough after we gave them the opportunity."

Gordon was developing a healthy dislike of the tankers. Mash suspected that much of it was to do with the fact that there was not an abundance of Scots among them and that left them open to being 'bloody Sassenachs' in Gordon's mind. But there was also a growing frustration in how the tanks seemed incapable of getting themselves to the right place at the right time. And when they finally did they were much too cautious. Mash felt the frustration too but he knew that there were two sides to every argument and if the infantry and armour worked together then they could be an impressive force.

He voiced this thought to Gordon but no reply came, just a rhythmic snoring from the other side of the lorry. Mash smiled and made himself more comfortable on the bucking ammo boxes before he too fell into a deep sleep.

Whilst the distance back to camp was not great, the traffic jams and detours made the journey longer than they expected. Finally, the lorry stopped and they jumped out, stretching their legs. After waving goodbye to the driver they made their way to Company HQ to find out where the others were.

"I strongly advise that you do not attempt to go up there until nightfall," said the duty sergeant without looking up at them. "We're getting all sorts of reports of sniper activity and we've already lost some men."

"But we need to get back to the lads," said Gordon. "We were sent on detachment and they'll have no idea whether we're alive or dead."

The sergeant looked up at them.

"Look, I'm far too busy to get into a debate so it's your call. All I'm telling you is that we've already had casualties and the Aussies told us not to make any movement in daylight. If you guys think you can waltz over there then that's your call but don't blame me if you get one between the eyes," and with that he looked back down and started to write, signifying that the conversation was over.

"What do you think?" said Mash when they were outside.

"I'm all for getting back to the boys," said Gordon. "I can't believe it's as bad as he's saying. I'm sure the two of us will be able to slip in unnoticed."

"I want to get back as soon as possible as well. But let's be really careful as we'd be daft not to heed the warning. Let's grab some grub and top up the water bottles before setting off."

They knew where the others were and how to get to them so navigation would not be a problem. To begin with the trenches around Company HQ offered ideal protection. But it was not long before the trench petered out and there was only open desert; flat and featureless. They knew that up ahead of them were the trenches of the Camerons and a couple of hundred yards beyond that, the enemy.

"I'm starting to get worried," said Mash. "I can't see any movement from our positions. You would expect to see someone moving around or at least the odd head."

"Perhaps that Sarge was right," replied Gordon. "What do you think, should we keep going?"

Mash stared into the blank desert.

"My senses are jangling," he said. "It's too quiet."

"Well, let's go on but treat it like it's a potential contact; up together and down quick."

"OK," agreed Mash. "You go left and I'm right, on the count of three."

As soon as the word three was out of his mouth the two of them were up and running. They zigzagged desperately before dropping to the ground a short way ahead. No shot rang out and nothing disturbed the silence other than their heavy breathing.

"You ready?" called Mash

"Aye, whenever you want," came the reply.

On the count of three they both rolled a couple of yards to one side so they would rise in a different position from where an enemy could have seen them go to ground then they were up and running again. Down they came again a few seconds later, although to them it felt a lot longer. Still nothing. On they went, repeating the pattern as they got closer to their colleagues. Soon they were drenched in sweat and panting as though they had run a marathon.

"Jesus, this is hard work," shouted Mash. "I'm glad we topped up on our water."

"Aye, I'm absolutely knackered," panted Gordon. "Nothing from Jerry, do you think we can risk taking it a bit more gently?"

"No, we're getting closer to them as well as our mates so don't risk it," replied Mash. "Let's keep going, are you ready?"

Seconds later they were up and running again. Sweat stung

Mash's eyes and he was gasping for air. The heat seemed to bounce off the ground. He looked ahead to spot his go-to-ground point. At that moment, out of the corner of his eye, he saw Gordon fall forward, and a split second later heard the crack of a bullet. Mash dived down and looked across at the inert body of Gordon, partly obscured in a cloud of dust.

"Gordon, Gordon, are you alright?"

For a couple of seconds there was no reply as Mash stared across, willing Gordon to answer.

"Aye, I'm fine," croaked Gordon eventually. "I tripped on a rock that sent me flying. Saved my life though, that bullet was exactly where I would have been."

Mash breathed a sigh of relief

"I feel a bit weird, I hit my head when I fell," continued Gordon.

"At least it confirms there are snipers. I don't suppose you saw where the shot came from?"

"I was too busy eating dirt at the time," came the rather disgruntled reply.

Mash paused and thought about how best to proceed. He was not sure how badly concussed Gordon was. The sniper would assume he had hit Gordon as his fall had been very convincing. So the sniper's focus would now be on him. If he stood up and ran forward he would be a dead man. The only alternative was to try and fool the man into revealing his position.

"I'm going to see if I can use my helmet to get him to fire at me, see if you can spot where he is."

He pushed a small mound of sand up to one side of him before drawing out his bayonet. Very carefully he placed his helmet on the tip and then, at arm's length, revealed the helmet over the top of the mound. The seconds went by with Mash tensed up, expecting the shot at any moment. But there was nothing; the sniper was not going to fall for so obvious a trick.

"I'm going to crawl forward and see if he fires. Keep your eyes open."

"Be careful," replied Gordon. "We've used our luck up for the day."

Slowly Mash rolled to one side, every second expecting a bullet. He rolled twice as far as he normally would in the hope that this might give him an extra split second. He had decided to crawl forward fast and then stop so his progress would be jerky and unpredictable. He had precious few cards in his hand and he needed to keep a cool head. He put himself in the sniper's position. How long would it take to spot where he had rolled to, take aim and fire? Three seconds he guessed. Summoning up his courage he slivered forward as fast as he could, counting in his head 'one and two and stop'. Just as he pressed himself down as hard as he could the rock no more than six inches in front of him dissolved, showering him in dust and sand whilst his ears were deafened by the crack before the round ricocheted away.

It was Gordon's turn to call out, "Are you OK?"

"Yes," he said shakily. "But that was bloody close. Did you see him?"

"No nothing. I don't have the first clue."

"This boy's way too good to take any more chances," replied Mash, only just beginning to get his wits together again. "He missed twice but one was pure luck and the other was too close for comfort. I think we're stuck here until nightfall."

"That's at least four hours away," groaned Gordon.

It was the longest four hours either of them could remember. They each tried to scrape a small depression under them with their hands. But it was a very slow and painful exercise as they could not raise themselves one inch in fear of being dispatched. All the time the sun beat down on them, scorching any exposed skin. Beneath them the rock and sand heated up so that they felt like they were in a frying pan.

Insects and flies added to their misery. Their only defence was to try and cover exposed skin with clothing or sand as best they could.

"If I remember correctly this was your idea," croaked Mash.

"I didn't hear you complain very much," retorted Gordon. "Anyway I thought you were in charge?"

"We're both as stupid as the other. That's the last time I ignore any good advice."

Gradually the sun started to lose its heat as it slid towards the west. Dusk could not come quick enough for the two but they knew they would have to wait until it was fully dark. Finally, when the air was blissfully cool and black, they deemed it safe. They stood up and stretched their aching limbs, moving slowly, partly from the pain from lying for so long and partly because they still expected a bullet at any second.

They were closer to their destination than they thought and they managed to reach the section fairly quickly. The reaction was one of shock and, Mash was touched to see, joy.

"You're alive!" said an excitable Drillbit. "We thought you guys had bought it."

"Last we saw of you was when you were volunteering for some secret op," added Kipper. "You gave us a right fright."

"I'm sorry guys," replied Mash. "It's a long story. Put the kettle on and we'll tell you all about it."

Mash and Gordon relayed the story of the engagement at Snipe and how close they had come to being killed by the sniper. In return the others told them how they had taken over the position in the early hours that morning.

"It's been bloody terrible with those snipers," said Callum. "You daren't even peep over the top of the trench in case you get your head blown off."

"Mind you it has had one upside," chipped in Kipper. "That thug Dougie caught one. It was first thing in the morning and

Mitchell said something to him, he looks up and bang that was it. So fast you couldn't believe it."

"He's dead?" asked Mash, not sure how he felt about it.

"Nah, he was lucky, he swayed back for some reason as the shot was fired so it didn't hit him in the head but smashed up his nose and cheek. He got carried back that night so I doubt we'll see him again."

"Well I'm not sad he's gone," replied Gordon, still remembering the blows he had taken behind the NAAFI. "Just a shame it wasn't the other way round with Mitchell."

"They're all good shots but there's one of them who's really good," added Finnean. "He could shoot a flea off a camel's backside at 200 yards. I reckon that was who nearly got you."

"He certainly got my attention," answered Mash. "Come the morning we'll have to see what we can do."

After stand-to at first light, Mash started to think about his plan of action. It was clear that there was more than one sniper, but one was definitely better than the rest and Mash had an argument to settle with him. His first problem was that he did not know where the sniper concealed himself. The only good news he had been able to ascertain was that the sniper seemed to operate in their section of the line and was active every day. Maybe it was because the Germans were dominating movement on their sector but this made the sniper bolder than he should be, as normally a sniper would fire and then disappear, not reappearing in the same place for some time. It was good to know that the sniper could be relied on to be active in their area, but without knowing his location Mash would be exposing himself badly if he tried to spot him.

Putting this problem to one side Mash turned his thoughts to potential firing points for himself. Gordon and Mash were sharing a trench with Drillbit. Sniper activity had made the digging of a trench complex impossible and three-man trenches were the best the Aussies had been able to do.

"Drillbit, tell me everything you can remember about the surrounding ground. No fact is too small, let me have every detail," said Mash.

Drillbit did not need a second invitation; he missed Gordon's look of undisguised horror and started into a full monologue, giving minute details of every piece of rock and sand that he could remember in that way of his that just seemed to gnaw its way into the head. Mash, who would normally not tolerate Drillbit for long, was transfixed, hanging on his every word and occasionally asking questions. With a groan Gordon conceded defeat and buried his head under his greatcoat in the bottom of the trench.

From the flow of detail coming from Drillbit it occurred to Mash that there were few opportunities for a good hide and firing position. The best points seemed to be presented by wreckage from the earlier engagement between the Aussies and Germans. There were various destroyed vehicles and debris scattered around. After probing Drillbit's mind, a burnt-out lorry seemed the best option.

"I'll say this for you Drillbit, you have a bloody good memory," said Mash as Drillbit finally drew to a close. From the bottom of the trench Gordon uttered another groan whilst Drillbit beamed with pleasure.

"If we go through what we know," said Mash, as much to himself as to the other two. "The Germans are about 200 yards away from us. It's good that our man is always active for most of the day in the same area and, from our conversation, I think I know where I can set up a hide, although I won't know that for sure until this evening. The big problem is that I'll have no idea where he is and if he has had enough time in this area to build one or more good hides then I'm likely not to find him. I've got to find a way of at least reducing the options."

"There's one other thing you should know," piped in Drillbit. "We're not sure what sort of weapon he's using."

"What do you mean?" asked Mash. "He'll have the standard K98k that all their snipers have won't he?"

"We don't think so. There's been a fair bit of debate about it amongst the lads," replied Drillbit. "When he fires there's a sort of 'snip' noise that you get from an automatic weapon. But he's only firing single shots so we reckon it's some form of semi-auto."

Mash thought about this new piece of information. Most infantry rifles were bolt action, including the British Lee Enfield and the German Mauser, from which the K98k was descended. When a bullet was fired all the charge went down the barrel behind the bullet and then a new round was loaded by manually opening and closing the bolt. An automatic weapon used some of the gases from the charge to push back the firing parts, ejecting the empty casing and loading another round. The movement of the firing mechanism as the gun reloaded itself, along with the release of some of the gasses backwards, made a distinctive 'snip' noise that was different from a bolt action.

"Good to know," said Mash. "It means that he'll be able to fire much quicker than I can if it comes down to it. I always thought it would be a one-shot decider but that confirms it for me."

★ ★ ★

The day ground on and the men endured the tedium of being confined to their trenches. Occasionally a shot rang out to show that the snipers were still present but, so far, no one seemed to have been hit as the Highlanders were learning to keep their heads down.

Mash thought on about the problem of how to locate

the sniper, but with the heat and the boredom he could not help his mind from wandering and before long he was daydreaming about being back gamekeeping at Greystone. He thought about all the times he had built a hide to shoot foxes and other predators in an effort to protect the poults as they grew ready for the coming season. It had become a battle of wits between him and the fox, where understanding the opponent and attention to minute detail were the keys to success. His forthcoming duel with the sniper would be similar; the slightest oversight being the difference between success and failure – only this time the fox could shoot back.

As he thought about the fields of home he was jerked back into reality by a shot followed almost immediately by a cry. The shot had the characteristic 'snip' noise they had been talking about and immediately all of Mash's senses were straining. Soon a voice started calling for a stretcher bearer and this, after a matter of seconds, was joined by a scream not of someone in pain but someone in panic. Mash peered out as far as he dared to survey the scene. All the time the screams intensified, piling pressures on those all around. Then finally Mash saw the man who had been screaming try to climb out of the trench and run to the rear. He got to his feet before another shot hit him in the centre of his back and he dropped like a stone. Instantly the last man in the trench jumped up in an effort to pull his comrade back only to be hit in the neck, sliding slowly back into the trench, leaving a bloody smear over the sandy wall.

Instinctively they all ducked down.

"Shit that was fast," said Drillbit, his eyes wide in his head, as they looked at each other in shocked horror.

"You're right about the semi-automatic," said Mash eventually. "There's no way that he could have got the third round off in time with a bolt action rifle."

"And he's bloody cold and ruthless as well as being good," added Gordon.

No one could move until dusk started to hide them. As soon as he dared risk it Mash was over the side of his trench and ran crouched double. In the last of the light he was able to see what had happened. The first man had been on the right of the trench. He must have been talking to his two colleagues and had raised his head without realising it. The bullet had hit him in the right temple before blowing the left side of his head apart. The person who was shot as he climbed out was covered in the blood and brains of his mate. He had been the one screaming, he must have been overcome with panic. Mash could not blame him. The man had spent all day stuck in a hole in the ground in fear of his life, then his mate's head was blown off in front of him, leaving him covered in gore. It was enough to send anyone over the edge. He had a bullet hole in the left centre of his back, exiting out of his chest, a heart shot. Finally, the last man, who had been calling for the stretcher, had tried to pull his mate to safety only to get a bullet in the neck. Quickly Mash lifted up the man who had been shot in the back and then jumped into the trench to do the same with the other two. As he was lowering the last one a voice rang out.

"What the hell are you doing?"

"I don't want these poor buggers to have died in vain," said Mash to the dark silhouette above him. "Together they've told me that the bastard who did this was somewhere over there." He pointed out slightly to the right of the trench.

The soldier grunted then bent to help Mash retrieve the bodies from the trench. When all the bodies were clear Mash left and went to see Sgt Robertson. Calmly he explained what he wanted to do and got Robertson's permission to proceed. He then walked towards the remains of the lorry Drillbit had mentioned. He was careful to approach it from the eastern side so no fresh footprints would be visible from the German side. He felt Gordon's presence beside him.

"Are you going to use the lorry as your hide?" he asked

"No. The guy we're up against is good. He's shown it at every turn. He might expect some form of retaliation; almost welcome it as a chance to show his dominance. Under a lorry is one of the first places he'd look and I wouldn't last a second. What I'm thinking is that you might look under a lorry but you wouldn't look under the debris blown from the lorry."

In front of them was the remains of the load the lorry had been carrying. Boxes were strewn around along with old tarpaulin and rope.

"It has to look exactly the same from the front as it does now, but I want to build a hide using that tarpaulin and those boxes that face in that direction," he said, pointing on the bearing he had worked out the shots had come from.

"We have to do it in the dark and we have to get it right; there'll be no chance to check that we've got anything wrong in the daylight."

"Why don't you wait another day and check it out tomorrow?" asked Gordon

"Because tomorrow this bastard will have taken care of some more of our boys, and anyway I don't know how long we'll be here."

The two worked on into the night using only the moonlight and trying to remember every detail of the scene the German would see. Carefully they removed sand and rocks from underneath the tarpaulin, gently replacing them with bits of wood from the boxes so that the tarpaulin lay in the same way as before. They made an entrance from the rear and ensured that Mash would have as good an arc of fire as possible whilst both he and his rifle remained hidden by the tarpaulin. Eventually they were done and they made their way back to their trench.

After a meal and a couple of hours' sleep the two rose early, well before the dawn, and made their way back to the hide. Gently Gordon held up the entrance while Mash, with only his rifle and water bottle, crawled inside. Gordon carefully lowered the screen back into place and, for the last time, checked around him for any detail or mistake that would reveal Mash's presence. Then with a whispered "good luck" he was off back to his trench, leaving Mash alone with his thoughts.

Inside the hide Mash tried to make himself as comfortable as possible. He knew that once the sun was up he would not be able to move at all until he was either victorious, dead or the day proved to be a blank. The first signs of light began to appear from behind him. Gradually he became very still and slowed his mind, entering into an almost trance-like state. It was a trick the older gamekeepers had taught him, a way of detaching yourself from the discomfort of having to keep still whilst remaining alert to the slightest movement or noise.

Slowly the sun began to cast its light across the battlefield. Objects started off black against the grey of the dawn before gradually filling in form, colour and definition. At first Mash was only able to make out the Highlanders' trenches, but soon the light revealed features in no man's land, then on towards the German lines. Mash tried to keep his peaceful state of mind but it was difficult as the sun would also be illuminating his position, revealing any flaw he and Gordon had forgotten.

*There's nothing I can do now if we've made a mistake. The first I'll know about it is when I die.*

*Am I facing the right direction? I think I got enough of a clue from the three bodies to have a reasonable bearing. It's a narrow field of fire though.*

*Am I going to get him first shot? Well I've placed my bet now; I'll just have to see how the cards fall.*

And all the time that these thoughts went through his head the most important one was at the back of his mind – where is he?

Mash gazed out from the hide along the line he believed would reveal the sniper. He stared as hard as he could at the German lines, searching for any clue. Suddenly he was aware of a flash of light before it was gone a second later. He almost did not see it as it was only 100 or so yards from the Highlanders' lines. He stared at the point. All he could see was a broken box half buried in the sand.

*What was it? Was it him or just the sun shining off some broken glass? It can't be him, it's too close to our lines, he would have been seen. Don't waste time looking here or you'll miss him.*

Mash stared around until his eyes hurt but nothing else moved or gave any clue as to what the flash was. Then he saw another glint of light, only this time from much nearer the German lines.

*That's got to be him. It's bang on where I thought he would be. Now careful, don't give your position away and don't fire until you can see the target.*

For the next hour Mash stared at the point as hard as he could, but nothing, no sign of a target. The sun's heat was starting to rise and Mash was sweltering under the tarpaulin. It stopped him from being burnt by the sun but it was a heat trap and Mash felt like he was being boiled alive.

He tried to distract himself from the heat, pretending that he was in a hide back in the Scottish countryside. More often than not he was too cold there and wishing for some heat, but now it was the other way round. He imagined that he was lying on wet leaves, the smell of soil filling his nostrils and rain dripping onto his head.

*Just pretend you're waiting for a fox.*

*A fox with a gun.*

On and on went Mash's vigil. Still there was no activity and no sign of the sniper. Mash scanned the German lines and stared at the spot he thought could have been the sniper's lair until his head hurt. Nothing, nothing to give the smallest clue of the sniper. All the time Mash's discomfort grew and he was struggling to resist the temptation to move.

★ ★ ★

Crack!

Mash almost jumped out of his skin at the sound of the shot. He was sure that he had disturbed the tarpaulin as he fought to regain his senses. Quickly he stared at the point he thought the sniper was hiding, nothing, no hint or clue. Desperately he scanned the German lines for a sign but there was none. Everything was calm and quiet. Then he saw a tiny patch of dust out of the corner of his eye.

*That can't be anything, just the wind. Hang on it's dead still out there. Wait, that dust is a couple of feet from that first flash of light. It can't be him, he's too close. But it's on the line you thought he would be on. Why are you discounting it just because he's too close? Mind you from that range no wonder he was deadly efficient. Look again.*

Mash stared for what seemed like hours.

*There, something, the smallest movement. God it's him. He's so close to our lines.*

And as Mash looked, this time believing, he started to make out the tell-tale signs that showed he had found his prey. The box he had seen should not have been half buried when all around were not. It had been carefully positioned so that it was the apex of two banks of sand and debris. On top was some form of cover, either made from wood or tarpaulin, scattered with sand so that it looked exactly like the desert around it. It had been very skilfully done and you would need to be on top of it before you saw any sign of what lay beneath. Inside would be the sniper, far enough back in the hide that the tip of his rifle was well inside. From there the sniper had an uninterrupted view of the Allied lines and from that close he could pick off victims with impunity and not be seen.

*That must have taken some skill and hours of effort at night to build. I've been bloody lucky to spot it and I've only done that through his carelessness.*

The German was an accomplished sniper but he had grown careless over time, too used to having things his own way. Apart from staying in one place for so long he had made two mistakes that morning. The first was that as the hide faced east, the early morning rays from the low sun were able to penetrate under the rim of the hide and flash off the sniper's telescopic sight. It had only taken a second and Mash had missed the clue, partly because he could not believe the sniper was so close and partly because another, genuine, reflection had drawn him away. The second was that sand and dust are constantly moving in the desert and, over time, some had settled on the box through which the shot would come. When the shot was fired, although the barrel was inside the hide, the blast from the round sent some of the dust flying. Two tiny errors but they were the difference between life and death.

The cards were now in Mash's hand. He had seen the enemy without being seen himself. The range was only 150 yards, a distance where a skilled shot like Mash would have no problem in hitting the target with iron sights and there would be no appreciable drop in the trajectory of the bullet. There was no wind and the shot was flat so no allowance needed for shooting up or downhill. All of these factors flashed through Mash's mind. It should be an easy shot, but the only variable was pressure and Mash was feeling it.

It was stifling hot in the hide. Mash felt like he had been in a bath fully clothed and sweat dripped down his nose and stung his eyes. He knew he would only have one chance. If he missed, the sniper would either see the shot and return fire – and with an automatic it was a fire fight he would win – or back away out of sight. Slowly Mash raised his rifle into his shoulder. He already had a round in the chamber but with the safety catch on to prevent an accidental discharge. He edged his thumb to the left side of the rifle stock and pushed the safety catch forward. He had already flicked up the ranged sights and ensured that they were set to 200 yards, the minimum setting. He eased himself into a comfortable firing position and looked down the barrel. The round back sight and the blade foresight looked huge against the tiny target. He started to take regular deep breaths, trying to oxygenate his blood as much as possible. Finally he breathed out slowly, allowing the sights to settle on the target. He now had up to five seconds to shoot before he would start to feel his heart beat and his body would tell him to breathe.

*Be calm, pretend you're on the range or shooting foxes back home.*

He started to take the first pressure on the trigger. He had imagined how the man would be lying, visualising where his head would be, willing the bullet to the target. He squeezed the trigger.

The shot seemed excessively loud in the confined space of the hide. As fast as he could Mash chambered another round and stared at his target. Nothing. No sign of a hit or miss, just desert as it had been before. There was nothing for it but to wait and see if there was any hint of movement. Mash stared at the sniper's hide, willing there to be some indication, but for the next thirty minutes he did not see or hear anything. He did not know what to do; if he moved and the sniper was still there then he would be shot. But if the sniper was dead then Mash could release himself from this hell.

Then from his left he saw the extraordinary sight of Gordon leisurely climbing out of his trench, moving across to the next and clambering in.

*What the hell is he doing?*

But no shot came. It would have been a gilt-edged shot for the sniper but it did not come. Mash waited another fifteen minutes and then slowly backed out of the hide. He knew he was taking a risk but he could not stand it any longer and Gordon had produced a strong indicator that the coast was clear. He crawled back a distance to separate himself from the hide and then ran as fast as he could, crouched as low as he could, back to his trench.

"You took one hell of a risk getting out of your trench like that," said Mash to Gordon as they got a brew on a little later. When Mash had got back he had been bombarded with questions and had been forced to tell the story of the engagement in intricate detail.

"Maybe I've got more confidence in your shooting skills than you do," replied Gordon.

"Well, putting aside the matter of whether I hit him or not, there are other snipers in the area."

"To be honest I had forgotten about them," gulped Gordon. "But at least it means you got him and there's been no more sniping this afternoon."

"It doesn't say that at all," replied Mash. "If I missed him he could just have moved to the back of the hide and waited for nightfall. He could build another hide and be back to work tomorrow. We'll have to see if we get shot at tomorrow."

"That reminds me, we were told at stand-to that we're moving out tonight. Apparently we're needed for the next big push so we're being relieved by some Kiwis."

"So we'll never know if I got him," reflected Mash. "If nothing else, he had a reminder not to be so cocky."

The afternoon gave way to dusk and then nightfall. The men came out of their trenches and talked in hushed tones. Word had got round about Mash's duel with the sniper and there were many slaps on the back and words of congratulations. Mash could sense the relief amongst the troops. They had been intimidated by the sniper, scared to make an involuntary move that could be their last. They were full in their praise for Mash and he, in turn, was somewhat embarrassed by it. He played down his actions and stressed that he did not know if he had got the sniper. Even Mitchell came over and thanked him. Mash immediately tensed when he saw him approach but, although the words were muttered, they seemed genuine. After a while Mash tired of it and went back to his trench. Gordon was not there so Mash busied himself by cleaning his rifle and preparing some food. After a while Gordon dropped into the trench.

"Where have you been," asked Mash. "I thought you were going to miss our departure."

"I just went for a walk," grinned Gordon as Mash looked at him sceptically. "I thought I would pop over and see if you got that sniper, can't bear not knowing."

"You did what? Christ man have you got a death wish?"

"It was no issue; the sniper was as close to us as his mates. I didn't alert or bump into anyone. Anyway, he made his way out there every night so I didn't see why I couldn't. God that hide was good. Even though I knew where it was and had a peak this afternoon I went by it a couple of times before I found it."

He was enjoying dragging it out and could see from the expression on Mash's face that he was impatient to know.

"You did get him. Straight through the left eye. Dead as a dormouse," Gordon said finally.

Mash felt a sense of relief, and not a little bit of pride.

"You were bloody daft to do it though," he said.

"That's not all," continued Gordon, with all the showmanship of a vaudeville act. "I brought you back a trophy."

And with that he unslung a rifle that he had been concealing behind his back.

"It's the weapon he was using and I also took the ammo he had with him. I've never seen anything like it before, have you?"

Mash gazed at the weapon in the moonlight. It certainly was an automatic and it had a telescopic sight fitted. The forestock was made of wood but the barrel emerged from low down in the forestock, not on top as with the Lee Enfield, and there was a large ring foresight as a result.

"I've never seen anything like it either. But it looks business-like and it's clearly a potent weapon in the right hands. Pass me some of that ammo."

He took the ammunition and studied it carefully.

"That's good, looks like it's the standard German 7.92mm round. Christ, I wish I could loose off a few rounds now."

"Best not," said Gordon. "The boys will think you're a Jerry."

"Aye, let's get this move out of the way and hopefully we can look at it in more detail tomorrow."

With that they finished their meal and quickly packed their belongings.

The changeover with the Kiwis was uneventful. There was some machine gun fire as the noise spooked the Germans, but nothing in their patch of desert. Soon they were heading south again and the morning of the 31st saw the Highlanders of 152 Brigade enjoying a rest and a make-ready day before the forthcoming push.

"Now let's have a proper look at this weapon," said Mash as the rest of the section gathered round.

"Funny-looking thing," said Drillbit only to be hushed by the others.

Mash shouldered the weapon and looked through the sights.

"They're good, times four magnification if you believe the stamp."

"The Jerries always were good at making binoculars and cameras and the like," offered Callum.

"If it's firing the standard German round then the range

and stopping power should be the same so that's as good as a Lee Enfield. It should be easy to come by more ammo, especially if we can get Jerry going backwards. From the size of the magazine I would guess it holds ten rounds which would make it a semi-auto otherwise you'd be through them in seconds," pontificated Mash.

"Anyway, the recoil would mean that it wouldn't be accurate as an automatic," chipped in Gordon.

"Good point," agreed Mash.

"Mind you it doesn't look as though it has a bayonet," added Finnean.

"So how many snipers do you know that stab their victims to death?" chided Kipper.

"All right, just saying," replied Finnean.

"So what we have here," summarised Mash. "Is a sniper rifle that we know is bloody deadly when used properly, but which can also lay down a lot of fire quickly when it needs to. Sounds like the best of both world's to me. I'm tempted to keep it."

"Well you are the best shot we've got," said Gordon and the others all murmured their agreement.

The men's encouragement made up his mind. "I'll use it for this next push and see how it performs. Gordon, you take the Tommie gun for now."

For the next twenty-four hours the Camerons relaxed and made ready for the forthcoming action. In the early afternoon of the 1st they moved up to their start positions ready for the battle that night.

## CHAPTER SIXTEEN

# OPERATION SUPERCHARGE

"Good of you to let me have some of your boys," said Major General Freyberg, commander of the New Zealanders. "I need top men to play a key part in the operation."

Wimberley smiled at the compliment. "I'm sure they won't let you down."

The two commanders sat around a map on which was marked the details of the forthcoming operation. Whilst he would have loved to be commanding it himself, Wimberley could understand the decision to pick Freyberg. He was a capable and experienced commander, whose personal courage was without question, having won the VC on the Somme.

Wimberley reflected that the battle had turned into the war of attrition, something that Montgomery had predicted. Despite the failure to break the enemy's line and the ongoing arguments between the infantry and armour as to whose fault this was, it was clear that the Axis forces were under pressure and starting to show the strain. The Allies had made gains, particularly in the north up by the coast where the determined and gutsy Australians had pushed deep into Axis territory. But the advance of the Aussies had slowed and Montgomery had realised that the reason for this was that Rommel had started to strip units of German troops further to the south so that they could be moved north to hold the Australians. In doing so, Rommel's plan to 'corset' the Italian infantry with German troops to strengthen their resolve had to be sacrificed.

Montgomery realised that if he could make a thrust at the increasingly isolated Italians then he could make the decisive breakthrough that had eluded him so far. His optimism was further strengthened by intelligence reports that the Axis troops were getting short of supplies. The time was right.

Montgomery considered Freyberg his most capable divisional commander and so had tasked him with what was to all intents and purposes a smaller version of Operation Lightfoot, which had opened the battle. Freyberg was to advance 4,000 yards towards the Rahman Track which marked the main line of the Axis defences. As before, it was to be an infantry attack behind a rolling barrage, with armour in support. The infantry would take the Axis positions, with the armoured support arriving to hold off any counter attacks, before the remainder of the Allied tank force broke through into the desert beyond. Montgomery had chosen to aim the attack at the junction between the German and Italian troops, just north of Kidney Ridge, but extending well into the Italian sector. The attack would be codenamed Operation Supercharge and the Highlanders' objective was called Neat.

As the New Zealanders had been in constant fighting since the start of the battle and in action since before the first battle of El Alamein in July, Freyberg was given British troops to augment his numbers. The Durham Light Infantry would be on the right of the attack whilst 152 Brigade of the Highland Division, including the Camerons, would lead the left side, with the 2nd New Zealand Division in the middle. Support would come from the 9th Armoured Brigade. At Freyberg's request the attack was delayed twenty-four hours to give the troops as much rest as possible. Zero hour was set for 01:05 on the night of 2nd November.

"So what do you think our chances will be?" asked Wimberley after Freyberg had finished going through all of the details as they studied the maps.

"Difficult to say," replied Freyberg. "We have a number of distractions planned to keep Rommel guessing; some patrol boats are going to pretend to do a landing further up the coast, and we've made sure we've been seen working on tracks to the north. We're pretty sure that Rommel is expecting the push from the Australian sector; that's where most ground has been made so those moves should help reinforce that idea. Hopefully he won't be expecting an attack this far south."

Freyberg surveyed the map that he had already studied so many times that it was practically emblazoned on his mind.

"A lot of it will depend on the armoured boys of course," he continued. "I'm confident that if we're up against the Italians, the infantry will stand a good chance of taking their positions, assuming there are no issues in navigation given the dust from the barrage. No, my biggest worry is the armour, both ours and theirs."

"What do you mean?" asked Wimberley.

"Well, if the Italians have armour with them then it could get messy – despite the quality of their tanks. If we get round that then we're bound to stir up a hornets' nest and I'm sure we'll have to beat off a counter attack from the Germans at first light. The key is going to be how quickly we can get the supporting armour up to the troops. We can't have a repeat of Lightfoot."

Wimberley nodded gravely.

"With that in mind," continued Freyberg. "It's been decided that we'll use tanks at night. 50th Royal Tank Regiment will be supporting your boys in the attack. The hope is that if there are enemy tanks out there then having close support will be the deciding factor. The aim is then to have 9th Armoured Brigade make a move before first light, just a couple of hours after the infantry have taken their objectives. I know they don't like moving in the dark but if we can get them to the Rahman Track before the sun comes up then they should be on top of those ruddy 88mms that they seemed to be so scared of, before they're seen."

"They see one behind every boulder," replied Wimberley. "They just need to close the gap fast and get in amongst them."

"I'm hoping they'll use the cover of darkness to do just that," said Freyberg. "They'll also have a rolling barrage of their own, but if they dally about as they did last time then your boys could be in for a hard time of it."

Both men stared at the maps in front of them and thought of everything that could go wrong.

"Simple but complicated," muttered Wimberley.

★ ★ ★

"We've been here before," exclaimed Gordon. "It's a bit darker but other than that it's just like last time."

"It certainly feels like it," replied Mash. Looking up at the sky he thought Gordon must be right; it was darker but it was ten days since they had last formed up and the moon was on the wane.

The Camerons were waiting, spread out along a white tape on the ground. The piece of desert it marked looked like any other, but it was in fact their starting point. Again, they had St Andrew crosses on their backs, but no one questioned them this time, they knew from experience the help they gave in the swirling dust of a barrage. Officers and NCOs wandered amongst the men, reminding them to keep up with the barrage, stay spread out, not to stop for the wounded and other words of advice they thought appropriate. It was just before zero hour and Mash felt the usual fear and restlessness. He tried to ignore the dread that pulsed in his stomach, but it was growing in intensity and he had the nauseous feeling that preceded a battle. It was the same as Operation Lightfoot, except they did not have Rod there to set them at ease.

It was the first action for half of the Camerons and all of the Seaforths. Mash wondered if it was better to be seeing action for the first time or to have experienced it before. It was a topic they had often discussed on the ship out to Egypt when only Rod and Mash had been in battle. It was said that your first battle was your best as you did not know what to be afraid of, so you were more courageous. Wisdom had it that once you had experienced war, seen the carnage and your comrades butchered randomly, you did not take risks and lacked the offensive spirit to carry a position. Mash was not sure. He thought the Aussies were the best fighters he had seen and they had been doing it for a long time. They combined years of experience with a steely determination that made them a foe to be reckoned with. Maybe it came down to the personality of the individual.

Mash's musings were interrupted by a flash to the east. The horizon lit up as the guns commenced the barrage. Seconds later the shells shrieked overhead.

"Hey Finnean, it's those geese again," shouted Kipper above the noise. "Do you think they're going south for the winter?"

A number of the men laughed. It struck Mash that they would not have done so before Operation Lightfoot, so perhaps it did get easier with time.

The bombardment quickly grew in intensity as all available guns added their voices to the din. The shells exploded with a clang on the hard ground and threw up great plumes of dust and debris. At the same time anti-aircraft Bofor guns started firing on set bearings, their tracer shells showing the troops the way.

They set off with the skirl of the pipes leading them. Mash felt good to be on the move; even though he knew he was marching closer to danger, it was better than the waiting. They walked, as before, at the slow, regulation pace. Officers and

NCOs were scattered amongst the men, carrying compasses, heads down, apparently oblivious to all that was going on around them. They marched on a bearing that would take them from a white tape on the ground at one end to an imaginary line in the sand at the other, just over two miles ahead of them.

All too soon the troops were enveloped by the thick, clinging dust and smoke thrown up by the shells. The men went from a clear desert night into something that resembled the worst London 'pea-souper' possible. Visibility dropped to a matter of feet, with only the silhouettes of the men revealed when an exploding shell made a red glow through the haze. On they walked; their ears were assaulted by the deafening cacophony, barely knowing if they were going in the right direction.

For the first 600 yards nothing happened. Mash's senses were strained, like a coiled spring. But then the first of the enemy shells started to fall. Mash could not quite make out which were the enemy shells and which were from the rolling barrage; he did not think they were many in number, but he became aware that explosions were coming from behind and to either side of him.

"Incoming!"

Barely were the words out of his mouth when a high-pitched screech instantly followed by a deafening crash came from just ahead of them. Instinctively Mash and the others flung themselves on the ground. Razor-sharp pieces of shrapnel cut through the air where they had just been standing.

"Anyone hit?" bellowed Mash. Negative replies came from around him.

"That was bloody close," said Gordon.

"That's an understatement," replied Mash. "Onwards lads, before we lose contact with the others."

But it was too late; within seconds the thick fog had swallowed up the rest of the Camerons and the section found themselves alone.

"Shit," said Gordon, staring pointlessly into the dust.

"No choice for it but to follow the explosions of the barrage," said Mash.

This was easier said than done; the dust was disorientating and the perpetual noise made it difficult to communicate. Red flashes from the barrage warped their view. Added to this, the enemy shells were bursting to their sides and rear. Mash bit his lip as he squinted into the haze; he was worried that they were going off track. They had not seen any other troops; they were blundering around in the middle of a battlefield as though they were blindfolded.

"Where the hell are we going?" shouted Kipper. "I'm sure I've seen that rock before."

"Belt up and keep moving," replied Mash. "Follow the flashes."

On they trudged, the sand sucking at their boots, making it tiring to progress.

"I don't know if it's me," said Gordon. "But those flashes look to be getting closer."

"I've been thinking the same," replied Mash. "Still, we have to keep up with the barrage."

But they were right; the fall of shells was getting closer. All of a sudden two shells burst very close to them, one just ahead and one slightly to the left. They threw themselves to the ground.

"Jesus," screamed Finnean. "That nearly got us."

As he spoke another shell exploded just to their right.

"What's going on?" cried Kipper as they hugged the ground, trying to push themselves into the sand.

"I think it's our own side," shouted Gordon. "Do you think the rounds are falling short?"

Realisation hit Mash; it had been planned that the barrage would pause for thirty minutes at the half way point. The idea had been to allow the troops to reform before continuing. In the confusion Mash had forgotten.

"We've reached half way and walked into the barrage when it stopped," said Mash before raising his voice. "Everyone, start crawling backwards, fifty yards!"

Slowly the section backed out of the barrage, crawling all the way. Having reached relative safety they waited for the barrage to start creeping forward again. No other units came into view and Mash's nervousness grew.

"Gordon, take Callum and Drillbit and make your way over to the left," said Mash. "Count your paces and don't go more than fifty yards. See if you can find anyone else who knows what's going on and which direction we're meant to be going in. Be no more than five minutes and whatever you do, don't get bloody lost."

Within seconds Gordon and the others were swallowed up by the dust. Mash stared at the spot where they had disappeared and wondered if he had made a major mistake in letting them go. For the next five minutes he fretted like a mother hen. Finally, he was relieved to see the trio return.

"Good to see you again," Mash said to Gordon. "I wasn't sure you'd find your way back. Any luck, did you find anybody?"

"I wasn't sure we would at one point, you can't see your hand in front of your face," replied Gordon. "Two things; I bumped into another section, scared the willies out of each other. They were just as lost as us, said that everyone they'd met was in the same position and an officer had told them that we all need to make our way to the objective as best we can."

"That's easier said than done," replied Mash. "I'm sure we've been zigzagging all over the place."

"Well I said there were two things," said Gordon with a smile. "Here, I've bought you a present."

He opened his hand to reveal a compass.

"We passed the body of a sergeant. I think he had been caught by the barrage as we nearly were. Anyway, I noticed he'd dropped his compass when he was hit so I thought I'd bring it back."

"You're a little gem," beamed Mash. "That's the second pressie you've brought me, ain't I a lucky girl."

Soon the barrage started to creep forward again. Knowing that the section was now half way to the objective and that they were not alone in having difficulties, Mash felt a lot better, especially as he now had a compass. They set off again, trying to keep as close as possible to the barrage as it moved forward.

*We must be getting close, we've been walking over half a mile since the half way point.*

They had gone about another 100 yards when Callum signalled everyone to ground. Mash went over to him.

"Trench ahead," said Callum pointing the way. The trench was just visible though the gloom, no more than fifteen yards away.

"I think I can see another one over there and there could be more in the murk," said Callum.

"If they're manned then they must be asleep," said Mash. "Let's watch them for a second and see if there's any sign of activity."

They stared at the trenches, but nothing moved.

"Throw a grenade in there just to make sure," Mash said to Callum.

Callum took out a grenade and pulled the pin. The distance was not great and Callum was able to throw the grenade into the trench. A second later there was a crash as the grenade exploded and immediately a human scream. For an instant Mash and Callum looked at each other in surprise before leaping up and charging the trench. There was no enemy fire as they rushed up and when they loomed over the top they were confronted by the sight of two very dead Italians.

Mash and Callum took cover and were joined a second later by the rest of the section. They waited, but there was no fire from the other trench.

"I don't understand it," said Mash to Gordon. "They must've known we were coming when the barrage passed overhead and yet they weren't even keeping guard."

"I'd have thought that we would have got some reaction from the other trench, but nothing. Do you think there's anyone in that one?" said Gordon.

"Come on, let's work our way round to the right and go and have a look."

He turned to the others. "Cover us as we check out the other, any sign of movement then let them have it."

Mash and Gordon crawled round to flank the trench. They were well camouflaged by the cloud of dust. By moving a few feet in either direction they could either be completely hidden from view in the dust or just make out the line of the trench. Very slowly they made their way to the edge. They were tensed for a reaction but none came. Very cautiously Mash peeped over the lip of the trench. He could not see anything. He raised himself up and as he did so he heard a noise; it sounded like someone whimpering.

"Hands up!" Mash shouted with as much conviction as his confusion would allow. "Come on, let's be having you."

Again there was nothing, just the continued whimpering noise, although it now sounded louder. Mash peered into the trench to see two Italians sitting in the bottom. They did not seem to be armed and both looked scared out of their wits. One of them was crying; he clearly thought that his last moments had come and was having difficulty holding it together.

"Hands up, get your bloody hands in the air!" shouted Mash.

But neither of the men moved; they just sat there, shaking. Their fear was not diminished when Callum loomed up beside Mash.

"What do you make of it?" asked Callum.

"I think they're just terrified," replied Mash.

"Boy you can see the difference between the Jerries and the Eyeties."

"Be fair. How would you feel if you just had that barrage go over your head and you knew that half the British Army was about to descend on you? I reckon it was the same in the trench we bombed."

Before Callum could reply, the rest of the section appeared. They all pointed their weapons into the trench, which brought about a renewed bout of sobbing from the Italian. Mash indicated for the men to get out of the trench. Very hesitantly the first clambered out, still shaking. The whimpering man refused and made no effort to move. At that point Callum reached down and physically ejected him from the trench. They stood there, sure that their last seconds on earth had come, while the section stared at them as though they were from another planet.

"What're we going to do with them?" asked Kipper.

"Search them then get down into the trench and check that there are no weapons," replied Mash.

The search revealed two rifles which looked as though they had seen better days, but other than that there was nothing that could be used as a weapon. Mash smashed the rifle stocks then he took out the bolts and threw them into the desert. He tucked one bayonet into his belt and gave the other to Gordon.

He surveyed the men in front of him; the crying man's sobs had subsided but he was still sniffling. Mash looked at him with a mix of distaste and pity, and also something else. A part of him felt understanding, the part of him that wanted to cower and hide when the guns started. But you could not give in to that part of you in battle, because it made you defenceless, like this man. Mash did not see a man before him, he saw a terrified child.

He sighed.

"I can't shoot them in cold blood, but we can't afford

to send anyone back with them," said Mash. He spoke his thoughts out loud. "They're unarmed and neither of them could fight their way out of a paper bag in the condition they're in. I'm going to leave them here and let them be picked up in the morning."

He looked around for any dissent, but the others could see the logic of his decision.

"I for one have had enough of this little comedy routine, so let's get to the objective. I reckon we only have about 600 yards to go so keep your eyes peeled."

They had lost a little ground on the barrage so they quickened their pace to close the gap. Before long another trench appeared out of the murk, only this time the occupants were up for a fight. It was very brief. Neither side could see each other in the dust until they were ten yards apart. The first Mash knew of the enemy was when Gordon's Tommie gun opened up and, almost at the same time, a round zipped past. Niall and Gordon then leapt forward and, before the others had a chance to recognise the threat, they dispatched two Italians in the trench.

"We were on top of them before we could see them," said Gordon. "The only good thing was that they were as surprised as we were."

"I'm just glad you've got good reactions," replied Mash.

"Aye, but having this Tommie gun helps, you know you're not getting it back," Gordon said with a grin.

Just then a machine gun opened up close to them. They all dived for cover.

"That's a Breda," said Mash. "And it's bloody close."

"It doesn't seem to be shooting at us. Hopefully that means more of the boys are nearby," replied Gordon.

They edged their way towards the sound of the firing. The Breda was still making sustained bursts as though it was under direct attack. They moved further and out of the gloom appeared the silhouette of a tank, hull down in a defensive position and side on to them.

"Shit," said Gordon as they hit the deck. "This is going to be difficult."

"I'm not so sure," replied Mash after looking around. "There's no infantry support that I can see and no return fire from whoever they're shooting at. We're side on so not in direct danger. I'm going to take Callum and Finnean round the back whilst you and the others stay here and give covering fire, but don't open up unless you see something."

The trio quickly worked their way round to the rear of the tank, making sure to check that it was not supported by more enemy from the rear. All the time the tank carried on a steady bout of machine gun fire; luckily this seemed to be the only active gun in the vicinity. Slowly Mash approached the tank. He recognised it as an Italian M13/40 from the innumerable lectures they had received on the subject. He pulled out two grenades and gave one to Finnean.

"When I tell you, drop the grenade down the exhaust pipe," he said to Finnean. "Callum, as soon as it goes off, you and I get up on the tank."

The two nodded and they gathered at the back of the vehicle. On Mash's word Finnean pulled the pin and slid the grenade down the exhaust. It was easy to do as the engine was not running and the effect was instantaneous. There was a loud metallic clang as the grenade went off. Immediately the hatch on the turret shot open and a head appeared, only for the man to collapse back into the tank as Callum's enormous fist crashed down on his skull. A split second later Mash's grenade followed through the hatch and dispatched the occupants of the tank.

"Nicely done," said Gordon as he came up with the others.

"We must be close to the objective," replied Mash. "So on to the next."

They were all thoroughly alert and peering into the dust. After only a few yards they came across another M13/40, hull down, to their left. This time there was a trench next to it. Immediately the section went to ground and Mash signalled for the others to crawl backwards until they were out of sight while he recced the position. The trench held four Italian troops, one of whom seemed to be having an animated conversation with the commander of the tank who was leaning out of the top of his turret. Mash could only guess at what was being said but most likely it was whether to retreat or not. It was clearly distracting both men whilst the others in the trench were only keeping half a lookout while they listened to the argument.

Mash went back to the others and quickly updated them on what he had seen.

"Right, we move forward a couple more yards until we're on their flank. I'll deal with the loudmouth in the tank. As soon as I've fired, Callum, Finnean and I will go round the back of the trench, up onto the tank and drop a grenade in the hatch before they can close it or turn the turret to face us. We dealt with the last one so we'll be quickest. The rest of you charge the trench and deal with the occupants. Be quick so that you don't hit us as we climb up the tank. Any questions?"

There were none so they quickly moved up and lay ready for the shot. Given the short range Mash would be certain of a hit with his Lee Enfield. Through the telescopic sight of his newfound sniper rifle the man filled Mash's vision; he decided to go for a head shot given the man's body was mostly covered by the turret. For a second he felt sorry for the man who had no idea what was happening. But then he took aim and fired. The round caught the Italian just above his right eye and, through his sights, Mash saw the spray of blood and brain as the back of his head exploded.

Instantly they were all up and running. The first thing

Mash was aware of was Gordon firing his Tommie gun from the hip as he raced towards the trench. The other arguing Italian stood frozen as he stared at the pulpy mess that had been his adversary's head. He was caught in the back by the Tommie gun and collapsed into the bottom of the trench. The other three Italians took a second to react; by the time they had swung round the Highlanders were on them and their bayonets made quick work of them. While this was happening, Finnean had reached the rear of the tank and sprung up onto the engine covers like a hurdler. The commander had collapsed back into the tank but his arm was still over the rim, almost pointing in the direction that the shot had come. As Finnean reached the back of the tank another arm reached up out of the turret and pulled the hatch down. There was a sickening crunch as the hatch was slammed onto the tank commander's arm. Finnean dropped his rifle and grabbed the hatch with both hands to try and pull it back up again. It was stalemate until Callum appeared beside Finnean and the hatch flew up like a cork out of a bottle. Immediately after, Mash threw the grenade into the hatch, past the face of the wide-eyed Italian who looked in horror as the grenade landed on the floor of the tank. Callum slammed the hatch back down, almost severing the still-pointing arm and the grenade exploded.

They had no time to rest after they completed their attack of the tank. They quickly formed up and moved forward at the ready. From nowhere, another trench loomed up out of the swirling dust in front of them. This time they had no option but just to charge and pray that they would be spared any incoming fire. They dashed forwards, firing as they ran. But when they reached the lip they found only bodies twisted in the bottom.

"I can't believe we got them all," said Gordon as he and the others went to ground.

"Someone's been here before us," replied Mash before

shouting to the others. "Keep your eyes open and don't shoot until you know it's the Eyeties, there're friendlies in front of us."

Cautiously they rose and resumed their advance. They quickly came across another trench and could just make out the outline of another a short distance to its right.

"Kipper, with me. The rest covering fire if needed but don't shoot any of our own side."

With that he and Kipper edged their way towards the nearest trench. Slowly they peered over the rim.

"Don't bother, we've already sorted that one," came a voice from one side.

Mash jumped and swung his gun round, but quickly relaxed as he saw another Highlander in the further trench clearly enjoying his discomfort. They had made it, they were at their objective.

★ ★ ★

As far as they could tell, even though they had all been split up, the objectives had been taken to schedule. It now remained for the armour to exploit the opportunity.

Mash and the others dug in or took over captured trenches and waited for the dawn. But it did not take the enemy artillery long to start pounding their position in earnest.

"I'm starting to take this personally," said Drillbit to no one in particular. "You'd have thought that we'd have taken these bastards out by now."

"They've probably heard that you screwed their girlfriend in Cairo," piped in Kipper. "Enough to get anyone upset."

"What I would give to have a go back at them," said Drillbit, ignoring Kipper's comment.

At that moment, as if by magic, the shelling stopped.

"You must have scared them," said Kipper.

"Be quiet and stand to you lot," shouted Mash. "If they stopped firing it's because they have something else in mind."

In the stillness they heard the squeaking of tank tracks. Before long enemy tanks could be seen moving towards them.

"Do you know if the anti-tank guns have been brought up?" asked Gordon.

"Don't think so," replied Mash, staring at the dark shapes of the tanks. "This could get messy."

"You just had to open your mouth didn't you Drillbit," said Kipper.

The tanks grew closer and closer. Soon the first fire from the Highlanders started. But it was small arms fire and all it managed to do was to annoy the tanks into returning fire with their machine guns and cannons. Bullets sprayed the top of the trenches, ensuring that the Highlanders kept their heads down.

"If they get any nearer we're toast," said Mash.

Sand and rock showered down on them as the tanks' machine guns continued to lay down heavy fire. As they moved on to another target both Mash and Gordon popped up and let rip at the nearest tank, only to see their bullets ricochet away harmlessly. They ducked back down into the trench.

"I think the only thing to do is to let them come over the top of us and then put a grenade into the engines," said Gordon.

"Yes but we'll be easy pickings for the tanks behind and anyway there's no guarantee we'll do anything but disable it, they could keep firing right on top of us," replied Mash. "I'm going to try for the slits and see if that does any good."

With that he rose up and started to take aimed shots at the observation slits of the nearest tank. His first two shots produced no reaction, but on the third shot the tank erupted into a ball of flame. The two looked at each other in open-mouthed amazement.

"Tell me you did that," said an incredulous Gordon.

"It wasn't me," replied Mash. "But I'm bloody grateful to whoever it was."

As if in response, a screeching track noise behind them announced the arrival of the 50th RTR's Valentine tanks. The Valentines had been coming up through lanes cleared by the Kiwi sappers to provide troop support.

"They must've heard the commotion and sent some of their guys to lend a hand," said Mash. "And for that I'm intensely grateful."

The Valentines started to fire well-aimed shots at the oncoming tanks and before long another enemy tank was hit. At the same time the artillery fired prepared heavy concentrations of defensive tasks for the southern flank. The enemy tanks soon realised that their opportunity had passed and melted away back to their lines. The Valentines then took up supporting positions behind the Camerons, whilst the enemy artillery renewed its pounding.

"I never thought I'd be so pleased to see a tankie," said Gordon. "Remind me to buy them a beer."

"I'll do the same," replied Mash. "But they're our support tanks, where is the armour that's meant to press on through, have they let us down again?"

What Mash and the others did not know was that they were in the front seat to watch one of the largest tank battles of the campaign.

★ ★ ★

Back at his Divisional HQ Wimberley monitored the progress of the battle with a maternal concern for his troops. A succession of messages came in and Wimberley was delighted to see that the operation was going according to plan. Whilst it was clear that many of the troops had become detached and disorientated, they had used their initiative and training to advance and the result was that messages were coming in thick and fast to say that the objectives were being achieved. Wimberley thought about the next phase of the Operation Supercharge plan, which would see 9th Armoured Brigade pass through the infantry's position and move a further mile forward to the Axis defensive line at the Rahman Track. Having made a hole in the line they would hold the gap until the 1st Armoured Division could come up and exploit the gap and move into the rear of the Axis forces. To minimise the risk from the enemy defences, the attack would be launched in darkness just before dawn.

Wimberley knew that the tanks had started to move forward from the railway junction at El Alamein at 20:00 on the 1st November, before the infantry had even started its advance. To the north of Mash's position armour from the 3rd Hussars and the Wiltshire Yeomanry led the way, while behind the Camerons the Warwickshire Yeomanry tanks were forming up. In the dark some tanks had got lost whilst others had been delayed as they went through the narrow channels in the minefields which were under fire from the Axis artillery. By the time the armour reached their start line over thirty of them were out of action or deemed as unserviceable. The combined attacking force would consist of only ninety-four tanks. Plus, the mines and enemy artillery had taken a toll on the soft-skinned trucks and vehicles behind the armour. At the request of its commander, Brigadier Currie, the start was delayed by thirty minutes so that the force could regroup. The Brigade set off at 06:15 and not 05:45 as planned, with the artillery having to correct their fire plans. As they commenced the first signs of dawn were starting to light the sky.

The Armoured Brigade advanced, ready to cover the 2,000 yards to the Rahman Track. But Wimberley realised from radio chatter and reports that the half-hour delay was proving crucial. In the north, as the Hussars and Wiltshires charged forward, they found themselves silhouetted by the rising sun and the Axis anti-tank guns started to pick them off one by one. But still they came on; they were in no man's land where to withdraw was just as dangerous as to advance. Wimberley found himself willing the tanks forward just as he would have listening to a sports event on the radio before the war.

The Wiltshire's tanks were the first to reach the Rahman track, easily identifiable by the telegraph poles that ran along it. They pushed on over this track before being stopped by enemy fire. Other squadrons of both the Hussars and Wiltshires also came under heavy fire, some short of the track with others over it. Their numbers dwindling rapidly, they went into hull-down positions and attempted to hold the position for the expected reinforcements.

The tanks managed to take and hold the position on the Rahman track. It was estimated that they destroyed thirty-five enemy anti-tank guns and took several hundred prisoners as well as some larger-calibre artillery. They had dented the enemy line and it was ripe for immediate exploitation.

# CHAPTER SEVENTEEN

# TELL EL AQQAQIR

"There're a lot of tank noises behind us," said Mash.

"Perhaps it's the cavalry you thought weren't coming," replied Gordon. "They're making enough noise to wake the dead anyway."

"It looks like they're coming right through us," said Callum staring behind him. "If we're not careful we'll be run over."

Grants and Shermans were appearing out of the darkness. 38 Warwickshire Yeomanry tanks had made it to the start, along with their support of anti-tank guns and lorried infantry. At first they were careful to pick their way round the Camerons' trenches. Mash could see the tank commanders talking to their drivers as they made their way through. As soon as the leading tanks were through the position they started to head south-west.

"I wonder why they're doing that," said Mash. "The shortest route to the track is due west."

"They're headed for the tanks the Valentines knocked out," replied Gordon. "Perhaps they think that's the way?"

At that moment there was a crack like a sledgehammer hitting a broken bell and one of the leading Shermans dissolved in a ball of flame. The shot was immediately followed by more rounds as the Axis defensive line opened up.

"Did you see that?" shouted Finnean. "It just went up; the poor buggers didn't stand a chance."

"Keep quiet," bellowed Mash. "And watch out for our tanks."

The tanks had closed up for action; their visibility was now much restricted and their focus was on the enemy, trying to spot targets away in the gloom. They were starting to get dangerously close to the trenches in front of them. Two more tanks were hit before any fire was returned as the Axis gunners used the rising sun to their advantage. One brewed up whilst the crew could be seen bailing out of the other.

"Move, move, move!" screamed Drillbit as a tank loomed up behind the trench he was sharing with Kipper. They scrambled out of one side as a Grant slammed into the other. They then stood like lost schoolboys as enemy rounds fizzed past. When the tank cleared their trench they dived back into it.

"I'm not sure the sandy edges will take the weight of a tank," shouted Mash to the section. "So have one looking forward and the other backwards. If a tank comes, get out of the trench, lie down and then get back in when it's passed."

The last of his words were drowned out by the deafening bang as a Sherman fired its opening round. More and more of the Warwick's tanks were moving forward into what felt like a wall of steel. The number of rounds from the enemy made it seem like they were advancing towards the whole of the German and Italian forces. Frantically the tanks manoeuvred to try and dodge the rounds whilst getting into a firing position themselves. Enemy armour piercing rounds screeched and whined as they ricocheted away. Dispersed among them were the explosions of HE rounds as they lit up the scene. More and more tanks opened fire in return as the first rays started to reveal the enemy positions.

"Looks like there're loads of the bastards," said Gordon as the morning sun started to show a concentration of anti-tank guns backed by enemy tanks.

"Behind!" screamed Mash as they dived over the lip of the trench, just as a Sherman charged at full speed over the spot where Gordon had been standing. They lay as flat as they could, feeling very vulnerable, before the tank moved on and they could roll back into cover.

"Cheers," said Gordon. "That was too close for comfort. I'd be bloody annoyed if one of my own side turned me into strawberry jam."

A second later another tank fired from directly over their heads and for a minute they were stone deaf as their ears tried to recover.

"Men to the front," shouted Callum. "Looks like some of ours."

Singles and small groups of men filtered back, survivors from the tanks that had been hit. Some looked unharmed whilst others were clearly injured. Two men, one almost carrying the other, stumbled towards Mash's trench and he waved them in.

"Are you boys OK?" asked Mash. He stopped at the sight of the injured man and the smell of burning flesh swamped the small trench. The man no longer had trousers to speak of, they had been burned away and the skin on his legs and hands was black and peeling. If this wasn't enough he had multiple wounds all over his body as the shrapnel, caused by the metal from the sides of the tank as well as the head of the round disintegrating as it penetrated the tank, had ricocheted around inside the tank.

"I'm fine but my mate isn't," said the uninjured man, his voice betraying the terror he was feeling. "It was an 88, I'm fucking sure of it, went through us like a knife through butter. I only just managed to get Fred out; he's going to be OK isn't he?"

"He'll be fine," Mash lied; Fred was already starting to slip away, in some ways a blessing given his injuries. "Niall,

Drillbit, get over here and help these two to the dressing station and then get back fast."

He pretended he had not seen the horrified look on Niall and Drillbit's faces and tried to push the image of the injured man from his own mind.

By this time, all of the tanks and trucks had cleared the Camerons' lines and were still pushing on. Mash surveyed the scene. In front of him were the wrecks of a lot of British tanks. A quick count confirmed that there were at least thirty out of action plus a number of trucks.

"They've taken a real pounding," said Gordon. "I take back what I said about the tankies, that takes a lot of balls."

"They've been handing it out too," replied Mash. "I can see a lot of tanks and guns have been knocked out by them and it looks as though they've reached the track."

Sure enough the tanks had managed to get to the track and had overrun some enemy guns whilst putting pay to others and their supporting tanks. But the toll was getting too heavy and the Warwicks were forced to withdraw to a position hastily made by the two surviving anti-tank guns and supporting infantry, half way between the Rahman Track and the Camerons' position.

The remaining tanks of the initial attack tried desperately to hold on to their gains. Of the ninety-four tanks that had started the attack only twenty-three remained. It was thought that the Hussars and Wiltshires in the north had sixteen tanks left while in front of Mash in the south there were only seven Warwick tanks left, with their support groups decimated. Whilst the attack had failed to open a permanent gap in the Rahman line they had done considerable damage to the Axis defences. They sacrificed themselves on the line and restored the reputation of the armoured units in the eyes of the rest of the Army. Whilst they had not knocked the door wide open they had at least got their foot in and it now needed the weight of 1ˢᵗ Armoured Division to barge through.

But the expected armour did not rush forward to kick the door down. In his HQ Wimberley pounded the table with frustration as it became clear that the same lack of drive was resulting in another missed opportunity to break through. As before, the delays started in the confusion behind the Highlanders' lines. Many vehicles had now passed through a small area, intermittently shelled, and there was considerable confusion as to where they were meant to go. When they finally did get into a position to advance, the airwaves were full of reports about enemy counter attacks and all they could see were the burnt out British tanks from the initial attack, showing that enemy resistance was strong. Despite Freyberg's pleas for them to take the opportunity, the orders they were receiving from their divisional commander did not stress sufficiently the need for speed and so the commander, Brigadier Fisher, took a more cautious approach, preferring to reconnoitre the ground and await orders. In doing so he slowed down other supporting armour behind them. It was not until nearly 09:00 that Fisher's tanks got to the Rahman Track. But then they came under fire and halted. And so in the north, rather than break through, the reinforcing armour merely joined with the remnants of the Wiltshires and Hussars and dug in with them.

★ ★ ★

Meanwhile, to the south, Mash and the others were relieved to see reinforcements.

"At last," said Mash.

"They don't seem to be in a hurry," said Gordon.

They looked on as the tanks of 10ᵗʰ Hussars crawled slowly forward.

"Don't you know your pals are down there?" came a cry

from somewhere to Mash's right, only to be sharply rebuked by an officer or senior NCO. Mash was glad the remark had not come from one of his men and he knew the Hussars were following their orders, but he had a lot of sympathy with the comment. After the heroics of the Warwicks this advance was puzzling.

"What the hell are they up to?" said Gordon. "They need to get down there and help the Warwicks drive through."

Mash stared at the snail-paced tanks.

"There has to be something we're not aware of," he said. "Not sure what it is but we're in grandstand seats to find out."

Gordon grunted, clearly showing that his opinion of the tankies had reverted back to his previous stance.

Slowly but surely the Hussars moved out to a position mid-way between where the Warwicks and the Camerons had dug in. They were joined by the 50th RTR who had been of such help to the Highlanders and, before long, the last of the Warwicks were ordered back to join this new line. Together they started to trade pot shots with the anti-tank guns on the track and the enemy tanks behind them.

"What're they doing?" asked Finnean.

"Fannying about, that's what they're doing," said Gordon.

"They've just missed the opportunity to break through," said Mash.

"Aye, it's just a stalemate now," said Gordon.

"I don't know for how long," said Mash. "I bet Rommel's going to try to turn the tide soon enough."

Mash was proved right not long after that. At approximately 11:00 the enemy advanced in a last-ditch attempt to turn the battle.

"Here they come," said Mash as he looked through the scope on his rifle. He could see a line of tanks, with the dust billowing out behind, advancing towards them. In front of the Camerons, the Hussars and others were hull down and had time to position their anti-tank forces.

"Looks as though they knew the attack was coming," said Gordon as he started to make out the enemy's advance. "Although I still think we missed an opportunity to push on."

"Yep, and now the initiative has gone back to Rommel. I guess we'll never know why," said Mash.

"I can hear aeroplanes," shouted Kipper. "I hope they're ours."

"Should be," replied Mash. "But keep your eyes open."

The drone of the engines increased and it became clear that they were British planes. The bombs began to fall at the same time that the tanks started to exchange shots. This began the largest tank engagement of the battle. To the Highlanders it was like watching a football match.

"Did you see that one get hit by a bomb?" said Gordon. "One minute it was there, the next minute gone."

"Our tanks are also taking them out," replied Mash. "It's amazing; you can almost see the rounds going back and forth."

A cheer signalled a hit, but it was then followed by a groan as one of the defenders was knocked out. All around, columns of black smoke showed where tanks had fallen victim and provided a means of keeping score.

"We're definitely winning this bit," said Mash. "But it's always easier for the defending side."

"Aye, and these planes are making a difference," replied Gordon. "Mind you, if you take this morning into account I reckon we're about even."

"Enemy tanks to the right!" came a cry as a group of tanks manoeuvred forward. Fortunately the Camerons' support units had come up at about 09:00 and the anti-tank guns were in position. With a loud crack they opened up on the distant enemy who had come within range. There was a cheer as one of the tanks was hit, but it then drew fire from the others. HE shells came close, causing Mash and the others to duck down, covered in dust and sand.

"They're spoiling the view," said Kipper. But soon the anti-tank guns had done their work and the enemy pulled back to probe in a different direction.

On and on went the fighting until finally the enemy realised they were not going to break through and started to withdraw, harried all the way by shells and bombs. Whilst the armour had failed in its attempt to break out, it had achieved its objective of finding and destroying the Axis armour.

It had been a battle of attrition and one that Rommel could not afford. Both sides had lost over 100 tanks, but it was a loss the Allies could easily take and one that the Afrika Corps could not. The writing was on the wall and, unbeknownst to the Allies, that evening Rommel requested permission from Hitler to withdraw and started in motion the process of disengaging. Key to his withdrawal would be to leave a rear-guard to repel any advances whilst the bulk of his forces got away.

Wimberley's HQ was a hive of activity as there had been a change in the chain of command. Montgomery had seen from reconnaissance and other sources that the weakest part of the Axis line seemed to lie to the south-west of the salient. This view had been reinforced by the success of the Royal Dragoons' armoured cars in piercing the enemy line and causing havoc to their rear. Speed was of the essence and so Montgomery had split the command of troops in the salient, Freyberg retaining command in the north but giving Wimberley command in the south with the instruction to enlarge the ground captured to the south-west. At present the Camerons were the most southerly troops in the salient; if all went well they would end up in the middle. However, Wimberley soon found himself trying to sort out communication misunderstandings as plans were rushed into place, with the need to move troops about quickly and with well-intentioned involvement of senior officers not helping at all.

Wimberley had finally decided to make two advances. In the

first, the Seaforth Highlanders, with tank support, would head a mile and a half to the south-west from their current position behind the Camerons to take a position codenamed 'Skinflint.' At the same time lorried infantry with tank support would take the position at Snipe where Mash and Gordon had fought so hard. Wimberley was delighted when both advances went very smoothly and it was obvious that the Italians had no stomach for a fight. The Seaforths advanced and took 100 prisoners without a single casualty. Further south the Italians defending Snipe had seen Skinflint being taken and were worried about being outflanked, so they surrendered without a fight and sixty prisoners were taken. So, despite the confusion, the salient was successfully extended and the focus was now on the breakthrough.

Over the night of 2nd November, the Armoured Division made an attempt to move troops up to and beyond the beleaguered tanks on the Rahman Track. In the north, attacks were made which got some early gains. But then they ran into anti-tank fire which threw the attack into confusion and they withdrew. In the south, the 2nd Battalion King's Royal Rifle Corps were to pass through the Camerons and attack a small rise in the track at a place called Tell el Aqqaqir.

Mash and the others were still in their trenches. The first they knew that something was happening was when a barrage started screaming overhead.

"Someone's in for it," said Mash. "I'm just glad that's not coming at us."

"Aye, it's strange though," replied Gordon. "I haven't heard or seen any attacking forces gathering, yet that barrage is going down right opposite us."

"Perhaps they're just softening it up," pondered Mash. "But there can't be anything coming through our lines if they aren't here yet."

The barrage finished and relative silence returned. There was some action going on further to the north but in their sector it was quiet. Then, about an hour later, they heard and then saw the trucks of the 2nd KRRC crawl through their lines, working hard to avoid the trenches in the dark.

"They're a bit late if that barrage was for them," said Gordon. "I hope they know what they're doing."

They watched on as the trucks moved out from the lines and disappeared into the darkness. At first all was quiet and then muzzle flashes lit up the line of the track. A second later came the noise of the guns firing; explosions amongst the advancing trucks and the whine of ricocheting solid shot burst into the night.

"They look as though they're taking a battering," said Mash. Through the light from the explosions he could see men leaping from the trucks and taking up defensive positions. "Looks as though they're going to ground."

At that moment they were showered with sand as the anti-tank guns of 2KRRC sped past them on their way to support the troops. After that the fire slowly died down and relative peace returned.

At stand-to in the morning the Camerons were able to see the result of the night's activity.

"You can see what's happened," said Mash as he and Gordon looked out towards Tell el Aqqaqir. "They've taken up a defensive position but they're at least 500 yards short of the track. I'm surprised they didn't fall back; they're right under the noses of the Jerries. Look, you can see that they could throw grenades at each other over there."

"Why are the armoured boys always late?" mused Gordon. "That barrage must've been over a good hour before they started. They might have stood a chance if they'd followed up straight away."

"That seems to be the way they're doing things at the moment," said Mash quietly.

★ ★ ★

It was mid-morning on the 3rd November and Wimberley was frustrated; intelligence had come through that the Axis forces were pulling out. He knew that they needed to strike hard with the armour to break through the rear-guard and trap the enemy before they had a chance to escape. If they could ensnare them then there was a real opportunity to deliver a knockout blow. But still the armoured boys were unwilling to make the drive that Wimberley felt would unlock the door and win the day. After the withdrawal of the infantry in the north of the salient, the planned armoured attack had been called off.

"At least we have a chance at Tell el Aqqaqir," said Wimberley out loud to no one in particular. In front of him was a message from the 2KRRC Brigade HQ which had been forwarded to him, stating that they had managed to take the Tell and were through the track. He was thankful that they had some troops on the track; they could use them as the lever to open the door. Fisher's armour should be pushing up to exploit 2KRRC's position with other tanks pushing forward further to the south.

The Highlanders HQ was still incredibly busy. The 5th Indian Brigade had been brought under Wimberley's command. The idea was to make an advance with the Gordon Highlanders just to the south of Tell el Aqqaqir that evening, with the Indians making a nighttime attack further south. Finally, the Argyll and Sutherland Highlanders were to move through and mop up any opposition. The door would then be truly open. But the plans were going wrong before they were even issued. Tell el Aqqaqir was not in Allied hands.

Meanwhile, Mash was watching the first of Fisher's tanks. They had come through the Camerons' position on their way forward. A tank commander had given Mash and the others a cheery wave as he went by which they had returned. Very soon the first rounds were fired by the defending Germans.

"They're never going to break that line," said Mash. "There're too many guns."

"Look, the tanks are already starting to take casualties," agreed Gordon.

The tanks had made it up to 2KRRC but had stopped there and gone defensive, trading shots with the defenders.

"Look at the artillery," said Gordon. "They're miles off."

"Well, if the armour boys' map reading is as poor as it was when we were at Snipe then it doesn't surprise me if the gunners are shooting at the wrong place," muttered Mash.

Before them the fight was petering out. The tanks were not advancing and the position had become static. The afternoon settled down to nothing more than the defenders at Tell el Aqqaqir taking occasional pot shots at targets of opportunity.

"Well that was a let-down," said Gordon. "I was really hoping they'd crack the line."

"A pretty poor show," replied Mash. "I hope there's something lined up for tonight."

Even as he spoke, the Gordon Highlanders were forming up behind them with their tank support. Plans had been carefully made with a massive barrage waiting along with the R.A.F. ready to carpet bomb the target. The mood amongst the attacking troops was optimistic, but back at Divisional HQ Wimberley was a very worried man. Throughout the afternoon he had been receiving reports from artillery observers from his own division and from some tank units following a recce before the attack. They told him that Tell el Aqqaqir was still in enemy hands and 2 KRRC was not in possession. If this was true then the Gordon Highlanders would be very badly exposed and the barrage and bombing would be desperately needed. However, 1st Armoured Division was adamant that they were in possession of Tell el Aqqaqir and were against the barrage being fired. Wimberley's logic was that as the troops and tanks supposedly on the Tell both reported into the

Armoured Division then they should know. If he unleashed a barrage and bombed those two units when told they were in possession then he would massacre his own side. Finally, there was an urgent need to break through before the Axis forces retreated too far. Montgomery was pushing hard so a delay was not an option. While Wimberley was pondering the issue a clerk brought in a message. It said that 152 Brigade HQ had received an unconfirmed message that Tell el Aqqaqir was in British hands, although they could not confirm the source of the information. In Wimberley's mind it tipped the balance, and he decided on a compromise. Fire orders were changed; the barrage and bombing were called off. In their place a smoke screen would be fired. If the position was in British hands then no one would be injured; if it was in the enemy's hands then he hoped to cover the Highlanders' advance.

And so at 17:45 the attack started.

"Give'm hell!" shouted Gordon as the tanks carefully manoeuvred through their position.

"Where are you off to?" Mash asked a sergeant.

"Next to the Rifles on top of the Tell," came the reply

"But the Jerries are up there in strength," shouted Mash. "The Rifles are a long way short." As the words came out, the driver of the Valentine tank gunned the engine to get round another trench and the words were lost. The sergeant simply waved back as the column moved forward.

"Shit, they're headed for a death trap," said Mash to Gordon. "Hold the fort; I'm going to see WB."

"So you see Sir, if they think the Rifles are on the Tell then their whole flank is wide open and they'll be slaughtered," finished Mash as he relayed the events of earlier.

"You're right," said WB. "In addition, the smoke screen will hide both sides so they won't know until it's too late. There's also a danger that in the smoke they might think the Rifles and tanks are enemy as they aren't where they should be."

WB paused for a moment and cracked his knuckles, something he did when he was nervous. Mash was about to ask him what to do when he suddenly got up.

"Hold here for a second," he said.

A couple of minutes later he was back.

"There's no time to stop the advance. I want you to get out there on the double and warn them. Tell them where the rifles and tanks are and to expect lots of trouble from the Tell. Now go, fast."

Mash did as he was told and was gone in a flash. As soon as he got to the line he could see that the Gordon Highlanders were already well out. He sprinted after them, thinking if he went flat out that he might catch them as they were coming up on the Rifles.

"Aye aye, are you late for the party?" shouted someone as he raced away.

Smoke was still being fired by the artillery and a thick blanket covered the Tell and the Rifles' position. It was hard work running in the sand but he was gaining. As soon as he was close enough he started shouting but he could not be heard. Finally he managed to catch up with the rearmost troops; as he did so he was aware that the smoke was thinning – the barrage had finished.

"Where's your OC?" gasped Mash.

"He's over there," said a thoroughly startled Highlander.

Mash dashed forward. All the time the visibility was improving as the smoke dispersed.

"Sir!" shouted Mash and he saw the officer turn towards him. At that second one of the lead tanks on the right erupted in flame. The force of the blast was tangible and they all went to ground as a hail of anti-tank and machine gun fire descended on them. Mash was too late.

Machine gun fire poured from the Tell. On the flat desert there was little the men could do other than hug the ground as closely as possible. Rounds zipped and buzzed around their heads as the bullets sought them out. The anti-tank guns added to the maelstrom as their solid shot cracked overhead, whining as they ricocheted away or found their target with a sickening crump and explosion. They were in a killing field and the casualties started to rack up quickly.

Mash was with the other Highlanders, trying to search out any cover whilst men died all around. He managed to find a small scrape which gave him some shelter. The Tell was about a mile away and the nearest part of the track about 600 yards. Mash breathed deeply and tried to calm himself as he sheltered behind his cover, which was barely a bump in the ground. He could not just sit there doing nothing; he had to feel like he was fighting back. He started to fire a couple of rounds at the nearest anti-tank gun which was on the track opposite him. At first it just felt good to be doing something, but then he noticed that his weapon was actually hitting the gun. He could not look out from his cover for long and, at first, he thought the gunners were ducking down from others' fire, but he soon realised that they were ducking when he shot at them. The magnification through his telescopic sights made understanding what was happening easier. He started walking his rounds onto the target and before long he had the first man down.

"Bloody stupid place to be zeroing a rifle," he said to no one. "But this one's worth keeping."

He carried on shooting, reluctantly marvelling at the German gun, and prayed that the assault would soon be over.

★ ★ ★

Wimberley was furious when he heard about the mistake. Whilst the Gordon Highlanders' wireless was put out of action early on, the commander of the tanks was able to get a message back to his HQ telling of the desperate position. They in turn asked the Highland Division HQ for the original barrage to be fired but, as there was still confusion over the Rifles' whereabouts and given 1st Armoured's objections to a barrage, this was denied. Eventually it was agreed to fire more smoke. Before long the smoke rounds whirred overhead before starting to lay a thick blanket which obscured both sides. This and the onset of nightfall meant that the Gordon Highlanders and Valentine tanks were saved from more punishment and they dug in.

As the engagement raged on and men died, 1$^{st}$ Armoured had finally signalled Wimberley's HQ to admit that their troops were not on the Tell and that they were wrong in their map references that caused them to object to the barrage.

Wimberley was seething with 1$^{st}$ Armoured and thoroughly worn out from the lack of sleep and strain of the battle. But most of all he was angry with himself; he should have known that the armour boys would make an error on their map reading; they had done it throughout. The artillery and his own people had told him differently; why had he not gone with them?

Wimberley had a genuine affection for his troops; he ensured they were trained, he instilled a passion and a cause in them and he looked after them like a father. And now ninety-eight Gordon Highlanders were killed, missing or wounded, along with twenty tanks destroyed or damaged. On the verge of victory he took the loss personally.

But he also knew the attack had to go on and mistakes happened in war. So, a wiser man, he went back to his duties and to ensuring the next two attacks were successful. First would be the Indian Brigade and they would be attacking further south. All the time feedback was coming through of the Axis withdrawal and so the Allies needed to be quick.

At 02:30 the Indians set off behind their artillery barrage, supported by tanks. There had been much concern prior to the attack as the Indians had not been trained to follow a rolling artillery barrage and it was only after some improvisation by Brigadier Weir that it was deemed possible. In addition, there was an hour's delay in the attack due to considerable difficulties in getting all the required troops into position in time. All of which did nothing to sooth Wimberley's nerves. But, in the end, the attack went faultlessly. The barrage worked perfectly and the Indians came across dazed and disorientated defenders. Many troops were captured, mainly German, with almost no casualties. Whilst the Indians received much praise for the attack, they privately thanked the artillery. The final attack on the line was to be conducted by the Argyll and Sutherland Highlanders with the job of taking Tell el Aqqaqir once and for all. They formed up in the same position as the Gordon Highlanders had, opposite the Tell. Now that the artillery knew where the armoured troops were, they were able to lay down an effective barrage. This started at 05:15 and the Highlanders moved forward an hour later, just as the sun was starting to reveal the dawn. They passed through the Camerons' lines once more to the usual jokes and well wishes and on into the desert.

The rolling barrage went before them. Sporadic enemy shelling caused some casualties but on the Highlanders went. And as they reached the defences of the Tell they braced themselves for the fire that had so badly cut up the first attack. But they found nothing; the enemy had gone. The German rear-guard had judged that they had given the withdrawal enough time and knew they could not stop a co-ordinated attack and so, in considerable haste, they too had begun the long withdrawal back across the desert.

Back at Divisional HQ Wimberley was in a reflective mood. It was clear that the battle was won and for that he was relieved and grateful. As with all battles there had been mistakes and he had vowed to learn from them so that they would not be made again. He sat and thought about the events. They had taken place in such a short space of time; so much had happened that it almost felt like months. Two thoughts settled in his mind; firstly he felt the losses. Only the Australians had more casualties than the Highlanders which reflected how central these divisions had been in the fighting. In total the Highlanders had suffered 2,495 men killed, wounded or missing. Among them were friends and colleagues of Wimberley. There would be many a hard letter to write over the coming days.

But the other thought that stayed with him was one of pride. The division had performed well. They had come through their first battle with honour and had evolved into an effective fighting force. Above all, they had their revenge. Rommel had been beaten and the Highlanders had played a key part. His air of invincibility was dented and he was now on the run. The Highlanders had their revenge for St Valéry.

★ ★ ★

Mash had watched the armour going forward without opposition and could see the Highlanders on the Tell. As it was safe he slowly stood up and stretched his cramped body. He had spent the night in a shallow trench he had been able to dig once darkness had fallen and the fire had dropped away. Around him the Gordon Highlanders were starting to get up too. They had gone through hell the previous evening and yet with the dawn there was peace.

"What do you think we do now?" asked one of the Highlanders, who was also emerging from a dug-out shelter.

"I'm not sure about you but I need to get back to my unit," replied Mash. "So I guess I'll be seeing you boys next time, hopefully in slightly more pleasant circumstances."

"Good luck," he said.

Mash waved farewell before setting off.

"Hey, don't you know you're going the wrong way?" the man shouted. "Our lines are over that way."

"I know," replied Mash glancing over his shoulder. "I've got something I need to do first."

He walked off, heading straight for the Tell.

When he got to the Tell he found that the Highlanders were enjoying themselves. Some form of German HQ had been there and, as the enemy had left in a hurry, there were lots of things for the men to play with.

"Here you go laddie," said one man, walking round with a box of Iron Crosses, presenting one to everyone he came across.

"Thanks," said Mash as he stored the medal in his tunic. But he did not stop, he had other plans.

At last he found what he was looking for. Fortunately the door of the sturdily constructed storage hut was open and he went inside. In one corner he found what he needed, stacks of what looked like wooden suitcases with rope handles. Stencilled on the top was 'Patronenkasten 900'. They were ammunition boxes and inside were 900 Mauser 7.92×57mm rounds in five-round stripper clips. This was the standard German bullet and the same as used on his new weapon. He swung his rifle over his shoulder then picked up two of the boxes. Carrying them he made his way out into the sun and headed back to the Cameron lines.

"Wotcha," said Mash cheerily as he returned to his trench. "Did you miss me?"

Gordon looked up.

"We were about to send out a search party," he replied.

They talked for a while, each bringing the other up to speed.

"So what's in the boxes?" asked Gordon

"Ammo, this rifle is proving to be the dog's bollocks," answered Mash as he cradled the gun in his lap. "Accurate out to 800 yards but it can lay down a lot of lead quickly when needs be. I'm aiming to keep hold of it and I don't want to run out of ammo. If you see any more as we wander about then pick it up for me."

"Will do. Does that mean I can keep hold of the Tommie?" said Gordon. "I've taken a shining to it as well."

"Aye, that's fine. Between us we'll have a fair amount of firepower," agreed Mash. "Don't ditch your rifle though as we'll need to go back to normal when we're not in the field. Oh, that reminds me, I brought you a present."

With that he produced the iron cross and presented it to Gordon with an exaggerated salute.

"After the way you rescued Rod and I back on the Ben, I thought you deserved a medal," said Mash.

Gordon smiled and muttered his thanks, but the mention of Rod's name put them both in a solemn mood.

"You know it's weird," said Mash. "He died less than two weeks ago and yet it feels a lifetime."

Gordon nodded.

"He was like, this huge part of our lives," he said, gesturing with his hands. "And I honestly don't think we would have got this far without him. But, it feels like we've moved on."

Gordon scrunched up his face in distaste as he heard his own words.

"Shit, that sounds bad. I'm being disloyal to him by saying that."

"You're not," said Mash. "It's how we survive. After Colette." He paused and Gordon glanced at him. Mash rarely said her name voluntarily.

"After Colette," Mash continued. "I beat myself up over her death; I guess I stopped living too. But in all that's happened to me and this battle especially I've learnt that life's a lottery, and you can be gone in a second. There's not much point on dwelling on the past. Doesn't mean I wouldn't love to know who did that to Colette and pay them back in full." His knuckles wrapped around the gun and went white for a few seconds as the familiar but never easy vision of her lying in a pool of blood came to him. But he breathed deeply and flexed his fingers.

"I guess I mean you've got to do what you can to survive, I try to remember the good times I had with her and not the bad. It's the same with Rod. He was a top man. But he's gone and we can't bring him back, so better to remember him for the friend he was."

Gordon let out a low whistle.

"Blimey," he said. "That was deep."

Mash smiled. "I suppose it was."

"You're right though," said Gordon. "I feel I've aged ten years in this battle. Think we've all done a lot of growing up recently."

They were quiet for a while. Mash actually thought Gordon had nodded off, but then he heard him whisper.

"Makes you think how many more of us won't be here by the time this is all over."

Mash looked at him but Gordon did not look at Mash. Mash saw Gordon's fear and felt his own; the fear that was always there, sometimes simmering, sometimes boiling. He thought of the man with the burnt legs and wondered if he was still alive. He prayed to God that he was not.

"I s'pose it means we've got to pack as much living as we can into the time that we're here," he said.

Gordon looked at him.

"Easier said than done," he said.

"Yes," said Mash. "But worth it in the end I reckon."

Gordon smiled falteringly, then let it settle on his face.

"After all, we all make a pretty good team," said Mash.

"Aye and it also shows how well you've picked up the mantle."

Mash shrugged.

"So, what do you think happens from here?" said Gordon after a moment.

"Well, we've won the battle. But it's clear that the Jerries have done a bunk which means that they're not beaten yet. So we have to chase them back across the desert, only kick them out for good this time. Once that's done we can see about sorting Adolf."

"Seems like we've a lot to do," said Gordon.

He paused for a minute and picked at his fingernails; an array of emotions flashed over his face. Gordon could never hide his thoughts. Mash saw he was stealing himself for something. Finally he turned to Mash.

"We're even on the life debt now," he said to Mash.

Mash resisted the urge to roll his eyes as he could sense that the Scotsman was working himself up to something and he liked a sense of occasion.

"But even still, you and me we're… well what I mean is… I'm proud to…" He paused again and scratched the back of his neck. "What I'm trying to say I guess is that it's good to know you're going to be there beside me."

Mash looked at Gordon's slightly red but solemn face and did the only thing he felt appropriate in the situation. He reached forward and took Gordon's hand in a firm shake.

"There I'll be," he said. "And I'm glad to have you with me too."

Gordon smiled and shook his hand back.

"You're alright for a Masher," he said.

# AUTHOR'S NOTE

This book is an historical novel. As a result, although the central characters in it have been invented and did not exist, it is based on true events that took place in the Battle of France between April and June 1940 and at the second Battle of El Alamein between the 23rd October and the 4th November 1942.

To make the story flow we have had to take a number of 'liberties' to ensure that Mash and his section were in the thick of the fighting. In particular:

We wanted to include the Battle of France and the disaster at St Valéry as it is so pivotal to the history of the division. To do so we needed to start our characters in the 4th Battalion of the Camerons and then transfer them to the 5th Battalion once they made it back from France.

The story of what took place in France is true as we understand it. It was a very chaotic time and many of the details are not fully recorded. However, we have taken two liberties. We have taken considerable artistic licence with the amount of freedom both Colette and Mash would have had during their time on the Maginot Line. We needed to do this as we had a very short time in which to develop their romance. The Camerons were actually based in Ising Camp and not billeted with the local inhabitants. As movement in and out of the camp, especially at a time of high alert, would have been difficult we chose to use the time-honoured method of billeting.

Secondly we have changed the point of the attack on Caubert. The Camerons were the only ones to achieve their objective in the Battle of Abbeville before being driven back once the Germans rallied and redirected forces from elsewhere on the battlefield. Caubert was a small village to the south of Abbeville and next to the village of Mareuil-Caubert. Today Caubert has been absorbed to be part of Mareuil-Caubert. Given the original Caubert was too small to serve our story we have based the action in Mareuil-Caubert using, as our background to the action, the real church and the village school as the house where Colette lived. In practice this means that we have moved the Camerons assault about 600 metres south of where it really happened.

Moving to El Alamein, whilst two companies of the 5th Camerons did take the objective codenamed Inverness on the first night, we are not aware that any Camerons went forward to help the Black Watch storm the objective Kirkcaldy. We needed to do this to ensure that Mash had a good view of the battlefield so that he could join the advance to objective Snipe.

It would be highly irregular for staff officers from the infantry and armour to have an argument about the battle in front of the troops, or for Wimberley to allow it to happen. However, relations between the infantry and armour were strained with each side blaming the other and without it we would not have been able to have Mash volunteer to show the way to Snipe.

The action by 2nd Rifle Brigade at Snipe was the stuff of boyhood heroes and has rightly gone down in the annals of the British Army. Whilst the Snipe engagement is not generally well known, it played a major part in the outcome of the battle in that it cost Rommel a confirmed thirty-two tanks and five tank destroyers along with a further estimated twenty tanks that were put out of action but recovered by the enemy. To put this into context that was more than 10% of Rommel's total of available tanks at El Alamein. Of the tanks the Germans were able to recover it is unlikely that many, if any at all, could have been repaired before the Axis forces withdrew. It also forced the Axis to use precious fuel and news of the victory went round the 8th Army like wildfire, raising morale at a key time. Lt Col Turner fully deserved his Victoria Cross for the action and it is strongly arguable that others should also have been awarded the VC, particularly Sergeant Calistan. Indeed, as was typical of the man, Turner claimed that his VC was a team award and that Calistan should have been given one. The recommendation for Calistan's VC was approved by everyone up to Montgomery and there are a number of theories as to why he downgraded the award. Again we are not aware that any members of the Camerons were with 2RB but we felt this was too critical an action not to be included.

The Camerons did come under accurate sniper fire when they were in the Australian sector. The war diary of the Camerons states that the sniping was day and night and that the Highlanders were under continual observation with any movement being greeted with artillery, mortar and machine gun fire. Therefore we had to limit ourselves to daytime sniping and restrict the artillery fire to allow Mash and Gordon to return to their mates and build the hide. We wanted Mash to have something to stand him apart and came up with the idea of the Gewehr 43 semi-automatic sniper rifle with a ZF 4 telescopic sight. This had legitimacy once the Seaforths described being sniped at with an automatic weapon and we learned of Major Otto Burckhardt and his Experimental Battalion field-testing some of the Wehrmacht's latest weapons on the rim of the Quattara Depression, including small arms that were twenty years ahead of their time. We hope that it is not too big a leap of faith that one of these experimental weapons ends up thirty miles to the north.

During the course of the battle there was much discord between the infantry and the armour, each holding the other responsible for many of the shortcomings in performance.

Whilst there are always two sides to every story and mistakes made by all in the heat of the action we have, perhaps because we have been following the Highlanders, leant towards the side of the infantry. Certainly the incorrect reporting of the situation at Tell el Aqqaqir and Montgomery's threat to remove various armoured officers for a lack of drive are true. In saying this we do not intend to diminish the bravery of any of the armoured forces in any way and the advance of the 9th Armoured Brigade in Operation Supercharge serves to show the extreme gallantry and courage of the tankers.

Whatever the rights and wrongs of the argument it is true that the differences in map reading were a major issue, although this is explained to some degree by the flat and featureless ground. It is, however, interesting to note that the 2RB war diaries confirm that 51st Division's map reading was correct. It is also true that, at this stage of the war, the infantry and armour acted independently. Although exercises were done together there was still a long way to go before they were one cohesive unit. Had this been in place then the battle would have been over quicker and Rommel may not have been able to live to fight another day.

Whilst the distances were only a thousand yards or so, it is unlikely that Mash would have had as clear a view of the later stages of Operation Supercharge as we have described due to the flatness of the terrain and the debris of war. However, we needed to include him in the gallant advance of the Gordon Highlanders. Once more we are not aware of any Camerons included in the advance of the Gordons.

The message saying that the 2nd King's Royal Rifle Corps had taken Tell el Aqqaqir is true and did cause the issues described. However, it is not known why or by whom this message was sent. The same is also true of the later message to 152 Brigade and both messages must be put down to the confusion of war.

Throughout we have tried to ensure that the facts are correct and apologise in advance for any factual errors, which are ours alone.

Paul and Victoria Richman – aka Paul Tors

# MAPS

1) The Situation on 11th June 1940

Source: *St Valery, The Impossible Odds* – Bill Innes and reproduced with the kind permission of Birlinn Publishing.

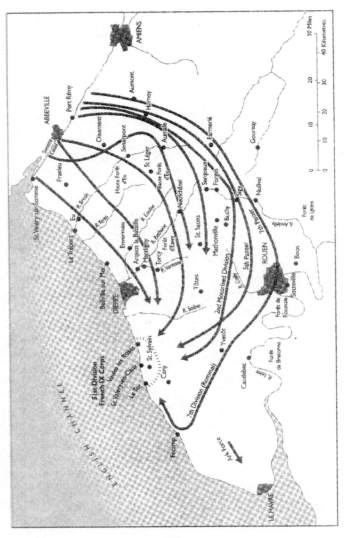

2) Positions around St Valery

Source: *St Valery, The Impossible Odds* – Bill Innes and reproduced with the kind permission of Birlinn Publishing.

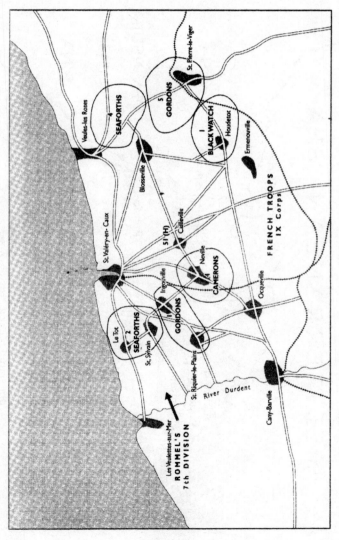

3) The Journey from Port Twefik to El Alamein 11th August to 23rd October

Source: *The History of the 51st Highland Division* – J.B.Salmond and reproduced with the kind permission of Librario Publishing

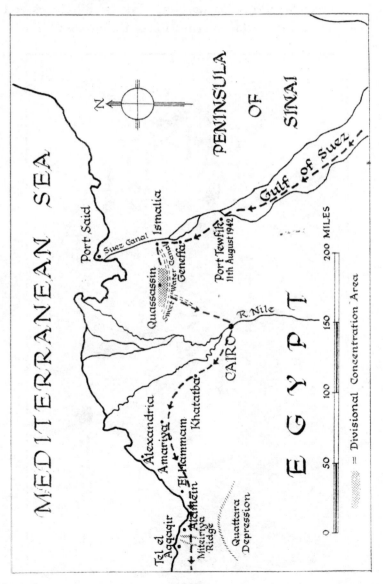

4) Highland Division's Objectives – Operation Lightfoot

Source: *The History of the 51st Highland Division* – J.B.Salmond and reproduced with the kind permission of Librario Publishing

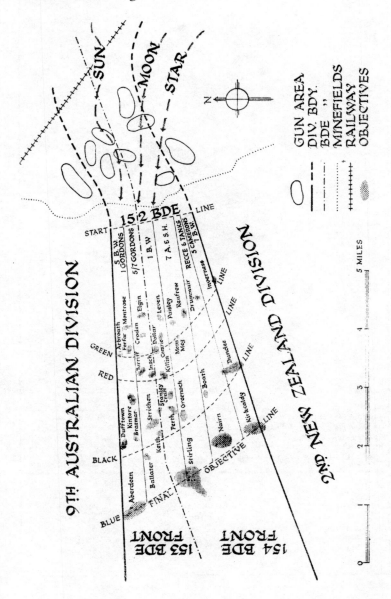

5) Six-pounder Anti-Tank Guns at 'Snipe' and Their Victims
    Source: *Last Stand* – Bryan Perrett and reproduced with
his kind permission.

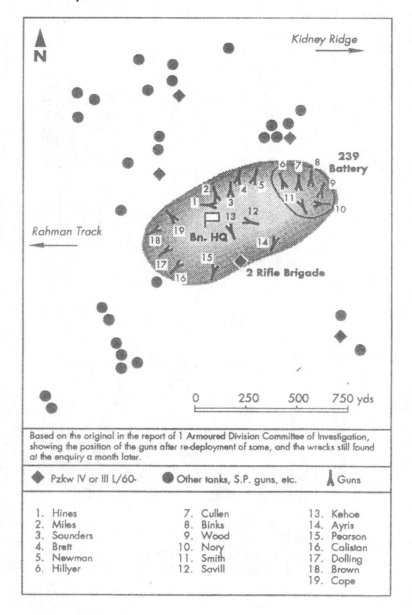

Based on the original in the report of 1 Armoured Division Committee of Investigation, showing the position of the guns after re-deployment of some, and the wrecks still found at the enquiry a month later.

| ◆ Pzkw IV or III L/60- | ● Other tanks, S.P. guns, etc. | ⋏ Guns |
|---|---|---|

| 1. Hines | 7. Cullen | 13. Kehoe |
|---|---|---|
| 2. Miles | 8. Binks | 14. Ayris |
| 3. Sounders | 9. Wood | 15. Pearson |
| 4. Brett | 10. Nory | 16. Calistan |
| 5. Newman | 11. Smith | 17. Dolling |
| 6. Hillyer | 12. Savill | 18. Brown |
|  |  | 19. Cope |

6) Operation Supercharge, Night 1 – 2 and 2 November
Source: University of Wellington – *Official History of New Zealand in the Second World War 1939-1945, Chapter 30 Alam Halfa and Alamein, Operation Supercharge* and reproduced with the kind permission of the New Zealand Ministry for Culture and Heritage.

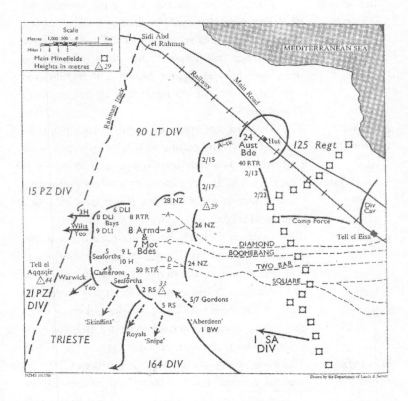

# GLOSSARY

2 inch mortar    The SBML 2-inch mortar was a lightweight and versatile mortar that could be fired by a single soldier. It threw a variety of bombs up to 500 yards and gave greater range and firepower than rifle grenades. Its main weakness in France was that it had limited stopping power and was ineffectual against any form of armour.

3 ton 4x2 Bedford OY    The Bedford OY was an Army lorry based on Bedford's O-series commercial vehicles with a 3-ton payload. It was widely used as a general transport.

5.5 inch guns    The BL 5.5 inch was a medium artillery gun with a crew of ten. It could throw a 100-pound HE shell over 1600 yards.

6 Pounders    The Ordnance Quick-Firing six-pounder was the primary anti-tank gun for the middle part of the war and had arrived in the desert in time for the Battle of El Alamein. It had a crew of six. It was more than a match for the latest German tanks and was a relief to gun crews who were used to seeing their old two-pounders bounce off enemy armour.

8cm Heavy Mortar    The 8-cm sGrW 34 (schwere Granatwerfer 34) was the standard heavy infantry mortar used by the Germans in the war. It was simple, easily portable and well built. Capable of firing high explosive, smoke and illuminating mortar bombs it was well respected by the Allies for its accuracy and rate of fire.

88mm    The 88 was a German anti-aircraft and anti-tank gun. It was widely used by Germany throughout the war, and was one of the best and most feared weapons of the war. Originally designed as an anti-aircraft gun it was realised that the high muzzle velocity required to throw a shell into the sky also made a perfect anti-tank weapon. Its range far exceeded those of the Allied tanks and the round easily penetrated all Allied armour. The gun went on to be used as a very successful tank-based gun, arming many of the later German tanks.

| | |
|---|---|
| Air Burst | An artillery shell that is fused to explode in the air above the target and not on impact with the ground. The effect is to throw shrapnel over a wider area and is particularly effective against troops and soft-skinned vehicles. |
| Ark Force | Ark Force was an improvised formation of the B.E.F. sent to Le Havre to hold and prepare for the evacuation of the 51st Highland Division. In the end it was not used as Rommel's 7th Panzer Division cut the road to Le Havre. The Ark Force was evacuated and arrived back in England on the 16th June. |
| Armour Piercing Round | Fired against a tank or armoured vehicle. At this time it was a solid shot designed to penetrate armour through high velocity. As it entered the tank the shock waves would cause multiple pieces of red-hot and razor-sharp pieces of shrapnel from both the round itself and the steel of the tank to destroy the tank and its crew. |
| Battle of Flodden | The Battle of Flodden was fought between the English and the Scots in September 1513. It was a decisive English victory. In terms of troop numbers, it was the largest battle fought between the two kingdoms. It was a particular disaster for Scotland as not only was King James IV killed, but the Scots lost most of their officers as they placed them in the front line, medieval style. Nearly every noble family in Scotland would have lost a member at Flodden |

as well as many families from the small Highland community. In total the Scots lost between ten and twelve thousand men out of a force of 60,000. The dead are remembered by the song and pipe tune 'Flowers of the Forest'.

B.E.F.

British Expeditionary Force was the British sent to help the French in 1939/40. It was commanded by General Lord Gort. The B.E.F. was deployed mainly along the Belgian–French border during the so-called Phoney War leading up to May 1940. When the Blitzkrieg advance started on 10th May they were driven back through Belgium and north-western France, forcing their eventual evacuation from Dunkirk and a number of other ports, such as Ark Force from Le Havre, along the French northern coastline.

Blitzkrieg

Blitzkrieg (literally Lightening War) was a new concept in military tactics developed by the Germans. They had learnt from their own storm trooper tactics from 1918 and based it on an attacking force spearheaded by a concentration of armoured and motorised infantry formations, and heavily backed up by close air support. A key feature was movement; if a well-defended position was located the attack swept around it to maintain momentum, leaving it to be dealt with by others when surrounded. Modern historians question if Blitzkrieg was a formal doctrine or created to resolve practical tactical issues. Certainly the freedom used by exceptional leaders such as Guderian and Rommel was often taken rather than given.

Bofor

The AB Bofors 40mm gun, is an anti-aircraft gun designed in the 1930s by AB Bofors. It was one of the most popular medium-weight anti-aircraft systems during the war, used by most of the Allies as well as by the Axis forces.

| | |
|---|---|
| Boatswain | A boatswain (or bosun), is the senior crewman of a section and is responsible for his area in the ship. The boatswain supervises the other members of the ship's crew. Other duties vary depending on the type of ship, her crewing etc. |
| Boys .55 rifle | Issued in the early part of the war as an infantry carried anti-tank weapon. It could knock out the early Panzer I and IIs but was very quickly obsolete. It was disliked by troops, partly due to its very heavy weight (35 lbs), but also because of its massive recoil which could break a shoulder if fired incorrectly. |
| Bren gun | The Bren Gun was a light machine gun used by Britain throughout the war. Firing a .303 round at a rate of 500 rounds per minute it was loved by troops as being tough, reliable and accurate. Indeed its only criticisms would be the magazine limited to thirty rounds and the fact that it was too accurate, gunners wanting more of a spray than precision from a machine gun. |
| Bren Gun Carriers | The Bren Gun Carrier (named from the light machine gun armament) was a light and small armoured tracked vehicle built by Vickers Armstrong. It was widely used for transporting personnel and equipment, mostly support weapons, or as machine gun platforms. By this stage of the desert war it often had a number of other armaments added as they were 'acquired' through the campaign. |
| Brylcream boy | Slang term used for someone from the Royal Air Force. |
| Char B1 | The Char B1 was a French heavy tank armed with a 75mm howitzer in the hull and a 47mm gun in the turret. It was one of the most powerful tanks on the battlefield in 1940 and was very effective against German tanks of the period. However, limited numbers, slow speed and poor mileage worked against it in a war of movement. |

| | |
|---|---|
| Eyetie | Slang term used for an Italian. |
| F.O.O. | Forward observation officer. He was forward with the troops on the front line (and sometimes in front of it). He would then communicate back to artillery batteries, selecting targets and directing fire. Well known for being a very dangerous role as the enemy would often seek them out to prevent shelling. |
| French 75s | A French 75mm artillery gun that was seen by many as best artillery gun of the First World War and was still in wide use in the Battle of France. Quick firing and accurate, it could fire up to 7,500 yards. |
| Frog | Slang name for a Frenchman |
| Grants | The M3 Lee tank was bought from the US by the British, where it was known as the Grant. To solve the issue of needing to fire both armour-piercing and HE rounds it had two main weapons, a two-pound gun in the turret for anti-tank fighting and a 75 howitzer mounted in the hull for anti-personnel. This gave it a very high profile but it worked well in the desert and filled a gap until it became outclassed at the end of 1942. |
| H39 | The Hotchkiss H39 (Char léger modèle 1935 H modifié39) was a small, light two-man French tank. It was well armoured but suffered, as most French tanks, with being slow. Armed with a 37mm gun. |
| H.E. | High Explosive. Here the shell is designed to burst throwing shrapnel over a wide area. Very good against infantry but of no use against armour. |
| High port | The rifle is held parallel and across the chest. |
| Hull Down | A position taken by a tank so that only its turret is visible to the enemy, thereby retaining its full fighting capability whilst protecting the main body of the tank. This can be achieved either by using a natural fold in the ground or, in a static defensive position, by driving the tank into a pre-dug trench. |
| Iron Cross | There were three levels of German medal each with |

a number of levels within the main group. The Iron Cross was the lowest level of decoration with the Knight's Cross and the Grand Cross being the others. It is estimated that some 4.5 million 2nd Class Iron Crosses were awarded during World War II, and 300,000 of the 1st Class. The Iron Cross (unlike the other awards) would have been awarded in theatre.

| | |
|---|---|
| Jacob's Ladder | A flexible hanging ladder consisting of vertical ropes or chains supporting horizontal wooden or metal rungs. Used by the Royal Navy and others to allow people to board a ship from small boats. |
| Jerry | Slang name for a German (also Kraut). |
| Jerry Can | The Germans had a much better design for petrol containers which were stronger and more durable. The British used the 'Jerry Can' in preference to the disposable petrol tins they were issued with which could not stand up to the rigours of the desert. |
| Kraut | Slang name for a German (also Jerry). |
| Lee Enfield | The Lee-Enfield bolt action, magazine-fed rifle was the main rifle used by British and Commonwealth forces in the war. In the First World War it was known as the Short Magazine Lee Enfield (SMLE). By the start of WW2 it was still in service known as a No. 1 Mk III. The No. 4 Mk I started to be issued in 1941. The main differences were that the No. 4 barrel protruded from the end of the forestock and a new bayonet (a spike, essentially a steel rod with a sharp point) which replaced the long-bladed bayonet of the No. 1. ten-round magazine, loaded with .303 by 2 x 5-round charger clips. |
| M13/M14 | The Fiat-Ansaldo M13/40 was the main tank the Italians used throughout the war. The M14/41 was a slightly improved version of the M13/40 with a more powerful diesel engine. By the Battle of El Alamein the M13/40 and the M14/41 were completely |

surpassed, and their armament was all but useless against the British Grant and Sherman tanks at all but point-blank range (however, both could easily destroy an M13/40 from a distance).

**Maginot Line**

The Maginot Line was a line of concrete fortifications, obstacles, and weapons installations that France constructed running from the Swiss border along the borders of Germany and Luxembourg during the 1930s. Crucially the Line did not extend through to the English Channel because the French military did not want to compromise Belgium's neutrality. The line was a response to France's fear of another surprise attack from Germany and was designed to buy them time to mobilise in the event of attack. The Germans did not waste time and resources attacking the Line; instead they simply invaded through Belgium, going around the Maginot Line. The Maginot Line was impervious to most forms of attack (including aerial bombings and tank fire), and had state-of-the-art living conditions for garrisoned troops, air-conditioning, hospitals and underground railways.

**Mauser K98k**

The Mauser Karabiner 98 Kurz (K98k) is a bolt-action rifle using the standard German 7.92mm cartridge and was the standard rifle of the Germans used throughout the war. Fed by a five-round stripper clip the K98k rifle was widely used by all branches of the armed forces and saw action in every theatre of war involving German forces. Although comparable to the Lee Enfield, its disadvantages in rate of fire became more apparent with the introduction of semi-automatic weapons.

**Mills Grenade**

The Mills grenade was a grooved cast iron fragmentation bomb with a lever held by a pin operating a central striker. Originally designed by William Mills it was used throughout the war by the British. It could be thrown about fifteen yards but the blast area was greater so the thrower had to take cover once used. Originally the fuse was set for seven seconds but in the Battle of France this was seen as too long and reduced to four seconds.

NAAFI    The Navy, Army and Air Force Institute is an organisation created to look after the needs of service men. In wartime it ran clubs, bars, shops, supermarkets, launderettes, restaurants, cafés and other facilities on most British bases and also deployed into the field to help soldiers near the front.

N.C.O.    The term non commissioned officer in the British Army refers to two categories: lance corporals and corporals are junior NCOs, sergeants are senior NCOs. Warrant officers are often included in the senior NCO category, but actually form a separate class of their own. Senior NCOs and WOs have their own mess, which are similar to an officers' mess (and are usually known as a sergeants' mess), whereas junior NCOs live and eat with the unranked personnel.

Neptune ceremony    All ship passengers and crew were required to attend a King Neptune ceremony the first time they crossed the Equator. King Neptune along with his Queen Amphitrite and assorted helpers would ensure that all first-timers were educating 'in matters of the deep'. In practice it involved dressing up and having to undergo a number of initiation rituals that varied from ship to ship. Originally used as a morale-boosting event it has become a custom when passing the Equator.

Panzer II    The Panzer II (from the German Panzerkampfwagen), was originally brought in as a stopgap until more advanced tanks were introduced. However, by the invasion of France in 1940 it was the most numerous German tank. With a crew of three the Panzer II was quick and manoeuvrable. It was armed with a 20mm cannon and an MG34. Its main weakness was its armour which was designed to stop infantry rounds and not anti-tank rounds.

Panzer III A medium tank, the Panzer III was initially intended as the main tank of the Germans. By the time of the Battle of France it had only been introduced in small numbers and was armed with a 37mm gun but was superior to British and French tanks it encountered. By the time of El Alamein the Panzer III was the most numerous German tank; by this time the armament had been upgraded to a 50mm gun. Originally the Panzer III had been designed to destroy opposing tank forces with the larger Panzer IV providing infantry support. However, as tanks grew bigger and more formidable the roles were reversed.

Panzer IV Special The Panzer IV was a medium tank used throughout the war. Robust and reliable, it saw service in all combat theatres and was notable for being the only German tank to remain in continuous production throughout the war (indeed some historians have said that if production was concentrated on large numbers of Panzer IVs and not diverted to the much more complex Tiger and Panther the outcome against Russia might have been different). Originally designed as an infantry support tank to operate alongside the Panzer III, upgrades and design modifications involving increased armour protection and upgraded weapons extended its service life. By August 1942, Rommel had only received a small number of Panzer IV Specials, armed with the long-barrelled 75mm gun, which he deployed to spearhead his armoured offensives. The longer gun could penetrate all Allied tanks at ranges of up to 1650 yards.

Panzer 38(t) The Panzer 38(t) started life as a Czech tank. When

Germany occupied Czechoslovakia they discovered the tank was considerably better than the Panzer I and IIs in service and so they adopted it. Armed with a 37mm gun and with a crew of four, the Panzer 38(t) filled a gap until the Panzer III and IVs arrived in numbers and were numerous in France.

Petty Officer  In the Royal Navy, the rate of petty officer comes above that of leading rating and below that of chief petty officer. It is the equivalent of sergeant in the Marines, the Army and Royal Air Force. Petty officer is the lowest of the senior rating grades

Phoney War  Commonly known as the period between the 3rd September 1939 when war was declared and the end of April 1940 when the Germans increased their activity resulting in the Blitzkrieg advance across France starting on the 10th May. In this time there was very little military activity on either side with each not wanting to provoke the other. For example in this time the RAF dropped many more leaflets than bombs. The fact that it was one of the worst winters on record did not help. The term Phoney War caught on with the Allies whilst the Germans referred to the period as the Sitzkrieg or sitting war.

Point  The lead position. The normal formation to cross open ground is an arrowhead. The point man is at the tip or furthest forward. In file it is the first man in the column. It is the first and most exposed position in a combat military formation and the soldier on point is frequently the first to take hostile fire. Given the risks and need for constant alertness, point position is often rotated periodically.

Pollywog  Someone who is crossing the Equator for the first time and, therefore, has to go through a number of initiation ceremonies.

Priests  The 105mm Howitzer M7 was an American self-
105mm  propelled gun vehicle bought by the British. It

was given the official service name 105mm Self Propelled Gun, Priest, by the British Army due to the pulpit-like machine gun ring and following on from other self-propelled guns named after religious figures.

R35    The Renault R35 (Char léger Modèle 1935 R) or R35, was a French light infantry tank with a crew of two. As with most French tanks it was well armoured but slow. As it was armed with the short-barrelled 37mm gun it had poor anti-tank capabilities.

Recce    Reconnaissance.

Sappers    A sapper is a combat engineer, who performs a variety of duties such as bridge-building, laying or clearing minefields, demolitions, field defences and general construction. They are also trained to serve as infantry personnel if needed. The phrase "sapper" comes from the French "saper", to dig or to trench.

Semovente    The Semovente 75/18 was an Italian self-propelled gun. It was built by mounting the 75mm gun on the chassis of an M13/40 or M14/41 tank. Although these machines were not widely known, the vehicle performed well in its role, serving as divisional artillery instead of a pure assault gun. The Semovente 75/18s were deployed in the desert alongside M tank units to provide additional firepower.

Shellbacks    Someone who has crossed the Equator before and is given a certificate to prove it and to ensure they do not have to undergo the ritual again. Shellbacks make up King Neptune's helpers.

Sherman    The M4, known by the British as the Sherman, proved to be reliable and highly mobile. Thousands were distributed to the Allies and it was the second most produced tank in the war. The M4 Sherman evolved from the interim M3 and retained much of the previous design but had its main 75 mm gun in the turret. When the Sherman arrived in North Africa in 1942, it was clearly superior to both the German Panzer III, and the short-barrelled 75mm gun on the Panzer IV (but not the Panzer IV Special). At the time of El Alamein its only weaknesses were its high profile, which made it vulnerable on a flat desert and its ability to burn, resulting in the Germans calling it the 'Tommie cooker'.

Spandau (M34)
Sometimes called the Spandau by British troops the MG34 (from the German Maschinengewehr) is a recoil-operated air-cooled machine gun. It fires the standard 7.92 round. The versatile MG34 was arguably the most advanced machine gun in the world at the time. The combination of being light enough to be carried by one man and high rate of fire (of up to 900 rounds per minute) was unmatched. It could have a drum magazine holding 50 or 75 rounds or, in a defensive role, the gun was mounted on a bipod or tripod and fed by belt. Belts contained fifty rounds and belt lengths could be linked for sustained fire. The MG34 was the mainstay of the Germans until it was supplanted by the MG42.

Stand-To
Short for 'Stand-to-Arms', the process of Stand-To was observed morning and evening by both sides. Each man would be expected to be ready, rifle loaded, bayonet fixed. The theory ran that most enemy attacks were mounted either before dawn or shortly after dusk under cover of darkness. Consequently both sides took care to ensure adequate preparation at such times, manning the fire step an hour before dawn and dusk. Stand-To lasted between half an hour and an hour, after which each man would be ordered to stand down; breakfast would follow in the morning. It became generally used as an expression to get ready to be used throughout an engagement.

Stick grenade
Model 24 German hand grenade (Stielhandgranate) was very distinctive with a metal grenade on the end

of a wooden handle. It led to it being called a 'stick grenade', or a 'potato masher' by the British troops. The stick provided a lever, significantly improving the throwing distance. The Model 24 could be thrown approximately 30 to 40 yards, whereas the British Mills bomb could only be thrown about fifteen yards.

Stuka    Junkers Ju 87 or Stuka (from Sturzkampfflugzeug) was a two-man German dive bomber. Easily recognisable by its inverted gull wings and the sound of its sirens called Jericho Trumpets, designed to cause fear and panic. The Stuka's design included several innovative features, including automatic pull-up dive brakes under both wings to ensure that the aircraft recovered from its attack dive even if the pilot blacked out from the high G-forces. It was also used as a tank buster, particularly on the Eastern Front. Very vulnerable to fighter aircraft.

Tam-O-Shanter    Tam-O-Shanter is a 19th-century nickname for the traditional Scottish bonnet worn by men. It is named after a character in a poem by Robert Burns. It is made of wool and has a pom-pom in the centre. The Tam-O-Shanter is best known as the headgear of a number of Scottish infantry regiments.

Tommie    Slang name for a British soldier; all Commonwealth soldiers tended to be grouped together.

Topee    The pith helmet (also known as the safari helmet or topee) is a lightweight cloth-covered helmet made of cork. Designed to shade the wearer's head and face from the sun. They were hated by the troops as they marked them out as newcomers.

Valentine    The Mk III Valentine was a British infantry tank and was extensively used in the North African Campaign, earning a reputation as a reliable and well-protected vehicle. The Valentine shared the common weakness of the British tanks of the period; its two-pounder gun lacked HE (anti-personnel) capability and soon became outdated as an anti-tank weapon too. Its relatively low height was an advantage in a battlefield with little cover such as the desert, allowing it to take up a good hull-down position in any fold in the ground.

# ACKNOWLEDGEMENTS

When we started to write this series of books we thought we would need to invent a whole battalion. However, we found the 5th Camerons who, as the saying goes, had a factual history that was better than fiction. The more we delved into the history of the battalion the more we were amazed at exactly how often they were at key battles in World War Two, and were astounded at the raw courage and tenacity that the Highlanders displayed. As a result this book and the others in the series are dedicated to the brave men, not only of the 5th Camerons, but also of the 51st Highland Division, to whom we are all indebted.

The key to writing an historical novel is to try and get the balance right. The characters are all fictional and so there is a need to give them life and use them to tell a story. However, the events that they operate in are true and we need to ensure that they are correct whilst entwining our characters into them.

On the first only you, the reader, can judge if we have brought our characters to life. However, the need for historical accuracy is challenging, partly as much of the detail and records of the Battle of France have been lost, and partly because the Battle of El Alamein was very complex, lasting the best part of two weeks and involving men from many different parts of the world.

Firstly we are grateful to the staff of the National Archives who provided a wealth of source material and for their help in our research across the book. We are indebted to the Highlanders' Museum (Queen's Own Highlanders

Collection) at Fort George near Inverness for their assistance. Also to the Royal Green Jackets Museum and the Hampshire Record Office, both in Winchester, for their expert knowledge of the Snipe engagement.

With respect to the Camerons as part of the 51ˢᵗ Highland Division, J.B. Salmond's *The History of the 51ˢᵗ Highland Division* is a must-read. Alastair Borthwick's *Battalion* gives a hugely personal and insightful view of the 5ᵗʰ Seaforths, a sister battalion in 152 Brigade. Richard Doherty's *None Bolder* and Patrick Delaforce's *Monty's Highlanders* both add significantly to understanding the life of the division. On the web, the 51ˢᵗ Highland Division Online Museum provides a reference for the division interspersed with many and varied personal accounts.

With respect to the Battle of France, *The Highland Division, The Army at War* by Eric Linklater is, rightly, seen as the authority on the campaign, something all the more impressive given the above statement on the scarcity of information.

In addition *St Valéry, Impossible Odds* edited by Bill Innes gives an excellent summary in its introduction followed by a personal insight into the Camerons' struggle.

With respect to the Battle of El Alamein, the Alam Halfa and Alamein section of the *Official History of New Zealand in the Second World War 1939-1945* as held online by the Victoria University of Wellington is a brilliant study of the battle and a must-read for anyone interested in the subject. Richard Doherty's *A Noble Crusade* has a chapter on El Alamein, which is a valuable summary. In addition John Bierman and Colin Smith's *Alamein – War without Hate* has an excellent section on El Alamein which includes a very good description of the Snipe engagement. Also on the Snipe engagement, Bryan Perrett's *Last Stand* provides an excellent and thorough overview, as does the web site of the Royal Green Jackets. Adrian Gilbert's *Sniper One on One* along with *Sniper Training, Techniques and*

*Weapons* by Peter Brookesmith and *The Sniper Anthology* shed light onto the world of snipers and their personal duels.

We would like to thank the following family members and friends for reading the first draft of this novel and providing invaluable advice: Hazel Bird, Tim Farrow, Paul Preston, Andrew Richman, James Richman, John Richman, Nicola Richman, Sue Richman, and Nayomi Skinner. We also need to thank our partners for the patience and understanding they have shown whilst we have endeavoured to tell the story of the Highlanders' Revenge.

Finally we are grateful to the two Highlanders in the Royal Regiment of Scotland, on duty at the Olympics 2012, and the duty sergeant at the Royal Scots Dragoon Guards who were all kind enough to confirm that an Englishman in a Scottish regiment is and has been called a 'Mash Man,' from which our character was born.

# BIBLIOGRAPHY

http://nzetc.victoria.ac.nz/tm/scholarly/tei-WH2Alam.html
http://51hd.co.uk
http://convoyweb.org.uk/ports/index.html?arhome.htm~armain
http://www.bayonetstrength.150m.com
http://www.reocities.com/Bohemiabhoy/elal.html
http://www.flamesofwar.com/hobby.aspx?art_id=578
https://www.youtube.com/watch?v=Ly2Ps0Actpg
http://www.2ndbn5thmar.com/history/SUPERCHARGE.pdf

*Alamein, War without Hate* by John Bierman & Colin Smith

*Monty's Highlanders, 51st Highland Division in the Second World War* by Patrick Delaforce

*A Noble Crusade, the History of Eighth Army 1941-45* by Richard Doherty

*None Bolder, The History of the 51st Highland Division in the Second World War* by Richard Doherty

*Battlefields of the Second World War* by Richard Holmes

*The Imperial War Museum Book of the Desert War 1940-1942* by Adrian Gilbert

*The 51st Highland Division at War* by Roderick Grant

*The History of the 51st Highland Division 1939-1945* by J.B. Salmond

*A History of the Queen's Own Highlanders (Seaforth and Camerons)* by Lt Col A. Fairrie

*Battalion, A British Infantry Unit's actions from El Alamein to the Elbe 1942-1945* by Alastair Borthwick

*The Highland Division* by Eric Linklater

*St Valery, The Impossible Odds* edited by Bill Innes

*Last Stand! Famous Battles Against The Odds* by Bryan Perrett

*Drawn In Battle Sketches of the 51ˢᵗ Highland Division* by Aston Fuller

*Monty The Battles of Field Marshall Bernard Law Montgomery* by Nigel Hamilton

*Companion to the British Army 1939-1945* by George Forty

*Sniper One on One The World of Combat Sniping* by Adrian Gilbert

*Sniper Training, Techniques and Weapons* by Peter Brookesmith

*The Sniper Anthology Snipers of the Second World War* with numerous contributors

## ABOUT THE AUTHORS

Paul Tors is the pen name of Victoria and Paul Richman, a niece and uncle team.

Victoria, also known as Tors, is a freelance writer who has worked for a number of magazines. She writes for her local paper, the East Anglian Daily Times, among others.

Paul is a retired, successful businessman whose passion is military history. Following a career in the IT and Telecom sector he now devotes himself to writing factually-based military novels.

Together they have co-authored *Highlanders' Revenge* as the first in a series of World War Two fiction that will take their lead character Mash through North Africa and the invasion of Sicily, onto the D-Day landings, the battles around Caen before the liberation of the Low Countries, the Battle of the Bulge and the crossing of the Rhine before ending the war in Bremen.